THE MAGDALENE CONSPIRACY

The Apostle Jesus Loved

(First Nicolina Fabiani novel)

By

Yvonne Crowe

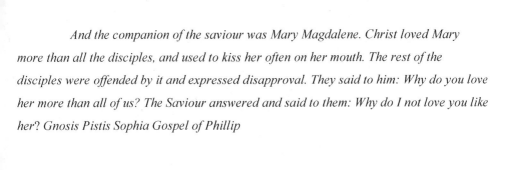

And the companion of the saviour was Mary Magdalene. Christ loved Mary more than all the disciples, and used to kiss her often on her mouth. The rest of the disciples were offended by it and expressed disapproval. They said to him: Why do you love her more than all of us? The Saviour answered and said to them: Why do I not love you like her? Gnosis Pistis Sophia Gospel of Phillip

Simon Peter said to them: Let Mary go forth from among us for women are not worthy of the life. Jesus said: Behold, I shall lead her that I may make her male, in order that she also may become a living spirit like you males. For every woman who makes herself male shall enter into the kingdom of heaven. Nag Hammadi Coptic Text Gospel of Thomas Saying 114

Chapter One – The Confession

"Bless me Padre for I have sinned. It has been six days since my last confession."

"No," a ragged whisper came from the other side of the confessional, where the old friar sat. "I don't want to hear your confession." His gnarled hands twisted and twisted in his lap.

"Come now, Brother. It is your duty to God and me as your superior," the arrogant voice responded.

"No. I will not hear it." Agitated, he shook his head from side to side.

"Bless me Padre for I have sinned," the voice mercilessly continued. "It has been three days since I last helped a sinner to their just reward on the other side of the great divide."

"I will *not* listen." The elderly friar's quavering voice sought to repudiate what he was forced to hear once again. Raising his arthritic trembling hand, as he devoutly crossed himself repeatedly, he raised his eyes to heaven, seeking redemption.

"You must Padre," the hated voice continued. "It is your duty as a friar. Remember, what is said in this confessional is sacrosanct. You cannot break your vows."

The dreaded voice cut through the roaring in his head, as the old priest tried to find an escape. "Then I will not hear you," his voice whispered so softly it could hardly be heard, as he clutched his rosary to his breast so hard that it tore into the thin skin of his hands, weathered by age and a lifetime of hard work in the monastery's gardens.

A glacially cold smile slashed across the penitent's face, as he relaxed in the booth of the confessional. "Hear me you will Padre, for I have been tasked to carry out the Lord's work again and you will not fail me, as I have not failed him," he hissed in a sibilant whisper.

"No," wailed the listening voice, unable to comprehend that anyone could be so deluded to believe, that the loving Christ he worshipped would want this monster in the confessional booth, to carry out such deeds in his name.

"Yes. I am directed to rid this world of the evil Magdalene. This is my sacred duty and my confession and penance, are my release from sin." This was no penitent, but someone glorying in his vile act.

"Stop, please stop," the friar's voice whispered piteously.

"The testament confirms, that I am glorified in my quest and am doing the work of the Lord," the abhorrent voice of the psychopath in the next booth persisted. "There is one less evil Magdalene in this world and within the next weeks, there will be more."

"No," whispered the old friar, as he raised cupped hands to his face, as though he could block out the sight and sound of his nightmare. "You must stop this killing. It is against God's law." He shook so violently, his breath came in short gasps, as he hyperventilated.

"Ah yes," the voice triumphantly continued. "It was ....

As the old priest tried to close out the voice, he sobbed and clapped his hands over his ears, to block out the horrendous confession he was trying to avoid hearing.

Still it seeped through and he was forced to listen, as he had six days prior, when the same penitent had told him of his plans to murder innocent women.

"Then my brothers and I ....; and the Lord was pleased with my work."

The burden was too great for him to bear, so the old friar thrust aside the curtain and staggered out of the confessional, sobbing until he reached the high altar in the magnificently decorated chapel and there he prostrated himself, begging redemption from his Saviour.

"How can this be? How can you let this happen?" His deeply reverent, simple faith was rendered asunder. "Do not test me so."

As a figure joined him at the altar he shuddered.

"Padre, you forgot to bless me and tell me to go in peace. You forgot to give me my penance," a figure whispered in his ear, as the old man prayed and sobbed. "Keep this secret of the confessional. Do not be tempted to break your holy vows."

"God will strike you dead if you defile his Holy Church," the devoted friar whispered.

"Oh, I rather doubt that," was the arrogant reply. "I simply rise higher and higher in his eyes."

The figure slowly rose, walked over to the side altar, chose a candle, lit it from another burning brightly in the glittering firmament of other candles offered in hope and faith on behalf of loved ones, then sunk to his knees before the statue of the Virgin Mary.

"Hail Mary, Mother of God, blessed art thou amongst women and blessed be the fruit of thy womb, Jesus. Bless me Mary now and at the hour of my death."

"Hail Mary, Mother of God, blessed art thou amongst women and blessed be the fruit of thy womb Jesus.

Bless me Mary, now and at the hour of my death."

As the rosary beads moved between his fingers he felt the power surging through his entire body. From the corner of his eye he saw the frail old friar rise and stumble unsteadily towards the sacristy, his senses ravaged.

Glancing at the walls and ceilings lovingly painted by local artisans, yet so finely wrought, they could have been attributed to one of the master painters; he allowed his eyes to wander.

Behind the magnificent marble altar with its relics of St Gerard, the 11th century saint, who was the founder of an order created in Jerusalem to provide care for poor, sick or injured pilgrims to the Holy Land, was a 3 foot high triptych, portraying the adoration of the Christ child.

"Bless me Mary, Mother of God, for I am about thy holy son's work as directed by my vows."

Rising he moved to the high altar and knelt, to offer the prayer of the Blessed Gerard:

"O God, who exalted blessed Gérard, because of his care for the poor and the sick, and through him founded in Jerusalem, the Order of St. John the Baptist, confer on us, the grace of seeing, as he did, the image of your Son in our brothers and sisters. We ask this through our Lord Jesu Cristo your Son, who reigns with you and the Holy Spirit, One God, for ever and ever. Amen."

Rising from his knees, he genuflected then turned away, the pectoral cross suspended from a chain around his neck and the scarlet zucchetto on his head denoting him to be a Cardinale of the Church of Rome.

His black trimmed black cassock, with its fringed sash of red watered-silk ribbon swirled around him, as he followed the old friar into the sacristy of the chapel of St Gerard and thence into the monastery itself, which was situated in the hills outside Italy's capital city, Eternal Rome, where he dwelled in the Vatican City, the sovereign city state beholden only to itself.

Chapter Two – Arma dei Carabinieri Headquarters Rome

The unbelievable had happened. Unshockable Rome, who thought they had seen it all over the centuries, was in shock. Paralysing total shock. Strangers in the street stopped and spoke of it with each other, trying to exorcise it from their minds, which simply refused accept the truth.

The *Arma dei Carabinieri*, the darlings of the people, who had been tasked with solving this heinous crime, as it was outside the remit of the Polizia Stato, were having a meeting.

"This has the highest priority," *Primo Capitano* Carlino Fanelli said, to the assembled group of carabinieres of the Rome Headquarters Division. Turning to a man standing beside him, he gesticulated to introduce him to his elite squad. '*Carabiniere Ispettore* Orsini from del Centro Nazionale per l'Analisi dei crimini violenti (NCAV) has joined us today to help us profile this offender."

The crème de la crème of the paramilitary force, had assembled together in the squad room at their headquarters in Rome's leafy Parioli neighbourhood. Many people in high places were screaming blue murder at this outrage. The assembled men nodded as a short swarthy man acknowledged them with a gesture.

Chairs faced the lectern up front, where whiteboards on one wall outlined the crime and the progress that had been made to date, although all was pretty sketchy at the moment. Plain painted walls did not lend much to the ambience. No colorful frescoes here, for these were hardened men, who were used to working with the bare necessities in a crowded working environment, despite the pride the Roman citizens felt for their Carabinieri.

At every smoke break, the squad would stampede outside and unhappily puff away, to relieve the stress etched on every face. Without access to their constant nicotine fix, as they endeavoured to solve perplexing cases, they were restless and irritable, cursing the day public workplaces were made smokefree.

Umberto Orsini was as unlike the usual elegant slim built Florentine male as you could get, despite his having born there. In fact, many, upon first meeting him, judged his origins to be in Sicily or Catania, and he could well have applied for membership in the local mafia. Nevertheless his reputation went before him and carabinieri and villain alike knew this was not a man to be trifled with.

Neither was his compatriot in the Rome Headquarters of the Carabinieri, Primo Capitano Carlino Fanelli. An extremely good looking, tall man who towered over Ispettore Orsini, he could have been a movie star had he been able to act. Sadly this talent had not been bestowed upon him, although every day he felt as though he was on stage. However he was dedicated to his work and loved the job when it was not driving him completely insane.

Coming from an impoverished aristocratic family, he was well aware of the propensity for the patrician families to sweep under the carpet, any taint of scandal, particularly if it was one of their own that was guilty. This made every move the Carabiniere made more difficult, as they were blocked at every turn, the investigation usually being dealt with at the highest levels, and a severely filtered version of interviews trickling down to squad.

Carlino Fanelli had to step lively to avoid the bureaucratic handwringing. An emotional tornado was sweeping through Rome and he was firmly in the hot seat, which allowed the upper echelon to heap on to his head, any mistakes that were made.

Every day since the incident, he felt as though he had been tied to a stake, the fire raging around his body, with the heat he was receiving. His phone rarely stopped ringing with calls from the PM, the Secretary of State from the Vatican. He fielded calls from other bureaucrats and members of the Parlamento Italiano who were endeavouring to milk any political gain out of this tragedy. Not to mention the Direttore Generale della Pubblica Sicurezza. "Madre Mio."

Life had left him with very few illusions.

Carlino nodded to the team leader, *Tenente* Ferdinand, who took an arrow and affixed it to one of the whiteboards between the point the victim was found on Aventine Hill to an unknown with an unknown destination. "We all believe the crime was committed elsewhere."

No-one argued with that summation, as Ferdinand picked up another arrow. "Then the body was taken up to the Rose Garden on the Aventine Hill," and he affixed another arrow.

"Yeah," agreed his *sottotenente*, "but the garden is closed until next May, so they obviously chose this place, knowing it's more or less deserted at this time of the year and they were pretty safe on the hill late at night."

Another carabiniere picked up the thread. "I can't believe the gall of using such a public place."

"Capo," one of the more outspoken carabiniere put his hand up. "She wasn't dead when she was nailed to the cross. They jammed a crown of thorns on her head and speared her in the side and these wounds bled." Hardened as he was, from the terrible sights he had seen in his career, he shuddered. "She would have been alive at that point."

"You're right." Carlino ran his hands through his hair in frustration. "The victim was transported alive up to Aventine. From where and in what condition, we cannot determine at this point."

"The autopsy showed atropine in her body, which rendered her paralysed, not dead," his Sottotente, Rocco leaned back in his chair.

Heads raised, chills running down their spines at the thought of what the woman had suffered. *"Che cavolo."*

"Bastardos," muttered the carabiniere in unison. The victim would have been utterly helpless, yet know everything that was done to her.

The Comandante Generale dell'Arma who was on good terms with the well connected, had demanded this was sorted and quickly. If there was another incident, Carlino's head could roll. His entre into society was on shaky ground.

"*Christo*, these bastardos are phantoms," commented Ferdinand who was leaning against the back of a chair, desperately wishing he could puff furiously on one of the cigars that was never out of his mouth before the smokefree edict was made law. "It must have taken more than one person to pull this off."

Again, the group agreed and Umberto interrupted briskly. "It would have taken precise planning, by more than one person, to achieve what they did."

The carabiniere looked at each. *Who in the hell would be so twisted, they would involve themselves in such a horrific crime? Dio sa (God knows), there were some crazies running around Rome, but this was outside the pale.*

One of the group raised his hand. "How the hell did they get the cross up and erected, ready for the kill and the crucifixion."

Primo Capitano Fanelli nodded to Umberto who stood up and looked around the group. "I think they brought the victim from another location once she had been rendered comatose. And we don't have a clue as this point."

"It could be anywhere," Vieri looked perplexed. "Where the fuck would we even begin to look."

"There are so many tyre marks around the area we'll never trace a car," Gianfranco contributed, dismayed by their helplessness.

"But you took casts?"

"Of what?" the carabiniere shrugged helplessly. Everyone knew it was futile. "There are a million footprints on the Aventine. Tourists are constantly trampling all over the goddamn hill." He scowled at the thought. "Somehow they must have gotten the site ready, then brought the victim and the cross to the site." His mind sought desperately for an answer to this perplexing murder.

"Yeah, there were no scuffmarks," agreed Guido Sevilla. "Nothing definite. Nothing for forensics to pick over. It was weird."

"I think they laid large sheets of plastic around and obscured the marks afterwards," one brave lad, Mateo, conjectured.

"Fuck, don't be stupid," *sottotenente* Rocco Testa, turned his head in disgust. "People live on the hill. Don't you think they would find something unusual in a group of bandits running around with sheets of plastic and erasing footprints. What? They used branches to sweep the area?"

"Hey, this is Rome. Everyone is crazy here." Stung by Rocco's remark, the carabiniere gave him the fingers. "You think they dropped the whole fuckin' thing by helicopter?"

"OK, settle down." Carlino Fanelli stood up and looked at the group who looked back at him glumly. "We can't have women picked off like this. Crucified for God's sake. It doesn't look good in the same city as the Vatican."

"But you would think we would see heavier tyre marks on the ascent," Baldo frowned, deep in thought as he tried to figure out the logistics of the crime. "The cross must have weighed a ton. What did they use?"

"Probably a tour bus," Lapo snickered nervously. "Those bastards are up and down the hill all the time."

"Do you know how many people travel up the fuckin' hill every day?" Andreas moaned,as he tried to erase the cloud of tiredness that sat with them all after thirty hours without sleep. So much for the Seven Sisters of Rome. One of them was turning into a bitch of the first order.

Primo Capitano Fanelli held up his hand, as things were getting out of control with half a dozen cops tried to speak at once. "The perpetrators must have wrapped something around the tyres."

"How? It would have come off as they travelled." Carabiniere Aldo tried getting his head around that one.

"You would think so. I don't know." He glared at them in frustration. "That's what I'm asking you to find out."

"Has anyone looked for fragments of plastic or material that might have shredded if they did that?" Umberto asked.

Hands clenching and unclenching in frustration, Roberto shifted his backside to get more comfortable. "We combed that fuckin' area with toothbrushes and never found a thing."

"Jesu Cristo, if we had gotten down and licked the fuckin' soil, we would have, but nothing."

They all looked as miserable as when they carried out the search. "Sniffer dogs brought up nothing."

"Why the Aventine? What's the significance?" Luca scratched his head.

"Okay," said Fanelli. "Settle down guys. I know it's frustrating and the Comando Generale is demanding answers. We're getting hammered."

Umberto nodded. "We have no idea why the bastardos took her to the Aventine. It doesn't make a lot of sense. What sick statement are they trying to make?" He looked at the group. "If we don't crack this case, it will be handed over to (NCAV)."

There was a collective groan throughout the room.

"Hey, we're not the enemy guys," Ispettore Orsini hurried to reassure them. "We're happy to work alongside you, not take over from you completely. At this rate, we need all the help we can get. The next step is to get the profilers in, to see what kind of sick mind has dreamed this up?" His unit had seen it all over the years, but most of the crimes he visited, still had the ability to sicken him to his very soul.

"Let's break it down to the essentials," their boss continued, shaking his head as he moved over to a whiteboard with photos of the victim, and the scene. "Let's find what else we have."

Sighing, everyone turned to the board, as he linking arrows between points of interest.

"What about the cross?" Eligio looked around the room, as he asked the question.

"What about it?"

"Where is it now?" Umberto chimed in.

"Forensics. Try getting near it," Massimo grumbled. "The way they're crawling all over it, you'd think it was the original and they're going to going to solve the mystery of mysteries."

"So what are their findings?" Umberto thought it was time to get curious about the method of her death.

Ferdinand took out his notebook and found the notes he was looking for, then attempted to lighten the atmosphere a bit. "It's your regular crucifixion cross made from sturdy oak? Beams and bolts out of the middle ages."

Carlino gave Ferdinand a hard look, while many of the men grimaced at the remark and a cacophony of insults rained down around the team leader's head, resounding off the walls of the room.

"So where the hell did they come from?"

"Where did they get those?"

"Smartass."

"Shutup." Umberto held up his hand for silence, while he looked at Rocco. "What did you say?

"From the middle ages probably."

The men looked back at him. "Where would you find oak beams and bolts from the middle ages in Rome?"

"Practically everywhere," Ferdinand snarled. "The whole damn country is awash with them."

Not to be cried down,Umberto tackled them again. "Check around and see if any sites are being renovated and if any studs and bolts are missing."

A collection groan was torn out of eight throats simultaneously. Surely he wasn't serious?

"Well that should only take a dozen teams a couple of decades, give or take, to work their way through that," Mario said sarcastically. "Those are not just laying around Rome, waiting for someone to pick them up. They're protected as heritage sites," he managed to get in, before Carlino shot a filthy look his way, which stopped Mario's mouth for a moment or two.

"Maybe they went into the country and got them from some deserted farmhouse or something." Luca thought he might as well put in his sixpence worth. Couldn't be any worse than the others.

More than one of them was scratching his head over this one. One even scratched his balls in frustration.

Carlino Farnelli looked around at his team, knowing they were going to protest at his next instruction.

"OK we're going to have to do some legwork."

The room erupted with groans and whinges, the men knew this meant days and even weeks of foot slogging. The direction this case was heading in, they'd all be in the divorce courts, if such a thing was within the realms of possibility. As it was, they were in for a lot of shit and breastbeating. Their families would be lucky if they saw them at all over the next six months. Oh well, it was a well known fact, a policeman's lot is not a happy one, no matter what country he resides in.

"Check on some derelict churches and monasteries, or some that are under renovation," he suggested, while his team looked at him aghast. Add another fifty years to the legwork and they might, just might mind you, uncover something.

"Might as well check the sodding Vatican, while we're about it," someone muttered sotte voce.

"Well we could start with Castel sant'Angelo," the clown of the group sniggered.

"Or Castel Gandolfo. Just tell Il Papa (*the Pope*), he can't have it for a while." Luigi joined in while the others groaned in dismay.

"Well he only goes there for his summer holidays," the clown tried again.

"How about the Priory of the Knights of Malta?" Rocco chipped in. "It's up on the Aventine, where the murder took place."

"When you've finished with your smartass remarks," Umberto interjected, knowing they were frustrated and just letting off steam, but trying to restore some order to the place he suggested, "you could get started," while they looked at him with such contempt, he exited smartly.

This was the beginning of another long day and they all desperately needed some sleep, or a break in the case. They would take either.

Chapter Three – Lina & Edoardos

Lina Fabiani was a freelance journalist, currently on assignment in Rome. Christened Nicolina, she loved the Eternal City, birthplace of her parents, and spent many pleasant hours roaming the ancient streets. As her eyes feasted on the symbols of former glory, her mind would take her to those ancient times and her fertile imagination would see, and hear the city, as she believed it would have been.

Now it appeared Rome was under attack. Or to be more precise, a highly connected, aristocratic woman of the city had been abducted, tortured and murdered. In fact, flagellated and then crucified, on the crest of the Aventine, one of the seven hills of the city, in the southern district of Rome, just beyond Trastavere.

Aventine, with its beautiful sweeping views of the Eternal city and directly below the circus Maximus, the historical site built in 600 BC, which could hold an audience of 385,000 and was used for chariot races and contests between gladiators and wild beasts. Here, in a manner that had horrified modern Romans, but would have been great sport in ancient times, the victim had been crucified.

Found at daylight, the pathetic sight of her body crucified in the manner of Jesus Christ, with a spear wound in her side and a crown of thorns placed upon her head then pressed down, so the blood ran down her face, made the citizens of Rome's blood run cold. Around her neck they hung a sign. *The Magdalene – Whore.*

Naturally the sensationalist media were calling the murderer, The Magdalene Killer.

With her Italian heritage, Lina counted herself fortunate to have spent a year studying at the Universita of Rome with its Centuries old buildings. Founded in 1303 by Il Papa Boniface VIII, essentially as a University for ecclesiastical studies more under his control than those of Bologna and Padua, it was now the primary university in Rome.

Here she met Edoardos, scion of an aristocratic Italian family and destined for a life of celibacy in the rarefied atmosphere of the Vatican. His ancient lineage provided one son from each generation to serve the Church, and had done so for centuries. Edoardos was perfectly happy with his lot, and had remained good friends with Lina, meeting up again, when he had attended Harvard University in the United States.

Lina thought it was wonderful, having a male friend who did not want to 'jump her bones' at every opportunity. Having an inside track to the Vatican and upper echelon of society in Italy, was a heaven sent opportunity for a freelance journalist.

On a typical summer's fine balmy evening in Rome, she was seated at a table on the terrace of the Pauline Borghese restaurant which overlooked the gardens of the Grand Hotel Parco Dei Principi, flirting outrageously with a Vatican priest.

"Thank God Edoardos; I have an aristocratic, handsome priest who treats me to the Roman high life instead of starving in a garret on my meagre earnings." This was an exaggeration as she was highly paid for her stories. , "And I don't even have to worry about you having designs on my ravishing body," she taunted him.

This was debatable but they both ignored the possibility.

Edoardos merely smiled condescendingly. "Oh you are perfectly safe with me, Cara mia."

"But do the locals know that?" she whispered conspiratorially. "Or do they think something untoward is going on? If this was America, we would be attracting curious glances."

"When in Rome." Edoardos made a sweeping gesture that took in all of Rome, and probably extended throughout Italy, "The problem with you Americans," he continued as Lina blew an unladylike raspberry at him, "is that your country is still so young and obsessed with sex."

At this, Lina could not help herself and interrupted him. "Oh, and the Italian men who cannot keep their hands to themselves in public, aren't on the make every minute of every day."

"As I was saying before I was so rudely interrupted," Edoardos continued as though he had not heard her comment, nNor has your country learnt to be comfortable with wealth. Your nouveau riche squanders their money, endeavouring to impress the world, as they indulge in extravagant, vulgar displays, or hoard away collections of stolen art that they alone can feast their eyes on."

"Oh My God, E." The abbreviation of his name, was a measure of her affection for him. "Firstly I'll thank you to remember I am as Italian as your aristocratic self. Albeit without the privileges of your noble lineage," Lina protested. "They have to work hard to gain a position in the Vatican, not have one ceded to them from the Old Boys' Network."

Edoardos had been given a shoe in but still had to climb to the lofty heights within the Vatican's hierarchy on his own merit. Receiving a yearly stipend from his wealthy family was a big help.

The family's fortunes had never declined over the centuries, as they went from courtiers to Doges and Emperors. With the benefit of education they built a dynasty which adapted to the needs of each age. For the past three centuries theyhad been one of the foremost bankers of Venice.

Their links to the Vatican bank brought them respect and privilege. The Roman branch of the Guilianini family, had provided the Holy See with a Pope and couple of papal chamberlains over the centuries. Appointments of expediency than of faith.

The petite, dark haired, olive skinned woman sitting opposite him was a beauty in her own right who could disarm him with one direct look from her large brown eyes.

Edoardos sparkling brown eyes drew one deep into their depths and he had one of the most charismatic personalities she had ever met. She wouldn't be surprised if he ended up as Pope.

Personally she thought it was a waste of good male material. It was a mystery to her why he preferred her company to that of the stimulating, intellectual and intelligent people he associated with in The Vatican and Italian high society

"While we're throwing stones at bastions of power." Edoardos waved his hand in the air disdainfully. "Are your dreadful television evangelists truly men of God, or breast beating fundamentalists, in many cases bent on feathering their own nests?"

"And the publicity machine of the Big V is not grinding out propaganda every day as they rake in the tithes to add to one of the largest wealth bases in the world." Lina's retort was fast. This was an old argument both of them enjoyed and rendering the Vatican to the status of the Big V in no way diminished its power.

"You have to admit, that your TV evangelists have a propensity to get caught spectacularly." At this Edoardos leaned forward in his chair, grinning like a Cheshire cat from ear to ear.

Lina could not argue with the first part of his comment, but met his challenge full and tackled his second. "And the great Church of Rome is not fleecing the gullible and pitiful?"

"Well of course Lina," he agreed, leaning forward and smiling superciliously, "but we are Italians, and do it with such style that the pitiful and gullible are grateful to be a small part of such grand theatre."

Lina made a moue with her mouth. "Reverendo Padre, do forgive me," she mocked him.

"Furthermore," he continued playfully. "I can prove my lineage without a shred of doubt."

They both laughed at each other, having played this game out many times before. Edoardos had never hidden from Lina, that he accepted the machinations of the Church's power. After all she was a small untouchable Sovereign state with absolute powers, situated in another large nation, yet with a reach that spanned the globe and held millions in her thrall.

Mother Church had held onto her Empire for two thousand years, rivalling the Egyptians at their zenith. This was the dizzying heights of empire building and he loved being part of it.

"No-one in the Big V believes that God and his angels are sitting around on big fluffy white clouds, playing harps and eating grapes." His eyes glowed at being part of such a hierarchical power structure, with a central bureaucracy that controlled over one billion parishioners throughout the world. "This is big business at its best – and it's been business as usual for two thousand years. What an achievement."

"Yes. Called to serve, it came to rule. Let's order, I'm starving." Lina picked up the menu. "Phew look at these prices. I can't afford to blow off my rich friend who has taken a vow of poverty so I can spend his money as my own."

"I'm a pragmatist, you know that." Edoardos raised his eyes from the wine list he was studying, to meet her gaze. "My family is no different to other influential families,who made it to this present day." Shrugging diffidently, he dropped his eyes to the wine list once more.

"What, you're admitting it?" Lina threw down the gauntlet.

"Why would I bother to hide such common knowledge?" Edoardos grinned at her.

"Not many influential Italian families come with mani pulite (clean hands)." Lina's thoughts drifted to her own family who had emigrated to America for the opportunities it afford them when their own country, stultified in history did. It had paid off and they were loved their new country.

"True, piccione viaggiatore - *homing pigeon*," he admitted, using the familial endearment. "I do penance every day for our sins for the exhaustive manoeuvrings and side stepping of daily life at the Big V."

"I find your frankness refreshing after the stuffy atmosphere at my place of work. If it costs me a meal, then that's the price I have to pay," he shrugged with typical Italian insouciance. "Anyway you're not as expensive as a mistress would be."

Lina played along with him. "I'll have to order up a couple of diamond bracelets then. You tend to the wine while I spend your money. Deal?"

"Get thee to a nunnery," he parodied Shakespeare's Hamlet, while grinning cheekily at her.

"Never," Lina told him emphatically.

Edoardos gestured to the menu and suggested, "Perhaps we should take a look."

"God E. You are so frank for a priest, especially one who works at the heart of the Big V." Lina leaned back and scanned his face.

"Only with you Lina, and I know you keep my secrets close to your heart." Wagging his finger at her in mock warning, he grinned mischievously.

"Of course you must be absolutely out of your mind, trusting a reporter to keep your secret." Lina laughed out loud.

Chapter Four – Edoardos

Edoardos worked for the *The Administration of the Patrimony of the Apostolic See*. This part of the Roman Curia dealt with the properties owned by the Holy See in order to provide the funds necessary for this body to function. The Roman Curia can be loosely compared, to cabinets in governments of countries with a Western form of governance.

After the previous President Domenico Delgano's unexpected death, Cardinale Vendetto, to whom Edoardos reported was elected President of the Administration of the Patrimony of the Apostolic See.

He had replaced the former Secretary with his own man Monsignor Galasso, whom Edoardos thought aptly named, as it meant steep side of the mountain. An unapproachable and difficult man, Edoardos privately felt that as the conduit to the Cardinale, the secretary guarded his power jealously, which was not always in the Patrimony's best interest.

At the end of the Second World War the International Monetary Fund considered this August Body to be the Central Bank of the Vatican.

Under the Patrimony's guidance sits the Committee of Vigilance, composed of a Cardinale and members who audit the accounts of *Istituto per le Opere di Religione,* more commonly known as the Vatican Bank. A privately held institute located inside Vatican City, it is run by a professional bank CEO who reports directly to the committee of Cardinales and ultimately to the Pope. Since its assets are not considered property of the Holy See, it is not overseen by the Prefecture for the Economic Affairs of the Holy See.

Shrouded in secrecy and beset with financial scandals, its balance sheets are complex and less than transparent. Furthermore, the IOR is not subject to European anti-money-laundering rules and controls. It is also free of supervision by the International Monetary Fund, as it has declined to join that organisation. Unlike other states, the Holy See is not recognised as a European state and has no border security or control, therefore the IOR is a useful tool for money laundering and tax evasion.

Neither is it a central bank responsible for a country's monetary policy and for maintaining the stability of a currency and money supply. Its ultimate purpose is to provide for the safekeeping and administration of movable and immovable property, transferred to and entrusted to it, by physical or juridical persons and intended for works of religion or charity.

Thus it is not a department of the Roman Curia and is therefore, not among the departments of this central administrative structure of the Roman Catholic Church, enabling the latter to erect a Chinese Wall from which it can, and does, deny culpability in any misdoings.

In nineteen twenty-nine a conciliation treaty was established between the Italian Government headed at that time by Benito Mussolini and the Holy See.

The Administration of the Patrimony of the Apostolic See is a body of the Roman Curia which is composed of two sections.

The Ordinary Section entrusted with the administration of the property remaining to the Holy See after the complete loss of the Papal States in 1870, and The Extraordinary Section which manages the funds generated from the 1750 million lira, about US$100 million, transferred to the Holy See by the Financial Convention of the Lateran Treaty, to offset any claims by the Roman Catholic Church for which Edoardos labored.

"A Royal Court appointee if you like," Edoardos commented archly to Lina.

"It doesn't demand a lot of me and I can lead an indolent life," he said self deprecatingly.

Which Lina dismissed. A self effacing man, she knew this hid a brilliant incisive mind. "It takes a Machiavellian mind to survive in that jungle," Lina rose from the table and came to stand behind him. Leaning forward she ruffled his hair.

"Oh absolutely," Edoardos agreed, catching her hands and rising to face her. "We're born with it and my family has had centuries to perfect it. It allows me to indulge myself in the Vatican library, tinkering with history," he sighed contentedly. "It is the most wondrous place." His face lit up thinking of that treasure trove to which he had unlimited access.

He fully understood the Church of Rome and Vatican City were not about religion, but power and wealth. It was business and his family had always had someone on the inside. His duty to his family was foremost in his life and he took this and his role at the Vatican very seriously.

The political influence and parties of Italy might fluctuate and change, but the Church of Rome and Vatican City were a constant, and had maintained its power base against all threats throughout the centuries.

He might have been better off in the banks his family controlled, Lina thought as they tussled verbally. 'Pity,' she thought whimsically. Excusing herself, she sauntered over to the ladies room, while Edoardos seated himself once again and patiently waited until she returned to her seat.

"Speaking of mistresses," Lina said archly, leaning back in her chair.

"Oh were we?" Edoardos countered.

"What do you think about this appalling murder?" As the waiter brought their meals and placed hers in front of her, she leaned forward with a frown on her face.

"I don't know." A shadow passed across his face, darkening his countenance. "Everyone's at a loss to understand what is happening, including the police." Edoardos looked down at his plate. "This looks good. Why did you bring that up? I'll lose my appetite. We knew these women and their families personally. It's ghastly."

"Have you any theories?" Picking up her fork, she speared a piece of the duck to hold it secure and then used the knife to separate a piece. Lifting it to her mouth, she sighed contentedly while tasting the game bird, "Mmm this is delicious."

"Cara Mia, can we please speak of something else while we eat our meal? This is most distressing for all of us."

"I'm sorry Edoardos," Lina said contritely. "I didn't think," and they turned the subject to more trivial matters, as they enjoyed the meal and wine.

"Would you like some dessert sir/madam?" the waiter enquired, hovering expectantly.

Edoardos looked at Lina, who shook her head, "un caffè per favore."

"E per me," Edoardos also settled for a coffee. "That is my contribution towards my vow of poverty and humility."

The meal completed, after having left a generous annuity for the waiter, they leisurely wandered arm in arm back to Edoardos' Black Ferrari.

"How can you possibly drive up to the Big V in this?" Lina gestured at the magnificent, atrociously expensive vehicle. "It's an insult to your vow of poverty," she laughed.

"I hide it in a corner of the courtyard where it cannot be seen," Edoardos grinned as he opened the door. "Anyway Il Papa has his very own Il Papa mobile," he defended himself.

"Sure. But he's the head honcho and you're just a lowly clerk." Ducking into the car, she waited until he got in on his side and started the motor. As the engine growled furiously, he changed gears and they moved through the streets of Rome like a sleek black panther on the prowl for its next meal.

Lina raised the subject again. "How am I supposed to grill you over that?"

"Grill me about what?" Edoardos answered, wondering what she was on about.

"This murder, I'm going to investigate it," Lina said resolutely.

"Oh Lina, don't go there," he warned her."You're treading on dangerous ground."

She jumped on him. "What do you know about it?"

"Nothing," he countered. "Other than it's dangerous."

"And when have I ever shrunk from danger?" she reminded him. "I covered the Balkan war. I went to Bosnia. Now I go to Iraq."

"I know." Every day she had been there he had been concerned for her safety. "I have a feeling about this. Sometimes Italy can be more dangerous than a Slavic war." Biting his lip he changed gear to take a corner.

"What is it E? What are you not telling me?" Looking at him, feeling something imperceptible was casting its shadow over everything.

"Lina, do you know how untouchable this woman was?" Taking his eyes off the road briefly, he glanced at her.

"Yes I do." It was no secret the powerful men protected their spoilt wives, sheltering them from the outside world with its tempests and vulgarities.

"I don't think you do understand. For her to have been taken is outrageous. This is the work of a lunatic,who is being hunted by forces you can't begin to imagine and yet he manages to elude them." Changing gear once again, a frown crossed his face and he growled at her in tune with the powerful car. "Someone like this would swat you aside like an annoying fly, if you got in his way."

"If he is an Italian he knows the repercussions will destroy him. What makes him think he is invulnerable is beyond me. The very earth he walks upon will become narrower and narrower each day, as he is hunted from within."

"He has to be stopped by any means," Lina protested. "There could be more than one assassin." ."

"Lina, stop it!" E began to wish he had not eaten a rich meal as his stomach turned over. "Desist I say."

"You know I won't." Lina's back was bristling. Being told what to do was not her forte. "Listen E, the body must have been nailed to the cross first, in order to speed up the process," Lina shuddered at the thought. "This could win me a Pulitzer Prize if I crack it open."

"Find another story for your aspirations of a prestigious award." Angrily he dropped gears again, as they rounded yet another corner in the narrow winding streets on the way to her apartment in the Centro Storico of Rome.

Lina loved living in the historical quarter, with its warm interesting artistic environment. Every year, the *100 painters of Via Margutta*, a traditional arts festival which helped critics discover new artists, was held there and she revelled in the atmosphere.

"Damn you Lina, you don't know what you are up against."

"You sound as though you do E." Lina looked at him sharply.

"I know many historical secrets, some of which have never died out." He reached out and put his hand on her arm, as though beseeching her. "Please stop Lina."

"E, a woman you know died, horribly. What do you know?" She was dismayed at his rejection. "These women are not disposable tissues, dropped on the pavement when someone has wiped the dog shit off their shoes. This is Rome, not Southern Italy, where their stupid blood feuds ensure somebody disappears constantly. If you will not help me to prevent this happening to another helpless woman, maybe another one you know, I'll do it by myself."

Edoardos knew she would not stop once her mind was made up, but was not about to help her self destruct. "No, I won't and that's an end to it."

Pulling up on the pavement below the sixty-nine steps that were required to access her apartment in the old quarter of Campo Marzio, she angrily opened the door before he could help her out.

"Don't bother coming up."

He reached out and caught her arm. "Don't be like that." Taking a deep breath, they began the ascent through the narrow alleys and steps shaded by walls overgrown with wisteria, bougainvillea, palms, figs, and roses which shut them up.

At the top Edoardos emphasized. "I mean it Lina. Don't be a naïve meddling American. Leave it to the experts."

Shocked Lina drew back and looked at him in consternation. In all the years she had known him, he had never spoken to her in this manner before.

Watching whilst she opened the door he kissed her on the cheek. "I'll see you next week for dinner." With that, he turned and began the trek back down the steps, to his luxury vehicle that hunkered there menacingly, reminding him of the murderer of the woman who moved in at the pinnacle of society. Shuddering at the thought, he paused as he put the key in the lock, whilst ruminating about the pernicious underbelly of the city he loved with all his heart.

Chapter Five – The Brotherhood of the Cross

They had met in the sacristy of the chapel of the Monastery of the St Gerard thirty kilometres south east of Rome. Some with tenuous links to the men charged with tracking down The Magdalene, her offspring and their followers, and eliminating them centuries before. They had not counted on the followers of the Church of the Nazarene forming a secret society that passed on the flame. Generation to generation, which fanned the subversive ideology that Christ was not celibate and bore children with *The Magdalene* of all people.

Eight of them garbed in a black habit and a camel-hair cloak of the same colour with a white eight-pointed cross adorning the breast of the black habit. Normally the cloak of this order was only worn for ceremonial occasions which the Protector had deemed this was.

This order which had a chequered history and whose fortunes had strengthened in the twentieth century, was now a key player in the struggle for the future of the Roman Catholic Church.

All were dedicated to their objective of stamping out the rumours that abounded on the Internet, citing Jesus as mortal. He survived the crucifixion for a brief time with his spirit broken. As a Rabbi he was married to Mary Magdalene.

Far from being the prostitute that Pope Gregory I labelled her in 591AD she was a woman of power. Pope John Paul II had apologised for the slur in 1969, which had driven the Protector into a frenzy.

'What was the matter with the man?' A man he had admired had plummeted to below zero on any scale.

"The problem with educating the masses," he sneered, "results in them sniffing around in places they should not be and exposing secrets that have been long buried. The Internet is an absolute menace these days."

"How did this rumour begin?" queried one of the group?

"There are too many people sticking their noses into matters they have no business with. The Emperor Diocletian destroyed most of the Christian scriptures, including the Nazarean Gospels and documents from a group of followers of the despised Magdalene. He relegated her to her rightful place in those days, as submissive to man and based on the original sin."

The Protector had no truck with this modern thinking, which in his opinion had upset the natural balance of things.

The men around him nodded in agreement.

"It is time the Holy Mother Church returned to her rightful status and has a political voice." This was one action of the Pope John Paul II he agreed with. "I have my spies and news has reached my ears about a group of well connected women belonging to a group called le Donne in Azzuro. They revere Mary Magdalene and claim to hold a casket that contains a secret about Our Lord Jesu Cristo that they are going to reveal to the world."

The group of men assembled looked at him then at each other, wondering what these ridiculous women had to say, that would be important enough to declare it to the world at large.

"What secret?" one ventured.

"You may well ask." His face a mask of fury the Protector sneered in derision at the thought of these women believing they had something of importance to share. "They are claiming they have the betrothal contract that proves Jesus and Mary Magdalene were married. Heresy," he hissed, wishing it was the Middle Ages and he could burn these heretics alive at the stake. "We are tasked with finding that contract, which is surely a forgery, and destroying it."

The group shuffled their feet looking decidedly uncomfortable and one soul braver than the other ventured a comment. "What effect would this have on the Church if it was widely acknowledged?"

"You fool." The Protector rounded on the unfortunate man who was now cowering in fear before him. "This could destroy the Holy Roman Catholic Church which has stood invioable for two thousand years. I," and he took his right hand and placed it on his heart, "will never let this happen. I will hunt down these heretics and destroy this contract. "

The highly disturbed monks and clerics clamored in unison.

"But the Reverendo Padre?" It was understood that all matters of the testimony for and against the church, must be referred to Il Papa, who would make a decision on the matter.

The Protector was not about to trust the current Il Papa, Callixtus IV. "That specious do-gooder."

A collective gasp when up from the group.. Hopefully the cellar didn't have ears.

The Protector's face darkened and his eyes grew even colder. A chill that told of death and despair circled through the room.

"I have not heard anything about this," one of the group spoke up. "Surely people will ignore it. I have not read anything on the Internet."

"We are going to pre-empt any announcement of any kind," the Protector promised. "We are going to silence these imposters." He had selected those hangers-on who wouldn"t have a problem with this.

"Now." He crossed himself. "I want your commitment to this cause."

"We are at your service Vostra Eminenza - *Your Eminence*," and they bowed their heads in obeisance to him.

The Cardinale for such he was, delighted in the power he held as a member of the Curia, being a Prefect who directed one of the liturgical Offices of the Holy See.

"It must never see the light of day." Nor was he averse to using his power to gain his own ends.

Poor man, he couldn't help it, as he came from a long line of coat tailers to the Papacy, from which his family had derived power and wealth. Unfortunately they had fallen on troubled times and as a group were not nearly as powerful, nor wealthy, as they had once been.

Without solid connections he had to make extraordinary efforts to suck up to those who matter, in order to rise in the ranks of the Vatican Hierarchy. His fanatical devotion to the Holy Roman Catholic Church and its liturgy had helped him advance to his present post.

"It must be destroyed, burned, condemned to hell for all time," one breast beater angrily shouted.

"And it will." The Cardinale looked at them, knowing the church had discovered such documents before and rather than destroy them, had buried them deeply in the vaults located in the basement of the Tower of Winds, which were very difficult to access.

"To achieve our goal we must destroy the followers of the Magdalene Whore."

Once again his face twisted in a mask of fury. He simply was unable to contain his emotions where Mary Magdalene was concerned.

"Surely they can be written off as some deluded new age group."

Whirling around to find the speaker, the Cardinale shot out his arm and pointed with his index finger to the unfortunate man.

"They are not one of these modern cultists. One of their number claims a connection with the Trencavel family of the Languedoc. They offered protection to the Cathars who settled there and in Northern Italy."

"I thought the Cathars were all destroyed by Il Papa Innocent III in the 12th century."

"Of themselves, they are unimportant. It is the Trencavel family that kept this legend alive. The memory of the Magdalene whore that has persisted since the last of them, died in the Languedoc in the 14th century."

"How is this so?"

"When the Cathars were hunted down and burnt at the stake a few of them escaped and took refuge in Cordova. The Trencavel family sent their women and children with them."

"Why did the church not track them all down and destroy them?"

"They no longer posed a threat. For some reason, this ridiculous cult have chosen this place and time to make themselves and their supposed secret, known."

His cold eyes raked the gathered assembly. "This heresy has infiltrated and corrupted our noble Italian families and I will not countenance this. Now that I have discussed the matter with you and have your full agreement, we will proceed with my plan."

The group murmured amongst themselves as they waited to see what the Protector would say next.

"This heresy," he spat the words out viciously, "was passed down by the followers of the subversive ideology of Arian Christianity, which the Emperor Constantine stamped out."

"The woman we crucified did not reveal the whereabouts of the contract."

"No, she did not." The violent psychopath who was leading his merry little band of equally vicious psychotics, looked at each of them in turn. "Therefore we will take another of them. We will force them to abandon their plans and destroy this outrageous cult." Eyes like those from the fiery hell of Dante betrayed his madness.

"We will never allow our Holy Mother church to be destroyed. Take this vow with me before our Lord." The Protector's face darkened further, until his evil soul emanated from his being, chilling even these soulless men, as his gaze rested upon them, one by one

The group looked at him searchingly. He revealed only as much as he felt they needed to know, and had kept back most of this information. However, they were quite willing to follow him into the jaws of hell, if it would gain them kudos in Heaven.

"The Church has weathered many a storm before, Protector," one eager beaver sought to be heard. "Can she not do so in the face of this tempest?"

The Cardinale's head seemed to extend forward like a snake's seeking its prey. "Only if we make sure of it. It has been the brave men of the Roman Catholic Church that hasvekept the doctrine pure and unadulterated over the centuries. They did not hesitate to take whatever measures were necessary." His physical form seemed to change even further and those gathered almost expected him to grow horns upon his forehead. "This heretical doctrine will die once we discover the secret and destroy it along with the keeper; and I know who she is." Locking his steely gaze with the groups' collective one, they looked shocked and one or two hissed their dismay.

"She is here?"

"Here in Rome?" one stalwart queried.

"In Rome, the Eternal City?" another exclaimed incredulously.

"Yes she is," the Protector's visage infused with an uncontrollable rage, "and her bastard whelp."

Heads shot up and eyebrows climbed to the ceiling. This was news, something they had not counted on.

The Cardinale was alarmed to suddenly see, a less than steely determination to follow him into the fires of hell if need be.

"A child?" Whispering amongst themselves. Some did draw a line in the sand and expressed their reluctance to take the life of a child.

"It must be done." A shadow passed over the Cardinale's face and his raised his hands appeared like talons, ready to tear the very fabric of society into minute pieces. If it would protect the church his soul belonged to he was prepared to murder a child, even one of his own kin. The doctrine of the church was woven into every fibre and cell of his diseased mind and body.

"We must seek them out and destroy them." The Protector watched each face to see if there were serious objections. His personality carried the day and as one, all heads nodded in agreement. They were with him in this.

"Most assuredly," one particularly nasty being agreed wholeheartedly.

"They will be hunted down and killed."

Now they noticed him mulling something over in his mind.

"I know who this woman and child are but I do not know where they have hidden the so called secret. Before I deal with them we must take another from their group and make her tell us."

No-one objected.

"The Church must return to its origins. Il Papa John Paul II worked so hard to bring this about and I will not see it fail," he promised the gathering.

Alluding to the dogmatic absolutist Biblical morality of feudal times, he was in agreement with John Paul II's desire to see the Church of Rome return to a time when it shared hegemonic power with the State and the Pope was the coequal of any king in power and wealth.

"We must complete this mission in our lifetime." Again his gaze raked the group who continued to nod. "Put an end to it." A pleased smile creased his face. "Then we will make our pact now," and he walked to each of the group of eight men and shook their hands. "Follow me to the altar in the chapel, my brothers. Testify with me and dedicate your life to the Lord."

A few of them looked at each other a little uncertainly, as the Protector's cold gaze bore down on them, but quickly changed their minds. They would rather not be on the receiving end of his wrath. He had shown what he was capable of.

"Is your love for your Lord and Saviour strong enough to testify in front of him? Think of your families before you, who served the Church for centuries. They never hesitated to do what was required."

Two or three of them swallowed hard, but after glancing furtively at the others, nodded along with the others. It was too late to turn back now.

"Then declare with me. You were specially chosen because of your families' commitment to Mother Church. Do not let her down now. There is no room in he Brotherhood of the Cross for anyone who is not totally committed," he hissed at them, looking around like a cobra about to strike, should one of them show any sign of omission.

"We are committed." Crying out in unison, they were well aware the alternative was less than desirable. "We will do what is required of us." Now they were party to the Protector's scheme, it would be madness to resist. He was far too powerful in the hierarchy of the Vatican to cross.

It helped that they were as mad as he. Religious fanaticism will do that to a certain type of person. Furthermore, many of them owed their present positions in the world and church, to him. Nor did they want to meet with some unforeseen accident before their time.

"Then follow me to the chapel and in the presence of our Lord, testify that you will stand with me in ridding the earth of this heresy."

The men rose and did as he asked, clerical robes rustling as they followed him out of the cavern into the chapel, then rearranged themselves in a semi circle in front of the high altar ready to make their vow.

"Now, you will turn to each other and testify that these evildoers will be sought out and destroyed along with this bogus secret," the Protector commanded.

The eight men did as they were bid and yet another secret society bent on wreaking havoc, conspired in the bowels of the earth.

"We have our secret sign by which we know each other. It seals our brotherhood and its commitment to do whatever is necessary to defend the Holy Roman Catholic faith."

The gathered men nodded solemnly and turning to each other grasped hands in a parody of the masonic handshake with the thumb pressing against the first knuckle joint and the little finger pressing against the outside of his fellow conspirator's little finger.

"I personally will strike them down. I make this vow to my Lord and Saviour." The Protector turned to face the altar and raised his face to the cross above, as he put his hand on his heart. Then he turned back to face the men.

"I know I can trust each and everyone of you." Without a doubt. After all, he had them by the cojones now. His co-conspirators had willingly colluded with him in murdering the first woman. They were his, and he could bend them to his will whenever he chose.

The group once more assured him of their loyalty, as they nodded in agreement.

"The Church and her ideology must be protected at all costs," a Monsignor stated.

"Is the Reverendo Padre aware of this?" one of the friars asked.

The Protector held up his hand. "There is no need to trouble the Reverendo Padre with such knowledge." Hell would freeze over before he informed the spineless interloper about his deeds and intentions.

After all, *he* was a descendant of an ancient family who had produced one Pope and controlled the destiny of the Church and state for many centuries. They had let nothing get in the way of their ambition and neither would he. Their blood ran in his veins. They had answered to no-one but their own. He was no lesser a man than they.

"His burden is heavy and it is my job to protect and shelter him from such heresy. It would not be seemly for him to challenge this in public."

No-one was left in doubt as the Cardinale's smile was replaced by an implacable determination. An honest man now wore St Peter's crown, but make no mistake, everyone was aware of the steel that lay beneath the gentle heart

"In the past we had the Holy Office of the Inquisition to stamp out such heresy," one ventured, thinking some of the devices that Office had employed,would be quite handy now.

"We will implement such methods as are necessary to get hold of this contract." Turning to look around at his cohorts he challenged them once more, "Are you with me on this?"

It was too late to back out now. To attempt to do so would be suicidal and no-one in this group was looking to suffer an early demise. They were having too good a time. Raising their right arm, they brought it around in front of their chest until their hands rested against their hearts. "You have our pledge Protector."

"Dying is too good for them," the Protector hissed sibilantly. "Rest assured, they will reveal secrets before they pass out of this life."

"They are heretics," the Abate of the monastery declared, "and they must be treated as such. They are not worthy of our Lord's love."

"I have devised the way we will deal with them, and you must all be committed to it," the Protector's eyes gleamed, as he began to outline his plan to them and his willing group of psychotics listened eagerly.

Chapter Six – The Monastery of St. Gerard

Returning to the monastery, the Cardinale felt relief in flagellating himself on the floor of a cold cell, a ritual he looked forward to. In his twisted mind, it proved his dedication to his Lord and his willingness to suffer as much pain as he could inflict on himself, as he would never be able to experience that of his Lord.

Was not the Blessed St Dominic exemplary in mortification, doctrine and contemplation? Three times each night, he would whip himself to blood, once for his own salvation, a second time for sinners, and a third for departed souls. Later, other Dominican saints would do the same.

Dominic habitually wept for sinners in the towns he passed, while celebrating Mass, and during his vigils. He was heard crying: "O Lord, what will become of sinners?" Often on the road, he would either instruct his companions, or wander off to pray. His most evident characteristic was that he always spoke to God in prayer, or about God to others.

The Cardinale had not realised he would take such pleasure in the role of the assassin. Perhaps it was because his victims were women. He was well aware he had acquired a pathological hatred of the fairer sex, fuelled by membership in the Brotherhood, whose main reason for existence was to stamp out the Magdalene legend.

Searching through France and Italy, even Germany for their victims, it was known the bloodline had found its way from Egypt and Judaea into Europe. Prominent families had been involved and the secrets had been passed down through the ages. Secrets that were locked in the vaults beneath the Vatican had revealed this to him. His was such a high office, that access to all of these secrets was his to command. Nothing was denied to him.

How easy it had been, to convince the victim to take a trip with him. Why not? He was a well respected Cardinale, who moved with ease in aristocratic circles. He was the last person anyone would suspect of murder.

The brotherhood had been waiting for him in the mausoleum not far from the Priory of the Knights of Malta, and when the victim had seen the assembled group, she had turned to him, puzzled. How satisfying to see the look of trust, replaced by awareness of her danger, then turn to terror as they took hold of her and stripped her. An altar had been set up in the mausoleum and after telling her they knew of her secret, that she was one of the followers of the Magdalene's 'Donne in Azzuro,' they had told her she would be offered as a sacrifice to their Lord and Saviour, as the ancient Jewish tradition had demanded.

Denials were useless, as he had meticulously proven these women were keepers of the flame. In that position they should have not trusted anyone from the Church, but who amongst the well connected circles would have dreamed of the heresy these women were perpetrating. And who amongst these women in blue, would have believed they were in danger.

It did not matter that there were lesser beings in the circles. Once their leaders disappeared, the circles would dissolve without the strength to hold it together. Then they would seek out the circles in France and Germany, which they had uncovered, as they made their presence known in this so called enlightened age. The brotherhood would form in these countries as well. Who in Catholic countries, would dream of these vipers in their bosoms. There had been Chamberlains in the Vatican, amongst the group these heretics had moved in.

Affixing gloves to their hands, they had stripped the victim and tied a loincloth around her hips, as was the custom with crucifixions in ancient Rome and as Christ had been clothed. "It is the Magdalene who should have been crucified, not our Lord," they cried as one.

"She should have been crucified as a common criminal," the Protector hissed at her, as the victim looked at him in stark terror. "You will take her place." Bringing his face right up to hers, he revelled in the fear she showed, as she tried to draw back from him."You will be crucified as our Lord was."

No band of cloth was affixed across her breasts, to maintain a modicum of female dignity. These crucifiers of women, wanted every shred of dignity to be stripped from this woman.

"How dare you worship a prostitute, a common whore." His spittle sprayed over her as she fainted.

The victim had screamed and her body thrashed around as the group had dragged her to the altar and laid her before the Cross, while the Lord looked down upon their actions. The Protector then took a cat of nine tails and lashed her across the back until her back bled.

"Let us see how strong your faith in The Magdalene is now?" he had hissed as the victim's screams had rent the air. He timed it precisely so she did not die from shock.

Nodding to the dottore, he stood back as a dose of Atropine was injected. This paralyzed every muscle in her body, including her throat and eyes, but she was still fully aware of what was happening to her.

"Now we take her to the Priory."

A risky maneuver, but they knew of secret passageways beneath the Villa, which had been used by Benedictine monks in the tenth century, and after them the Knights Templar.

After reviving her, they had taken her bleeding body to a prepared cross and lain her on it.

Again he nodded and the group covered her with a sheet of plastic to ensure there would be no trace of DNA on her body, as they spat and jeered at her, as they held her down.

Each one took turns at hammering in the nails to the hands and the feet, delighting in the terror they saw in the woman's eyes. If she was not already paralyzed, this indeed would have finished off the job. When the woman saw what they were about to do, she fainted. To no avail. Cold water was splashed on her and as she revived, the nails were driven in to her hands and feet. Once again, she passed out with terror and shock, her mind unable to accept what was happening to her.

"Are we prepared?" he had asked.

"Yes," his deranged sycophants responded. Eight lifted the cross and the victim silently cried out as her body was strained and twisted.

An underground tunnel built to facilitate Nazi escapes through the Vatican ratline, it served as a timely route to the site of the old Jewish cemetery.

At the exit he dialled a number connecting him with a member of the Brotherhood stationed outside. "Is all clear?"

"Yes, there is no-one here at this time."

They had chosen the spot carefully. Above the glorious Il Roseta (Rose garden) where the remains of the imperial palace could be seen on the Palatine.

No curious passersby was likely to interrupt them late at night as the garden was only open from May to July when the roses were in full bloom.

"Dig the hole quickly and pour in the quick setting cement," he ended the call.

Turning around, he looked at the group in the back and the victim who would know her fate to the bitter end.

The cellphone rang a prearranged signal of three rings. The clerics lifted the cross and carried it to the hole. Before they erected it, he walked over with a crown of thorns and thrust it on the head, watching as the blood ran down her face.

The Protector delighted in thrusting a crown of thorns on the victim's head and hanging around her neck a sign which read 'The Magdalene-Whore'.

Putting their shoulders into it, they grunted and strained as they placed the cross into the quick drying cement and held it upright until it was set hard.

Bending down the Protector picked up a spear that had been dipped in poison and thrust it into her side, watching as the blood streamed out of the wound.

Satisfied they stood back from their handwork.

"Quickly," he said. "Back to the Villa. Make sure we cover up our tracks as we go."

Each took a leafy branch they had brought with them. Stripping them from the Villa's trees would have been alerted the police. Walking backwards they brushed their tracks from the ground. Into the tunnel, emerging once again in the cellars of the villa, flushed with their success.

Lesser mortals' hearts would have given up the ghost along with their victims, but these men were made of sterner stuff.

Excitedly, the Protector turned to the group. "Good work. Now you must disperse quickly and quietly one at a time, so that the movement from here will not be noticed."

Turning to the Abate of the Monastery of St. Gerard, he said. "You will stay the night with me my friend. You have given a reason for your absence?"

"Yes Vostra Eminenza," the Abate confirmed. "They do not expect me back tonight."

"Good, good." The Cardinale's heart was pounding and his entire body was tingling, he wanted to go back to his apartment and relive the scene over and over again. Little did the group know, that under his cassock he had recorded the diabolical scene on a video camera, which he could play at his leisure to satiate his bestiality.

"We meet two days from now at the monastery to consecrate our sacrifice to our Lord." Smiling with self satisfaction, he congratulated himself on using his charismatic power to mould a group of fanatics who would do his bidding.

Chapter Seven – Those who had the most to lose

Eight men clothed in business suits, sat around the large round wooden oak table in the beautifully appointed room of the spacious Priory of the Knights of Malta, together with the Cardinale clad in his ecclesiastical robes.

"What in the name of God did you think you were doing?" Leaning forward, his face a mask of fury, the spokesperson for this rogue group from the Order, attacked the Cardinale. "Are you completely deranged?"

He was now regretting using him for this job, which required a more delicate touch than that of the maniac seated across from him, had employed.

Remaining poised the Cardinale responded to the attack calmly. "I did what no-one else was willing to do." Leaning forward he glared at each and every one of them. "I sullied my hands when none of you would have had the guts."

"Sullied your hands?" the spokesman's voice rose as he thundered across the table at the Cardinale. "You were told to quietly and I emphasise this word *quietly*, question one scared timorous woman and then once again, *quietly* dispose of the body, *if* necessary."

Sitting upright in his well upholstered chair, he banged his hands on the table. "What do you do? You *crucify* her, for God's sake," his voice was incredulous, the look on his face one of outrage, "in full view of the entire city of Rome."

"The entire city of Rome was asleep at three am." The Cardinale studied his meticulously manicured fingernails.

"Don't play with me," the spokesman warned. Here was a ruthless man of great power, that he did not hesitate to use when the occasion demanded it, but even he had a problem getting his head around the Cardinale's actions. "Jesus wept, there are security guards on patrol in this area. In fact they are designated to protect this villa in particular." Throwing himself back in the chair he remained glowering at the unrepentant Cardinale."How the hell did you get past them?"

The Cardinale merely smiled codly.

All the men at this table were at the pinnacle in their chosen field of endeavour, either through their own determined efforts or by the accident of birth. Many of them highly visible and recognisable in the media. Exposure as perpetrators of this unsavory plotswas unthinkable. However, this was precisely the situation this lunatic had placed them in.

Financiers, heads of state, directors of intelligence agencies, bankers par excellence, major and minor heads of royalty and aristocratic lineages, were all at risk because of the whim of one man. His position within the Vatican hierarchy was not one of a minion.

"A firm message needs to be sent to this group of stupid women who must be stopped by any means at our disposal," the impertinent churchman challenged them all.

"A stern message?" A minor royalty personage, whose family's history was steeped in murder and mayhem raised his eyebrows. "Why didn't you just cut off her head and send it to them like the Mafia do." His own house ha, cleaned up their act. Well in public anyway.

"I considered that."

"Jesus Christ." One of the highly recognisable top bankers of the world muttered in despair.

The Cardinale, who remained unfazed as he was under attack from this group of powerful men, did not miss a beat. Leaning forward, he placed both hands on the table and admitted, "I now know the one who keeps the contract safe."

"So crucifying the woman wasn't for nothing then." Sarcasm dripping from every word, the head of an entire country's intelligence service,cast a scathing glance at the man in the crimson beretta.

"Far from it." His languid tone continued to offend the other men in the room, as the Cardinale enjoyed every moment of his time in the sun. "She and her mother happen to be members of my family, albeit by a most unfortunate marriage."

As he dropped the bombshell, the jaws of the other eight men dropped open, despite themselves.

"I am in the perfect position to see they disappear, never to be seen again."

"Oh God." The man from tan intelligence service who had not hesitated to employ torture when required, put his hand to his head, as the others recovered their composure. "What mad scheme do you have in mind now? I really think we should get someone else to deal with this," he appealed to the assembly at large. "He's unhinged and could expose us all."

The spokesman raised his hand to stave him off and motioned for the Cardinale to continue.

"I will meet the mother and tease out the location."

"Meet with her? What you're going to take her out for lunch at Quinzi & Gabrielli and question her over the table whilst all the other diners and restaurant staff listen in," the spy chief protested heatedly. "You think she is just going to sit there and admit everything, then hand it all over to you, a Cardinale of the Church of Rome, whom this group despise."

"A stroll in the gardens of the palazzo will suffice," he responded disdainfully.

"And then what? Another crucifixion." Lip curled between a snarl and a sneer, a Head of State shook his head.

"No, I have other plans for them."

"Oh something high profile I have no doubt," the last speaker pointed his finger at the Cardinale. "If you do anything to further endanger this Order, you will meet an untimely death."

"Tsk, tsk." The Cardinale remained completely unperturbed. "This will never see the light of day."

"You," the spokesman pointed a finger at the Cardinale, "after you have found if, and I emphasise *if*, there is any evidence to be recovered, will do nothing more more than arrange an unfortunate traffic accident. This dies with them and goes away."

The Cardinale nodded agreement. "As you say," but having no intentions whatsoever, of abiding by their directive.

The spokesman waved him out of the room and the group looked at each wryly.

Chapter Eight – Office of the Doctrine of the Faith (formerly known as The "Holy Office" and previously the "Holy Roman Inquisition)

Giovanni Contardella was now one of the most powerful men in The Vatican, being appointed by the current Pontiff to the position of Prefect of the Office of the Doctrine of the Faith.

Following the assassination of Benedict XVI that had shocked a world weary of political murders, Callixtus IV had ascended to the Throne of Peter. The College of Cardinals had surprised the Roman Curia in a rare burst of wisdom, electing a good, wise and humble man, the incumbent Callixtus IV.

Not without his detractors, the rumblings in the front seats arose. It now appeared Il Papa Callixtus was another liberal, cast in the same manner as Popes John XXIII and John Paul I. Already concerned glances were being directed at him and eyebrows raised at some of his intended changes, which smacked of ultra liberalism.

He had taken his papal name from one of the first popes who had served his Lord in perilous times. Born a slave he had worked in the mines before ascending to the papacy and been martyred. The only record of him had been written by his bitter rival.

Giovanni Contardella had been viewed as the natural successor to the Papacy as the late Pope had trusted him completely. However the brass ring on the merry-go-round had eluded his grasp this time.

If he was disappointed he hid it well. Following the early demise of Angelo Amato, Prefect of the Office of the Congregation of the Doctrine of the Faith, the new Pontiff had appointed the Cardinale to this important Office.

Heads turned as the tall handsome man from the aristocratic family of Contardella, walked into the Offices of the Doctrine of the Faith which were housed in the Palazzo del S. Uffizi. In his red-trimmed black cassock buttoned down the front, with its sash of red watered-silk ribbon, and the scarlet zucchetto (skullcap) on his head, he made a striking figure.

His family had served and influenced The Holy See for centuries, back to the time of Il Papa Alexander V1 of the colourful house of Borgia.

As he entered his personal suite, Cardinale Contardella braced himself for another demanding day. Nodding to Cardinale Latham, the Cardinale of New York, who was waiting for an interview with him, he swept past him into his luxuriously appointed office. His private secretary had followed him into the inner sanctum and placed the leather bound folder with its impressive seal on the desk in front of the Cardinale.

"When would you like me to show Cardinale Latham in, Vostra Eminenza?"

The latter was weary of the church in America with its ongoing scandals about paedophile priests, homosexuality and priests conducting affairs with their parishioners. Some had even left the church to live with women. It was true St. Paul established many small communities and left them in the hands of married priests and bishops, but this was before the establishment of the Holy Roman Catholic Church.

None of these thoughts showed on his face. The Contardellas had learned long ago, to mask their thoughts and feelings.

"Do we have the most up to date reports on the matters I wish to discuss with him?" Opening the folder, he perused the agenda and papers relating to the matters at hand. Raising his head, he met the young priest's eyes and held them.

"Yes Vostra Eminenza, as you requested."

Dropping his eyes to the paper once more Cardinale Contardella skimmed the details quickly.

It was the same story worldwide. The Church's inability to attract new priests to a life of celibacy; those that remained were rebelling against the strict rules; and women were demanding the right to become priests, for God's sake. These modern times were exceedingly tedious what with women's expectations rising above their station, in his opinion.

Quoting unsubstantiated literature they claimed proved women were priests in the early Christian church, the women of America were beating their breasts and demanding equal rights. Not while he was in the driving seat.

Then there was the ongoing thorn in the side of celibacy. Unfortunately they could point to the early days of the church when priests and popes had taken wives in the early days of the church. Thirty-nine popes having been sexually active before the Roman practice of abstaining from marital relations to conserve energy before a battle or a sporting event had found its way into liturgical practice. Celibacy ensured the wealth of the Church *stayed in the Church*.

The cleric cleared his throat to remind him. "Here is your schedule of appointments for the day, Vostra Eminenza. I have kept most meetings to 15-20 minutes, except for the visitation from the African nations' Cardinales, for whom I have allotted one hour."

Cardinale Contardella sighed and turned his attention back to the task in hand. His eyes skimmed over the appointments. "All the relevant documentation is here?"

"Yes Vostra Eminenza. There is a brief covering each appointment."

"Thank you for your diligence. Please give me ten minutes to peruse this and then show Cardinale Latham in."

The Contardellas were aristocratic gentlemen who treated their underlings with dignity and respect. In the viciously contested cut and thrust of the Vatican politics this was a rare quality indeed.

"Yes Vostra Eminenza." The secretary bowed stiffly and backed away from the desk, before turning and exiting, returning with Cardinale Latham at precisely the correct time.

At the back of the Cardinale's mind was the state of the church. It was true, the attendances in America and other Western countries had decreased drastically and there were lawsuits pending against the Church for sexual abuse.

'Why on earth did John Paul II ignore the scandals and allow Ratzinger to shelter the guilty by moving them to other parishes where they continued to offend,' he reminisced. 'The effect on the Church has been nothing less than ruinous." With explicit media coverage nothing could be swept under the carpet. They were like ravenous dogs feasting on the bones of bodies already picked clean.

He looked at Cardinale Latham with distaste. A stronger hand than his was needed to pull the American priesthood together.

Cardinale Ratzinger had formerly been the Prefect of the Office that Contardella now held. His attitude towards the sexual scandals had been seen by critics as at best indifferent, and at worst, complicit in covering it up, both in specific cases and as a matter of policy. During his tour of England in Two thousand and ten his apology to the children that had been abused was criticised as not going far enough.

The aftermath of the attacks on the World Trade Centre on 9/11 had seen a brief resurgence in attendances at mass, but there was no doubt that the Catholic Church of Rome was not the flavour of the month in the United States.

"Vostra Eminenza." The Cardinale from had never been able to read the Prefect nor get close to him. Italians were extremely class conscious and the aristocracy held itself aloof, even in the Church.

'How am I going to get him to agree to some of my requests?' he asked himself. Concord with his ideas seemed as remote as the man himself. Still he had to try if he wanted further power in the church.....and he did.

The day went by, with the African bishops also wanting more of the church than the institution was prepared to give.

A lot of emphasis was being placed in this area, as the work of John Paul II over the past ten years before his demise had dramatically increased their fold in third world nations. The Cardinale's mind wandered off for a moment. *'Pity they were as poor as church mice, and the contributions to the Church were not even worth mentioning.'*

However as their nations were wealthy in mineral rights, once the corruption could be stemmed and more of the wealth found its way to the hands of the masses, Holy Mother Church would benefit. Thry had understood this from time immemorial. Conquer the minds and hearts of the masses whilst they were illiterate and confused and they will grasp out for the hand of a saviour. Give them some hope; something to live for, even if was the promise of greater things when they died.

'It's all about the great hereafter. Promises are made to the faithful by all the great religions of the world, because no-one was in a position to refute the afterlife did not exist,' he thought sardonically. *'Step up and receive the first prize for being the lucky contestants who abided by the tenets of the faith.'*

Unable to guarantee a prosperous and happy life for the teeming masses on this earth, they settled for the assurances of their various Gods and Prophets that the hereafter was what one really should be aiming for.

Diplomatically reassuring all of his visitors that he would give their requests every consideration, he sighed with relief when the last had left his presence.

"Vostra Eminenza," his private secretary had returned with the rest of the day's schedule. "You have three meetings this afternoon, beginning with a luncheon for the emissary from South America."

"Have my car brought round for me," he said brusquely, rising from his desk. No Roman worth his salt, would work through the day without the essential long Italian lunch.

Walking briskly to the side entrance where he knew his car would be waiting to drive him lunch and back to the Vatican for his scheduled meetings, the Cardinale's mind wandered back to the days of Constantinople and Saladin, the Warrior King, whom he admired greatly. He could not help but feel regret for the regression of one of the most intellectual and enlightened nations in the world, to the state Islam was in now.

Rome had fallen from her former heights, but the Vatican was still a powerful force in these modern times.

Europe was well versed in the art of corruption and diplomacy. The new kid on the block, the United States of America was a babe in the woods when it came to corruption and diplomacy, but was a willing learner. Another century or so and maybe she would not be so clumsy in her overtures and stances.

As Cardinale Contardella was driven to his luncheon appointment he was content.

Chapter Nine – Lina strikes out on her own

Lina was feeling slightly pissed off with Edoardos.

"Godammit. He is my conduit to these people. I thought it was a shoe-in." Angrily she kicked off her shoes, threw herself on to the sofa and sulked while her mind busily sought another way.

It was two days since their dinner and she had tapped into her source at the Carabinieri, to no avail. Apparently they were as baffled as anyone else.

"Oh, to hell with it." Feeling cross, she leaned forward and looked at her feet for inspiration. Finding none there, she frowned. "If E won't help, I'll do it on my own. Didn't need him on any other assignments I covered." Rising she crossed the room and moved over to the terrace, with its amazing view of the Villa Medici. Opening the french doors she stepped outside. It never ceased to amaze her, that she had been lucky enough to score this amazing apartment, on the second floor of a XVI century building, where she could look down at the astonishingly peaceful garden in the midst of this most frantic of cities.

She only needed to turn a corner and walk a hundred metres to the famed Spanish Steps to see the tourists milling around.

"God I've had enough of that for one day," muttering to herself, she gazed over the park and reflected on the Medici history.

"Two popes from one family. Albeit one was an antipope," she continued the conversation with herself. "Not bad going." Leaning over the low parapet she gazed on the tranquil setting of the park and let it lull her from the bad mood she had arrived home in. "From the Godfather of Florence to head honcho in the Big V. Hmmm. Although their fortunes waxed and waned over the centuries, but whose didn't?"

Letting the late sun warm her, she walked over to the wrought iron chair where she spent many lingering hours basking in the heat. Pulling it back from the small wrought iron terrace table, she let herself drop into it and pulling her cargo pants up to her knees, stretched her legs out in front of her, letting her thoughts run free.

"They were certainly bright boys, that Cosimo and his old Dad, building a princely dynasty on banking and commerce rather than through warfare or marriage. Pity about Cosimo's son though, who did his best to lose his inheritance. It's so often the way." Lina had visited the Medici Laurentian library in Florence and boned up on the history of the family.

The Vatican library was established by Cosimo Medici and Pope Nicholas V who shared a common love of Greek culture and Plato in particular

"Shades of E's family," she mused contentedly letting the warmth from the golden orb in the sky warm her. "The Medicis gave their son Giovanni to the Vatican as a boy Cardinale in 1512, with the ultimate goal of him achieving the Papacy, which he did. I wonder if E will make it to the top job." With that thought in mind, peals of laughter emanated from her, "Serves him right."

"Then there was the rebellious antipope, Clement VI, the Medici whom King Charles of France established in a new papal palace in Avignon, to further his own ends, after falling out with Urban VI."

Shaking her head at the duplicity of it all, she recalled how the greed of the King determined him to take over the wealthy area in the south of France where the Knights Templar had settled with their fabled treasure.

Using the excuse they were wiping out the heretical Cathars who lived in the South of France and had penetrated into northern Italy with their dualistic Arianism beliefs, they mounted a cavalcade of bloodthirsty Crusaders to carry out their dirty work.

"And so began the Inquisition." Lina expressed her disgust at the lengths the Roman Catholic Church had gone to in order to preserve their power. "Nasty bastardos," she swore. "Driving people from their homes and burning them at the stake because they would not conform to the dogma of the Catholic Church."

Lifting her right foot and pointing it, she made small circles with it. "Think, think!" she commanded herself. "Connect the dots and see where they take you." Scolding herself for forgetting a journalist's main rule, she rose and going inside picked up a pad and pencil laying on the coffee table and which were always at hand to jot down ideas before they slipped away and were lost forever.

Retracing her steps, she sat down and pulled the chair up to the table. Placing the pad in front of her she began to write down what was known of the murders.

The victim was a woman, a wealthy well connected woman. This was a very risky move.

Mary Magdalene. Why?

A crucifixion. Again very risky. Why? What was the purpose?

Nasties. Who are they?

Location. Aventine Hill.

Proximity to?

Access to?

"It's time to fill in the blanks. I have the what, who and where," she muttered to herself, "but who *are* the Who?" Frowning she raised the pencil to her lips and nibbled until she realised what she was doing. "Great, give myself lead poisoning soon."

"Oh to hell with it!" Throwing the pencil down on the table, she rose and looked back out over Rome. "The Aventine, why the goddamn Aventine?" Her eyes scanned the horizon, trying to make sense of it all. "They couldn't have dragged the body through the city." Something in her mind clicked, "Who on the Aventine?" she exclaimed excitedly.

"Right I'm out of here." Turning back inside, she picked up her trusty enormous shoulder bag that contained her world in it, slung it over her shoulder, grabbed her car keys off a credenza by the door, and ran down the sixty-nine steps as though she was a seasoned athlete.

"Boy, these steps will do it for you every time." Laughing gaily as she reached the street and headed towards her car which was kept in a locked garage a block away, she saw one of her neighbours about to make the climb and waved. "It's better than an hour at the gym three times a week and less expensive," she tossed at him, as he gazed back at her wondering what the hell she was on about.

Jumping into her Peugeot, which was small enough to survive the suicide mission that is Roman traffic, she started the motor. Nosing out of the parking area, into the mayhem, she headed in the direction of Trastavere and thence up the Aventine, passing the homes of the well heeled, many occupied by Ambassadors from foreign countries.

"Yep, this is a high-rent district allright!" she murmured.

Driving into the parking area on the south side of the Santa Sabina monastery, founded in 425 AD and one of the oldest Christian churches still in existence, she told herself, "I'll only be five minutes," as she locked the car.

Running inside, she feasted her eyes on the glorious interior of the basilica, with its beautifully decorated marble friezes and flooring, noting the well lit nave. Her mind flickered on and off like a light switch, as she made a 380 degree turn. "Nothing like the murders could happen here. It's far too open."

Making her way outside, she meandered through the shady walkways of the Giardino degli Aranci, the tranquil Garden of Oranges, with its fantastic views of the many monuments roof tops and domes of Rome. Quickly glancing at the scowling face of Giacomo Della Poretra's fountain, which some say is a reference to Oceanus, a River God, she recalled it had been moved around from various locations, including the Forum and Lungotevere Gianicolense, before finally coming to rest in the peace of the Aventine.

Her eyes roamed over the remains of a wall which once surrounded the 10th Century Savelli Castle, which eventually became a Dominican monastery. Legend has it that the Spanish St Dominic brought the first orange tree from his homeland, and planted it close to the cloister where St Catherine of Siena picked the fruit and made candied fruit, which she gave to Pope Urban VI.

Lina smiled as she thought of the summer theatrical productions she loved to attend in this beautiful setting. With its romantic ambience, it made a favourite trysting spot for lovers. Smiling at the thought she sighed wistfully thinking of E.

"Now don't be such an idiot," she remonstrated with herself, "it's never gonna happen." Then shaking her head emphatically she decried, "Oh damn it, I can daydream when there's no one around."

Making her way out of the garden, a few steps away was the Piazza del Cavallieri, which was surrounded by green cypress trees. Named for the Knights of Malta, on her right hand side was the large white sculpted entrance facade to the Order's priory.

Her eye was caught by the ever present tourists, being shepherded to the view of St Peters through the keyhole in the gate of the Villa Malta.

"Through here," a tour guide told her flock, "it is possible to see three sovereign states: Italy, the Vatican and Malta."

"OK." Looking around she saw a large Texan with ruddy cheeks and a loud voice. "Get the Vatican and Italy. What's this about Malta?"

"This is the Grand Priory of the Knights of Malta," the tour guide tossed at him patronisingly.

"Yeah, so?" the belligerent fellow bellowed. He was more than a match for any haughty Roman female.

"This Order is an extra territorial sovereign state, which enjoys diplomatic immunity," the guide retorted smartly, hoping to shut him up.

"Holy shit," The Texan exclaimed. "How the hell did they get that sort of autonomy? Wish I could declare myself a sovereign state with all the perks."

Other tourists shook their heads at the man's crassness and the guide, looking smug, turned away and beckoned to the rest of her flock to follow her. Refusing to be deterred by the boorish man, she continued with her history lesson. After all, it's what they were here for.

"Originally this was the site of a fortified Palace owned by Alberico II. In 929 it became a Benedictine monastery. In the 12th century it passed into the hands of the famous Knights Templar until they fell out of favor with Pope Clement V. It was then given to the Knights Hospitaller, who were the original order that, led to the present Knights of Malta."

"From the 15th to the 17th centuries, a lot of radical rebuilding went on and at one stage, in the 1600s, it even became a coffee house and was the favorite haunt of the artists of the times."

Looking straight at the obnoxious Texan she repeated with great satisfaction. "In 1869 the site was granted extraterritoriality by Italy." Turning from him, she encouraged them all forward to peer through the keyhole one by one. "Come, come," she beckoned. "If you look to your right you can see the Church of Santa Maria Aventina and in front of us to the left, the Villa with its rooms full of portraits of previous Grand Masters and many valuable paintings."

"Through here, you can also see the wonderful secret garden with cypresses, palms, pathways that lead one through low box hedges and into the wonderful fruit yards."

Lina gazed at the goings on, her mind racing at 100 rpm. "Another merda secret society attached to the Roman Catholic Church." Fairly seething at the conspiracies that had abounded in that institution for centuries; she smacked her palm against her forehead.

Moving forward amongst the tourists, who were lined up waiting to gaze through the keyhole in the green gate set in the wall at the front of the villa, she firmly pushed her way in.

Putting her eye to the keyhole, she looked through to St Peters Cupola, and then let her eyes rove to front, left and right. Drawing back she uttered exasperatedly, "Oh I don't know. What else is here?" Her eye fell on the Church of St Sabina and then travelled on to the famous Garden of Oranges.

Leaning against the wall, she tried to follow niggling thoughts that danced through her mind like busy bees gathering nectar from the flowers.

"The Aventine." Muttering to herself, she was beginning to attract attention. "Why the Aventine? This is all there is up here," and she looked around her at the wall, decorated with obelisks and military trophies and dedicated to the Knights Templar, the monk-warrior defenders of Christianity, as she tried to get her brain into gear. "Home to the Knights of Malta. An extra territorial sovereign state. Untouchable."

At the back of her mind something niggled, trying to get through to the frontal lobe and put its hand up. "A law unto themselves eh? Their standing in the Catholic Church is seemingly on a par with that of Opus Dei. Both organisations are favorites of past popes." She mentally shrugged. "So what?" Still she gazed at the wall, until pins and needles in her left foot told her it was time to move on.

Walking back to the car she opened the door, climbed in and sat there looking back at the Priory.

"What the hell's the matter with me?" Her mind began to sort through the information she had stored in the brain over ten years of being a journalist. "Anything in there about the origins of the Knights of Malta?" she asked her brain. This brought little response from that overburdened receptacle of information.

"Apparently not." Shrugging her shoulders she tried to get into the recesses. "I don't know much about them really. Never been any reason to." Focusing once again on the wall and the buildings behind it, she cocked her head to one side and pulled her attention away from the Villa Malta.

With a last look at her surroundings, Lina put the car into gear and eased out of the parking lot, then drove down the hill busy with tour buses hauling more sightseers up to the top of the ridge. Out into the Roman traffic, dodging accidents waiting to happen, she heaved a sigh of relief when she finally made it home to the enchanting loft apartment on the Via Margutta, a quiet and central street full of antiques, painters and artists, and just a few steps from the Piazza del Popolo and the Spanish Steps. Once she climbed the sixty nine steps to the apartment with its extra high ceilings and spectacular views she would arrive at her haven in a busy area of Rome.

Chapter Ten –The Sovereign Military Order of Malta (SMOM) The Knights of Malta

After securing the Peugeot in its garaging, she gathered her bag from the seat, heaved it over her shoulder, locked the vehicle, and then walked the block to tackle the steps to her apartment.

"Talk about the stairway to heaven." Gasping when she finally made it, she stood for a moment to catch her breath. "It'll be a snip for me when I pass on, sprout my wings and I've a head start." Selecting the front door key on her key ring, she inserted it into the lock and turned until she heard it click.

"What is it about the keyhole in the wall damn it?" A stray thought still niggled yet again. Nothing astounding came to mind, so she parked it in a small compartment of her brain where she could retrieve it at will. "It's probably just another bit of useless information that will clog up the cells I have left."

Walking inside she threw her car keys onto the credenza then wandered into the kitchen and busied herself making an espresso. "No cappuccino or cream for you today madam, not after that tiramisu you had this morning. Oh well," she comforted herself, "there's always a price to pay for indulgence and boy that dessert was the best. However, exceptions can be made for the adventurous and I have earned this."

Grabbing a chocolate biscuit from a glass jar on the counter, she let herself enjoy a warm and fuzzy moment. Carrying the coffee into the living room, she sat down at the dining room table and picked up the pad and pencil which lay there having brought it back inside.

"It's time to get to know you boys whoever you are. Come out, come out wherever you are?" Idly tapping her pencil against her teeth, she realised how little she knew about the Knights of Malta. "No reason to until now."

"What do I know about the modern Knights? Do I care?" Realising she was now tapping the pencil on the table with the lead end, she harumphed as she saw she had made a mark. Scolding herself for being so careless, she wet her forefinger in her mouth and then rubbed the mark off the surface of the table. "Just as well no-one's around to see *that*."

Returning to her comment about the Order, she answered her own question. "Well obviously I do or I wouldn't be looking them up would I?"

Standing up, she moved over to her laptop on the coffee table. Turning it on, she waited until it booted and typed in her password. "Don't know what on earth I'm looking for. Why is my gut feeling pushing me towards this? Exactly what am I looking for?"

Starting with a blank canvas, she brought up Google and typed in Knights of Malta.

"God, that's vitriolic, a waste of time," she recoiled from the first website she opened then ran through some others and continued to scroll down. "Let's see if I can find something less venomous."

"No smoke without fire," she decided, as her eyes skimmed the comments in the banner for a lot of websites.

Fingers flying, she returned to one banner that caught her eye and opened it. "Gesu," she exclaimed in Italian.

"In Italy, the order is entirely Roman Catholic, and its higher ranks must document an aristocratic lineage and coat-of-arms of at least three centuries, she read.

The Grand Master of the Order is both a secular prince, and a cardinal of the Church. Reflecting its history, its membership is still heavily comprised of individuals with a military or intelligence background."

"That's interesting. Now how did a chivalric order which was formed to care for the sick in hospital, devolve into a military encampment? OK, let's have a further look at this."

Caught up in historical backwater eddies, the Hospitallers of St John have a very convoluted history going back to the time of the first crusade in 1099, where they cleaned up the mess the psychopathic Crusaders had left behind them.

"Here's the answer to my question," she remarked, noting the order had made their headquarters on the Island of Rhodes and became corsairs, attacking Turkish merchantmen in reprisal for Muslim pirates becoming the scourge of Christian commerce. "Tit for tat," she murmured softly.

Valiantly attempting to maintain their foothold, after two centuries they lost ground and their territory to the Muslims, so they decamped to Malta. This brought about another name change and by this time they had established themselves as a military order. In 1834 Pope Leo XIII allowed the Knights to establish their headquarters in Rome.

"So that's how they ended up in the Eternal City."

Coming across photographs of different Knights in the ornate costume with its ostrich-plumed hat, gold spurs and a uniform with gold epaulets, sashes and the medal with the eight-pointed Maltese cross, she had to admit it was very impressive.

Their involvement with Fascist Italy during the WWII began to emerge, so she skipped on until she found something else that caught her attention.

"The Black Prince, Julio Borghese himself was a Knight. Well to be fair to the man he was a brilliant strategist. Unfortunately he was just on the wrong side by the end of war. The victor writes the history and he was cast as a villain in the Allies' version."

Reading on, she learned the Black Prince had planned a coup d'etat against the legitimate Italian government in 1970, but aborted at the last moment.

Wondering about the family's devolution into anonymity, she searched for the modern day kin. "What a sad end for such a famous and powerful family." Dallying with lingering thoughts, she recalled the loss of the family's fortune in the late nineteenth century through bad investments. Their legacy to the city was the wonderful Borghese Park and Villa, which cojoined the Medici gardens and Villa.

There appeared to be four remaining branches of the family. One residing in America, peddling the high end cosmetics their grandmother Marcella Borghese had designed. The grandson Lorenzo appeared to run a company selling high end spa body and skin products for pets and was very active in animal rights.

Shrugging her shoulders she considered it all a bit of a comedown for a once infamous and powerful family. "Good for him. His heart's obviously in the right place."

However, when she read Lorenzo had appeared on the reality show *The Bachelor* she grimaced with distaste. "Oh well, they say any publicity is good publicity."

"I mustn't deviate. It's back to the Knights." Lina pulled herself together and continued scrolling through website after website, culling out the crazies, the more radical conspiracy theorists and the plain sadistic. "There are members of P2 who are also Knights."

Another website enlightened her to the involvement of the infamous P2 pseudo-Masonic Lodge which had operated illegally in Italy and had been implicated in numerous Italian crimes and mysteries, including the nationwide bribe scandal Tangentopoli. This was a term coined to describe pervasive corruption in the Italian political system, which had been exposed in the Mani Pulite investigations between 1992-6.

"The doors of all bank vaults open to the right," Licio Gelli the Master of P2 had boldly stated at the height of his power.

Harboring few illusions about politicians in any country, she recalled the Tangentopoli that had led to the collapse of the powerful Christian Democrats and their allies.

"Mani pulite, Italian for *clean hands*" She threw back her head and chuckled with amusement, "That's a contradiction in terms."

"Hmmm, here's Berlusconi, a member of both organizations. There are some rough players amongst their members." The self serving Prime Minister of Italy had finally been deposed, but the mess he left in his wake would affect the citizens for decades to come.

"Openly referred to as a *shadow government* because of its power, other members are members of parliament, industrialists and military leaders and prominent journalists. I wonder how many of them also belong to the SMOM?"

"This begs the question of how a masonic lodge become accepted by the Roman Catholic Church?" she puzzled, leaning back in her chair to relax and think. "For centuries they were mortal enemies."

She took a deep breath and as she let it out she stretched her arms and linked them behind her neck as a small thought niggled at her. "Maybe P2 is behind the murder. There were certainly shady goings on between them during the Vatican Bank scandal."

"Why do I think any Catholic order, lay or otherwise is involved? Because of the crucifixion I suppose. It's beyond weird." Returning to her question, her fingers flew over the keyboard and her eyes followed the screeds of information available.

Membership in the Knights of Malta entails obedience to one's superior in the order and ultimately to the Pope

The Italian police are not welcome on its territory. It issues its own stamps, and has formal diplomatic relations and exchanges ambassadors with a number of countries.

The 13,000 members of the Knights of Malta ALL have diplomatic immunity. They can ship goods across borders without paying duty or undergoing customs check.

"Good grief, they are a power unto themselves and answerable to no-one. How did this come about I wonder?"

As a member of the Knights of Malta, and by virtue of your blood oath of obedience to the Pope, you are required to support to the death the desires of the head of the Order of the Knights of Malta - in this case, the Pope - over and above any other allegiance you may feel or pretend to feel toward any other loyalty-such as a loyalty to the Constitution for the United States of America.

"I wonder what the President of the United States thinks about that," Lina thought as her fingers flew across the keyboard.

In 1927 a branch of the Sovereign Order of the Knights of Malta was established on the East Coast of America. Most of the 1500 founding members were tycoons of industry and finance who strongly opposed Franklin D. Roosevelt's New Deal and saw an opportunity to set up a new seat of power.

Discovering in 1941 that Cardinal Francis Spellman was the Protector of the American branch of the Order, she cried out excitedly, "ah ha, the link with the Vatican." After the war, Spellman worked with then-bishop Montini who was undersecretary of state at the Vatican and would become Pope Paul VI, and was the handler of the infamous ratline.

On November 17 1948, the Knights awarded their Grand Cross of Merit to Reinhard Gehlen, who served as the German Chief of military intelligence on German's eastern front during the WWII. Fearing communism, the allies involved themselves in a free for all scramble to snare for themselves, any and everything that could help them halt its advance. Rumours abound that Gehlen's organisation became a paid subsidiary of the CIA.

James Jesus Angleton who firstly formed the OSS during WW11, then later would become the CIA chief of counterintelligence, was a member of this Catholic order.

In this century Knights have been involved in such unsavory activities as helping Nazis escape justice at the end of World War II, she read. Opening another website she tried to stop her stomach lurching, as she discovered paragraph claiming; '*nor did the allies ever attempt to destroy the railway lines leading to Auschwitz. Despite mounting a raid on a factory five miles from Auschwitz, out of 227 planes of the RAF and the American Airforce, not one was diverted to bomb the death camp.*"

"Ideology is truly the enemy of humanity," she muttered bitterly, having read the quote somewhere recently. "Bitter enemies are perfectly willing to band together when it serves a common interest."

Chapter Eleven – The Members of the Knights of Malta

"Diavolo! Let's see if I can find the members of this Order," she muttered to herself as her fingers continued to dance around the keyboard, her eyes and mind trying to keep up with the pace.

The Knights of Malta is a world organization with its threads weaving through business, banking, politics, the CIA, other intelligence organizations, P2, religion, education, law, military, think tanks, foundations, the United States Information Agency, the United Nations, and numerous other organizations.

Former prime ministers of England were Knights, together with generals from WW1 and WWII, particularly from the UK and the USA.

"Here's an attempt to name some of them." Bringing up the list, she cast her eyes over it. "Presidents of the US are well represented and I shouldn't be surprised at some of these names. J Edgar Hoover was a Knight and the Bush family is well represented."

Drilling down, she discovered heads of the CIA over past decades as well as members of the European and British royalties and the Vatican numbered many cardinals amongst members of the Order."

"And of course here are many of the great American robber barons. Well, I can't say I'm surprised there. Balzac got it right, *"Behind every great fortune is a great crime."*

Chairmen of some of the largest banks in the world were well represented as well as well as the boards of directors of large American corporations. Senior officials of many governments' intelligence and military services were on board.

"The Knights are in bed with some of the most infamous people in modern history." Whilst not surprised, she was disappointed.

"Mind you," mentally shrugging off her dismay, she looked back on the history of the Catholic Church and declaimed, "Mafia dons are made Knights of the Roman Catholic Church, so why would they flinch at an Order composed of many unsavory people."

Taking time to read the names on the list thoroughly, it became obvious the Octopus's tentacles reached into every corner of the spectrum of society.

"Il Papa Pius XII joined when he was Cardinale Pacelli and his legacy to the world was the Nazi Ratline." Wrinkling her nose in disgust she whispered to herself, "Here's the late Il Papa Benedict who was knighted prior to being elected to the papacy."

Discovering, retaining, discarding that she considered detritus, slowly she began to build a profile of the Knights that she could begin to form opinions about.

Taking her fingers off the keyboard, she sat back and thought about what she had learnt.

"What does it all add up to? Let's have a look." Flexing her fingers she leaned forward again and began drawing up a profile of the Knights and their connections to events that had shaped the world.

"Gesù pianse - *Jesus Wept*," she muttered to herself as she took a well earned break, turning her neck from side to side to ease the tension. "It's the Synarchy, a veritable Who's Who, making darn sure those who aint, don't get a look in."

"It's an exclusive old boys network for European aristocracy, the *black nobility* and the political right of the US and Latin America. Italy is well represented by those the Smiling Il Papa called The Ancients of Venice."

A thought sneaked through her mind and she grimaced. "Vacca Sacra - *Holy Cow*, E's family is one of the Ancients. I wonder if any of E's family are members of SMOM? I could be treading on dangerous ground here."

The Knights of Malta maintained its exclusivity by refusing to accept members from Europe and Latin America who were not of the nobility or heads of state. In recent years the ruling has been relaxed for Latin America, but even as late as the 1940s the order refused to admit Eva Peron as a dame because of her proletarian background.

'Why would they want to admit her to this cosy little club anyway?' she wondered.

"I can understand them making an exception for the United States as its political, economic and military power rose." Sighing with exasperation, she sat back and contemplated what she had learned.

A broad picture began to emerge and it soon became apparent the Knights of Malta, had been involved in shaping the outcome of world events to their masters' liking.

Contenders for the crown of the intrigue and corruption that stalked the corridors of the Vatican and other bastions of power, it sat firmly and comfortably on their collective heads.

Owning men in positions of power, there appeared to be amongst them, the soulless predators feasting on the flesh of the world, leaving the bones and pickings for the hyenas, who stalked the levels beneath their own exalted status. Those that pulled the strings and their puppets danced.

Pushing the laptop aside, Lina sat back and gazed out the bifold door, across the terrace and to the late autumn sky.

A shiver went down her spine as she thought of the order created back in the mists of time and suborned until it became a perversion of the original intent, an order of hospitallers to shelter pilgrims on their journey to the Holy City of Jerusalem.

"They've blossomed into this bloated octopus whose tentacles reach into every level of society on planet earth. This is what it's like to walk with the Beast. I need a drink to get the unpleasant taste they've left in my mouth." Pushing herself away from the table, she stood and crossed over to the credenza. Taking down a large brandy balloon, she located the Napoleon brandy in the cupboard and poured herself a large snifter.

Wandering over to the window she watched a sulky watery sun trying to make its way past the fast roiling clouds. She stood there for a moment breathing in the wonderful aroma of the alcohol, took a sip and speculated on the information she had gathered.

"It's time to get back to business." Turning around, she returned to the table and seated herself before the computer. "Let's try and build a profile."

Bringing up another screen she let her hands drop in her lap and stared hard at the screen.

In addition to the Roman Catholic SMOM, there are four Protestant orders of the Knights, all founded within the last 150 years or so, and all run by ruling houses of Europe. The Sovereign Head of the British Knights is Queen Elizabeth, while the late Prince Bernhard of the Netherlands (with his ties to the SS) was the head of that country's Chapter until his death.

'Why would the Catholics and Protestants band together?' Lina wondered. "Some common cause brings them together. Power!"

They remain a sovereign state, run from their headquarters at 68 Via Condotti in Rome. They maintain their own fleet of aircraft, have diplomatic relations with 92 nations as well as the United Nations and the Holy See, and enjoy diplomatic immunity.

"This makes them untouchable." Her brow furrowed, as reality sank in. They must be incredibly wealthy to run a fleet of aircraft to transport aid to the Third World," she reasoned and blanched at the next sentence. "They enjoy diplomatic immunity which makes them exempt from searches."

"That leaves the Order open to abuse by anyone with dishonest intent."

"They can cross borders without official bodies searching their aircraft or vehicles and with diplomatic immunity no-one can be detained despite any suspicions. They're heavily involved in humanitarian aid but," she hesitantly acknowledged, "I'm well aware not everything is as it seems at first glance."

Relaxing back in her chair, she worried at a strand of her hair, as she picked up her glass again and this time drained it. "If a fraction of this is true, they certainly have friends in high places, other than the Big V."

Putting her head in her hands, she sat gazing at the notes strewn around the table, finally deciding she needed another cognac.

Slowly rising and strolling back to the Italian hand painted credenza, her thoughts were clouding over with tiredness. Reaching down, she opened the moulded door to the cabinet, took out the bottle of Napoleon and once more poured a generous amount of cognac into the balloon. Appreciatively taking a sip, she immediately felt the warmth permeate her body and began to relax her muddled brain.

Turning she leaned back against the credenza for a moment, contemplating what she had learned. Pushing herself away from the piece of furniture, she returned to the laptop, seated herself, and thoughtfully took another sip, wondering what was to come. "Better keep a clear head."

As she followed the trail of the American chapter, her attention was caught by an article about New York's Cardinal, Francis Spellman, who at one time, was the most powerful Catholic Churchman in the United States. His involvement with the American branch of the Knights, almost from its inception, saw him acting as the Order's official church patron in the United States when he was auxiliary bishop of Boston.

For some reason Spellman enjoyed the support of the right wing of the Curia and had a cosy relationship with Cardinale Nicola Canali, who dominated Vatican finances. He funneled the American Knights' contributions into Canali's coffers, rather than to SMOM headquarters in Rome. When SMOM's Grand Master demanded an accounting from Spellman, he was ignored by the arrogant Cardinal and no action was taken against him because the order was fighting for its life against Canali who wanted to gain control of its wealth.

His access to the economic and political elites of the US, some of whom were Knights, gave him immense power, and by World War II he had become the Vatican's go-between with the White House, and its proconsul in Latin America.

What was the payback for Spellman? With the support of the right wing of the Curia in the Vatican, Canali endorsed Spellman's authority over all of the Knight's appointments in the United States and because of his financial contributions to the Vatican; Il Papa Pius XII extended his friendship to him.

More than any other person, his influence was responsible for the USA supporting the Roman Catholic ruling class in Vietnam, which ultimately involved that nation in the ruinous Vietnam War.

An egotistical man, upon his elevation to Archbishop of New York in 1939, he changed his Knights of Malta title to Grand Protector, whilst King Leopold and Queen Wilhelmina remained mere Protectors of the Belgian and Dutch branches of the Knights.

"These boys play rough," Lina decided, feeling the greatest contempt for all the players in the nasty game. "This proves the Knights have no qualms whatsoever, about getting their hands dirty when it suits them and will stop at nothing. They take no prisoners by the looks of things."

"Let's sum it up, some of the Knight's members have been involved in fascist plots and CIA covert wars, and while the majority of members are dedicated to charitable work in the Third World, their status and access to other countries makes this a very attractive proposition for anyone who has a hidden agenda."

Lina was elated with her efforts and believed she was making a pretty good case for her suspicions of the Knights of Malta. "Now how do I get E to come around to my way of thinking?" She needed his help if she was to dig deeper into the links between the Knights of Malta and the Vatican and she was determined to convince him.

Rising from the chair, she decided it was definitely time for a pick me up. So she wandered out to the kitchen, made an espresso and took it out on to the terrace, looking across the rooftops. Taking deep breaths to help her concentrate, she began to mull around in her mind the information she had already gathered.

Moving to one of the wrought iron terrace chairs, she pulled another towards her and put her feet up on it. Cradling the cup in her hand, she gratefully sipped the fresh coffee, wondering where all this would take her.

Respite over, she wandered back, delivered her cup to the kitchen, rinsed and put it in the dishwasher, then moved back into the lounge to her labors.

Diving back into the fray, she realised it would take a brave editor to stand by her and print the story when she uncovered it, but it made her even more determined to write the story that could win her the Pulitzer Prize. "If I don't try, I certainly won't have a chance." Encouraging herself to follow this line of reasoning, she pushed down any unease she felt.

In 2010, the Vatican Bank was investigated by Italian prosecutors for money laundering, and a new scandal arose in 2012 with the closing of their account by JP Morgan.

"Am I barking up the wrong tree?" she questioned. "Could it be Opus Dei or the Vatican Bank again?" Her mind raced in a thousand different directions. "Why am I so fixated on the Knights of Malta? God, I hope this isn't just an exercise in futility."

She began to worry her theory, like a dog with a beloved old mouldy bone he had dug up for the umpteenth time. "What's the connection to the Aventine? Because of the location," she told herself. "There *is* a connection; I can feel it in my bones." And they had seldom let her down before.

"Have I uncovered enough to convince E? Or myself for that matter?" Time to question her reasoning again. "All I know is that the stench appears to be reaching to heaven."

"Perhaps I should get E on to it for me. It's time to get his sanctified undies in a tangle." Squirming at the thought of it, she hopped up from the sofa and walked over to pick up the telephone. "Somehow I need to convince him to let me dig deeper into all the Vatican Offices." She realised this would take some doing, as it meant dragging up the ancient history from World War II and the Vatican's involvement in less than acceptable spiritual behaviour.

Reaching out to pick up the phone, she hesitated before depressing the buttons that would call Edoardos' private line at the Vatican. Putting the instrument down again she reconsidered "He'll get the shits, I know he will." He wasn't some source she could trample all over and she valued their friendship. Was she about to lose it? "Come on, you're a reporter, don't be such a pussy," she berated herself.

"Oh well," letting out a massive sigh she picked up the phone and waited for him to answer, "in for a penny in for a pound, as they say. Won't be the first time I've upset E." Tensing, she was already wincing at the reception she knew this would engender.

Nor was she disappointed. "Are you out of your mind?" he flared up immediately.

"E." she sighed dejectedly, "you have to admit I've got good cause. Please don't be so close minded." She softened her tone hoping this would sway him. "Women's lives are at stake. Just get me into the Vatican Archives so I can have a look at them."

"Get you into the Vatican Archives," Edoardos whispered furiously down the phone. "Are you crazy?" He was losing patience with her.

"But they are taking conducted tours in there now. Why can't I be in one of them?"

"Those tours are very tightly controlled and monitored. Only scholars are allowed in, and then only to the reading room and the Tower of Winds," Edoardos retorted smartly. "How do you propose to pass yourself as a scholar?"

"I'm a scholar of humanity. I have a degree in journalism."

"Oh, great, they'll love that."

"Well, I have to get in there somehow."

"No you don't and you're not going to."

Lina winced. Oops, obviously big mistake. "Please E, I need your help," she cajoled. "It's the logical place to look."

"And how do you propose I smuggle you in?" he answered, sarcasm dripping from every word. "Dress you in the robes of a Cardinale?"

"Well there's a thought." Joking seemed to be a good try at diffusing the situation, or she could be buying her own lunches next week.

"Don't be flippant Lina. You'll be the death of me yet," Edoardos retorted and hung up the phone, while Lina stood looking at it from her end.

"Well, that didn't go so well." Licking her wounds she retired to consider another approach.

Chapter Twelve – The Cardinale remains steadfast

After being dismissed from the meeting in the Priory of the Knights of Malta, the Cardinale returned to the Vatican,striding through the corridors of the citadel which was the heart of the doctrine he had killed to preserve. Nothing escaped his gaze as he took in the splendor that was taken for granted by those that worked in these magnificent buildings of the Holy See while it went about its daily business and held worship for their Holy Trinity.

Sensing his mood, eyes furtively followed his progress through the opulent surroundings that were the antithesis of the simple doctrine of Jesus Christ.

His Undersecretary raised his eyes from the workload on his desk as the Cardinale passed him imperiously, without acknowledging his presence.

Entering his office through the tall gilded doors he settled behind the magnificent desk from the renaissance period and bent his head to the tasks that awaited him. Working assiduously through the remainder of the day to clear all the appointments in his diary, he met with the undersecretary to sign any documents that required his signature. They covered off any remaining issues and discussed his agenda for the next day. Heaving a sigh of relief, he relaxed in his chair and making a steeple with his two hands ruminated on the meeting at the Priory of the Knights of Malta.

'They do not have the devotion to Our Lord that I have. All they are concerned with is their own selfish interests and how the exposure of the secret will affect them and their grandiose plans to further line their pockets by illicit means,' he deliberated. 'I will uncover the secret if I have to destroy every one of these whores who follow the Magdalene. They are the scourge of the earth in My Lord's eyes'.

His stomach rumbled reminding him of the late hour and he pushed down the feelings of hunger.

'How can I possibly consider partaking of food when I am about My Lord's work?' he castigated himself. 'I will fast tonight. And thought of how he would flagellate himself again to remain steadfast in his duty.

Hurrying to St. Peter's Basilica, he prostrated himself on the floor before the altar.

Oh my precious Lord, in the name of your suffering on the cross, I make you this solemn promise that I will cleanse the world of this heresy and their damnable secret that threatens you.

"I feel your pain my precious Lord," he whispered. "Every day I live with your pain. How I wish I had been at your feet on that day so I could have taken your pain from you." And his diseased mind transported itself back to the time of the crucifixion.

Chapter Thirteen – Yeshua the Nazarean

Aaagh! The cross was incredibly heavy on his back as the merciless heat bore down onto his tired body, burning him with its intensity, while the crowd mocked him and the soldiers beat him. He had been singled out by the Sanhedrin as a threat to their authority.

As a descendant of King David he could not allow their corruption of the Temple and its teachings to continue. Ufortunately his connection had made him more dangerous then any other of the many messiahs roaming Judaea in these apocalyptic times.

Enough to convince Pontius Pilate, the Roman Governor, to hand him over to the people to be crucified. A punishment reserved for insurrection.

Slowly he staggered along the dusty road to Golgotha the place of the dead.

"Thank you Yahweh for protecting Miryai," his mind whispered to Yahweh, as he thought of the nefarious practice of stoning of women and how she would have suffered. "My beloved is safe for the time being, but danger awaits her."

At the time of his execution, there was to be no peace for him, as Miryai was with child, his progeny.

Yeshua was descended from the royal line of King David through his father Iosef – *Joseph*. He was schooled in the teachings of Beit Hillel (the House of Hillel). Hillel was a great Jewish rabbi who lived in the second half of the first century, one or two generations before Yeshua's birth.

Mariam his mother, was descended from the house of Levi, the priests of the Sanctuary whose role it was to protect the mysteries of the Golden Ark and the Torah.

Miryai, his wife, was descended from the Hasmoneans. The Maccabeans who led the revolt in some two hundred years previously against the Zadokite High Priests of the Temple.

The most important symbol of Jewish life was the Temple and it was here that the greatest conflict arose. Through their corruption, the Zadokite priests had led the Jewish people astray and opened the doors to the Selucids.

Jonathan the Hasmonaean, from the house of Hashmon was not of the Zadokite line, yet had been proclaimed high priest and leader of the people.

Viewing them as heroes, the Jewish people wanting change, had rallied behind the Hasmonaeans, whose goal was to bring back the purity of Jewish worship in the Temple and fought courageously with them. The Maccabean dynasty ruled until 63 BC, until the Romans arrived in town.

Yeshua was a Rabbi, whose life path had been determined prior to his birth. As a religious teacher, he could not ignore the injustice he saw all around him. As a liberal and reformer, he believed in equality for all people and sharing of the wealth of a nation, their right and he strongly objected to it remaining in the hands of a wealthy few, with the complicity of the priesthood.

It was Yeshua's duty to challenge their greed and endemic corruption then drive it from the Temple. Now he was to be executed for spreading sedition throughout Judaea. If he was to be sacrificed, so be it.

Miryai, his wife and the mother of his child, *must* survive to ensure the purity of the Davidic bloodline, which Herod the Idumean, feared greatly.

His bleeding, cracked feet moved slowly, too slowly for the soldiers, so they beat him again, until he felt the blood from his back trickling down the side of his body to land in the dust. "The burden is too heavy," his tortured body told him and his mind accepted this truth.

"I do not want to die." Thoughts of his wife and child were all that kept his battered body moving forward. "I have failed in my main task. I do not want to minister any longer. I want to live in peace with my wife and child, far away from this torturous land where religious factions tear the Jewish people apart."

"This is what keeps them from Yahweh and enables others who crave power to enslave them." As he struggled on the bitter thoughts rose to drain the strength from his mind and body further. "I cannot help them if they will not help themselves. If they are content for the rich to exploit them and break their spirits so a few can live in luxury, so be it."

They had arrived at Golgotha, the place of the dead. Here the soldiers roughly grabbed the cross and threw it to the ground, as Yeshua gasped in agony. His body rose with the impact and thudded against the unyielding wood of the cross, shuddering with the force of the pain.

Casting down his tired eyes against the glare of the sun, he was unable to brush the dust from them, as his hands and feet were lashed to the cross. He could not help letting forth a terrible scream, as a soldier hammered nails into his hands on the crossbars.

Mercifully he fainted, as his body went into shock while they hammered his feet onto the stock. Then they threw water on to his face, so he would be conscious whilst they rammed the base of the heavy wooden cross into a hole that had been previously dug into the ground. Piling stones and dirt around it, they hammered it in further as he groaned with despair; his body feeling as though was tearing itself apart.

"Hah, King of the Jews," the Roman soldiers taunted.

"I did not realise it would be as bad as this." Tears ran unbidden down Yeshua's cheeks, as he looked upon the faces twisted with hate leering at him.

"You call yourself King of the Jews, but where is your crown?" they mocked him.

Pain lanced through him, as the soldiers dragged a wooden ladder over and slammed it against the cross, so one of them could climb it with a crown of thorns in his hand. Reaching the top, he rammed it on Yeshua's head, while another cry of agony was torn from him, as rivulets of blood ran down his face to mingle with his tears.

"Now you've got your crown. Enjoy your reign," and the legionnaire clambered back down to the ground.

Glancing off to the side, the agonised man saw a group of people approach. His beloved Miryai sank to her knees beside the cross and wept. His mother Mariam, her ravaged face showing signs of her pure grief, put her arms around his wife and knelt beside her while James, his 0x0d (*brother*) wept with them.

Alongside him two thieves were being crucified, as this was the normal punishment in ancient Rome for criminals whose offence might simply have been stealing a loaf of bread to remain alive. All Yeshua could feel was pain, agonising pain.

As his body took the strain, his shoulders dislocated, which was common during crucifixion. Shuddering from the agony, his body went into shock and he knew it would take him three days to die a horrible, painful and lingering death. Mercifully he passed out with pain again.

The heat and the pain took their toll and when the family was allowed to take his body down on the third day, it was so lifeless they believed they were burying him.

Iosef of Arimathea, Yeshua's uncle had offered the devastated family his own tomb, for this member of royalty of the House of David. Iosef was a member of the Sanhedrin, the Council of the Temple, and was also descended from the same line as Yeshua, so it fell to him to offer them succour. In the coolness of the tomb, Miryai and Mariam washed Yeshua gently with scented water and anointed him with fragrant oils. Myrrh and frankincense were burned in lamps burning lamb fat. They smothered him with kisses and cried over his broken body.

"Move back," Iosef commanded and they cleared a way for him. As a respected physician, he knew he must put the dislocated shoulders back in, for they were determined his body would be straight before they wound him in his burial shroud. Beckoning Joses and Shimon, Yeshua's 0x0d's, forward he had one hold

Yeshua's arm at a certain angle and the other to hold his body. Then he manipulated the arm back into place.

A groan emanated from Yeshua and they looked at each other in bewilderment.

"It cannot be," Miryai whispered as she put her hands over her belly to reassure their child. "It cannot be he is still alive."

Iosef bent his head to Yeshua's lips, then to his chest "I believe his heart beats, but so feebly I do not know if we can save him," He shook his head sadly, as he looked at the shattered wreck before him. "I dare not shock his body any more by trying to put his other shoulder in. For now we will wait and see. Prepare healing herbs quickly." He told Miryai and Mariam who hurried to do his bidding.

"Please Yahweh, save him. Let him live. He has suffered enough," Miryai cried. "We have done your bidding and I carry the seed of David. I need Yeshua, his love, his spirit and his strength to be with me, and help keep the lineage alive."

For three more days they tended his broken and battered body. Miryai applied unguent of spikenard, which was well known to heal deep emotional wounds, as well as calm and balance his nervous system. He would need all the help she could give him.

Then she applied her amazing healing powers, which were part of esoteric wisdom that had been passed on to her during her training since childhood. Through visions and revelations, she possessed mystic knowledge and teachings, far superior to that of the public apostolic tradition.

Teachings that went as far back as the Hindu Vedas, had found their way to Persia, then into Judaea. The Dao (the Way) had crossed the continent from China, teaching that the cosmos was composed of opposites that attract and align, to create the balance and harmony of the world and man's persona.

Both Miryai and Yeshua had been educated in the mysteries of the duality of the spiritual and earthly worlds, as well as the essential balance between the masculine and feminine aspects of man's nature.

As well as being holders of wisdom, in ancient times women were also recognised as priestesses.

The mysteries had been corrupted over the centuries, until Judaean women had been relegated to the status of inferior beings to men. Jewish Rabbis in the 1st century BC were encouraged not to teach, or even to speak with women. Jesus broke rank and Miryai taught alongside him, further inflaming the Sanhedrin. Their union was to be the catalyst that was meant to return the ancient knowledge back into the world.

Now she called on all her training. Using her powers, she blended the feminine with the masculine, and merged with her own etheric, mental and physical bodies. Calling on the Law of Opposites to balance and harmonise his being with that around him, she willingly gave of her energy, knowing she could replenish it at will. As the spiritual bond between them was so deep and powerful, Yeshua unconsciously drew upon it.

On the third day he opened his eyes and looked into those of his Ftn0lw (*wife*), Miryai and his OmO (*Mother*), Mariam's. Dropping to their knees, they kissed his hands and he felt their tears wash over them. Now it was time to heal his mind and spirit, for they knew that if they could not, he would not survive the terrible ordeal he had been through.

They had to be wary of the Herod's soldiers and the Pharisees and priests, who would kill him if they knew he was alive, so they left him in the tomb until a month had passed. He was still terribly weak, but alive and able to hold light broths and bread. After a second month, they moved him into Iosef's house, lovingly tending to him for another three months until the tide turned. He lived although shattered and weak.

During this time, Miryai lived with Mariam and Yeshua remained with Iosef and his family. When the child was born, they brought her to her Jwhyhb0 (father), whose face shone with delight and love as he cradled her in his arms, drawing strength from the miracle he and Miryai had wrought.

"Shall we name her Tamar, the name of the mother of us all?" Mariam looked at Yeshua and Miryai who smiled and nodded in agreement and so it was.

They brought Tamar to him as often as it was safe, but Yeshua chafed at his child growing up without him by her side.

"It is not safe Yeshua," they told him.

"I cannot bear to be apart from you. You are my strength," he cried out to Miryai in sorrow and pain. "I have failed in my duty to the House of David, now I want to lead a simple life."

Unfortunately, Kepha's – *Peter's* - jealousy of Yeshua's love for Miryai was too great for him to be told of the miracle, so they told him and the other disciples that Yeshua had risen and gone to his father in Heaven. This they felt would suffice for Kepha to leave Miryai alone.

In this they were wrong, as Kepha's love for Yeshua and his guilt for failing him in his hour of need, fuelled his jealousy and hatred of Miryai, and it festered and roiled within him.

Harassing and haranguing her, although he knew she carried the royal child, he sought to punish Miryai for his own failings. Joses, Yeshua's 0x0d (*brother*), and some of the other disciples remonstrated with him, as he should respect Yeshua's Ftn0lw, who was deeply loved.

"Yeshua would not stand for you treating his wife like this," they protested.

Mariam, Yeshua's mother also attempted to reason with him, but Kepha would not be moved from his stance and the situation was becoming dangerous. In his heart, he knew that it was essential the royal lineage continue, but his jealousy was so intense, it blinded him and he could not bear to see her belly swell.

Being a simple fisherman and a blowhard, Kepha told the disciples he would bring the soldiers and kill Miryai and her child, as it was a betrayal of his sweet master.

No matter how the disciples protested and begged him not to be so vindictive, no-one could reason with him. No matter how they reminded him the child was Yeshua's, he would not be swayed from his purpose. As he watched the child grow in her belly, and the contentment this brought Miryai, his hatred festered in his bitter, twisted mind.

His life had been a miserable and non eventful one before Yeshua came along. Every day, he struggled as a simple fisherman to survive and keep his family fed. He had gained authority and become important when Yeshua had called upon him to become one of his disciples, where he had experienced a camaraderie and brotherhood that he had never hoped to have in his life. Now it had all been swept away and once again he was nobody. He could not bear it.

A council was called, and they decided they could never tell Kepha that Yeshua was alive, with his spirit broken and he would never preach or lead them again. Kepha's simple mind would not accept the times of glory were over and that Yeshua only wanted to be with his family, living a simple life. If he could turn against Miryai and the child, eventually he would turn against Yeshua as well, so they planned to get them out of Judaea.

When the baby was four months old and Yeshua was physically stronger, they decided it was time to move them, before Kepha acted against Miryai. His mind was shattered from grief and despair, hatred and jealousy, and it would not be long before it broke and being an impulsive man he would carry out his threat. No-one knew why it had taken so long for him to act and they lived in dread each day. When they showed him the child they thought it would soften him, but instead it had hardened his heart even more as he saw Yeshua in the child, but denied to him forever.

Chapter Fourteen – The Escape from Judaea

The knowledge that the baby was Yeshua's drove Kepha to the brink of insanity. He had lost the man he had loved with all his heart and believed he would have followed into the fires of hell, but when it counted had denied him. His guilt racked his empty soul. He had nothing of Yeshua, but Miryai had his child.

He went to the Pharisees to tell them the truth. The Royal House of David lived on through Yeshua's child. The gall nearly choked him as he admitted it.

The Pharisees conferred and beat the truth out of him, as he had been claiming the child was not Yeshua's, so how was this suddenly so? He admitted he had lied and the Pharisees knew that if the truth was known and this child grew into its heritage, it too would have its own followers in the future and they would be challenged once more.

What to do? Deal with it themselves, or take it to Herod? Involve the division of soldiers from Rome whom Herod commanded? Herod believed Yeshua dead and the growing unrest and gentle revolution Yeshua had led, had been quashed. His anger would be great. It would be best if they hunted him down, then took his body to Herod, to show him the threat was over and he would reward them.

Miryai had given birth to a girl-child, which Herod would not fear as much, but she in turn, could give birth to a male child, who would become a threat to his own line of Kings. It would be best to deal for them to deal with it themselves. It would not be the first time they had blood on their hands.

"They must go tonight," Mark ran to Lazarus, "as the Pharisees and Priests have paid assassins to kill them."

"Bring Miryai and the child here immediately," Iosef of Arimathea ordered and turned to Yeshua, who made to run to his FtnOlw and child. "You must not be seen, you must remain here."

"I must go to Miryai."

"No," Iosef told him. "You will impede them and put them into greater danger."

"We must flee tonight then." Yeshua weakly moved across the room.

"You are lucky to be alive, Yeshua, but you are still not strong enough to stand the rigors of a difficult journey. You need another three months."

"But they will kill my family," he cried.

"No, we will hide you all in the tomb," Iosef told him, "and let Kepha and the priests think your family has fled. When all is quiet again, we will pass you through the escape route we planned."

Chapter Fifteen – Yeshua and Miryai's flight

Miryai sat by the embers of a fire nursing her child, when Yeshua's Ammi El-Lih (*father's brother*), Iosef of Arimathea arrived at the house. His heart went out to her, as she looked so wan and pale. He had watched her grow from a young child, into the beautiful, strong and confident young woman, who had married his nephew. The crucifixion had damaged her, as much as Yeshua.

"You must gather up a few belongings and come with me," he told her, "and swiftly."

"What is wrong Ammi El-Lih?" Seeing the concern in his eyes, she rose at once.

"The Sanhedrin is sending soldiers to arrest you and Tamar." Iosef was one of the most important members of the Council and was privy to the most confidential information.

"Why would they do that?" Distraught she looked at Yeshua's uncle despairingly.

"Because they are afraid that the followers of Yeshua will turn to you both as descendants of the House of David and the child will foment rebellion when she is older," he told her.

"That is ridiculous," her spirit returned as she became angry. "A female child is no threat to them." Turning from him she comforted her child who, sensing the fraught mood in the room was beginning to whimper.

"How can they do this?" Mariam cried as she turned to Iosef. "Is it not enough that they have destroyed my Oydyly? Must they persecute his wife and child now?"

"They still fear your 0ydyly and his mission," the concerned man pressed them, "so hurry, hurry. They will be rounding up the soldiers and Kepha will lead them here."

"Kepha," Miryai spat out. "I should have known he was at the back of this." Despairingly she looked at the child, "Is his hatred of me so great because Yeshua's love for me was so deep, that he would kill an innocent child, one of royal blood?"

"I am afraid so, my dear. Yeshua challenged the Sanhedrin's power and many of the people followed him. It is in their interest to destroy him. We must hurry."

"But where will we go?" Perplexed at the turn of events, she looked beseechingly at Mariam, Yeshua's OmO, in whose house they were living, as was the wont in this era. "How do you know this is so?" Turning back to Iosef, she was becoming dazed.

"I was at the Council when the vote was taken and mine alone was not enough to sway the decision. Come Miryai, Yeshua's daughter must survive and so must Yeshua, because he is King David's heir."

Miriam's concern for her daughter in law overcame her. "Iosef, he must not be discovered and die now, not when he is getting stronger." Hurrying around she threw a few clothes into a bundle and urged Miryai to leave.

At this moment Joses, Yeshua's 0x0d, (*brother*) ran into the house.

"Kepha is beside himself with jealousy of you and grief, from what he believes is Yeshua's death. He is leading the soldiers here to capture you and the child." Joses was distraught. "We must leave here now."

Miryai finally rose then taking Joses' face in her hands, she kissed him on both cheeks. "We know. Iosef came from the council to warn us. You are a wonderful 0x0d and friend," she told the older man, "let us depart."

Turning, she stooped and picked up her child, wrapped her in a shawl and slipping on her sandals, picked up her robe and drew it over her head, then followed Iosef and Joses out into the cool night air, as they urged her to hurry.

Miryai looked back sadly at the home she had known all her married life.

Slipping away from the house, they swiftly and silently made their way to Iosef's home. "This is the first place he will lead them to, when he finds you are missing." This senator and member of the Sanhedrin was an intelligent man and had planned for this event, as he had not trusted Kepha.

He then went swiftly into the living quarters and appraised Yeshua of the situation. "I have put provisions into the tomb. You must stay in there until I tell you it is safe to leave." Helping Yeshua to his feet he led them all out into the garden.

"Joses you will stay as well. Keep the baby as silent as you possibly can," he cautioned the anxious trio. "It will be crucial to your safety. Mariam," Turning back to the older woman, who was wringing her hands and watching them with tears in her eyes, he exclaimed, "You must pull yourself together, as we must explain to the soldiers when they come, that you are staying with me for now. Do not give anything away."

Nodding, she hurried to embrace them all and turned back to the house.

Hurrying from the tomb, Iosef motioned to a trusted servant whom Yeshua had helped through an illness and would never betray his saviour. Together they rolled the rock back into place. Although it was pitch black inside, air came from a shaft that Iosef had dug out. However they could not light any candles.

Chapter Sixteen – Donne in Azzurro - The Women in Blue

"In these enlightened times, we have followed our faith without fear of persecution. But somewhere out there, we have an enemy who is obviously bent on destroying us." The elegant, mature woman, dressed in Valentino, looked around at the other four women, as they sat together in a Palazzo in Rome's exclusive Monteverde Vecchio district.

The sisterhood of the Nazarene doctrine in Rome, had gathered in the luxurious surroundings of this palatial home, with its drawing room decorated in the Italian Renaissance style. Pieces of furniture dating back to the 16th century graced the room.

The woman, whose husband was the Marchese of another famous Italian family, who could trace their lineage back to the days of the infamous Borgia popes, had been contented with her life. Her own family lineage, went back to the days of Venetian power. She had been aptly named Savina, which meant *follower of another religion*, by her mother, who had passed on the mantle of le Donne in Azzurro to her.

In front of each woman was a Venetian glass goblet, containing a light refreshing Italian wine. A small tray of exquisite Italian pastries was set in front of them, but none of the assembled women had any appetite for them.

"Why?" A slender attractive woman in her thirties looked at them puzzled, as she placed her goblet on the table, after taking a sip. "No-one has ever bothered us before. Why should we pose such a threat now, that one of us has been murdered?" This woman was also married to a high profile, well connected husband.

"I don't know, nor do I know who *they* are." Turning her head to look at them all, Savina's face was traced with sadness and grief. "I cannot believe Fabia died in such a horrifying manner. The Apostates will not remain with us with this danger hanging over our heads."

"Why now? It is not as though they were unaware of us for centuries," Adelina, the wife of a well known politician asked, lifting her goblet and sipping the delicious wine from the magnificent cellar Savina's husband kept. "We've been tolerated."

"Not quite tolerance. Centuries of subjugation and hiding," Savina replied. "Now that women have a stronger voice in the world and are no longer burned at the stake, they can enjoy the different beliefs in which they hold positions of power."

"Is it because this is Rome, the heart of the Roman Catholic Faith?"

Savina waved this view aside. "The Reverendo Padre does not concern himself with us. I fear our sisters in France could be murdered also. This is some sinister outside force."

"Why? It is not as though we declare our belief to the world. We carry on the faith quietly and unobtrusively. We are hardly a danger to the mighty seat of power of the Roman Catholic Church."

"I know, it is perplexing," Savina agreed, as her gaze lingered on Adelais. They both knew a secret they were not sharing with the others in the group for now, which would place them in jeopardy. "More wine?" she looked around the group.

Heads shook in refusal. "Are we sure they are targeting the sisterhood of the Nazarene faith?"

"It would appear so with one of our number being killed."

"Should we announce ourselves to the world?"

"I don't think we would get airtime or newspaper exposure."

"The reporters would listen if it was an interesting enough story. They will do anything for a sensationalist twist."

"And that is precisely what we do not want. That is not what we are about. We simply carry on the faith quietly and in our hearts."

"Our families would not tolerate exposure," Giada chimed in. "Many of our families have links to the Church and have had for centuries."

"What does that say about us? How strong is our faith then?" Another queried and the others looked at her.

"Oh come on Sylvia," Michela protested. "This is not an age where one suffers and martyrs themselves for their faith. I've seen beggars in the streets of Rome and I don't intend to join them."

"Our families would disown us, for making them a laughing stock," Another voice insisted.

"Sisters," Savina interjected quietly. Such was her dignity and personal power, that as she held up her hand to quell them, the chatter silenced immediately. "We only want to be left in peace to practice our beliefs as we see fit, and to ensure the flame is passed on."

"That appears to be the problem," Luciana interjected whilst raising her head from contemplating the floor, her mind far away. "Whoever is behind this seems to bear us a grudge, but perhaps the publicity will scare him off."

"Perhaps Luciana is right," another slim blonde in her mid thirties, attired in Giorgio Armani, implored the others. "I am afraid. When I am out alone, I am constantly looking over my shoulder."

"I know." The last woman, a sophisticated blonde in her forties, looked at her trembling hands. "However, psychopaths are very rarely scared off by anything. Their need for recognition grows stronger as they continue to kill. Somehow we have to find him and expose him as a murderer of women."

"Where do we even begin to start?"

Eyes turned to Savina as their rightful leader. Hers was the oldest of the Roman aristocratic families amongst those assembled and the flame had been passed to her by her mother.

The men of the doctrine had long since faded from the group, preferring secular power and that of the Roman Catholic Church. Knowing of their belief in the doctrine, they indulged their wives, as long as it did not impair their influence in the corridors of power.

"Where are our enemies?"

"In the Church, but surely you don't think…" Guilia started and her large blue eyes grew even larger. "Not in this day and age?"

"There are twisted minds everywhere, even and *especially* in this day and age," Savina emphasised. "In Karol Wojtyla's time as Il Papa, he steered the Church back into politics and never hesitated to voice his opinions. It was his desire and Ratzinger's, to see secular and church power, combined once again."

"Oh why did Il Papa John XXIII and Il Papa John Paul I have to die?" Nunzia bemoaned. "The world welcomed their liberal ideas and the changes they intended to make to the Curia and their Offices. They truly loved ordinary families throughout the world and sought to simplify the church doctrine to make their lives easier."

"This new Il Papa brings great hope," Sylvia commented quietly.

"Providing they do not assassinate him as well," Luisa answered dryly. "He is cast in the same mold as Il Papa John Paul I."

"In the meantime," Sylvia looked at them one by one, "we have to be very, very careful in our daily lives and also in our plan to release Miryai's secret to the world, as I am sure they will strike again."

Her words struck terror in the hearts of the small group, as they sat in this well appointed room which was decorated with murals of the Catholic Christian faith on the ceilings. The very structure of their well cushioned lives was threatened, and their thoughts went to their daughters and other apostates, who were young and vulnerable.

"This is the age of enlightenment, where men can no longer hold women back," Carla spoke out boldly. "The time for Mary Magdalene and Yeshua's mother, Mariam, to be recognised in their own right, has come. Women's power in the world *is finally* increasing. The feminine influence must be felt in this world, if we are to avoid its total destruction."

"When the legacy was left to our ancestors, it was predicted there would be 2000 years of darkness before the feminine flame would burn again so brightly, that it could not be ignored. That time is here. Are we afraid to claim it?"

"Who has the most to lose if the feminine power becomes a force to be reckoned with, particularly in the name of Mary Magdalene?" Athena leaned forward to address them forcefully, "The Holy Roman Catholic Church, who for centuries have buried the truth about the early Nazarenes. Perhaps they fear our faith could throw its structure into disarray."

Adelina, the wife of the popular politician Donato Mariani spoke up. "Already they are unable to attract young men and women to their doctrine that shackles minds and bodies. It is an unnatural doctrine, with its insistence on celibacy, which has led to all sorts of perversions and atrocities in the name of their unbalanced faith. Once they excised the feminine equation, they set this world on a path of destruction. It must be returned to the natural balance of the cosmos."

"The Gnostic sects worship openly now and the church ignores them, so why would they bother with us?"

"Because we hold a secret they do not want revealed to the world," Adelais proclaimed.

"Well they could easily dismiss that," Athina countered.

"Noone else holds the proof that we do, and they will fear that," Adelais was adamant.

"We are restricted by our families' ties with the Vatican. Perhaps I will call a meeting with the French Chapter and enlist their help as well." Sighing Savina elegantly rose from the exquisitely tapestried sofa she was seated upon. The other women rose with her, each to return to their lives as the upper strata of Roman society.

Chapter Seventeen – Lina reflects

It was one of Rome's autumnal October days. The skies above the Eternal city were sunny and clear as usual, with the weather bureau promising a high of seventy three degrees and a low of fifty three.

Lina awoke and stretched contentedly, deciding to luxuriate as it was Sunday, her day off from her busy regime. As a freelance reporter this was a myth. As her thoughts kept returning to The Magdalene killing, her mind was not cooperating with the idea of a day off.

Rising from the super king sized bed she descended the steps from her loft bedroom, padding into the small kitchen to turn on the espresso coffee machine, which was her morning wake up call.

Whilst the machine fired itself up she wandered over to the stereo set up in the drawing room which also served as a dining room, to push the CD button, which allowed the strains of Panchelbel's canon to waft through the air.

The acoustics of the high ceilings in the room, caught and caressed the tune, as it emitted from the Bose speakers, her other extravagance. The wonderfully light and sensual melody filled the entire apartment, as she walked over to the bifold doors leading to the terrace, throwing them open to the morning light and air, before returning to the kitchen.

With the strains of the music resonating throughout her entire body, every cell responding to the exquisite notes, she made herself a Vienna coffee. A long black, with whipped cream piled on the top, and cinnamon sprinkled over. Sometimes she stepped up the flavour boost, by taking a small piece of a fresh vanilla pod, scraping the seeds out and popping the small fragment of pod into the bottom of the cup as the espresso drew. Once she added the whipped cream, the seeds she had scraped from the pod, were sprinkled over the top. Add sugar. Stir. Heaven in a cup! Pure indulgence by self.

Carrying it out onto the lounge, she stepped out on to that most treasured of all delights, a terrace, where she could look over the famous Trinita dei Monti church that sits atop Rome's famous Spanish Steps. Seating herself at the small round wrought iron table and two chairs she had set up, she reflected on the proposed changes to the Sacred Heart School for girls, which was attached to the convent.

For one hundred and seventy eight years, the school had been run by nuns, but when the French government demanded they increase their presence, the church found it as difficult to attract young women to the vocation as a nun, as young men to the priesthood. The world was changing, even in Rome. So the nuns had agreed to vacate.

Her gaze fell on the window boxes full of azaleas and contentedly sipped her coffee in the calming atmosphere. Edoardos loved the compactness of her apartment, after the vastness of the Big V and his family's palazzo, so they would often sit on the terrace sipping coffee, or inside the drawing room with the terrace doors wide open. It was all she required, as she ate more often in the trattorias and pizzerias, that were a step or two away and a vivid part of Italian life.

Very much a Roman now in her habits she would arise around 10am on leisurely days, then wander down to the Piazza Picolo. Finding a trattoria or café, she would treat herself to one of the irresistible Italian pastries and a frothy cappuccino, then sit down to watch the passing parade of Romans, indulging in one of their favorite pastimes, the passegiatte, or long walk, with many of them so elegantly attired, it was like a tableau out of a play.

Without complaint, she paid the extra money to sit at a table and watch the pasegiatte, unlike the tourists, who bemoaned the fact they had to pay for the privilege of sitting at a table, whilst just sipping coffee in the midst of an exhausting day. Obviously they didn't understand that the restaurant needed to turn around the tables, preferably with the extra sale of a meal, to generate their profit margin.

If tourists wanted only a coffee, they could go to one of the excellent espresso bars in the city and stand whilst they sipped. Of course this did not give one a view of the *goings on*, nor did it rest weary feet and bones, after pounding the pavements around the historic sites, but hey, choices were choices.

Eating out in the many trattorias and mixing it with the locals, was where reporters gleaned their information and discovered stories, not by sitting on their backsides in an apartment or preparing meals. It was amazing what she picked up, by listening to conversations around her and who she noticed, while watching the world go by.

Many a story she had lodged, had begun in just that manner. Edoardos' expensive restaurants, which he delighted in taking her to, knowing it was beyond her budget, did not furnish nearly so many tidbits. These were passed on to her by Edoardos himself, bless his little aristocratic heart. Gossip abounded in Rome, usually before the event had finished taking place, either locally or throughout Europe, as mobile phones sped up the process. They were certainly quicker than pigeons.

Sited on the Via Margutta in an eighteenth century building, her apartment was reached by narrow staircases and alleys shaded by walls overgrown with wisteria, bougainvillea, palms, figs, and roses. After the climb of sixty nine steps from street level, which was her fitness regime, it was a small price to pay for a reasonably quiet spot in the middle of this city that never slept.

A mere five minute walk from St Peters, which was handy for Edoardos unless they were going further afield, when she reached street level it brought her to an ideal spot between the Piazza di Spagna and the Piazza del Popolo. Surmounted by the Pincio Garden, a very ancient part of the Borghese Gardens, at sunset this was one of the best views of Rome.

In just fifteen minutes she could be in the centre of the historic city. Perhaps she would go to the famous Rosati café, the hangout for the modern literati, or maybe Canova, which had been Fellini's favorite.

Or she could wander through the lively Via della Croce, with its trendy cafes, fashionable boutiques and Italian grocery stores, where it was a pleasure passing time in the Pedestrians Only zone.

She could also join the tourists on The Spanish Steps and wander around to the famous Antico Caffè Greco, one of the three most ancient cafes in the world with its classical atmosphere. The haunt of such noticeable, as Byron, Shelley, Keats and Goethe, it was easy for her to daydream that she could be sitting on the very seat one of them had used. Of course it was so expensive she would have to put cardboard in her shoes for the rest of the week.

Romans will tell you, the best coffee is to be found in the Piazza Navona near the Pantheon, a Greek word meaning literally *all Gods*. Originally part of the Baths of Agrippa in AD25 the rotunda was rebuilt early in the second century by the Emperor Hadrian and dedicated to the seven major gods worshipped by the Romans.

This two thousand year old temple was later consecrated as a Christian church by the Emperor Constantine and houses the tombs of the painter Rafael and several Italian Kings.

Truth be known, Lina was a bit pissed off with Constantine, feeling he should have left well enough alone and the Pantheon should have remained dedicated to the Gods it was built to honour. Oh well. What men will do to for a monument to their own greatness.

The Sant' Eustachio il Caffè is where you stand to drink your coffee, and a couple of thousand Romans who wander in and out of here each day for their delicious brews can't be wrong. Its house specialty, the *gran caffè*, comes with a *crema* so thick and rich, it is a meal in itself. The owner swears the secret is that he roasts his beans slowly in a wood fired oven. Whatever he does it works.

And his rival, the Tazza d'Oro where one could put one's feet up, or backside down, also makes a mean cup of coffee. One Lina had enjoyed many times.

'We Italians know how to get it right.' She winced at the thought of the excessive roasting of coffee beans in other countries which made it so bitter they had to drown it in milky froth to make it drinkable. Quite forgetting that coffee was to be sipped, a little burst of flavour, not to be gulped down, the world was drowning in bullshit *designer* coffee, adding syrups and God knows what else to a less than perfect brew.

She still laughed when tourists ordered caffe latte as they did back home, only to be served with a glass of milk.

'A little smattering of the language before arriving in the city would help,' she conjectured. It never ceased to amaze her, that English speaking people expected everyone in the countries they visited to speak English for their benefit. 'So arrogant and inconsiderate, no wonder the French snub them for their rudeness.'

*

Of course driving in the eternal city is an absolute nightmare, with the motorists making up their own rules, driving and parking on the sentiero (*footpath*) whenever they felt their progress was impeded. Safety was definitely not a priority in Rome.

If one decided to follow the Romans' example of driving on the sentieros as well, with the pedestrians scattering in all directions to avoid being severely injured, if not killed outright, one could move around these narrow streets with ease. Well that was not strictly true, but it made the passage faster. However, Lina found this so nerve racking, that she mostly caught public transport to retain her sanity.

The area was well served by public transport so she could catch the metro, the nearest Station being the Ottaviano (St Peters), or a bus or taxi. Lina figured this was less expensive than six months in a clinic after suffering a nervous breakdown, trying to cope with the madness of the traffic in Rome. As parking was merely a dream in this area she kept her dark blue Peugeot 206 in a locked parking garage a five minute walk away.

Lina loved the Via Margutta, which had been home to Italian and foreign artists' studios since the late seventeen hundreds and she needed no more than this. Located on the third floor of an historic building, thankfully serviced by an elevator the size of a wardrobe like most in historic buildings in Italy and France worked most of the time.

Not that she would have moved out if it was unserviceable. It was a way of life, created over centuries of history, culture and tradition. All things considered, life was absolutely smashing.

Today being Sunday Edoardos would attend morning mass before having a long Italian lunch with his family. Very much the Roman custom it was one she missed with her family living in America.

Thank goodness Edoardos was not caught up in the Vatican City's Sunday activities. After all Sunday was a day of rest, except for the officiating priests who were ministering to faithful flocks throughout the city and all of Italy.

Normally they would catch up in the evening and have a late meal at another of his favorite restaurants, but this weekend he had intended to forego the family luncheon to spend the time with Lina.

"Bzzz Bzzz." The insistent tone of the telephone interrupted her reflections. "Hi, it's Lina, I'm not available right now, leave a message and I'll contact you as soon as I'm able. Ciao." Feeling lazy, she let the message run and waited to see who was on the other end.

"Lina, its Edoardos. Pick up if you're there."

Ambling back inside, she walked over to the glass coffee table and picked up the cordless telephone, acknowledging the call as she fell into the large cushioned white sofa.

"Hey E. What's up?"

"Do you mind if we revert back to our usual routine of dinner together, rather than the luncheon we had planned today?"

"Sure, non c'è problema."

"They have some notables coming for lunch, including Cardinale Contardello and would like me to attend. I don't think I'm in a position to be able to snub His Eminence. That could be extremely bad for my future prospects." He laughed and she knew his deep brown eyes would be merrily sparkling and crinkling around the edges. "So I wondered if we could do dinner as usual. OK with you?"

"What are you suggesting here Reverendo Padre?" she teased, thinking *if only* quietly to herself, "and then come back here for a long Roman siesta? Naughty, naughty."

"You know Lina, you should have a nice young man of your own, to squire you around to lunches and dinners on weekends, instead of spending the time with a stuffy old priest like me."

"Yeah, right." Lina swung her feet up on to the sofa and lounged back on the rolled arm with a big soft plump cushion to support her back. "If they were as stuffy as you're not, and not so damn full of themselves, I might be interested," she shot back, "but they're all such a monumental bore."

"Well, how about a nice rumpled journalist that has been on dangerous missions?"

"God, one's enough." she groaned theatrically. "That's no basis for a long lasting romance."

"You'd probably have a better chance with your own kind, than some nice young aristocratic banker with steady hours, who would spend his time wondering where the hell you were and what you were up to."

"Well, there you have it in a nutshell, the story of my life. You should see the havoc it wreaks on these nice young banker/businessmen."

"In Italy they're probably all terrified they'll be the subject of your Pulitzer prize aspirations." Edoardos roared with laughter. "Try a country lad, whose aristocratic father is a Count with a vineyard and olive grove."

"Yeah, right! Most of them are poverty stricken." Lina winced at the thought of it. "I could spend my time turning the olive press or making beds, as they probably run a high priced guest establishment."

"Probably." He deftly turned the conversation back to the original subject. "Pick you up at 7pm?"

"Sure, I'll come down from the Mount and meet you at the bottom."

"Bring the tablets of stone with you. We all need a bit of guidance in these immoral times."

Lina giggled, thinking how irreligious Edoardos was for a Vatican Priest. "More likely I'll arrive with my sheep in tow. I've always fancied myself as a sweet little shepherdess."

Edoardos snorted. "Don't kid yourself, I don't think it was all it was cut out to be." He merrily chortled at the thought of Lina, as a lowly shepherdess driving her flock up and down mountains. Somehow he couldn't picture it. "How's your yodelling?"

"Not too good. I would fare as well as you would, in a monastery in the countryside."

Her gaze fell on an ancient pitcher that stood in a wall alcove and had cost her almost a year's salary to purchase. However, it allowed her imagination to run riot. Maybe it had been used in an ancient Roman's home. Or perhaps it had been used for ceremonies, in one of the temples where women presided as priestesses. It was a wonderful thought, one that she often entertained. "You would have probably been a priest of Jupiter or Mars in ancient times. They had a lot more fun you know, no celibacy."

"You're such a sacrilegious woman," Edoardos rejoined. "They'd stone you back in those days for making comments like that."

"They'd stone me in Sicily, for making utterances like that today." Lina curled her legs up under her and happily took part in the repartee she shared with this open minded Roman priest.

"That's very true," Edoardos agreed. "Let's have dinner down by the Forum and I can throw you to the lions."

"Nah, they only eat dedicated Christians." Lina's thoughts flashed to the bloodthirsty sports of the ancient Romans. "They'd spit me right out. Only lions I've seen around there, are the mangy alley cats and some of those are two legged."

Edoardos roared with laughter again. "I think you're right. See you at seven tonight," and with that, he rang off.

Lina hung up, wondering what the other priests in the Big V would think of his conversations with her, if they were overheard.

'Gosh, what life could be more wonderful than this,' she thought contentedly. Her parents, delighted she was living back in the old country, nagged her about settling down with a nice young Italian man.

"If you keep running around with Edoardos all the time, people will wonder about you," her mother would complain. She adored Edoardos, but he was not a candidate for domestic bliss. Italian mothers couldn't be expected to understand, an attractive young woman spending so much time with a priest from the Vatican. "You'll both start rumors, with all the time you spend together."

"You're absolutely right." Lina would throw her arms around her mother, whom she dearly loved, and laughed. "It certainly perplexes people."

Her mother could understand that. "I think you use him, to scare all the eligible young men off," she would scold her errant daughter.

"I'm in no hurry to settle down and breed Mamma." Lina would gaze at her lovingly. "I know you want some bambinos scampering around, but a roving journalist would make a terrible mother."

"Oh you," and her mother would swot her on the arm and look at her with such deep love it made Lina feel totally complete. She was first generation American Italian and it was difficult for those from the old country, to understand young women who wanted a career.

So many young Italian women of Lina's generation, were breaking with tradition and seeking their independence from a stifling male dominated culture that had continued for centuries. As the Italian men became confused about their role in the scheme of things, this led to some out of order behavior on their part.

The parents were confused and she rather suspected the young women were confused also.

Sighing, Lina contentedly picked up her coffee cup and with one last lingering glance at the view went back into the apartment, took it into the kitchen rinsed and placed in the dishwasher.

Lazily moving through the drawing room, on the way to the bathroom, her eyes checked out the room. Hmm, cushions needed straightening. A couple of magazines she had glanced at the night before, were lying haphazardly on the coffee table, so they were tidied up. No control freak, her. Yeah right! Happily climbing the stairs again, she wandered through the bedroom into the bathroom and opening the glass doors of the shower, turned on the hot water.

When she could not drive, she walked or rode her bicycle, a rather dangerous occupation given Roman drivers and their proclivity to drive on any part of the road, or footpath that took their fancy.

"Who would be a traffic warden in Rome? God forbid." Her laughter tinkled over the sound of the water and she basked, letting it massage her body.

Chapter Eighteen – The Guilianini Family

Sundays in Italy were generally church and family time. After rearranging his lunch with Lina, Edoardos was wending his way to his family's ancient palazzo in the exclusive Parioli district. Passing the Duke Hotel, he turned right at the Villa Borghese and continued into the residential area, turning at a high wall that enclosed the family mansion and pointing the car at the large wrought iron gates, changed gears to slow the vehicle down, as he depressed the automatic gate opener.

Snarling like a stalking panther, the luxury vehicle moved forward around the entrance of the circular driveway that led to main entrance of the home, which was surrounded by beautiful gardens. Stopping at the parking area to the left of the main entrance, he smiled and gave his keys at the elderly gentleman who came out to greet him.

"Ciao Benito, how are you?" he greeted the family's major domo.

"Padre. I am very well and yourself?" replied the white haired maggiordomo who had been with the family ever since Edoardos could remember. Smiling warmly at the young man whom he adored, he recalled the happy times that were now behind them, when he bounced this same young man on his knees and despite the dignity of his position, had crawled along the floor after him pretending to be a lion.

And when the young fella had clambered onto his back, they both pretended he was riding a great golden lion to show how brave he was. Rather undignified for one in a house steward's position, but wonderful nevertheless.

These wonderfully warm paisan servants were the mainstay of aristocratic European families. Their upbringing was left to the istetutrices - *governesses* - whilst the parents were dutifully engaged in the pursuits demanded of them by their position in society. It hadn't hurt any of them as far as Edoardos knew.

He placed his arm around Benito's shoulder. "All the better for seeing you poco babbo (*little father)*," he fondly remarked to his substitute padre. Benito's wife, the equally elderly housekeeper who ruled the 'below stairs' servants with a firm hand, tempered with affection, was his piccolo mama (*little mother*) and he treasured the love that had been showered upon him by them both.

Due in part more to these two, a warm atmosphere had pervaded the family home at all times. Filial duty and social mores had been bestowed upon the siblings by Edoardos' parents, passing on the baton with the same expectations of their children their parents imposed on them. This was not to say they did not love their bambinos, they certainly did and the Guilianini had endeavoured to relax the formality normally associated in an ancient family, when it came to their children.

Entering through the front door, Edoardos glanced affectionately around him at the magnificent foyer with its marble floors, columns and sweeping staircase. His gaze travelled up to the wrought iron balustrade and railings of the landing that encircled and overlooked the entire foyer, leading off to the rooms on the second floor.

Leaning against this at the top of the stairs was his sister Alegra, who when she saw him, ran down the stairs and flung herself into his arms.

"Edoardos you're home again." Alegra nestled her head into his shoulder, as he held her tight. The baby of the family, the soon to be Princess, was twenty three years old and betrothed to be married. To be sure she loved her fiancé from another of the acceptable families and it was quite understood he would continue to indulge and love her, but in some ways she was quite unsophisticated and immature.

Whilst excited about the grand wedding that was planned, similar to a fairytale in which she was starring, she had her reservations about stepping over the threshold, to become mistress of her own home and leaving behind that of the family where she was adored and treasured.

"Cara mia, it has only been one week," Edoardos teased her and held the beautiful young woman away from him to look into her eyes.

"I know, but you are away so often now and soon I will no longer be part of this family, but of another, where so much is expected of me," she complained.

"Well I cannot move in with you, can I?" he teased her, trying to lift her spirits. "I do not think your husband, or your future parents in law would consider that appropriate."

"Ooh," she breathed out, as she moved beyond his reach, the smile of delight she always felt in his presence radiating from her. Moving back in close, she took hold of his arm, as though he anchored her to this earth, which he had always done, as he sheltered and protected her through life.

He was the next youngest in line and his two elder brothers were five and seven years older than him. They had long ago made appropriate marriages, established their own families and were deeply entrenched in the family businesses of pharmaceuticals and finance.

When he had entered the church and moved into an apartment close to the Vatican, Alegra had been heartbroken. You are deserting me," she had wailed, knowing full well the expectations the family had of Edoardos and that he had no option.

"Far from it," he had cajoled her. "I am merely reserving a place in heaven for an angel like you."

Standing on tiptoes she had kissed him, "I will miss you so much. Promise you will come and see me often."

"Cara mia I am around the corner and you only have to call me and I will be here." Placing her hand on his chest, he vowed, "you know you have my heart."

Now they moved together across the vestibule and into the drawing room where the family awaited Edoardos; and the arrival of his two brothers Antonio and Giovanni.

The drawing room was elegantly furnished in antique Rennaisance pieces and was painted in a soft glowing yellow. Grouped around a huge marble fireplace were two large comfortable sofas and six armchairs upholstered in tones of fuchsia/yellow Italian linen, matching floor to ceiling drapes framing the large arched doors that ran the length of the room letting muted light in, and led out onto the large terrace.

Gilt edged chairs from the Renaissance period were grouped around the room, with matching tables. Matching marble and cedar credenzas held magnificent arrangements of flowers that would have fed the average Roman family for a week. No expense was spared to create the tableau.

Stepping forward towards one of the straight backed antique chairs, Edoardos bent to kiss his mother el Duchessa, on each cheek. At fifty five years of age, Caterina Guilianini was still considered one of the beauties of Roman society. Breathing in her unique scent, he could identify her favorite perfume, Coco by Chanel, which she had worn since its release in 1987 and he always associated with her. Her heart shaped face had broken many a heart when she was a young woman, being courted by aristocratic young gentlemen from all over Europe, whom she rejected for his padre.

"Madre," he murmured adoringly to this elegant woman, whom he held in the highest esteem.

"Babbo," Edoardos addressed his padre, El Duca, as he turned and walked over to kiss him on both cheeks. As the older man held him at arms length to look at him, the younger one could see the dignity and bearing that had attracted his beloved madre, together with the deep intelligence that shone from his dark brown Roman eyes. Together they remained one of the most striking couples in Europe.

"Come, stroll out into the garden with me Edoardos." As his madre elegantly rose from the chair, she took his arm and they strolled together through one of the open doors onto the terracotta paved patio that ran the length of the building.

Fluted columns held the second floor balcony and placed at strategic intervals were huge tubs of cyclamens, smiling beatifically as they showed what a loving relationship they had with the sun. The deep patio led out to two wide steps that accessed the garden, where yellow and violet crocuses preened with the arrogance of models waiting to be admired for their beauty, reluctantly sharing the space with bright yellow daffodils.

Quietly content in each other's company, they descended the steps and strolled together past beds of gentle bluebells nodding quietly to each other. White and blue stately iris mingled with the vibrant orange of Tuscan poppies gently quivering in the slight breeze, spring gentians, asters, cornflowers, cosmos and dahlias created a wonderful tableau.

Caterina, his madre, abhorred structured formal gardens, preferring the riotous beds of flowers, which were a departure from her very formal lifestyle.

"I can breathe freely here," she remarked, and as if to prove it she now closed her eyes for a moment and allowed the scents to soothe her

Edoardos smiled at her lovingly, knowing the waves of longing buried inside, that beat against the dignified exterior she presented to the world

"You have created a paradise madre," he assured her.

Naturally there were a profusion of the most glorious roses, the air redolent with their sweet perfume, which were lovingly tended by Paolo the gardener, who had been with them for as long as Edoardos could recall.

The gardens fulfilled their intention of being a source of great pleasure, providing a symphony of harmony and beauty for the eyes to feast upon and the soul to absorb. Strategically placed stone benches allowed one to sit and muse quietly, shutting out the world beyond.

Meandering underneath arches, where sweet jasmine exuded its special scent at night; wisteria and lilacs tumbled over themselves, like floral waterfalls. Statues of ancient Roman Gods were dotted around the garden, gracefully proclaiming their right to exist, if only in their heavens, where they remained sulking after two centuries of being ousted from their privileged positions in favor of one man, which was enough to make any self respecting God feel out of sorts.

A riot of various colours of bougainvillea tumbled in profusion, ever ready to reach out and catch the clothing or person of the unwary should they venture too close.

'Like Vatican politics,' Eduardo's thoughts wandered to that Machiavellian gilded cage.

Their eyes alighted on the beds of the papery delicate flowers known as Lunaria o Moneta del Papa (*the Pope's money*), which he is not allowed to carry.

"Very apt Madre," he murmured to Caterina who smiled softly and nodded, allowing her thoughts to wander about the possibilities of her strong son becoming Il Papa one day.

"Now Madre, I know where you thoughts are taking you," Edoardos admonished her gently. "I'm not sure I'm that ambitious."

His madre just smiled enigmatically, recalling the role the family had played in the Vatican over the centuries. "Ambition has nothing to do with it my son."

Edoardos' thoughts wandered to Lina. "That would be the end of my being able to come and go as I please," he thought, shuddering slightly at the closeted life of Il Papa. However, these days they were travelling further afield than those that preceded them.

Interspersed around the walkways were huge tubs of geraniums, working in harmony with other plants to keep pests from devouring this wonderful reprieve from the busy world, which lived just outside its walls.

"Let's return now," his madre sighed softly. "I must be there to greet the Cardinale when he arrives."

Turning to face the palazzo to lead them back inside, Edoardos' thoughts turned to the privileges his family enjoyed, but mostly at a loss to their freedom, particularly in the older generation. It was time to put on his formal face for the arrival of Vostra Eminenza (*His Eminence*).

*

Antonio, Edoardos' older brother arrived with his beautiful French born wife Adelais. Their two children were sent off upstairs with their istitutrice (governess) once they had greeted their nonna (*grandmother*) and nonno (*grandfather*). Unlike most Sunday family lunches, today they would eat with their istitutrice in the playroom upstairs, as there were important guests arriving.

"So this is the first informal visit between the two families," Edoardos noted, wondering how informal it could be with Alegra's titled future in laws and the Cardinale in attendance. "I suppose Alegra will be dividing her time between both families on Sundays once they are wed."

One could call Cardinale Contardella family, as he was the Prince's brother-in-law and the marriage between the two children of the ancient families was drawing close. Edoardos doubted he would return regularly, as he would hardly be likely to want to attend the rather noisy family lunches with all the children running around.

"Cardinale Contardella," Benito formally announced as he led the aristocratic man dressed in black and red into the room. Immediately, he commanded the room, as he swept around the assembled group. With his regal bearing and his hooded emerald green eyes flecked with gold that seemed to plumb the depths of others and read their deepest desires, he had brought a delicious shiver to many an aristocratic lady, who had harboured lascivious feelings about forbidden fruit.

With his full sensual lips and an air of hauteur, perhaps a little danger, he was reminiscent of John Malkovich's Vicomte de Valmont in Dangereuse Liaisons. As he walked over to Edoardos' mother, everyone stood respectfully as befitted a Prince of the Church. This being a family gathering Cardinale Contardella would forego the kissing of the Cardinale's ring on his right hand, by the principals of each family. Instead he picked up Caterina's hand and kissed it, acknowledging her as the matriarch of the family his nephew was joining. Turning to his nephew's fiancé Alegra, he walked over and held out his Cardinale's ring for her to kiss.

After she complied, he kissed her on both cheeks then held her at arms length to look at her.

"Bene, bene, I see you are happy," he murmured with exquisite formality. It was not the first time these two families had forged deep links through marriage, but not all of the alliances had been happy ones.

Turning to the men, he nodded to them and they reciprocated in like manner, murmuring "Vostra Eminenza."

"Principe and Principessa Contardello," Benito announced formally once more, as the matriarch and patriarch of the Contardella clan entered. It was not difficult to see where the Cardinale had inherited his regal bearing, as his elegant brother and sister-in-law immediately dominated the gathering. Beautifully clothed and coiffed, they made the room their own, as they proceeded at a stately pace to greet and meet, expecting and receiving a slight curtsy and bow. One almost expected a retinue of servants in their wake.

Knowing his fiance would feel intimidated, their son Niccolo moved from their side to Alegra's. It might be an *arranged* marriage, but it was also a love match.

The Prince was an astute politician, whose family went back to the fourteen hundreds when they had aligned themselves with Lorenzo de Medici. Through their association with this famous Italian family, they had enjoyed the company of the artists of the day such as, Botticelli, Ghirlandaio, Lippi and Michelangelo. Their brilliant literary circle included Poliziano, Ficino, Pulci, and della Mirandola. To this day, the Contardella family were patrons of the arts and literature, and admired for their renowned library of Greek and Latin manuscripts.

During the Renaissance, the Roman branch of Edoardos' family had been aligned with the scandalously corrupt court of Pope Alexander VI, which had rocketed them to dizzy heights. No worse than any other corrupt Pope, of whom there had been many, Rodrigo Borgia shot to stardom as Pope Alexander VI, at the demise of Pope Innocent III, and the Guilianini's had held on for dear life, to this new star in the firmament.

Accused of many different crimes, including adultery, simony, theft, rape bribery, nepotism, incest and poisoning, Alexander VI was no different from many Popes who had ascended the throne of the Holy See. His main crime was to be born Spanish, the Italians despising him for this very reason. After all, the Papacy had been the dominion of Italians for centuries. Who did these upstarts think they were?

In their search for power, the Borgias made enemies of other powerful Italian families such as the Sforza's, the rival Borgia had defeated in the quest for the Papacy; and the influential monk Savanarola.

The Borgias were patrons of the arts and their support allowed many artists of the Renaissance to realize their potential. The most brilliant personalities of this era, regularly visited their court.

The Guilianini family had bathed in the reflected glory of this star, who had made the Earth, his own firmament.

The aristocratic Guilianini's were an ancient Venetian patrician family whose lineage reached back to the Emperor Valentinian III. One of the Venetian Vecchi - *old houses*, they were considered one of the foremost fabulously wealthy families in Venice, having built their fortune in maritime and finances, as Venice asserted herself in the trade routes originally established by the Phoenicians.

The Guilianini families were deeply entrenched in the governing bodies of both Venice and Rome, as well as the Papacy, making their presence felt over the centuries, enabling both factions to wield enormous power in the Eternal City and La Serenissima. Their tentacles of influence extended deep into the Papacy and they were well immersed in the Machiavellian machinations of the Papacy, by the time Edoardos was established in the Vatican.

With the decline of the nation's fortunes in the early nineteen hundreds the family had relocated to Rome, where another branch of the family had entrenched itself in commerce and as part of the *black nobility*.

A number of companies and banks were established in Venice during the early Twentieth century, enabling the Ancients of Venice, although diminished, to command important financial and intelligence power.

The Smiling Pope, John Paul I, who had been the Patriarch of Venice, as Cardinale Luciani, despised them and referred to them openly as the Ancients of Venice.

He was horrified when Archbishop Paul Marcinkus, who had been appointed head of the Vatican Bank, despite no previous banking experience, bought all the shares of the Banca Cattolica del Veneto which Cardinale Luciani ran the bank for the good of the people of Venice, and had merged it with Banco Ambrosiano, the bank involved in the Vatican Scandal.

Upon his election to Pontiff, Pope John Paul I immediately set up an investigation of the Vatican Bank, which sent shockwaves through the Institution. He intended dismissing those incumbents who were accused of financial and other misdeeds, and replace them new appointments. His papacy only lasted thirty three days, dying in his sleep amid rumors of assassination.

Today la Serenissima is hostess to myriads of tourists, who overwhelm the city like a plague of lost seabirds who stopped over for a respite from the long arduous journey. The average Venetian despises, but tolerates them with disdain, as they are reliant on their tourist dollars.

Peddling the beautiful Morano glassware for which the city is famous, it shamelessly flaunts its past, and flogs off exquisite masks to people who will never be fortunate enough to be invited to one of the fabled masked balls.

The wonderful Venice Opera House, much loved by Pavarotti, burned down and now lovingly and meticulously rebuilt, remains unnoticed by the majority of these squawking intruders, coming, on a shoestring, to one of the most expensive cities in the world.

Harry's Bar, made famous by the American writer Ernest Hemingway, is situated at Calle Vallaresso, to the west of the Piazza San Marco, attracting vitriolic reports from tourists, who can neither afford the prices, nor enjoy the ambience and history of the place. Perhaps they should have stayed away.

Reduced to such a sad state, elegant Venice reflects on her glittering history, sighs and carries on, for without this rude trade, La Serenissima would languish and becoming nothing but a backwater city, slowly sinking into oblivion as her foundations slither away.

But beneath her fabled exterior, remains the murky underbelly, in which the Ancients of Venice prolong their hold on the world's financial institutions. Corrupt to her core, she is a gateway for the ugly drug trade entering Europe from Iran and Lebanon.

She is truly the City of Masks.

Chapter Nineteen - The Office of the Administration of the Patrimony of the Holy See

Life in the Big V was a slippery slope and Edoardos would often joke that he needed skis to navigate his path. As there were few with a sense of the ridiculous in this meritorious, formal structure, his times with Lina were precious to him.

Edoardos was unsure where his sense of humour had come from. It was certainly not inherited by either of his parents, who of necessity adhered to the formal strictures of the society they had been born into.

Honed throughout centuries of tradition and the need to hold onto power in worlds of changing loyalties and masters, it was very difficult to break away. The family were well versed in survival under these conditions, and it had been essential for young Edoardos to master these very skills, to endure a career inside the Holy See.

As Edoardos strode towards the office of the Administration of the Patrimony of the Holy See in Vatican City, his shoulders tightened with tension.

The Administration of the Patrimony of the Holy See differs from The Economic Affairs of the Holy See and is the office of the Roman Curia that deals with the properties owned by them, in order to provide the funds necessary for the Roman Curia to function. It is comprised of two sections.

The Ordinary Section has direct responsibility for administering the property remaining to the Holy See, after the complete loss of the Papal States in Eighteen seventy during the unification of Italy.

These were not given up without a great deal of sulking by the Pope, as prior to 1870, the Papacy was the ruler in the civil, as well as spiritual spheres of these territories. This split the Roman nobility into two rival camps; the *White Nobility* around the King, and the *Black Nobility* around the Pope.

Believing this would diminish the power of the Pope, the opposite proved the case. So much so, that in 1929, Pope Pius XI signed the Lateran Treaty with the Italian Government. According to its terms, the Holy See received financial compensation $85 million, ($500 million in today's terms) for the loss of its territories and property. Also the full sovereignty of the Pope was recognised, where the Vatican State was concerned.

Now the Holy See was very wealthy indeed, with investments and huge landholdings around the world.

The Extraordinary Section, to which Edoardos was attached, administers the Holy See's cash and investments, including its patrimony and pension fund.

In 2010 the Vatican Bank had been rocked by yet another money laundering scandal, under Pope Benedict XVI, and had been investigated by Italian tax police.

A growing demand for public financial reporting had seen Pope John Paul II partly meet this demand. Now a report, *Consolidated Financial Statements of the Holy See,* is prepared by the president of the Prefecture for the Economic Affairs of the Holy See, who acts as the Pope's treasurer. This report, however, only reveals details of the financial administration in the Holy See, a partial disclosure that conceals details of other accounts such as the Vatican Bank and the Vatican City State. It is known, though, that about half the income of the Vatican City State is used to help finance the Holy See.

The Cardinale's office was reached through an antechamber, which was guarded by his faithful centurion, Monsignor Galasso, the Under Secretary, who was fiercely faithful to his Cardinale, his protector in the vicious politics of the Vatican. He would do anything for his master.

As he had worked his way up through the treacherous and difficult path of the Vatican hierarchy with its power plays, this man had earned the right to be seated on the right hand of Cardinale Vendetto. However, he could not hide his contempt for young political appointees and he never lost the opportunity to make their lives as difficult as possible.

Under-Secretary Monsignor Galasso had asked Edoardos to gather and correlate a report on some papers from the Secret Archives. The young priest always found this a delightful pastime, often taking the opportunity to browse some of the documents not readily made available to the thousand researchers who every year, apply for permission to examine them. The Secret Archives do not signify the modern meaning of *confidentiality,* but rather *that of the personal property of the Pope.*

The Head Archivist and his minions kept a very watchful eye on visitors to their special realm, but were used to Edoardos and other prelates coming and going to do their masters' bidding.

Hurrying along the corridor to an appointment with the Under Secretary, he glanced at the Philippe Patek watch that encircled his right arm, pausing in the doorway as he entered the antechamber, to gauge the reception.

The priest behind the ornate desk ignored him for three minutes as he walked towards him and stood waiting patiently, then looked up scowling and growled. "Well, do you have the papers I asked for?"

"I do Monsignor," he replied as humbly as he could manage. Whilst respecting the man's ability, Edoardos disliked the man intensely, considering him a boor. One who had not mastered the art of good manners, as he rose through the ranks in the Vatican. Nevertheless, he had to deal with him on a daily basis and could not afford to thwart him, or raise the man's ire.

The priest on his part resented Edoardos' parentage and lineage, knowing he was a *political* appointee. Not being born with Edoardos' aristocratic connections, his own advancement to the success he now enjoyed, had been a slow diligent approach. Treating Edoardos diffidently, he gestured for the papers to be placed on the desk.

"And your report?" His cold eyes bored into Edoardos, as the latter attempted to reply, in an effort to chip away at the younger man's confidence and, in the Monsignor's opinion, a hauteur, which was a result of his noble birth. Snorting with disdain, he ensured the atmosphere remained frigid as he listened, doing his utmost to shatter the young man's demeanour and make him falter.

Edoardos held his ground, with an easy confidence, which infuriated the Monsignor even more. If his obvious disapproval could chisel pieces out of the younger man's mind and heart, he would have done so. When he could not, his fury which he kept under tight control, continued to rise.

"This is inconclusive. I want you to return to the Archives and search harder. Write up a better report on this for me." Contemptuously, he picked up the report Edoardos had placed on his desk and threw it down in front of the annoyed younger priest.

Edoardos stared at the unpleasant man. "With respect Monsignor, I have diligently worked on this for two months now and the report is as complete as I can make it." This was a man who was sure of his own abilities and had been given access to the most secret of documents in the subterranean archives. His application to his work had been noted by the higher echelons.

The Monsignor knew this, which made him envy Edoardos even more. In his own bitter twisted psyche, he preferred to believe Edoardos had risen to such a rank and power because of his birthright, rather than his talent and ability.

Only just outranking Edoardos, but powerful because of his position, he rose and leaning forward placed his hands on the table, his face set in a cold mask and eyes glacial, he snarled, "do not argue with me, this is sub standard work and I will not put up with your impertinence. Do as you are told."

As far as he was concerned, he would bury the noble bastard in the Archives for as long as he could, preferably forever, to keep him out of Vatican hierarchy daily business.

Edoardos eyeballed the Monsignor, signalling he knew his game but would have to comply. Gathering up the report, he turned on his heel and left the antechamber, musing on the viciousness of Vatican politics. He could lead an indolent life of luxury if he chose, but this would not test his intelligence, nor keep the adrenaline pumping like life in the Vatican could and did.

Tomorrow was another day, he would return to the archives and like a mole in its burrow, work industriously. Whilst he was there, he might as well enjoy himself and delve into some of the histories of the Catholic lay societies, as Lina had suggested. It would be a little light relief for him as he was fascinated by the structures of the Catholic faith.

Edoardos sighed as he retraced his steps.

Chapter Twenty – Lina and E investigate the killing ground

"I must be out of my mind, letting you twist my arm," Edoardos grumbled as he hurried to keep up with Lina. Despite his better judgment, he had capitulated and agreed to look at the Knights of Malta Priory's juxtaposition to the killing ground.

"I have to show you how it does make sense," Lina insisted, looking back over her shoulder. "Don't lag behind. You look as though you're lurking."

He raised his eyes heavenwards. "What did I do Lord, that I should be subjected to this penance?"

Skirting the Circo Massimo, the home of the old gladiatorial games, Edoardos and Lina saw their target in front of them. Rome's famous Roseto Comunale di Roma (*Municipal Rose Garden*).

Every year, in late spring, on the eastern side of the Aventine Hill, next to the Circus Maximus' area, one of the most ephemeral natural shows takes place; the blooming of a thousand roses.

Rome's Roseto Comunale di Roma consists of two separate sections which are separated by a short via, di Valle Murcia. The upper section rises to the top of the ridge and the lower one down to the entrance, where two main gates provide access to the gardens.

It is not a large park when compared to many in other countries, around two and a half acres, yet the number of different varieties densely scattered over the garden's slightly sloping grounds is remarkable. There are over 1,000 coming from no less than twenty countries. As it was early autumn, the roses were not showing off their beauty. In fact they were readying themselves for the long refreshing sleep of winter.

Lina and Edoardos paused for a moment, to look back to the green field of Circus Maximus in the background and he could not help noticing how the moon illuminated her face, casting an almost spectral cast to her visage.

Presiding over the entrance was the impressive gigantic monument to Giuseppe Mazzini who had envisaged a republican future for Italy in the eighteen hundreds when it was composed of small kingdoms and determinedly opposed the Papal State.

"Look out," Lina couldn't resist a dig. "There's the enemy of the Vatican state."

The priest harrumphed and gave her a dark look. "Don't be such a smart ass," he shot back.

Considered somewhat of a father of the country, in 1949 when Italy was a very young republic the nation had decided to erect the large monument to his memory.

"I'll have you know smarty pants," Edoardos whispered aside to Lina as he gazed upon the statue, "that during most of his life, he was regarded as a dangerous conspirator. He was an instigator of rebellions and acts of terrorism."

"I know," she chortled, happy she had managed to elicit a response from him, "That's what reformers do."

"And did you know," he smirked at her, "his good friend Felice Orsini made an attempt on the life of the French Emperor Napoleon III?"

Lina nodded happily. "Sure, after the populace had been through the Revolution and the rule of Napoleon I, whom they finally got rid of, they were suddenly saddled with yet another Napoleon with empirical ideas."

Determined not to let Lina have the last say, Edoardos challenged her, "And he threw several bombs at the Opéra entrance, killing eight innocent people and wounding more than one hundred and fifty."

"I know," Lina was genuinely contrite. "It's an unfortunate reality that the overthrowing of theocracies, still results in the deaths of innocent people. This is the collateral damage the politicians and armed forces blab on about."

"Even after Italian unity was achieved," he started to say, when Lina chipped in.

"And God knows how they managed *that*. It's a mystery how it holds together today, with all the opposing factions we have now," she sniggered.

"Silencio," the priest rumbled quietly. "Mazzini spent many years in exile in France, Switzerland and England, and when he returned to Italy it was under a false name as he was regarded as a criminal by the police."

"Well he thumbed his nose at the Vatican didn't he?" an unrepentant Lina whispered back, as they moved on to the entrance.

"I don't know why I hang around with you." Edoardo was determined to have the last word as they went through the gate.

By the two entrances to the garden was a memorial pillar, with a plaque shaped as the Tables of the Law and a single Star of David. This was a reminder of the religious discrimination that had flourished in Rome, under the influence of the Papal Authority.

The moon hung in the sky, watching them as they carefully made their way along the pathway through the garden, where the tombstones of the Roman Jews used to stand.

Up to the first half of the sixteen hundreds, the local Jewish community had been using as a cemetery, the grounds located just before the old Porta Portuensis, one of the two ancient city gates in Trastavere district.

In sixteen forty-five the gate was rebuilt not far from the earlier one; on that occasion, the cemetery, which spread over the spot of the new Porta Portese, was removed.

The Jews were then given permission to use, for this purpose, an uncultivated patch of grassland on the Aventine, enclosed by the ancient Santa Price's church, the area where the old Savelli fortress once stood, at the top of the hill, by the remains of the Circus Maximus.

For two and a half centuries up to the late eighteen hundreds, the Jewish community kept burying its dead on the Aventine hill, which is the very location of today's rose garden. Meanwhile, Rome's main Verano cemetery had been opened in eighteen thirty-six but only the Roman Catholic were admitted. Religious prejudices rapidly subsided after the fall of the Papal State, and the Jews were able to use the main cemetery. The Aventine hill stopped being used for new burials in eighteen ninety-five

In nineteen-thirty four the road that now crosses the present garden, Via di Valle Murcia, was opened on the Aventine, thus necessitating the relocation of the Jewish graves to the Jewish section of the Verano cemetery.

Their eyes were attracted to the small mosaic beneath their feet and they saw in the distance, behind the trees, by the light of the moon, the remains of the imperial palace on Palatine Hill.

"So much history," Lina sighed as she gazed upon the site. "It's one of the reasons I love Italy so, and want to live here."

The Aventine, where they were headed, had been the site of the Temple of Flora, who was the Roman goddess of flowers and springtime. The first temple dedicated to her, according to official records, was in the Third century BC, where it stood on the Aventine, facing the Circus Maximus. Sadly there is no surviving trace of her temple.

Lina absorbed herself in the pagan history of Rome any chance she got, and was delighted by the tenuous link to the cult originally called *Floralia*, then *Ludi Florales.* In ancient times sacred rites were held every year from at the end of Aprilto the first days of May, to honour Flora.

The downhill section hosts the annual contest, to which the public are not admitted, before the committee has chosen the winners from the varieties that are arranged in the outer plots.

Lina and Edoardos passed under an arbor, where in the summer, climbing roses tumble around the frame, offering their beautiful faces to be admired by the throngs of visitors. Only one or two brave blooms were lingering in the early autumn sun.

"Be careful Lina," Edoardos warned her of the two seats to the right of them. "Do not run into the seats in the dark."

"I won't," she reassured him. "The moon makes them easy to see. It's so romantic really." Glancing sideways at him, she waited to see if he reacted at all, but he studiously ignored the last comment, not wanting to open up something he could not control.

The central oval is the hall of fame and features all the roses that were prize winners in previous contests.

In the uphill section, which they would pass through on their climb to the rear of the Knights of Malta Priory, the plants are arranged in different plots according to their several categories. Here the standard roses are the main feature. Surrounding them are climbing roses, ground cover roses, miniature roses and even English roses, all vying for attention.

In May when the gardens are opened to the public for two months, tourists and locals can be seen with cameras at the ready, snapping the magnificence of the roses in bloom.

"I think it was a lovely tribute to the Roman Jews, to preserve the memory of the old Aventine cemetery, by planning the pathways of the larger section of the gardens in the shape of a *Menorah.*" Lisa pointed to the section where the seven-branch candelabrum design was laid out.

"And those few tall cypress trees overlooking the garden here, are still the same ones that once grew in the old cemetery," Edoardos contributed to the history lesson.

As if in sympathy the silver disc in the sky cut a brilliant swathe in front of them, as though laying down the path for them to follow. Lina could feel the globe's sorrow, at the atrocities it had witnessed over the centuries.

"The darn moon is so bright," Lina whispered in conspiratorial tones to Edoardos.

"It is showing us the way," he whispered back. "Imagine what it has seen over the centuries.

"The darkest deeds were carried out on nights it could not follow the perpetrators, and weep at their horrific deeds."

"You're probably right there."

"Monsters cannot stand the light of day, or the gentle silvery beams of a benevolent moon, that lights the darkness for human beings to find their way," she romanticised, turning her head over her shoulder so her words would reach him.

"Wow, that's pretty lyrical." The priest was impressed.

"However," Lina smiled malignly and continued, "for those whose hearts are so blackened with malice and carry out these horrific deeds, they shrivel up if those same beams shine and expose them to the world for the malignant beings they are."

Edoardos looked at Lina, and pondered how wonderfully her mind conjured up scenes, painting them so brightly, he could imagine being there.

"You certainly have a way with words." Reaching out, he caught hold of her arm and guided her away from a bed of roses that she would have tumbled into.

"Right we have to put our backs into it, to push onwards and upwards."

They both looked up towards the Priory, with the tall tower of the former monastery clearly outlined across the sky.

"We need to be careful now, as the armed guards will be patrolling, even more so now since the murder." He took Lina's arm to help her up the incline, as they pushed on until they reached the spot where the horrific crime had taken place. It was still closed off as a *crime scene* but the cross and the appalling sight of the poor woman, who had been nailed to it, had been removed.

Both of them shuddered as the horror overcame them. Lina's eyes filled with tears, at the pain and suffering the woman must have endured. "It's beyond comprehension."

Edoardos moved close and put his arm around her shoulders. "I know. For a journalist, you have such a soft heart, but I agree. I cannot even begin to imagine such thoughts crossing anyone's minds, let alone carrying out such an atrocity."

Lina shook her head and wiped her eyes with a tissue she took from the pocket of her coat. "Let's scout around and see if we can find a trail."

"What do we hope to find?" Edoardos queried, as they stood for a moment, to catch their breath.

"I've got no idea, but you would think if a few people milled around this site, there would be traces of them."

"And it has since been churned up by many feet. Why do you think we can succeed where the carabinieri have failed?"

"That's because they are not linking up with Knights of Malta and the Priory," Lina insisted, whilst foraging around, searching the ground for traces of evidence or clues to the identity of the perpetrators.

"Lina," Edoardos tried to claim her attention. "Do you know how many police and other people have been crawling over this since the forensics were collected? There are bound to be tracks and traces all over the place. But of whom?"

"OK, I know, but nevertheless there may be something they have missed."

Edoardos sighed and began to search himself.

"If you look from here at the Priory, it is not a long way." Lina raised her eyes up to the building on the crest of the ridge. "If everything was prepared beforehand, all they had to do was raise the cross, and then nail her to it." Lina winced at the thought of it and continued gazing up at the building in front of them. "There is access there. Look." She pointed to the gate, set in the low wall that ran alongside the Priory's Church. "Maybe that's unlocked." Running over she tried it, but it would not give to the pressure. "OK, if you give me a leg up, I can get over that. Then I can try and get into the church, or even the Priory itself.

"Are you crazy?" Edoardos was aghast at the suggestion. Moving forward quickly, he grabbed her by the arm. "There are guys with machine guns, guarding the building and lights are on inside. God knows who is in there."

"Don't be a wuss E," Lina protested, trying to pull away from his grasp. Once she was on the trail, nothing would prevent her from going to any lengths to find the answers.

Edoardos held on tightly, as he hissed at her, "I'm using my commonsense, which is more than you're doing." Next he tried appealing to her sense of fair play. "When I agreed to come up here, I didn't agree to break into the Priory, nor its grounds."

Lina sulked and tried to pull herself away as he continued. "What do you suggest we tell them about a priest from the Vatican, crawling around in front of the priory with a journalist, in the middle of the night? That I want to pray in the church of Santa Maria del Priorato." He raised his eyes to the heavens and pleaded to the invisible. "So help me Lord. Save me from this crazy person."

"Get a grip." Lina was determined to bully him into it. "Look, I'll be really quick."

But he remained adamant in his refusal to buy into her plan. "And what if it's alarmed, which is more than likely."

Lina considered the possibility he could be right. That would bring the guards running for sure. "I still believe it's possible and highly suspicious."

"You can't go into their buildings. They have sovereign status. It would be like breaking into the Vatican." The priest was desperately trying to dissuade her from the crazy plan. "I'm not going to be part of it, without some proof of a motive."

Lina knew when to capitulate. "Then I'll find that proof and you have to help me with that."

Edoardos rolled his eyes upwards, beseeching God to help him out here. "I can't believe the Knights of Malta Order are behind such a bizarre murder."

"Stranger things have happened in this crazy world," Lina kept arguing the point with him. "In my mind, they are likely suspects. I can't explain, but I know they are behind this."

At this, she set off at a clip, to the back of the Priory while he followed reluctantly. Suddenly she stopped and he nearly ran into her. "What the hell compelled them to do such a thing? What's in their history that has brought this about? What are we missing here?"

"Maybe nothing, it's just your imagination," Edoardos suggested.

"It's just some lone psychopath."

"He couldn't have done it on his own."

"You may be right. Perhaps he enlisted the help of others, but we're not going to find out if we hang around here much longer, looking as suspicious as hell." Following Lina, who had surged forward again, he looked up at the Priory and the church.

"Then what the hell has he got to do with the Priory?" Lina would not be detracted from her suspicions, no matter what arguments the priest put up. "We have to track down someone connected with the Knights of Malta, who has access to the Priory and can come and go at will. Look at how easy it would be to slip out of there, with enough people to do the dirty deed." Lina gesticulated to the low wall bordering the Priory and the porta set into it. "It would be a snip."

"What about the guards?" Edoardos was apprehensive. "People live on this hill. Something that outrageous would be noticed."

"It could be done, and these are obviously very crazy people." Lina was not about to give up. "The gardens are closed and at night time the residents are about their own business, with the drapes drawn across their windows," Lina insisted, knowing the Roman need for privacy.

"Oh, so no-one would notice a group of people, digging a hole deep enough and pouring concrete into, that would hold up a cross, with the poor woman nailed to it,?" Ever the sceptic, Edoardos challenged her. "Really Lina, sometimes I wonder what planet you're from?"

She pouted, "Well someone did it E, and it would have been a damn sight more difficult if they *didn't* come out of one of these buildings." She made a broad gesture with her arm that included the buildings on the ridge of the Aventine. "I can't see the people that live in this high priced real estate, spying on their neighbours in the early hours of the morning."

"I don't know what to think Lina." He looked at her gloomily and then shifted his gaze to the Priory buildings. "Your entire suggestion is so outrageous, it's hard to take on board." Shrugging his shoulders, he turned from side to side at an angle of 180 degrees, to look at the other dwellings, and then turned to look at the wonderful view of St Peters and Rome.

Lina pointed to the remains of the Circus Maximus, which had been the site of many bloody encounters at the height of the Roman Empire. "We're just as much into blood sports as the old Romans were down there," she commented wryly. "Not much has changed."

"I know." His thoughts went back to his own family's nefarious deeds in their rise to power. Their hands were decidedly not *mani pulite*. The streets had run with blood as long as civilisation had existed. It would continue until the end of time, he reasoned.

"Let's go home Lina, tomorrow's another day. I'll think about how I can help you, but leave things for now please." Edoardos suddenly felt overcome by a wave of exhaustion.

The Catholic Church had taken a pounding over the last few decades, with sexual scandals, the faithful departing in their thousands and the lack of men and women being drawn to the vocations of priests and nuns. "It's a sign of the times," muttered to himself.

"Sorry, what did you say?" Lina turned to him.

"Nothing," he responded tiredly as he began to walk dejectedly back down the hill.

"What"s wrong E?" Lina came running after him.

"I don't want to see another scandal hit the church," he said.

"Then the church has to modify its behaviour and listen to how people feel." Lina had no patience with the Holy See's attitude to their flock. However she was very fond of Edoardos and looked at him searchingly.

"It's my *life* Lina," He replied morosely. "There are many good people in the Church, and I don't want to see them brought down by a lunatic."

"They won't be E," Lina moved closer and put her arms around him.

He flinched and moved back quickly.

"What's wrong?" she queried, hurt at his response.

"It's not you," he quickly reassured her, as he turned away from the feelings that arose when she was near. Not able to imagine a life without her in it, he was willing to deny and resist those feelings with all his being, rather than let her go. "Come on, I don't think we're going to find anything here. We have to go back and try and reason out *who* is behind this. Try to make some sense of it all, so we can hopefully find out why." Turning, he trudged back morosely through the gardens, with the moon providing a silvery path to follow.

"If only it was that easy." Provoked Lina reluctantly followed, trying to figure out why he was suddenly remote.

Chapter Twenty-one – Le Istituto per le Opere di Religione – (IOR), Vatican Bank

Lina had her own ways of convincing Edoardos against his will and she could always bribe him with the promise of a good dinner and delicious coffee. As the Carabinieri had made little ground over the murder to date, he cautiously agreed to come to the apartment for dinner.

"Now what about the Vatican Bank?" Lina turned over the pages of some notes she had in front of her. They were seated at the glass dining table in her apartment, as they could hardly been seen in public, discussing whether an office of the Curia could possibly be linked to such a tragedy. "There have been some very devious characters running this institution over the last few decades and it's not out of the woods yet."

Edoardos rolled his eyes. "God's Bankers scandal has been well documented over the past forty years. I think they've had so much exposure they would flay anyone alive who put them in a position like this. What would they have to gain? And they would be far more subtle than this guy has been."

But there was no deterring her. The terrier had a taste of the bone and it was firmly clenched between the jaws. "Not necessarily," she said, "they are still in trouble. Scandal after scandal. They don't seem to be able to clean up their house."

"Leave it to the new Papa. He will." Edoardos had great faith in the new Pope.

"Let's just have another look at them please?" Lina pleaded with him.

Reluctantly he nodded and they bent to the task.

The heart One hundred million given to the Holy See by formed the framework of the modern fortunes of the Roman Catholic Church, who created the IOR for the purpose of financing religious works from the tithes, gifts and offerings from the Catholic faithful.

However it soon became apparent that the Vatican Bank, which is not open to any individuals or corporations outside Vatican City, had evolved into a major financial institution. With its known main avenues of investment in banking, insurance, real estate, utilities, and construction, the Holy See also holds shares in private enterprise and had invested in a large amount of government bonds and debentures (*titoli* and *obbligazioni*).

The IOR effectively functions as a tax haven, set in the middle of Rome, which speculates in the stock, commodity and currency markets. Shrouded in secrecy, it is not subject to public scrutiny, nor is it subject to Italian and European Union banking rules.

So where did it all go so wrong?

Even Edoardos was disillusioned about the IOR. How could he deny the financial scandals that had dogged the Vatican Bank, in the last few decades? As Lina rightly pointed out, it had tarnished its reputation forever as it appeared the IOR had been one big Ponzi scheme in the eighties.

"You must understand Lina," Edoardos instructed her. "The Vatican Bank holds a unique position. It's a privately held institute, run by a professional bank CEO who reports back to a committee of cardinals."

"I know, but look at its sorry history."

And indeed it was.

Unfortunately the Holy See, which had been sulking about its loss of influence on European politics, was determined to regain a foothold once again. In its wisdom, the Holy See had chosen a brilliant but corrupt financier, Bernadino Nogara as its first director. They agreed to his condition, that his investments remain unrestricted by religious or doctrinal considerations. He was given carte blanche, and had shown no compunction about using the Vatican's funds to invest in munitions factories, banks and the manufacture of contraceptive devices.

This opened the door to the continuation of nefarious dealings over the next eighty years that still continue to the present day.

During the Second World War there were many questions asked about the Holy See's assistance to the Nazis. Fortunes stolen from the Jews as they were exterminated were secreted in Swiss Bank accounts and rumors abound that the Holy See was the recipient of some of the looted monies.

With the writing on the wall for the Nazis towards the end of the war, the Ratline was set up so they could escape retribution. A hungry monster that demanded more and more funding to keep it running, providing passports, shelter, monies and transport, for those war criminals wishing to avoid arrest and prosecution, the drain on the Vatican Bank's finances had been enormous, so they turned to nefarious deeds to generate greater profits.

In the postwar era, with a desire to finance its continuing attempts to influence European politics, the IOR appears to have plunged into organized crime. They were accused of evading Italian currency laws, laundering Mafia drug profits and serving as a front for fraudulent securities schemes. As early as 1948, a Vatican official named Monsignor Edoardos Cippico was arrested and imprisoned for evading Italian currency controls through money-laundering operations at the Vatican Bank.

In Nineteen-seventy an American Bishop foiled an assassination attempt on Pope Paul VI in the Phillippines. Archbishop Marcinkus was rewarded by being made Head of the Vatican Intelligence and Security. His career was upwardly mobile from there and he was promoted to the Secretary of the Vatican Bank. In nineteen seventu-one with no previous banking experience and with Cardinal Spellman's backing, he was promoted to Chairman of the Bank.

"See, here are the Knights involved in one of modern Italy's biggest political scandals," Lina turned to Edoardos, determined to make him admit there was a link between them. "Spellman was the Protector of the American Chapter."

The priest was well acquainted with the Bank's less than spotless history. Even he wondered why they had been allowed to continue unchecked, until once again, it brought them to the notice of the Italian and United States authorities.

Marcinkus had a free hand in running the bank and in nineteen seventy-three he engineered with Michele Sindona, the sale of the Catholic Bank of Venice to Roberto Calvi's Banco Ambrosiana which was suspected of being a mafia-controlled bank in Milan.

Church workers who could obtain low interest loans from the Catholic Bank of Venice lost their life savings and investments which they had purchased because of their priests' confidence in it. The profit made on an investment from these profits, was divided between Marcinkus, Calvi and Sindona.

At this time, Alberto Luciani was the Cardinale of Venice and upon investigating the sale he discovered the Vatican Bank held a fifty-one% interest in the bank. Outraged, the future Pope John Paul 1 took himself off to Rome immediately, to demand a meeting with Pope Paul VI, who adroitly avoided him.

Shunted off to Archbishop Paul Marcinkus, he was rudely told, "You cannot run the Church on Hail Mary's." Suspecting the sinister forces that he called the Ancients of Venice were at work, in retaliation the Cardinale closed all diocesan accounts at Banco Cattolica.

Things went from bad to worse. By this time Calvi, who was known as God's Banker because of his association with the Vatican, introduced Michele Sindona, a known associate of the Mafia to Marcinkus. This was a godsend for The Shark, as he was known in banking circles. The perfect tax haven, operating from a sovereign state that was unanswerable to Italy's monetary policy, or for maintaining the stability of that Nation's currency and money supply. As a private organization performing banking-like functions for religious institutions, it is not subject to public scrutiny.

By the late nineteen-seventies the Italian financial press was clamoring for Pope Paul VI to impose *order and morality* on his bank, and the Italian authorities were calling for greater transparency, after the crash of the Banco Ambrosiano.

When Calvi's Banco Ambrosiano collapsed, amidst a major political and financial scandal in the Nineteen-eighties, he Vatican Bank was one of its major shareholders.

As its Chairman during these crucial years Archbishop Paul Marcinkus was under consideration for indictment in nineteen eighty-two in Italy, as an accessory to the collapse. As long as he stayed within the Vatican City's walls, he enjoyed both the Pope's protection and diplomatic immunity from prosecution.

So, the Vatican Bank remained a secretive institution, which insiders had identified as controlling over $10 billion of assets. Whilst it was in the Pope's interest to protect the IOR, he would continue to deny the Italian Government the right to examine the records of the Bank, or serve arrest warrants against Archbishop Marcinkus and other officials of the bank.

The Vatican lost millions of dollars in its dealings with Sindona.

"It doesn't make very good reading does it E." Lina leaned back and pondered the intricacies of men and the world. "I wonder what motivated Pope Paul VI to protect Paul Marcinkus from the Italian prosecutors, when it came to the crunch."

"I think he had a fierce loyalty to the man who saved his life."

"Well that was pretty misguided thinking." Rubbing her forehead, Lina relaxed for a moment, "God, what feral mob they were."

It started with the death of Roberto Calvi, found hanging from Blackfriar's Bridge in London, after the collapse of his banking Empire. A few months after his mysterious death, Italian prosecutor Emilio Alessandrini was gunned down in the streets, as he was closing in on the facts of the Vatican Bank's criminal activities. When another prosecutor Giorgio Ambrosoli stepped into Alessandrini's shoes, he also was murdered. Lina was beginning to look a little green, as she documented all the killings.

In March 1980, a U.S. court convicted Sindona of 65 counts of conspiracy, fraud, and perjury, charging among other things, that he had siphoned $45 million from funds belonging to Long Island's Franklin National Bank, in which he had purchased a controlling interest, into other companies he owned, mostly in Italy.

Prosecuted in America, he pulled high level strings to get himself extradited to Italy for sentencing, believing he could escape. Much to his horror he was sentenced to life imprisonment and two days later was found dead in his cell of cyanide poisoning.

However, with the death of Pope Paul VI in 1978, it all changed.

On 5 June 1982, two weeks before the collapse of Banco Ambrosiano, Roberto Calvi had written a letter of warning to Pope John Paul I, stating that such a forthcoming event would *provoke a catastrophe of unimaginable proportions in which the Church will suffer the gravest damage.*

To everyone's surprise, especially one suspects that of Marcinkus, who thought he was in line for the papal tiara, the College of Cardinales chose a dark horse candidate as Paul VI's replacement. Albino Luciani, the Cardinale of Venice, was elected to the Throne of St Peter.

Chapter Twenty-two – The Smiling Pope

Pope John Paul I, who was a highly intelligent man, was well aware that all was not well within the Vatican Bank. It was brought home to him in no uncertain terms, soon after his election, when he received a notice from Italy's Office of Exchange Control, warning of illegal activities involving transfers to the *foreign* Vatican Bank, which violated the nation's currency laws.

Determined to clean house, he quickly ordered an investigation of the Vatican Bank.

This spiritual leader of all the Roman Catholics, Albino Luciani, was actually embarking on a revolution. He wanted to set the Church in a new direction, which was considered highly undesirable and dangerous, by many high ranking Church officials.

A supporter of Vatican II, the Smiling Pope was a staunch believer in ecumenism and the reduction of Church wealth, which he wished to share with the poor. He renounced the papal tiara and replaced the coronation with a simple ceremony, wearing the pallium, the white stole.

However, this kindly intelligent cleric had not forgotten Archbishop Marcinkus who had facilitated the sale of Veneto Catolitica Bank. At the time of his death, he was about to make a series of dismissals and new appointments, to remove those accused of financial and other misdeeds, in which Marcinkus was heavily involved.

Behind the scenes, the Pope had been investigating Marcinkus and his fellow robbers. He had uncovered among other things, the Archbishop's conflict of interests with his involvement in Sindona's company which made the contraceptive pill.

"Like Pope John XXIII, he was much admired by all peoples worldwide," Lina felt she should bring this to Edoardo's attention again.

"I know," he acknowledged.

What the Smiling Pope had set out to do, was to strip many of their powers, by dismissing them or reassigning them into harmless positions. He was found lifeless in his bed, after only thirty three days in office, following his quickly ordered investigation of the Vatican Bank. On the evening of his death he had reviewed final drafts of documents approving sweeping changes, which would, amongst others, have seen Marcinkus replaced immediately.

"He never lived to carry out his plans," Lina remarked sadly. "The Smiling Pope was silenced forever."

"Lina there's no proof of that."

"There's plenty of proof E, but let's beg to differ on the subject."

Astoundingly enough, when Pope John Paul II was elected, he reconfirmed Paul Marcinkus' appointment as President of the IOR and made him an Archbishop, as well as pro-president of the Pontifical Commission for the State of Vatican City, which ensured he was the third most powerful man in the Vatican.

"Why did he do that I wonder?" Lina turned the pages over looking for a clue.

"Perhaps he thought Marcinkus had earned it."

Lina looked at Edoardos out of the corner of her eye. "Or perhaps, as rumor has it, Marcinkus had a new ally, and later worked with the US government to funnel huge amounts of money through the Vatican Bank, to the Solidarity Union in Poland."

"You don't understand Vatican politics, in their continual fight against communism."

"And I don't want to," she retorted smartly.

This had left the way free for the Banca Ambrosiani, to merge with Banca Commerciale Italiana, Veneto, Cariplo and Banca Commerciale Italiana, forming Banca Intesa, and becoming the largest banking group in Italy and one of the largest in Europe.

The Vatican Bank effectively continued down the same murky path.

"Then there were a spate of other murders, when the government began investigating the irregularities in the Vatican Bank, with the public demanding answers this time. The Vatican's halo was badly tarnished," Lina brought these items of interest to Edoardos attention, who was trying to avoid them as best he could.

"And the scandals continued throughout Pope Benedict XVI's reign. Perhaps someone remains, who retains such old deep hatreds, they would stoop to the level of this atrocity," Lina postulated.

"The problem with that suggestion is, that person would be so ancient they would be physically, and perhaps mentally, incapable of carrying out such a deed."

Lina chewed on her bottom lip as she digested Edoardo's retort. "If he was in his late 80's, he could still be mentally alert enough to have planned it. He could be directing behind the scenes, not actively involved."

The sorely tried priest let go of a deep sigh, looked at her and shook his head in dismay. "Think about it Lina. What's he going to do to keep them in line? Beat them with his zimmer frame?"

At this point, Lina decided retreat was the better part of valor, but tucked it away in a small compartment of her mind, to be brought out at a moment's notice if necessary.

"Ultimately the Bank reports to Il Papa (*the Pope*), but he seems to have allowed incompetent directors to run it. Why is this?"

"Unlike my own Office, the OAPH and its overseer, the PEAH, (thank God for acronyms), it's assets are not considered the property of the Vatican."

"Why not?" Lina leaned forward and drummed her fingers on the glass table in front of them.

"It's personally owned and operated by Il Papa, making loans to religious projects all over the world." Edoardos set out to educate Lina on the finer points of the IOR. "It is stated mission is to manage assets placed in its care that are destined for religious works or works of charity. It also manages ATMs inside Vatican City and the pension system for the Vatican's thousands of employees."

"And in the end, it led to the assassination of Il Papa."

"Oh, Let's not go there Lina for heaven's sake." Edoardos was irritated that the subject had been raised yet again.

"We have to look at this E," she insisted. "His actions, in the short time he had in the Papacy, could still be festering in someone's twisted mind."

It brought back memories for both of them.

Albino Luciani was a liberal, following in the footsteps of Pope John XXIII whom he greatly admired.

Pope John Paul I, believed in greater power-sharing with world wide bishops. He planned to decentralise the Vatican structure, which had thrown the Curia into a frenzy. Nor did he believe in the church having temporal power, announcing that if the Church functioned on Jesus Christ's tenets, it should not have power or wealth.

As he took a strongly critical view of abortion, the Pope was an advocate of the anovulant pill developed by Professor Pincus, and appeared to be on a mission to reverse the Catholic Church's stance on birth control.

Tolerant of divorcees, he never hesitated to accept them. He sent his best wishes to the first in vitro birth, stating he did not have the right to judge her parents.

"We have to either eliminate the Vatican Bank, or discover its involvement and find out why."

"Oh, very well," Edoardos gave in with bad grace. The Vatican Bank had been dragged through the mire so many times by now, he was heartily sick of it all.

"They were certainly a bunch of cowboys. How on earth did they get away with it for so long?" Lina actually hoped the IOR wasn't involved, as it would be final straw and she seriously doubted the Vatican would ever recover from another scandal involving the Institution.

"Lina, I don't really want to dredge this all up again." Edoardos was weary of the subject.
"You know we have to look at all angles," Lina appealed to him. "Il Papa John Paul I *was* determined to reform the church."

"I know and I wish with all my heart he had lived to carry out those reforms. He wanted to make good on his promise to his padre, that he would never forget the marginalized and the poor." Edoardos had greatly admired the Smiling Pope, believing him to be a saintly man of great strength.

"He was stopped abruptly in his tracks."

"Why can't it be a normal death Lina?"

"It doesn't stack up. If you look at all the discrepancies, it just doesn't stack up E."

"I don't want to go over them again."

"Look at the deaths that followed his," Lina was determined to leave no stone unturned. "Many people who were close to him as well as influential outsiders. Too many died for it to be twists of fate."

"These things happen."

"I don't believe in this many coincidences." Turning to her ever handy laptop, she fired up a website and drew his attention to its contents. "Look at these statistics."

"In nineteen seventy-eight, a serious effort was made to combat world-wide war on poverty, with thirty three leading Roman Catholic liberals meeting to draw up a plan," Lina read out to Edoardos.

Within twelve months, it was all over, as a series of strange deaths cut back the numbers and frightened the hell out of those who survived. Many were Cardinals who were either potential future pope material, or at least electors of popes.

"It certainly killed off the plans for a war on poverty, and life went on as usual in the Vatican. It left a vacuum that has never been filled," she insisted.

Edoardos rolled his eyes again and beseeched heaven above to spare him from this woman.

"Then there was the death a few years later, of the nun who was his housekeeper, Sister Vicenza. She found him, but they covered that up at first."

"Oh come on Lina, she was an elderly nun who had received an awful shock when she discovered him. Some say she never recovered."

"Or she wasn't given a chance to. They shut her down real fast and packed her off to a nunnery," Lina said darkly.

"Well that's where nuns live," he replied archly.

"Well it's a hell of a coincidence that she died one week after David Yallop's book on Il Papa John Paul's death came out. Not to mention the death of his friend and theological ally, who was killed by a hit and run driver."

"Lina you're becoming a conspiracy theorist."

"Then," Lina pressed on regardless, "how come the apartment next to Il Papa's, where his valet resided, was empty on the night of his death, because his brother had fallen to his death from a sixth floor balcony and he was attending to his funeral arrangements out of Rome."

E suggested. "Let's move on."

"With the election of a new Il Papa Paul VI, no changes at the Vatican Bank were made. In fact, he promoted Archbishop Marcinkus."

"And what does this all prove Lina."

"Il Papa was murdered."

"I can't agree with you on that."

"Your body language tells me that."

Edoardos finally relented. "Look I know the Vatican has had anything but clean hands over the centuries, but we're not all murdering lunatics."

"I'm not saying you are, but we have to pursue this line of thinking so we can narrow our lines of enquiry."

"You're right. I'm sorry. The Big V has taken such a pounding over the last couple of decades and we're all a bit weary from it."

Lina bit her lip, in order to stop herself from suggesting to the priest that the Vatican had brought it on itself, with its less than holy behavior.

"The Bank did pay out over two hundred and fifty million dollars in reparation you know," Edoardos pointed out. In nineteen eighty-four the Vatican Bank agreed to pay two hundred and twenty four million dollars to the one hundred and twenty creditors of the failed Banco Ambrosiano, as a *'recognition of moral involvement'* in the bank's collapse.

"And so they should, but it was a mere fraction of the claims that amounted to over a billion dollars in losses, of innocent depositors in a Milan bank that the Vatican had helped to destroy."

"You're really laboring this point you know."

"And here we are in 2012, involved in yet another financial crisis. In 2010 the police seized over thirty million dollars of Vatican Bank funds. It just goes on and on E."

"But it isn't cause for murder Lina," He protested. "It's all out in the open so what would they have to gain?"

"I don't know. They've murdered before and I dare say it's won't be the last time."

Stung to the core, the priest immediately jumped to the Vatican's defense. "Much of this sensationalism about murder is without foundation."

Lina knew he had to defend the Big V against the accusations about Il Papa John Paul I's untimely death, but she had to move him past his loyalty to them. "The Vatican is in a unique position. It sits on two hundred and eight acres inside the Italian nation, operating as an independent country and not subject to that nation's laws and regulations. It would not be tolerated in any other country in the world."

Edoardos kept his counsel, knowing it gave the Vatican carte blanche to act as it desired,

"I think we're pushing a tired old nag uphill here," he grumbled.

"Let's just follow the trail a bit longer please E," she pleaded. "Look at the last President. He was a Professor of ethics in finance, but I don't think his ethics bothered him too much," Lina was scathing in her damnation of yet another failed head of this institution. "Reportedly he's close to Opus Dei, which makes him automatically suspect in my book. He also advised the Italian Finance Minister and look at the mess our finances are in. They're nonexistent."

Edoardos couldn't argue with that logic. Italy had a long road ahead of her, now that Berlusconi had finally been removed from office and an economist elected to clear up the mess he had left behind. "Still I can't see what they would gain by murdering women."

Lina was feeling weary. "You might be right. It does seem a dead end."

Edoardos held up his hands in protest. "Be fair Lina. Many banks have failed over the past few years. Countries are falling over like a stack of dominoes."

"I agree, its one giant mess. They've all got dirty hands in my book." It appalled her that Barack Obama had appointed as financial advisors to his administration, some of the cowboys of Wall Street, who had heavily profited from the Wild West derivative speculations, that had resulted in the $20 trillion financial crisis that currently held the world in its thrall. Tens of thousands had lost their livelihood, whilst the very perpetrators of these crimes had gotten off scot free. How on earth could they be entrusted with correcting the nation's financial troubles?

'Who are these people?' She asked herself silently.

"Look at this interesting parallel," Lina pointed out to Edoardos. "The Knights of Malta come really close to the autonomy enjoyed by the Vatican, including diplomatic immunity. The only thing they lack is their own bank, but then they count amongst their members, high profile bankers from established reputable banks."

"So we're back to the boys in the black cloaks now?" Locking horns with Lina whilst she was in full cry, could bring on the mother of all migraines. He sincerely hoped she was off the subject of the Vatican Bank and the untimely death of the Smiling Pope.

"We are getting a bit bogged down in one-up-manship here E," Lina admitted, shamefacedly

"OK. Let's pack it in and go out and eat. This has made me hungry," he suggested, hoping she would put an end to it for now. He needed the respite.

"God, I'm starving," Lina was only too happy to agree with this suggestion. "This is laborious work and I need a refill to top up the fire."

Packing away the papers they had before them, putting them in tidy piles and some into their briefcases, Edoardos held out his hand to her and helped her off the chair. An electricity ran between them, but before either could react, he turned quickly and beckoned to her. "Come on, race you to the bottom of the steps."

"I'll faint before I get there. I need sustenance, not exercise."

Halfway down the sixty-nine steps, Lina turned to him. "You know Il Papa John Paul II kept Marcinkus on, despite the allegations surrounding him; and whilst apologising for the sins of the world in 2000, he omitted financial malpractice. Many wondered what his personal view was of the scandal."

Edoardos remained silent and Lina left well enough alone.

After they had passed a pleasant couple of hours together, eating, drinking and ignoring the sins of the Vatican Bank, Edoardos wearily made his way home.

Sighing, he dropped into a favorite leather chair and bringing his hands up to cradle his head, he sat there feeling defeated by it all. "I thought I was made of sterner stuff," he berated himself. "I'm a Guilianini."

Chapter Twenty-three – The price of humility and goodness

Racked with guilt and remorse, the old friar in the Dominican monastery thirty kilometres south east of Rome, wondered how he could reveal his dreadful secret without breaking his confessional vow. There were forces at work greater than he, with his simple faith and love for his Saviour.

His Abate began to notice his decline and worried about his health, called him to his office.

"Brother, what is the matter? You are growing so frail, I notice you are not eating, you are constantly praying and you tremble. I think you should see a doctor," he said kindly.

"No, No," the old friar drew back in fear, trembling even more.

"Brother you have lost your composure. Look at your hands, they are constantly wringing and twisting and have been for some time. Tell me, what is the matter?"

"I cannot." His hands continued to wring and twist.

"Brother you cannot go on like this, you must see a doctor," his Abate insisted.

"No doctor can help me," the old friar replied miserably.

"Brother. You were an example to the other friars of this monastery with your gentle spirit, your devotion, your love for your fellow friars. You have practically become a hermit and avoid contact with your brothers. I must know what is ailing you," he said hypocritically, knowing full well what ailed the poor man.

"I must help you or I fail in my duty as your Abate." Deep down, he felt responsible for the steady decline and disintegration of this much loved friar and felt he should transfer the confession to himself, so the friar could die in a state of grace.

"Please do not concern yourself with me Abate. I am just a lowly friar, living only to be closer to my Saviour." The tortured soul put his head in his hands and wept.

The Abate stood up from behind his desk and came around and put his arm around the old friar. He could not bear to watch this further degeneration of the spirit of this loving person. "I must bring in a doctor or you will die."

"Then please let me die. It is time for me to go to my Saviour, but I do not know if he will accept me into his kingdom. I do not know if I can die in a state of grace," he whispered.

Now the Abate knew he had to weigh up the options. After all, he also had to die in a state of grace and make his own peace with God. "You of all people are the most exemplary friar of the Monastery of St Gerard. You must explain yourself to me. I demand this." It was important he be seen to do the right thing in the eyes of God.

The old friar was torn between his confessional vows and his duty to his Abate. "I cannot break a confessional vow," he whispered. "Please let me go in peace."

"But you are not at peace with yourself and have not been for the last two years. If you are determined to die, then I will not let you die unless you are in a state of grace."

"I will not be in a state of grace if I break my confessional vow," the old friar brought his head up and looked his Abate in the eye.

"You will not die outside a state of grace I can promise you that. I have watched your devotion to Our Lord Jesu Cristo and your fellow man for over 40 years. I will take your confession and you can pass the burden of your vow to me."

"I cannot ask this of you," the old friar was appalled. "My time is drawing near and it does not matter if I am disturbed." Never would he burden his beloved Abate with his terrible secret.

The Abate could not let such a devoted soul, believe he would die outside a state of grace. "I demand this of you and you must obey your Abate."

"No my Abate. I would rather die outside a state of grace." Deep inside the gentle friar, was a strength the Abate had always admired. He could have progressed further in the hierarchy of the Monastery but his humility was more important to him.

"And I will not allow you to." From a place he had not been to since this affair began, the Abate actually felt his conscience prick him.

With that, he led the old friar into the chapel and they entered the confessional box.

"Unburden your soul my friend that you might live in peace or die in peace and a state of grace."

"I must not burden you with this most terrible secret." Nervously the old friar's hand twisted around and around, as though he could wring out all the evil knowledge he had of the Cardinale.

"You took a vow of obedience to the Order and to your Abate. You must obey that vow of obedience."

So the old friar unburdened his soul and his Abate listened. Exiting the confessional, the two souls moved to the high altar and prostrated themselves and prayed to their Saviour to show them the way to the light.

From the shadows in the sacristy, a figure dressed in a red trimmed black cassock, with the sash of red watered-silk ribbon, with silk fringes at the ends and the scarlet zucchetto on his head, watched them for a moment, then turned and made his way to the Abate's private quarters.

When the Abate entered, he stood and they embraced, making the secret sign of the Brotherhood.

"You broke him."

"Yes, which means he is a danger to us all," the Abate confirmed.

"For centuries, the Monastery has kept the secret of the Brotherhood and sheltered its assassani." The Cardinale sat down and gestured to the Abate to be seated also. "The sacrifices must be made each generation and the testament decrees, confession of the sin to purify the assassani's soul."

"It was a mistake to use the old friar. I should have heard your confession," the Abate protested.

The Cardinale waved the remark away. "You are one of us and the brotherhood must control the monastery. My work is nearly done. The friar is dispensable and I leave it to you to arrange."

Despite his misgivings, the other man knew he must bow down to the Cardinale's wishes. "It shall be so Votra Eminenza."

Although he was genuinely fond of the old friar, he knew that drastic methods were required in the name of the cause.

After all, were not the Dominican Order a major force in the development and maintenance of the Inquisition Haereticae Pravitatis Sanctum Officium, the Roman Inquisition throughout the centuries, charged with suppressing heresy. Originally established in France to drive out and eliminate the Cathars from the Languedoc, the religious intolerance cloaked the real reason for the invasion, which was a land grabbing exercise that went very well indeed.

Following this success the Inquisition spread its wings into Italy and then Spain in their relentless pursuit of heretics.

*

The old friar's fitful sleep was marred by nightmares of his saviour turning his back on him and the damnation of hell fires. Black winged creatures of the night would appear to carry him off to the devil's domain. He whimpered and awoke with a start, to lay awake sleepless, until a merciful brief period of sleep overtook him once more.

Sharing his burden with the Abate had not saved him from his nightmares.

The wind stirred the leaves outside the monastery and they rustled in the night. A quiet footfall paused outside the friar's cell and listened. The door quietly opened.

"Who is there?" queried the old friar in an unsteady voice.

"It is only I," responded a well known voice. "I have brought you a cup of herbal tea to soothe and help you sleep."

"You should not have bothered. I cannot sleep the night through any more."

"Here, take the tea and I will sit beside you until you sleep again."

"Thank you." The old friar roused himself and took the cup. "I am so tired."

"Sleep my son," the voice soothed. "Sleep." and he sat beside the old friar as he drifted off to sleep – forever. The monastery's apothecary had an amazing variety of distilled plants, secrets that had been handed down for centuries.

The Abate anointed the old friar's forehead before his last breath and said the last rites over him. After all he had made his last confession the evening before.

The doctor came from the village and wrote out the death certificate from natural causes. His death was not unexpected. After all, the old friar was eighty eight years old. He had thrown off his earthly shackles and gone to meet his Lord Saviour whom he had worshipped all his life.

The friars said rosary in the chapel for the old friar, the Abate himself carried out the Service for the Dead. Then they carried him out of the chapel in a plain wooden coffin. They bury their own in the monastery's churchyard, and the Abate thought the rosary hanging on the cross above the grave, was a nice touch. The old friar would have approved.

Chapter Twenty-four – The Sack of the Languedoc

Pope Innocent III, who at that time was based in Rome, was obsessed with heresy and became known as the Crusading Pope, because of all the campaigns he launched.

Out came the teeth and claws immediately upon his election as Pope. His first order of business was to launch a crusade against the Cathars in the Languedoc, who continued to pose the strongest doctrinal challenge to the Catholic Church.

They believed the spiritual realm was that of heaven, the realm of God. The temporal realm was that of Satan and the flesh and he had created the earth and was therefore the God of the Genesis. The heresy the Catholic Church focused on, was that the Cathars believed both worlds and both powers to be coequal.

The Cathars had no doctrinal objections to contraception, euthanasia or suicide. They called themselves Bon Homme and Bon Femme, *Good Men and Good Women*, whilst others called them Good Christians who held fast to their biblical injunctions of refraining from killing, falsehoods and not swearing oaths. This got right up the Roman Catholic's noses, who were very big on the latter, given they were hell-bent on perpetuating the feudal system.

The Cathars who lived a simple life based on the Nazarene's teachings, found it hard to accept that the Catholic Church, who were some of the richest men in Christendom, preached poverty, whilst dressing in finery and jewellery and living in luxurious circumstances.

The Cathars also rejected the orthodox Catholic Church with its hierarchical structure, which preached official and ordained intercessors between man and God.

This meant in the Cathars' eyes, Popes, priests, bishops and other clerical hierarchy were superfluous. They also considered baptism and communion unnecessary, believing they had direct access to the creator.

They abhorred the opulence of the Roman Catholic Church and sought devotion through a life of extreme devotion and simplicity, worshipping in the open or barns, houses, a municipal hall and practicing meditation.

This put Pope Innocent III in a bind. Not only would he have been out of a cushy job had this belief persisted, he would also lose the very fancy roof over his head.

Fearing this heresy could conceivably displace Roman Catholicism as the dominant form of Christianity, he set out to rectify the matter.

The Languedoc was a place of tolerance, where the Cathars together with the Jews, enjoyed ordinary civil rights and were protected by the Counts of Toulouse, who showed an unusual tolerance to the sect. The Trencavel family wielded considerable power during the 11th and 12th centuries and were widely accepted as being the descendants of Mary Magdalene.

It was a land where learning and philosophy was encouraged and flourished. Troubadours roaming the land with their tales and poetry extolling courtly unrequited love, romance and chivalry, spread this culture across the South of France, and into the Carcassone. In an era where arranged marriages were the norm and an imperious Church's dictates stifled all feelings and ideals, it was a breath of fresh air, which in Pope Innocent's eyes, was not to be borne.

It was also the area the wealthy Knights Templar had settled with their enormous wealth and treasures.

The French King who was Innocent's pal, was only too willing to help bring the Cathars into line, as the French crown had long coveted the riches and goldmines of the Knights Templar, to whom they owed an enormous debt. So they put their minds and considerable forces to it, unleashing the first genocide in modern European history.

As they set about exterminating the populace, the Christians found themselves in the line of fire, despite seeking sanctuary in their churches. When the crusaders were asked how they would distinguish heretics from true believers, the Pope's representative replied. "Kill them all, God will know his own."

That must have been poor consolation for the Catholic followers in the region who were eliminated. It all sounds terribly familiar.

The Pope promised the crusaders an assured place in Heaven, remission of all sins, an expiation of penances and all the booty they could lay their hands on, so they set about ravaging the cities and crops, raping and plundering for 20 years. However, the first crusade was not the success the Pope had hoped for.

The second crusade, lasting another 20 years, saw the Cathars hunted down and burnt at the stake, until they were virtually exterminated.

So the fires raged, palls of smoke choking to death those who did not burn in the fires, and in Carcassonne, the Inquisition walled people up alive.

Indeed the techniques employed differ little from those used today in modern warfare. Sleep deprivation, trick questions, indefinite imprisonment in a cold dark cell on a diet of bread and water. They used threats against other family members and made promises of leniency in exchange for a confession.

Inquisitors and their assistants were conveniently permitted to absolve one another for applying torture, even charging people for the equipment used to execute members of their families. Instruments of torture, like crusaders' weapons, were routinely blessed with holy water.

Those Cathars that converted to Catholicism were few, as the majority preferred martyrdom.

Not content with the massacre of these innocents, with the collusion of Pope Clement V, Phillip IV of France, grasped the opportunity to destroy the Knights Templar for their fabled riches. Ancient parchments documenting his persecution of the religious order and covering the trial of the Templar Knights, can be found in the vault of the Vatican Secret Archives.

Chapter Twenty-five– The Taking of Another Woman

What do you want of me?" the terrified woman asked of her captors. Rivulets of tears ran down her cheeks and splashed on to her hands, which were folded in her lap.

"We want you to tell us where the betrothal contract is hidden."

Taking a deep breath and trying to calm herself, she haltingly replied, "I don't know what you are talking about."

The Cardinale stepped forward and leaning down brought his face close to hers and threatened "Don't you dare lie to me."

The woman sat there mesmerised by the look of hatred on his face. As she watched in horror, he brought his right hand up and slapped her hard across the face.

Her head snapped to the side, cheek stinging, head ringing, the pain of the blow beginning to work its way through her neck, while her entire body froze in shock.

"I really do not know what you are talking about," she stammered while her mind tried to recover from the horror of it all. "Why are you doing this to me? You know my husband has the power to have you hunted down, and he will."

How could he have done this to her? They had known each other for years. Her mind simply could not grasp the situation she was in. Two hours ago, she had driven to the monastery of St. Gerard, after a telephone call from the Cardinale who now stood in front of her, abusing and terrorising her.

Of course she had responded to what she believed was a mercy call to a dying monk, her confessor and friend. Why should she suspect or fear anything. Being by his side while he drew his last breath, would have been a privilege. Instead of being taken to his bedside by the Cardinale who had met her in the vestibule of the monastery, she had been brought down to the cellar, on the pretext that he had passed away and they had brought his body down here to carry out the embalming.

Not stopping to question why this would be, she had followed meekly, only to be attacked as she entered through the door. Hands on either side had grabbed her and roughly handled her to a chair, where they had bound her hands and feet.

Her eyes were dimmed with terror, nor could her mind comprehend what was happening to her, or why the Cardinale was asking her questions of a secret he could not have known about. "Ales….." she tried again, when he cut her short.

"Do not speak, unless it is to tell me the truth. I am warning you, one more refusal to tell me what I want to know and you will end up buried down here."

It was too much for her and her stomach revolted. Vomiting over herself, she fainted.

"Clean this mess up." Disgusted, the Cardinale turned to two of his lackeys and directed them to do his dirty work. "You," he pointed at another, "get warm water soap and a towel. I am not finished with her yet."

And he was not. Reviving her time after time, when she fainted as he tortured her, the same question rained down upon her befuddled mind. She was determined to resist his questioning and protect her dear friend, Adelais.

"I know you belong to le Donne in Azzuro."

Icy tentacles gripped her soul, while her heart leapt in her breast and thudded as though Thor's hammer itself was beating at her chest cavity.

"Tell me where the contract is."

"Ales…"

"Do not say my name," he thundered.

Sobbing with dismay, she tried to reason with him, but it was fruitless.

"Yes, I am a member of le Donne in Azzuro, but what harm have we ever done to you. We are pacifists."

"You seek to bring down the church."

"No Ales….."

"Stop."

Voice and body shaking with terror, unable to control herself, her bowels voided.

"Whore!" Slap. "Foul Whore!" Slap. "Magdalene Whore!" he hissed. "You will tell me where the contract is."

But she couldn't. She knew there was a casket, with a secret of Miryai's in it, but she had no idea where it was.

Eyes glittering, poised to strike like a Cobra, he mesmerised her with fear. His face was twisted with hatred for her. Placing his hand in the pocket of his cassock, he brought forth an ivory handled knife. Leaning close to her he hissed, "see how sharp it is. Feel!" and he ran the blade down the length of her arm, drawing blood, as she screamed in pain and panic. "Tell me what I know or I will carve strips from your body, starting with your arm."

As her body trembled with shock, her eyes rolled up in her head and she fainted once again. "Revive her." He instructed the psychopaths who were eagerly watching with bated breath, eyes glittering with excitement. They were really getting a taste for this now. The Cardinale had brought something exotic into their otherwise mundane world.

One placed a bottle of smelling salts under her nose, which did the trick. Gasping and sobbing, trying to draw breath into her lungs, she struggled to understand what was happening to her.

"Tell me," he demanded.

"I cccccant," she stuttered. "I dddddon't know."

Her scream of pain and terror stabbed the frigid air, which the monster before her appeared to breathe.

Taking the knife, he cut her blouse away from her body, and then he ran the razor-sharp steel from her shoulder blade to the top of her breast. As she fainted again with shock and pain, he cut another line between them at the top and bottom.

"Revive her again," he commanded, wiping the blood from the knife on a small towel.

Again smelling salts were applied and as she jerked awake, she was aware of the searing pain on the left hand side of her chest and the blood streaming from it.

"Tell me," he demanded again.

It was too much for this gentle woman. As he approached her again, she felt as though he had reached out his hand, plunging it into the centre of her chest and pulled out her heart. A tremendous pain suffused her entire being and her heart stopped beating.

"Revive her."

Again they applied the smelling salts, but it was to no avail.

"Revive her, I said."

"Vostra Eminenza, she is not breathing." One of the lackeys placed his hand on the jugular vein in her neck and found no beat. He then placed it under her nose. He felt no breath. "Eminenza, I fear she has died."

The Cardinale flew into a towering rage. His face diffused with fury. Throwing down the knife, he grabbed her by the arms and shook her, as the blood from the wound on her chest sprayed over him.

She had escaped him though. There was no doubt, she had passed away.

As the gathered men crossed themselves, the Cardinale turned on them in a frenzy. "May she burn in Hell." Turning violently, his cassock swirling around with him, he instructed. "Dig a grave and bury her. Get a lead lined casket. Spicciare *(hurry up)*. Throw lime on her body and destroy it, then bury her deeply. I do not want to see or hear of her again."

With this he strode out of the cellar, leaving a dumbstruck group behind him.

Chapter Twenty-six – Back to Arma dei Carabinieri Headquarters Rome

"Capitano, there is a call for you," his secretary popped her head through the door, awe on her face and in her voice. "It is Donato Mariani and he will speak only to you."

"Grazie Rosetta." Waving her out of the room, he lifted the receiver to take the call from one of the well known politicians of the Partito Democratico Italiano.

"Carlino?" a voice he recognised, queried.

"Donato, it is good to hear from you."

"Not so good Roberto. Not so good." With his voice rising in panic, the caller tried to calm himself.

"What is it Donato?"

"Adelina has disappeared."

"What do you mean disappeared?" The carabinieri always identified precisely what people were talking about.

"She has not been seen for two days."

"What happened?" His pulse began to race, hoping against hope, recent history wasn't repeating itself.

"We don't know," her panic stricken husband tried to remain calm, but his nerves were in shreds. "The servants saw her run to her car and drive away."

"Did she say anything to them as she left?"

"No, that is what we cannot understand. It is not like her to behave like that. Normally she tells them where she is going and when she will be back."

"OK stay calm Donato. When was this?"

"Tuesday morning." It was now Wednesday afternoon.

"Has she left home and stayed away without telling anyone before."

"Never," her concerned husband answered emphatically.

"Why haven't you called me before now?"
"I was out of town and the servants thought she would call or return that day. When she didn't they waited until morning. By afternoon when she had not returned, they rang me and I immediately returned home. Since then we have looked everywhere we thought she might be. We've checked with friends, relations."

"Have things been fine between you?"

"Of course, how can you ask that? You know how much I love her."

Yes, indeed he did. It was one of the great love matches in their circles. No dallying on either side, they were devoted to each other.

"What car was she driving?"

"The Audi."

"Give me the details, we will run a search on it."

"You can rely on me. I will find her for you."

"I know, I know." Carlino could imagine his friend being worried out of his mind. Wringing his hands and wracking his brain.

"As soon as we turn up anything, I will call."

"Thank you Carlino, thank you."

The lieutenant immediately dispatched a carabiniere to run a check on any reports of a missing woman, and calling three others into his office, instructed them they were on the case.

"You don't think?" one queried.

"I sincerely hope not," he replied, his brow creased with concern.

But it was. Two days later, the car was found abandoned in the hills of Tivoli, 30 km north east of Rome. Painted over it, were the words that were becoming synonymous with terror and murder. 'Magdalene-Whore'.

And the well connected families huddled together in fear, wondering who the next victim would be.

*

This second abduction really set Rome back on its heels. The reverberations echoed through all levels of society. As politicians went Donato Mariani was considered honest and his wife was popular with the voters.

*

Primo Capitano Fanelli bowed to the inevitable whilst his team sat outside his office looking at the two men, with resentment sketched across their collective faces.

Ispettore Orsini of the Unita di Analisi del Crimine Violento had the good grace to look troubled, as he sat across the desk from Carlino Fanelli. Shrugging his shoulders, he looked around at the assembled carabiniere and said his piece. "Look I know how it feels to have someone come in, trample all over your crime scene and try to take it out of your hands."

Primo Capitano Fanelli knew his division couldn't win this one. Not now the wife of a popular politician, and a close friend of himself and his wife, had disappeared. His heart bled for his friend and even more so for Adelina, whom they now knew, was now in God's hands.

The Unite dei Crimine Violenti had been assigned to the case that was disturbing Rome's equilibrium, as they needed to work up a profile for the killer, before they could even hope to begin to apprehend him. Both teams had been working closely together without any friction. Hell, Carlino Fanelli was only too pleased to have all the help he could get on this perplexing case.

A search had been organised that moved heaven and hell and they believed had left no stone unturned, but it had been fruitless. Political appointees and the nobility of Italy were notorious for their coyness, when it came to opening the doors into their world of privilege. It made the carabinieri's lives a nightmare, when it came to running an investigation involving one of them.

"I can't understand it," Rocco was annoyed and didn't care who knew it. "You would think they would want to cooperate with us, so we could find the kidnappers and murderers, but no they keep holding us at arms length, until the trail goes cold."

Chapter twenty-seven – Get ye behind me Satan

With the threat coming ever closer Edoardos had called in to Lina's, where she had invited him for some antipasto and wine.

"Thanks for coming E. This news is so shocking and I don't believe we can delay any further, if we are to uncover these people."

"You have a good heart Lina," he brushed her cheek with his hand, "but you are also after a Pulitzer Prize."

Lina put her hands up before her. "Truce. I'll make us some food before we start. Soothe the savage beast in both of us."

Walking into the kitchen she busied herself making an antipasta, calling out to the priest, "grab a bottle of wine and pour us a glass each."

"Oh, that reminds me," Edoardos gave himself a smack on the head. "I brought a bottle of Barolo and have left it in the car. I'll run down and fetch it."

"One trek up the stairs is sufficient for one day." Lina reached up and took a bottle of Valpolicella, from the winerack built into the corner, then showed him the label. "It's not as expensive as yours will be, but it is drinkable I promise."

Edoardos walked into the kitchen. "I know you have good taste, but I like to contribute to the feast."

"It's not as though you bludge off me E," Lina grinned at him. "You wine and dine me in the most expensive restaurants. I can afford to provide both food and wine sometimes."

"I know that but" he protested walking to the front door, "I feel I should contribute."

Lina put out her arm to stop him, blocking his passage. "Sit down. You can bring wine another day."

Still he protested. "It will spoil in the heat of the day. I'll be back in two minutes."

Sighing Lina relinquished her post and returned to her preparation of food as Edoardos commenced running down the stairs. "Hmmm. Bet the pace is slower on the return journey."

"Remind me never to do that twice in one day."

Turning from the bench, Lina saw Edoardos, standing in the doorway looking less than pristine and relaxed, his breathing rather ragged. Laughing at him, she couldn't help a dig. "You live an indolent life in the Big V."

Putting the wine down on the bench, he rebutted her statement. "Oh yeah. What about the hours in the gym and running every morning? Do you think I could keep the pace up without being fit?"

Knowing he put in the time every day to ensure he was at peak fitness, Lina couldn't resist a final dig at him. "What pace? Bench pressing your backside on those lovely padded velvet chairs?" Moving out of reach towards the fridge, she gathered up some zucchini and red and yellow peppers from a large bowl on the island in the middle of the room.

Opening the fridge, she grabbed some proscuitto and mozzarella cheese, closed the door with her elbow and returned to the bench. Taking down a wooden board and reaching out to the knife block to grab the appropriate knife, she began slicing and arranging the food on a large platter.

"Madam. You mistake me for one of the stately Cardinales." Edoardos was regaining his breath and jumped back into the fray. "They must affect a dignified walk, as befits their station, when they stroll from office to office." He was not averse to poking fun at the stuffy bureaucracy within the Curia office. "It is the underlings that carried out their bidding who are the speedy messengers."

Lina chuckled at the thought of a mass of priests in their black cassocks scooting around the Vatican halls. "With the miles of passageways in that place they should provide you with roller skates." The platter of food was ready, so she placed some basil leaves on the plate and chopping up the flat leafed Italian parsley, sprinkled this over the vegetables.

"Oh wonderfully dignified," Edoardos' eyes sparkled, as he thought of some of his colleagues at full pace throughout the endless corridors of the Vatican.

"If it was good enough for Princess Diana in Buckingham Palace, it should be good enough for the Vatican." Picking up the platter she handed it to him. "Take this out onto the terrace for me please E, I'll bring forks and plates." Reaching up into the cupboards she retrieved what she needed.

"Your every wish is my command," He teased her, as he took the platter from her hands and walked outside to set it on the wrought iron table. Returning he reached into a drawer, took out the implement required and expertly removed the cork from the bottle.

Sighing inwardly, thinking of things that might have been had he not been a priest, he watched Lina reach up and hand him two wine glasses.

"I'll let it breathe for a minute or two," he protested holding up his hand to stay her. "It should have been opened an hour ago."

"Oh well," Lina irreverently responded. "Let it have a quick gasp, it'll match your breathing." Dancing out of his reach, Lina ran into the living area, with Edoardos hot in pursuit.

"I can still catch you." With that, he reached out and grabbed her around the waist from behind.

Laughing, she turned her head and looked back at him, laughingly. "Only because I'm impeded with plates and implements."

"Right." Walking her towards the terrace, he retained his hold on her as she set them down on the table, suddenly reluctant to let go.

Lina felt the tension and leaned back into him, then gasped, "Are you just pleased to see me?" as she felt him hardening against her butt.

The priest let go as though he had been scalded, blushing furiously. "God, I'm sorry Lina. I don't know what happened." Dismay shot through him like a molten stream of lava, as she turned to face him.

Reaching up her hand, she softly touched his face. "E, you're only human." Softly she sought to reassure him.

"I'm not allowed that luxury." Dropping his head to look at his feet, he tried to hide his embarrassment and shame.

"E, It's okay." Lina reached out and raised his chin, looking directly into his eyes. "You're not superhuman. Celibacy is such a crock of shit. Don't feel bad."

Reluctantly he met her gaze. "But I took an oath, made a promise. I don't want to be a hyprocrite like so many others."

Tears welled up in Lina's eyes. "Oh E, man is not meant to be celibate, or the human race would die out. They're testosterone driven, it's natural."

"Not for me." Stepping back, he shook himself. "Let's have a drink."

Lina watched him walk back inside and felt for him, knowing he was shocked to his core at what had just happened. Slowly she walked back into the kitchen to collect napkins and cutlery.

Their gazes met. "It's OK with me E." Determined to reassure him, she didn't realise she was pushing buttons he would rather remained in the off position.

"I never want you to feel sorry for me," he said vehemently. "I couldn't stand that. We've been friends for so long and this has never come between us before. I don't want anything to happen now."

"Nothing has happened. Your body simply reacted normally." Trying to lighten the mood, she reached out to touch him on the arm and gasped, as he moved out of reach and walked away from her. Realizing he needed time to compose himself, she took down a tray and set it up with condiments before returning to the terrace. Placing it on the table, she walked over to where he was standing at the parapet gazing at St Peter's dome.

"Let's eat."

Turning towards her bemusedly, he was sure his feelings were written all over his face. How could he explain to her after all these years of platonic friendship, that he felt an overwhelming desire to take her in his arms and ravage her body.

Sensing the tension remaining between them, Lina walked back to the table, sat down on one of the chairs and patted the other. "Come on E, forget it and let's relax."

"I'll fetch the wine." With that, he walked past her into the kitchen, picked up the bottle and glasses, then returned to set them up on the table. Carefully he poured the beautiful red liquid into the glasses, handed one to Lina, holding his own up the light. Bringing it to his nose, he breathed in the bouquet deeply, in an endeavour to steady himself and feelings, then raising his glass to her, he sipped his wine.

Lina raised her own glass to her mouth and looked at him cautiously over the rim of her glass, giving him time to compose himself.

Offering a tentative smile, he seated himself. "I'm OK."

"I know you are."

Both fell silent, lost in their own thoughts until a cheeky sparrow landed on the table, an uninvited guest to the banquet. Before he could reach the food on the platter, Lina reached out and tore a piece off the Ciabatta in a basket she had brought out. Breaking it into small pieces, she tossed them on the terrace and both of them watched as Mr Sparrow's friends joined him, believing this to be an open invitation.

"That was a mistake," Edoardos laughed at the invasion of their quiet lunch.

"Wave them off if they try to get at the food." Lina hopped up and went inside, bringing back a supper cloth, which she proceeded to place over the platter.

Laughing together at the birds' antics, the tension disappeared and they relaxed together again.

Two hours and a bottle of wine later, their appetite for food sated, they stirred, knowing there an undercurrent remained between them, that spoke of other appetites for forbidden fruit.

To distract them, Lina once again raised the subject of the abductions. "E, please help me out here. The police are getting nowhere in uncovering the reason for these two atrocities. I just can't let this go. We have to work out whether this is a sadistic serial killer with female issues, or a nutjob. Or perhaps something deeper. I want to meet the family of Adelina Mariani, who has also been murdered."

"Lina, there's no way you will get near them. Let it go," Edoardos warned her.

Lina pleaded with him one more time. "E, I have to do something. I can't let this go. There could be other victims."

"I must get back to the office." He rose, avoiding the conversation. "Let me help you out to the kitchen with this."

Together they gathered up the debris and brought it back inside.

Lina tried one more time. "Please E."

"Lina, you have a good heart, but you also want a Pulitzer Prize. Ciao, cara mia. I'll call soon."

With that he raised his hand in farewell, took his leave and walked down the stairs to the street below, leaving Lina deep in thought behind him.

"I have to find a way to make him help me." Suddenly the phone pealed and she ran into the living room to answer.

"Lina. I'm sorry," Edoardos was on his mobile phone. "I don't mean to rebuff you, but this is starting to get us all down."

"E, I know it is and that makes it even more important for me to find the answers. I'm going to find out who the friends of these two women are and speak with them."

"I want to know they are all safe. I'll help you."

Her heart leapt in her chest and she caught her breath in her throat. "Oh E." She breathed a sigh of relief.

"I'll call you tomorrow and we"ll get together and work out a plan. Ciao." Putting down his cellphone he felt better knowing he did not have to avoid Lina and his unexpected sexual feelings for her that he did not want to get in the way of their friendship. Working with her on trying to resolve these murders, would put up a natural barrier between them in intimate situations.

Chapter Twenty-eight – Edoardos and Adelais

Another pleasant Sunday luncheon had been enjoyed by the Guilianini family, with the children in attendance, running around and enjoying themselves, while the adults benignly watched.

To find a little peace and quiet, Edoardos had invited his sister-in-law to take a stroll in the garden with him. Happy to spend a little time with him, she quickly accepted.

"We do not see enough of you Edoardos," Adelais remarked, as they enjoyed the afternoon sun beating down on their heads. "You must come to dinner soon."

"I would love that Adelais." E was genuinely fond of his brother's wife. He found her a strong, intelligent and interesting woman, with a deep insight into the nature of her fellow human beings.

"Tonio is seldom home in the summer months, following the yachts around the Mediterranean," she sighed. "It makes it difficult to host dinner parties."

"Then let's just have an intimate family dinner, I would prefer that," her brother-in-law assured her.

"I suppose you are extremely busy as usual." Adelais was always interested in his career at the Big V. Like Lina, she thought it was a dreadful waste of good husband material, but kept her views to herself, in the interest of family tranquility.

They enjoyed an easy camaraderie in each other's company and walked for a few minutes, without any discourse.

"Let's sit for a moment Adelais," Edoardos suggested, as they came up to a stone bench sheltered by overhanging wisteria.

When they had seated themselves, he broached a subject he did not want to. "Cardinale Contardella does not like it, that you do not attend mass with the rest of the family Adelais."

His sister-in-law looked at him calmly, "That is the Cardinale's problem Edoardos."

"The problem affects our entire family," he insisted, spreading his hands in appeal. "Alegra's marriage will unite ours with theirs, and as he holds a very senior position in the Vatican, he feels this besmirches him."

"Am I so important in the scheme of things, that the hierarchy of the Roman Catholic Church is concerned, if I absent myself from their services?" Adelais said doubtfully. "I am but an insignificant woman," she derided herself.

Edoardos smiled at the thought of this woman he admired, being insignificant in any way. "You are anything but Adelais, and you know it."

"Am I such an abomination in his eyes?" Her smile belied the concern she felt stirring at this discussion.

"I would not say that Adelais." He reached and out took her hands in his. "His status and dignity within the rarefied air of the Vatican, is paramount to him."

"And would he go to great lengths to preserve that?"

"As a Cardinale of the church, he has it in his power to make things a little uncomfortable between the two families, but I am not sure he would stoop to underhand practices."

Adelais was a shrewd woman and doubted the Cardinale would stop at anything, which did not serve his purpose in this world. "Could he make life difficult for you at the Vatican my dear?"

Edoardos shrugged. "Possibly, but don't worry about me, I can take care of myself."

"Goodness Edoardos, do you think he would have me burned the stake if he could?" she queried archly. "I can smell the fire and smoke already."

Beneath her flippancy she held a very real concern. It was quite impossible to put aside, after the crucifixion of her fellow devotee of Le Donne in Azzuro and the murder of such a prominent woman, her dear friend Adelina.

Reaching out she took his hand in hers and patted it fondly. "Edoardos, I love you and your family dearly, but they knew when Tonio married me, that I bend the knee to no-one."

"My God, they nearly died when my brother brought a heretic into the family," He shook his head at the memory. How he had admired his brother, for his courage and stand against his staunchly catholic family, particularly one hopelessly mired in the formal dance of aristocratic Italy. "I though they would have apoplexy."

"But Tonio stood by me at all times, until they understood I am my own woman, with my own beliefs and we would be together no matter what barriers were put in our way." Adelais loved her husband deeply, even more so for charting them both through these treacherous waters, until they had found safe harbour together.

"I know." He put his arm around the shoulder of this woman he was so fond of. Personally, he believed she was a breath of fresh air in the turgid pool of their family genes.

"Edoardos, I married Antonio, not his family, and certainly not the Roman Catholic Church." Adelais turned to face him and took his hands in hers. "You are all aware my family is descended from the Trencavels of the Languedoc, who are widely accepted as being part of Mary Magdalene's lineage. The Pope sent the crusaders against my ancestors in the 12th century and we were lucky a few survived with their lives, while the Pope stood back and let the French King take our wealth and lands which he had long coveted. We never bent the knee to King nor Pope, and I am not going to do so for a mere Cardinale."

Edoardos grinned at the thought of Cardinale Contardella overhearing this remark. A mere Cardinale indeed! Removing his hands from hers, he held them up before him in acquiescence. "I'm sorry Adelais. I know you are quite right. My career and my sister's marriage, are our own responsibility. I love you dearly, as you know and this is not meant to offend you. I wanted you to know what he is saying, as I do not want his enmity turning on you."

"Dear Edoardos." Adelais again took his hands in hers and standing pulled him up. "Let's walk." Tucking her hand under his arm, she turned her face to the sun, and moved closer to him. Passing under an arbor where lilacs tumbled in profusion, leaving their delicate perfume titillating their senses, she reassured him.

"Of course I am not offended. Our ancestors could hardly continue to be Roman Catholics after what they experienced and with their belief in Mary Magdalene. I want Alegra to be happy in her marriage. As happy as I am with Tonio." Her face creased with concern. "The Prince and Principessa are so rigid and dogmatic."

"Like the Prince's brother, our Cardinale," he agreed in all seriousness, although his eyes twinkled.

Adelais shivered, as though a cool breeze had arisen and brushed them with its hints of autumn. "I am very much my own person as you know Edoardos, and my own faith sustains me, but there is something about the Cardinale that disturbs me. I cannot put my finger on it though." She puzzled over her feelings. "I am not comfortable around him."

"He's very judgmental where his faith is concerned," he admitted, "and he is very ambitious." Ruminating on the Cardinale and his ambitions, he felt a tremor of fear which he dismissed. "He would dearly love the top job in the Vatican."

Adelais pursed her lips and her brows knitted. "I wonder what lengths he would go to for the opportunity."

"He could be quite ruthless I think Adelais. Be careful of him. Do not show him any disdain."

"I won't," Adelais reassured him. "He would be a tradition bound Il Papa like John Paul II." She sighed heavily. "Will we ever be free of these chauvinistic

Papa's? They enforce birth control on their women followers. It is so wrong to have these poor catholic families producing yet more children, who grow up in abject poverty, or starve to death, because of this outlandish dictate."

The priest kept silent, although in his heart of hearts, he agreed with her.

"How do Il Papas live with themselves, when they see the effects of their heartless dictates? It is as though the poor and weak are nothing in their eyes, or simply do not exist." Tears glistened in her eyes.

Her brother-in-law placed his arm around her shoulders and held her close to his side. "Adelais," he comforted her. "You cannot hope to understand, as they follow the teachings that have been set down for 2000 years."

"But they are not Christ's words Edoardos," she cried, pulling away from him. "He would never have inflicted such suffering upon poor people. He always strove to make their lot better."

"Adelais, my dear, you must be very careful at this moment. The connection between le Donne in Azzuro and the deaths of your friends is more than a coincidence."

She looked at him calmly. "I know but we are prepared."

"Prepared for what Adelais? What are you up to? For goodness sake, you must not invite trouble to come to your door"

"I am not a coward Edoardos." As Adelais turned to face him, he saw the fire in her eyes, the determination in the set of her mouth and was disquieted. What was afoot?

"I know you are not Adelais, and that is what worries me. Please do not try and take things into your own hands. Work with the Carabinieri and let the family protect you."

"Miryai, who you know as Mary Magdalene, will protect me Edoardos. She will protect us all."

He looked at her shining eyes and face, knowing he was seeing a faith far deeper than his own. "Your trust in her is to be commended, but please keep your feet on the ground. There is danger out there."

"We differ in our interpretation of Yeshua's immortality, his words and his meanings." Gently taking his face in her hands, she looked deeply into his eyes. "His wife was as powerful as he and I have full trust in her. I respect your opinions and love you very much, but I can look after myself."

Edoardos was still worried about her. "Adelais, if anything happened to you, Tonio would be so devastated he would never be himself ever again. Do not put yourself at risk."

"I won't do that dear Edoardos, but please remember I am my own woman."

"You're too much your own woman for any one to intimidate, but that courage could be your downfall." Reaching up he took her hands down from his face and put them to his lips and kissed them. "None of us could bear anything happening to you."

Adelais looked into his eyes, affection for him shining out. "You're a good man Edoardos. It's such a pity you're the family's sacrifice to the Vatican. You would have made a lovely husband for some lucky lady," she smiled cheekily at him.

He smiled back. "I'm content with my lot." His thoughts drifted, however, to a woman in an apartment in Via del Popolo area.

Chapter Twenty-nine – A brief respite

Lina was taking some precious time out, before she returned to the apartment to meet up with Edoardos.

Wandering the streets between the Piazza Navone and the Piazza dei Spagna (*The Spanish steps)*, she lingered in a doorway, idly gazing at the shoes in the window. The owner or salesmen, stood inside watching her. A limousine drew up to the kerb. The doors opened and an exquisitely clad family climbed out. Padre ushered in madre and figlia *(daughter)*, to be greeting profusely by the owner/salesman.

"Buon Giorno, Signore, Signora." Despite striving to hear their surname, she was unable to pick it up.

"Stupido," she rebuked herself, realising she had wandered into Edoardos' world of privilege. "The shoes in this store are handmade to order. Not on my earnings."

Looking down at her sneakers and well worn jeans she giggled, shrugged and sauntered out of the doorway, aware she was of no more importance to the owner/salesman than a gnat on his clean window. In fact, she realized, the gnat would hold more interest for him.

Despite herself her mind turned to the murder on the Aventine Hill. "While I'm here, I'm going to go past the headquarters of the Knights of Malta," she decided. Turning down the Via dei Condotti, she stopped before number sixty-eight and looked at the grey building. "What secret do I need to dig out from behind your façade? How can I get inside and find out what secrets you hide?"

"Not without great difficulty," she reasoned correctly. "Well, I'll just have to concentrate on the Priory, which should make the task easier."

As passersby were beginning to look at her oddly, she decided to move on.

Having arranged to meet Edoardos in the Piazza Navone, she took one last look at the renaissance palazzo and walked away, her mind deep in thought as to how she could penetrate the Priory on the Aventine Hill.

That reminded her she had not had lunch.

It was time for a pause and to take stock of what they had discovered and Edoardos had arrived around two pm.

"I'm ashamed to say I'm famished. The Vatican is in an uproar with the death of Adelina Mariani." He threw himself into a deep armchair and let it wrap itself comfortably around him, as he thankfully sank into its embrace. "My family is disturbed as well, she was Adelais' close friend. Needless to say she is deeply upset."

"I picked up antipasti on the way," Lina assured him. "Let me just put it together and we"ll talk."

"That would be most appreciated." Edoardos smiled at her fondly as she sauntered into the kitchen and returned with a tray of tempting cold cuts.

Edoardos walked to the edge of the terrace and stood looking at the Vatican, his face creasing in a frown.

"Sit down," Lina gestured towards the table and chairs. "I'll bring you a glass of wine."

"I'll fetch it," He followed her back into the kitchen. "What would you like?"

"There's a nice Pinot Grigio from Liguria, I put in the fridge about an hour and a half ago. It should be perfect by now." Lina tested the machine to see if it was hot enough to grill the bread, drawing her finger back quickly as she felt the heat. Popping the Italian sandwiches into the machine, she reached into the pantry and opening a jar of olives, placed them into a bowl, grabbing an olive spoon from the drawer in front of her.

"I'll take those out." He picked them up the bottle of wine and two glasses from the shelf and pulled the cork as Lina suggested. "Let's eat."

Edoardos could smell the aroma of the fresh perfume she was wearing and drank it in whilst thanking her, trying to resurrect a barrier against the emotions he was feeling, as he watched her move to her place opposite him and sit down.

Picking up the glasses, they toasted the food with a 'buon appetito' and appreciatively sipped the wine Edoardos had previously poured.

"Grazie, this is really good," he picked up a piece of the sandwich began to devour it. "Scusi Lina," he apologised, "I'm famished."

"Be my guest."

As Lina picked up a bread stick her eyes met his and one of their occassional electric moments hung between them. Knowing the friendship would never develop into more, she pulled herself together and cut through the atmosphere. "Who do you think this monster is?"

He looked at her gratefully as his thoughts were taking him to a forbidden place "God knows. There's no doubt he's a serial killer, but what motivates him?"

"We need to understand why he is killing them and the carabinieri don't have a clue." Lina picked up the linen napkin and dabbed at some oil that remained on her lips.

"They're under enormous pressure to find answers," he responded. "The families are closing ranks. No-one is more privacy crazy, than ancient Roman families."

"Don't they want the murders solved?" Puzzling over their reaction, Lina wondered what drove these people.

"Of course they do," he reassured her, "But it is not in their nature to allow commoners to trample through their lives."

"That's crazy," she said.

"Crazy to outsiders. Not to them," As Edoardos endeavoured to impress on Lina, the mores of his world, he said. "They all have secrets and don't want their lives turned inside out."

"Then where does anyone investigating this mess start?" Lina simply couldn't understand why the families were so reluctant to cooperate. Christ in pajamas, it was like throwing the Christians to the lions. Except these victims belonged to their friends' families. Still it wouldn't do to upset the man by voicing these sentiments.

"But everyone knows it is the plodder on the ground who will solve this in the end, not some highly placed bureaucrat sitting on his arse in his grand office." Lina was becoming angry, as she couldn't believe the families could stand by and watch their women be picked off.

"It's just the way it is." Edoardos turned to look out into the distance. "I've turned this over and over in my mind and whilst I cannot be seen to be interfering in the secular affairs of the State or the judicial system, I can't just sit by idly. This is too close to home." His voice dropped a register, as he uttered the last statement.

"What do you mean E? Close to home."

He expelled a deep sighing breath. "As a journalist, they expect you to stick your nose in where it isn't wanted and you will harangue people until you get answers. I can't behave like that."

"Oh E, please come on board with me." Lina knew it was important to remain professional and cool under the circumstances recognising that he had packed away those renegade feelings of impropriety and buttoned them down tightly. Jumping up and hugging him, would probably result in the horse crashing through the stable door and running through the Seven Hills of Rome, until he reached the cloistured atmosphere of the Vatican, where he felt untouchable.

"I walked past the headquarters of the Knights of Malta in the Via Condotti today," Lina tossed at him casually.

"Oh Lina, you're being ridiculous. Clutching at straws."

Lina's scowled at him. "You may see it that way E, but I just have such a strong gut feeling. I'll get the coffee."

Giving them both a chance to think about the situation, she walked back to the kitchen and made espressos. Grabbing whipped cream from the refrigerator she carried it out with the coffees.

"Cream?" she queried.

Edoardos shook his head and watched bemused, as she added cream to her own brew.

"My God. I don't know how you do it. All the sweets and cream you eat and you don't put on an ounce of fat."

"I burn it off," she shrugged nonchalantly. "It's in my genes."

Walking back into the kitchen she picked up a plate of Dolci Pesche (Italian Peach Cookies) from the counter and took it outside. "Would you like one of these Your Lordship?"

Despite himself, Edoardos grinned at her affectionately. "You know the way to a man's heart."

"With some Crema Pasticcera?"

"Of course." Grinning slyly at her, he winked.

Placing one of the beautifully formed Italian cookies in the shape of a peach, with the blush on it, she spooned a generous serving of the rich cream to which she had added a dash of Marsala wine and carried it over to him. Placing it down, she also set a napkin and cake fork in front of him.

"Grazie," he said, meaning every word as his eyes devoured the delectable morsel and he patted the seat next to his own, bidding her to sit down.

Reaching out, she placed another on a plate and gave herself a generous dollop of the cream.

"Yum," she exclaimed, as she took a bite.

His eyes twinkled as he watched her drink the concoction and tried to distance himself from wanting to reach over and hold her. Having promised her he would work towards a resolution of the mysteries, he knew he would have to remove himself from her life, if he couldn't control these urges that were coming between them.

"You know you only need one celibate religious nutcase to go over the edge."

"I know," Edoardos sighed and ran his hand through his hair in frustration. "The church needs this like a hole in the head."

"So the big question is. Why are they targeting wealthy, well connected women?" Lina arose, placed her feet apart and hands on hips and challenged him.

He leapt off his chair, strode around the terrace like a caged tiger, as he refuted her claims, his golden/yellow tiger eyes scattering lightning before him. "Well it's certainly drawn attention to their cause."

"And they'll be hunted down to the ends of the earth. Why take such a huge risk."

"No accounting for a homicidal mind." At this point, Edoardos knew it was time to employ the degree in psychology which he had studied together with Theology. If he was to help Lina resolve this conspiracy, he would have to analyse the situation and the motive behind it, then try and work out who was behind it. After all, he used his training, as he manoeuvred his way around Vatican politics.

"So what's Mary Magdalene got to do with all of this?"

"I wish I knew." Edoardos bit his lip as a thought struck him, but he had a hard time attaching any credence to it.

Lina suspected he was holding back on her now. "What?"

"Nothing," Edoardos dismissed her question with a half turn of his head, as he sat down again.

"No there is something. What is it?" Lina sensed a weakness in him, and pounced.

"It's my sister-in-law, Adelais." Hesitating for a moment he looked at the floor, deep in thought.

"What about her?"

"She is a descendant of the Trencavel family of the Languedoc."

"Soooooo?" Lina wasn't sure where he was going with this comment.

"She belongs to a group of women who call themselves le Donne in Azzuro."

Lina looked puzzled, as she exclaimed, "The Women in Blue?"

"Yes, it has something to do with Mary Magdalene."

"What sort of something?"

"I don't know," he admitted shamefaced. "We've never been interested enough to find out. We just considered it something harmless for a group of wealthy women to amuse themselves with."

"What the hell is this?" Lina was astounded as he had never told her about this before. Reaching up she turned his face towards hers. "E, look at me," she demanded.

He was unable to meet her eyes as she relentlessly pursued the elephant in the room that was casting its shadow over their relationship. "Did Adelais know this woman? Was she one of them?"

"Yes."

"So there is a connection here. Then why haven't you told the police?"

"It's being discussed."

"What with the police?" she demanded.

"Yes, her husband is too high profile for this to be swept under the rug." Edoardos felt extremely sorry for the man, one of the few honest politicians.

"Do they know about le Donne in Azzuro?"

"That's between her husband and the police."

"Well what about Adelais' involvement with them?"

"It has no bearing on the case."

"Of course it does," she exploded. "Don't tell me your family are hiding this from the police."

"Lina, this is my family's business. Not yours. Leave it alone. We'll work it out in our own way. We have done so for centuries."

"It may be the key to everything E. I need to talk to Adelais."

"Not a chance in hell Lina," Edoardos knew how the family would band together to protect his sister-in-law from the investigation into Adelina's death, and a nosy journalist with wild theories of her own would not be allowed within a mile of the Palazzo.

Arching one eyebrow, she looked at him disdainfully. "Is your family more concerned with their own privacy than solving these killings of women your sister-in-law knew?"

"Lina, back off," Edoardos warned her. "My family is very powerful. They are off limits to you."

"I have to speak with her. I can follow the trail if I speak with her."

"You do not have a chance Lina. My family will not tolerate the press looking into their life."

"God, what is the matter with these people?"

"Lina they have closed ranks around her and will be very selective as to whom they let near her."

"What about the Caribinieri?"

"We know Carlino Fanelli, the squad commander. He, and only he, will be allowed to question her about her friend Adelina, and their common interest in le Donne in Azzuro."

This was a defining moment in their friendship. The fragility hung tremulously between them, like the note from one of the temple bells in Nepal that sounded like crystal ready to shatter in the suddenly frigid atmosphere.

"Lina," he warned. "Do not cross my family. They are very powerful."

"I don't care," she cried and stamped her foot. "This is outrageous, protecting your family's honour, when lives are at stake. I will speak to them myself."

"You are no-one. The carabinieri will ignore you."

"Then I'm going to do everything I can to prove a connection."

"Doors will not open to you Lina."

"It won't stop me trying."

"Maybe so, but you will be stopped at every turn."

"What is your family so afraid of?"

Edoardos didn't answer. How could he admit he had his own suspicions that someone in the Church hierarchy could actually be behind these tragedies.

"Who are you protecting here E?" Searching his face for answers she knew he would not give her, she carried on recklessly. "Something else to be swept under the holy rugs of the Vatican?"

Edoardos stopped his bitter response and ran his fingers through his hair. He looked at her, then dropping into a chair, he put both hands to his head and cradled it. Lina had never seen him lose his composure before. "I don't know Lina," he whispered. "Don't make me question everything I've grown up with?"

"What and rock your boat E?" Lina was furious and not about to be swayed by sympathy.

Rising from the chair, he reached out and touched her hair, which was the closest personal gesture he would allow himself. "I have to go."

"E, don't run off," she begged him. "What are you going to do to help me?"

"I'm going to look for anything in the Archives that might point a finger to who is carrying out these atrocities. That is enough for now."

"But you have a direct link now."

"Lina that is what you asked me to do and that is all I am prepared to do for the moment." Picking up his car keys, he walked towards the door promising, "I will speak with Adelais myself again. Trust me."

Walking out the door, he turned and waved, before running down the steps to where his car was parked.

"Oh that man drives me insane, but I can't afford to alienate him now he has finally come around." Lina's thoughts were in turmoil and she felt her frustration and anger boiling over. "Damn him. Damn him," she cried aloud.

Running up to the loft bedroom, she pulled on a pair of running shorts, a tee shirt, socks and running shoes. Looking in the mirror, she pulled her dark, shoulder length hair back from her face and used a scrunchy to hold it in place. Turning on her heel, she walked down the stairs and out the door, pulling it to behind her until she heard the lock click into place.

Taking five minutes to warm up with stretching exercise, she jogged down the sixty-nine steps, until she came to the street. Stretching out she broke into a run as she turned towards the Borghese Park, "I'll have to run this off."

Settling into her pace, she strode out, feeling the lassitude that came over her as the adrenalin kicked in and the endorphins took her to that place that runners experience, between heaven and hell. Pushing hard, she blocked out reality, focusing only on the path ahead her.

All tension melting away, away, away, to some distant secret place that only she knew about, leaving her with a sense of peace.

Just like a little bird nesting safe and secure in its shelter from the coming storm.

*

Edoardos was having sleepless nights and it was not altogether due to his conscience over the murdered women. During the daytime it was easy to salve his conscience, by going about his business at the Big V. Nightime brought with it, a sense of guilt he could not throw off.

His first duty was to his family, his second to the Church. It had always been so and he had expected it would always remain that way.

Now he was in turmoil. Women his family knew, were being murdered. The insanity that lurked behind these murders was terrible to behold. He could not deny his admiration for Lina's persistence, and it bothered him he was unwilling to involve himself.

Then there was Lina. Finally admitting to himself that he was physically attracted to her, put their friendship in quite a different light. Did this mean he would have to stop seeing her? She was so much a part of his life, he didn't know if he could do that.

What could he do about it? The friendship had taken a turn to somewhere he began to suspect he had no control over. If he could not do so, he would have to cut her out of his life.

Making his way to a small chapel in the Basilica, he dropped to his knees and prayed to a higher being, that he had previously worshipped within the formality of the ritual of the Vatican. It had not touched him deeply in his soul until now.

"Forgive me Lord. My devotion to you has been clouded by my ambition. Help me to find a way through this mire. Guide me. Tell me what you would have me do. I am part of your church. How can I betray it by investigating your servants?"

His soul felt heavy, his heart burdened, as he knelt before the altar waiting for God to reply.

"I am tempted Lord. Please help me to resist temptation," he begged. "I do not want to lose my friendship with Lina, but help me resist the feelings I have for her. Why has this been put into my path now?" he beseeched his Lord.

"My family could be in danger. Please help me to protect them. Do not make me choose between my family and your Church, Lord."

Praying that he would be shown the way he remained on his knees, seeking an answer from his God.

"My son," a light touch on his shoulder made him flinch instantly on guard, "what is troubling you?"

Looking up, he saw Cardinale Vendetto before him. "There is nothing Vostra Eminenza."

"Come now Edoardos," the Cardinale remonstrated with him. "Your mien belies your answer. Have I not walked this path beside you, since you were a novice in the ways of the Holy See?" The Cardinale was well versed in troubled souls, which had been his stock in trade for many years than he chose to remember.

"Really Vostra Eminenza, I am fine," Edoardos assured the head of his department and was shocked at his reaction. He felt himself emotionally drawing away from the Cardinale, wondering whether the man before him could have anything to do with these horrific crimes.

"My son, something is weighing heavily on your heart and shoulders." Cardinale Vendetto sought to relieve the burden that was troubling the young man he had mentored for so long. "This is something that troubles your soul. Would you like me to hear your confession?"

Again Edoardos had to face his suspicion and realised he could not bear his soul to anyone who wore a cassock right now. Not about what was troubling him.

Feeling he was betraying the man who had mentored him in the ways of the Vatican, he shook his head, reassuring the Cardinale once again.

Rising from his knees, he genuflected before the altar and eyes downcast stood beside the priest in his red biretta and sash, not knowing what else to say.

"Edoardos, I know you well." The hand rested lightly on his shoulder once again. "Listen to your conscience. Let it be your guide."

Thanking the concerned man, who was watching him closely, Edoardos slowly made his way back to the office and immersed himself in his work, but his thoughts were with Sant Pietro, who had denied His Lord thrice.

"Am I no better than he was?" he asked himself, not wanting to listen to the answer that rung around the Citadel of St Peter's Basilica.

Chapter Thirty– The Escape from Judaea

The knowledge that the baby was Yeshua's drove Kepha to the brink of insanity. He had lost the man he had loved with all his heart, and believed he would have followed into the fires of hell, but when it counted had denied him. His guilt racked his empty soul. He had nothing, but Miryai had Yeshua's child.

He went to the Pharisees to tell them the truth. The Royal House of David lived on through Yeshua's child. The gall nearly choked him, as he admitted it.

The Pharisees conferred and beat the truth out of him, as he had been claiming the child was not Yeshua's, so how was this suddenly so? He admitted he had lied and the Pharisees knew that if the truth was known and this child grew into its heritage, it too would have its own followers in the future, and they would be challenged once more.

What to do? Deal with it themselves, or take it to Herod? Involve the division of soldiers from Rome whom Herod commanded? Herod believed Yeshua dead and the growing unrest and gentle revolution Yeshua had led, had been quashed. His anger would be great. It would be best if they hunted Yeshua down, then took his body to Herod, to show him the threat was over and he would reward them.

Miryai had given birth to a girl-child, which Herod would not fear as much, but she in turn could give birth to a male child, who would become a threat to his own line of Kings. It would be best for them to deal with it themselves. It would not be the first time they had blood on their hands.

"They must go tonight." Mark ran to Lazarus. "The Pharisees and Priests have paid assassins to kill them.

"Bring Miryai and the child here immediately," Iosef of Arimathea ordered and turned to Yeshua, who made to run to his wife and child. "You must not be seen, you must remain here."

"I must go to Miryai."

"No," Iosef told him, "you will only impede them and put them into greater danger."

"We must flee tonight then." Yeshua weakly moved across the room.

"You are lucky to be alive Yeshua, so you are still not strong enough to stand the rigours of a difficult journey. You need another three months."

"But they will kill my family," he cried.

"No, we will hide you all in the tomb," Iosef told him, "and let Kepha and the priests think your family has fled. When all is quiet again, we will pass you through the escape route we planned."

*

Miryai sat by the embers of a fire nursing her child, when Yeshua's Ammi El-Lih – *father's brother* Iosef of Arimathea arrived at the house. His heart went out to her, as she looked so wan and pale. He had watched her grow from a young child, into the beautiful, strong and confident young woman who had married his nephew. The crucifixion had damaged her as much as Yeshua.

"You must gather up a few belongings and come with me," he told her, "and swiftly."

"What is wrong Ammi El-Lih?" Seeing the concern in his eyes, she rose at once.

"The Sanhedrin is sending soldiers to arrest you and Tamar." Iosef was one of the most important members of the Council and was privy to the most confidential information.

"Why would they do that?" Distraught she looked at Yeshua's uncle, despairingly.

"Because they are afraid that the followers of Yeshua, will turn to you both as descendants of the House of David and the child will foment rebellion when she is older," he told her.

"That is ridiculous," her spirit returned, as she was became angry, "a female child is no threat to them." Turning from him she comforted her child who, sensing the fraught mood in the room was beginning to whimper.

"How can they do this?" Mariam cried as she turned to Iosef. "Is it not enough that they have destroyed my son? Must they persecute his wife and child now?"

"They still fear your son and his mission, so hurry, hurry," the concerned man pressed them. "They will be rounding up the soldiers and Kepha will lead them here."

"Kepha," Miryai spat out. "I should have known he was at the back of this." Despairingly she looked at the child, "Is his hatred of me so great because Yeshua's love for me was so deep, that he would kill an innocent child, one of royal blood?"

"I am afraid so, my dear. Yeshua challenged the Sanhedrin's power and many of the people followed him. It is in their interest to destroy him. We must hurry."

"But where will we go?" Perplexed at the turn of events, she looked beseechingly at Mariam, Yeshua's mother, in whose house they were living, as was wont in this era. "How do you know this is so?" Turning back to Iosef, she was becoming dazed.

"I was at the Council when the vote was taken and mine alone was not enough to stay the decision. Come Miryai, Yeshua's daughter must survive and so must Yeshua. He is King David's heir."

Mariam's concern for her daughter-in-law, whom she loved deeply, overcame her. "Iosef, he must not be discovered and die now, not when he is getting stronger." Hurrying around she threw a few clothes into a bundle and urged Miryai to leave.

At this moment Joses, Yeshua's 0x0d (*brother*) ran into the house.

"Kepha is beside himself with jealousy of you and grief, from what he believes is Yeshua's death. He is leading the soldiers here to capture you and the child." Joses was distraught. "We must leave here now."

Miryai finally rose, then taking Joses" face in her hands, she kissed him on both cheeks. "We know. Iosef came from the council to warn us. You are a wonderful 0x0d and friend," she told the older 0x0d. "Let us depart."

Turning, she stooped and picked up her child, wrapping her in a shawl, then slipped on her sandals, picked up her robe and drew it over her head, to follow Iosef and Joses out into the cool night air, as they urged her to hurry.

Miryai looked back sadly at the home she had known all her married life.

Slipping away from the house, they swiftly and silently they made their way to Iosef's home. "This is the first place he will lead them when he finds you are missing." This senator and member of the Sanhedrin was an intelligent man and had planned for this event, as he had not trusted Kepha.

He then went swiftly into the living quarters and told Yeshua of the situation, "I have put provisions into the tomb and you must stay in there until I tell you it is safe to leave." Helping Yeshua to his feet, he led them all out into the garden.

"Joses, you will stay as well. Keep the baby as silent as you possibly can," he cautioned the anxious trio. "It will be crucial to your safety. Mariam," turning back to the older woman, who was wringing her hands and watching them with tears in her eyes, he spoke firmly. "You must pull yourself together as we must explain to the soldiers when they come that you are staying with me for now. Do not give anything away."

Nodding, she hurried to embrace them all and turned back to the house.

Together Iosef and a trusted servant rolled the rock back into place. Although it was pitch black inside, a ventilation shaft let in some air.

*

Kepha led the *Speira* (*detachment of soldiers*), who were court servants, at the disposal of the Sanhedrin when necessary, for police purposes, through the village.

"Hurry, hurry," he urged them as they made for Mariam's house. "The whore will escape if she learns of our plans."

"Hah, we will find her," laughed one of the *legionnaires*. "She cannot escape. We will not let any bastard child of Yeshua live," and the group hurried noisily on, making enough noise to raise the dead, let alone the living. However, the latter stayed inside their homes when they heard the racket, knowing it was the safest place to be. Stick your nose outside and you could end up with it being cut off your face.

"Here it is, here it is." Kepha was beside himself, urging them forward. "They will be sleeping and you can kill them where they lie."

They entered through the low doorway into the courtyard and two of them swept towards the living quarters, while two turned towards the eating areas.

"There is no-one here," roared the decanus (*sergeant)* who led the contubemium, (*an eight man party)*, "What sort of wild goose chase have you led us on?" Roughly he turned on Kepha and grabbing a handful of his shirt, pulled him towards him, until his face was right in that of the bewildered man.

"But no-one could have known we were coming," Kepha protested, twisting and turning to free himself.

"You stupid fisherman." The contubemium's leader threw Kepha away from him. "You are good for nothing. Go back to your fishing," and they prepared to leave.

"Wait, wait." Kepha put out his hand and grabbed the man's shoulder, who spun around, dagger in hand, which made Kepha jump back quickly.

"Never lay a hand on me," the decanus snarled, "or you will not live to see tomorrow."

"I am sorry." Kepha was quick to humble himself before the angry man, but still blinded by hatred and jealousy, could not stop himself. "They have escaped. You must question Iosef of Arimathea. He must be protecting them. Make him tell you the truth."

"Don't be so stupid." The *decanus* looked at with disgust and signalled to his men to leave. "Iosef is a senator, a wealthy man and one of the most powerful members of the Sanhedrin. Why would he harbour this whore and her whelp?"

"Because Yeshua is related to him," Kepha cried out in desperation. "She will turn to him as family."

"Pah!" The *decanus* looked hard at Kepha, assessing whether he was leading them on another wild goose chase, then turned on his heel, motioning to his men to follow.

"Look, just follow me," Kepha would not give up. "I will prove it to you."

The decanus turned back and looked at Kepha, who was the very essence of a wild man in his fury. He didn't want to go back to the Sanhedrin and admit he had lost his prey and was defeated. They were not a forgiving lot and were determined to rid the world of Yeshua and his memory. A child would remind people and could foment future rebellion.

"Alright," the soldier agreed grudgingly. "We will follow you, but if we do not see them there, we will not follow you any further."

They made their way to Iosef's house, which was a very substantial dwelling one klick down the road. Banging on the door, they made enough noise to wake the dead, until Iosef came to the door, angrily demanding to know what they wanted, when the servant ran to tell him who was at the door.

"How dare you interrupt my rest," he spoke with such dignity, the *decanus* automatically drew back in deference to such an important personage. "You had better have a good reason."

"This man," the *decanus* indicated Kepha, "has told us that you are harboring Yeshua's wife, Miryai and her child."

"How preposterous," Iosef looked at the man with scorn. "Neither Miryai nor Tamar are here with me. Mariam, my sister-in-law is here and she is family. What business is this of yours?"

The soldier stepped back abashed. "The Sanhedrin has ordered that Miryai and her child taken to prison."

"So you descended like wolves, ready to feast on her blood." His mind was working furiously, as he sought to distract them. "You would take a defenceless woman and child?" Their impudence tried him sorely.

The *decanus* shifted his weight from one foot to another. "Your Honor, I know you must be upset, but you must have been at the Council when this decision was made. I have a duty to perform, or it will be the worse for me. Please step aside and let us in."

"What? Let you defile my home?" Desperately he sought to distract them.

"You must let us in." Despite his respect for the older man, the *decanus* brushed past the protesting Iosef and led his troops inside. "Search everywhere, leave no room untouched," he commanded.

After searching in every room, nook and cranny, they regrouped in the courtyard. No-one is here Basius," they informed the *decanus*.

"There must be," Kepha bellowed, desperately frantically casting his gaze around.

"Shut up." Basius told him. "We must look elsewhere."

"Where else could they be?" Kepha defied Basius and pushing him aside, ran through the rooms himself, turning over anything that got in his way.

"Get out of my house Kepha." Iosef stood in front of the angry fisherman, blocking his way. "Stop him right now," he commanded Basius, "or I will have you imprisoned, for treating the home of a senator in such a manner."

Basius motioned to two of his men. "Grab the fool. Shackle him and lead him away." As they rushed to do his bidding, Kepha fought them like the demons of hell possessed him.

"They are here," he roared, as he struggled, cursed and kicked. "Search the cellars."

"We have you, fool." Basius reached out and drove his hand across Kepha's face. "Shut up, or it will be the worse for you."

"I'll not have this rough language and behaviour in my home." Iosef's voice cut through the uproar. "Get him out of here. He is an unkempt ruffian."

Taking an arm on either side, two legionnaires dragged Kepha out of the house, whilst he continued to roar and curse. "I know they are here, you have to find them."

"Put a gag in his mouth, if he will not shut up." Basius said. The legionnaires cast around and seeing a couple of rags on the edge of the well, grabbed one and stuffed it in Peter's mouth, then tied the other around it.

"We'll push you into the well, if you do not stop it." Shaking him, they tied his hands behind his back, with leather thongs.

Basius turned to Iosef. "I am sorry Your Honour, but I had to do my duty." Sheepishly he began to walk away.

"I know you Basius and you are a good man. I understand, but never disturb my home again in this manner," Iosef ordered curtly.

The troop grabbed hold of Kepha and dragged him away, without looking back.

"We must get them out of Jerusalem as soon as it is safe, before someone thinks to disturb the tomb, where they believe Yeshua lies dead." Turning to Mariam Iosef motioned her back inside.

"They would not desecrate a tomb," she gasped, horrified at the thought.

"They may my dear. We only have a few days." Turning aside he looked up at the stars above them and reflected upon man's inhumanity to man.

*

After a week in the tomb, they could delay no longer. Yeshua's strength grew enough for them to begin the long and torturous journey.

"We must go to Nabatea (*Transjordan – Jordan in modern times*). Herod does not rule this area and the Nabateans are tolerant of other religions." Yeshua knew he could not travel far, as he had not regained his strength and will.

"We are still very close to Herod though." Iosef had misgivings.

"Rome does not care about Judaeans, or their religion, as long as we do not revolt against them," his nephew reassured him.

"You are correct about the Romans." Iosef thought for a moment. "I am still concerned about Herod though. He will not tolerate you being alive and will not rest until he has killed the first born son of the House of King David, fearing you will succeed in wresting power from him."

"I know." Yeshua hung his head in dismay, wishing he was not the heir to the Davidic lineage. Although he had enjoyed being a rabbi and debating with others, he was not sure he was king material. "He fears the messiah, the long awaited King of the Jews, who will challenge his false authority.

Herod was an Ibutean, not a Jew and had been fathered by Antipater. He was tolerated, because his mother Cypros was a Nabatean from Petra and he had married Marianne, a Maccabee from the Hasmonean dynasty, who were the titular rulers of Judaea.

Although the Nabateans were converted to Judaism 130 years previously, when John of Maccabee conquered them, it was a grey area and in the eyes of the Judaeans, he had no right to the throne of Judaea. For them, only the pure bloodline of King David was royalty.

"That is why we must leave," Yeshua sighed. "I have given it much thought and I think Nabatea is the best route for us." He stretched out a hand and touched Tamar. "She must be safe at all costs."

Miryai's love for them both reached out and enveloped the tomb. "I'm not sure we could resettle there," she said with misgivings.

"You will not have to resettle there Miryai." Yeshua looked at her sadly. "It is me Herod is after. You must leave me in Nabatea and then you must go on to Assyria, (Syria/Iraq/Turkey/Lebanon) and Egypt. Herod has no power there."

"What if the Romans want to please Herod?" Iosef stroked his beard, remaining doubtful. "Nabatea is part of the Roman Empire."

Yeshua looked sad. "The Romans do not care about pleasing their tame impostor Herod, as long as he quells any uprisings."

"That is true Yeshua," Iosef was a very learned man and a senator in the Sanhedrin. One did not reach this position without a very deep knowledge of Jewish history.

"Be that as it may Ammi El-Lih," Yeshua leaned forward. "The Egyptians are tolerant of us. Remember Egypt's beliefs, are the basis of the Nazarean religion. We learned from them."

"Yeshua is right, Ammi El-Lih." Miryai stirred and gathering herself, rose from where she sat and stood up. "In Egypt, we will be able to practice our religion in peace."

"My Omo (*mother*) and Jwhyhb0 (father) spirited me away to Egypt, when Herod was killing all the firstborn. We were safe there." Yeshua's pain was written on his face, as he thought of the destruction wrought in his name. "I have caused so much tumult."

Miryai came to him and softly cradled his head to her breast, "Yeshua, you know it was written. It is not your fault."

"It is so difficult. I feel such shame and guilt for much that has happened," he muttered.

Iosef reached out and lifting Yeshua's head gazed into his eyes. "Yeshua, you have nothing to reproach yourself for. You could have avoided nothing."

"Still it pains me. Once I am captured or dead, you will all be safe. Rome is only interested in me."

"I agree," Iosef nodded his head and looked around at the others. "I believe we must do as Yeshua bids us."

Joses drew in a sharp breath. "I will protect you with my life 0x0d," he promised.

"Joses," Yeshua drew back from Miryai and turned to face his beloved 0x0d. "I love you with all my heart, but I need you to survive for Tamar and also to carry on the ministry. You cannot be with me. You must remain with the family. Kepha will return to the flock, but he has a turbulent spirit and will need your guidance and spiritual strength, or he will falter again."

A wail escaped from Joses. "I cannot 0x0. You are too weak to protect yourself. I must be there."

"Joses, it is written I will die, but not by Herod's hands. My spirit will return to the Inner Realms, because it is time."

"Then why not remain here and die in peace," Joses cried out in grief.

"I must lead them away from my family. I will go as far as Nabatea with them. Then they can continue on to Egypt and safety."

Miryai looked at the man she loved more than life itself. "I will not be separated from you my love."

Yeshua reached out and touched the face he loved beyond all else and beseeched her. "Miryai, Tamar must survive to carry on the bloodline."

Miryai was as stubborn as she was strong and gentle. "Then I remain with you, as we are one." Turning to Mariam, she beseeched her, "I will put Tamar in your care. Please take her and love her. Bring her up in the truth of the Virgins of the Light."

Mariam drew in a sharp breath, "Miryai, you must be with Tamar."

"No Mariam," the woman in the blue robe said softly. "I must remain with your son, my husband. You know I must."

"My soul is dimming." Yeshua looked sadly around the group. "My time is over."

"No, my love," Miryai went to him and cradled him in her arms. "Your life is now beginning. You have no further duty to the Judaeans, other than to escape to continue the royal bloodline."

Yeshua rested his weary head in her lap. Miryai looked down at the scars on his body and where the crown of thorns had dug into his head. Picking up his right hand, she caressed the horrible scarring the nail had made. "I cannot believe they did this to you."

Mariam his mother rose from the ground and went to sit at their feet. Reaching out her hand, she gently picked up one of his scarred feet and bending down kissed it. "My son," she wept. "You have carried out your duty beyond expectations. Now you must live and only for your family."

Reaching out, she lovingly caressed his face and looking at Miryai, shook her head. Both of them despaired he would make the journey. It was a long and torturous one. He was still physically weak and his spirit was broken.

"We must wait until it is darkest," Iosef told them. "On the third night it will be a black night with no moon. You must leave then." Turning he left them. The stone that blocked the entrance had been moved enough for a man to slip in and out, but they only came at night fearing suspicious eyes would be watching in the daytime.

Chapter Thirty-one – Le Donne in Azzuro worship

"Oh Holy Miryai, you who are the bride of Yeshua, of the Royal Line of King David, and the bearer of his child.'

The Donne in Azzuro were worshipping their icon.

"You, who stood beside Miriam, his beloved mother, please guide us in our time of trial, as you were sorely tried before us.

You, whose purity is without question.

You, whose bloodline ranks with that of your husband's, Yeshua.

You, with your training in the esoteric mysteries, help us as we kneel before you.

Oh Miryai and Mariam, protect your children on this earth, we beseech you."

The women, old and young, stood before a plain white altar, where a golden sun studded with precious jewels rested atop it.

The head priestess, a beautiful older woman with a golden circlet resting on her shining grey hair, was dressed in a simple blue gown which fell from her shoulders to her ankles and tied around her waist with a thin golden girdle. She bowed to the first statue on the left hand side of the altar, which depicted Yeshua's mother, then turning to another statue on the right hand side, she raised her arms and implored,

"Oh Holy Miryai, we beseech you to shine your glory upon your followers and expose the murderer who would bring harm to your true believers and holders of your secret.

It is time for us to release your secret to the world. In this enlightened age we believed ourselves safe from harm, but it appears there are those who will destroy us, rather than let us give up the proof they have sought to bury, for so long.

Let us now fulfil our promise to you. We stand tall, as the slender but strong poplar trees that grow beside water, their roots deep in mother earth, who is the nourisher of life.

"Do not allow evil men to cut us down."

Turning to face the group of women and an adolescent girl, who stood around her in a semi-circle, facing the altar in this simple white temple, which had been built in the grounds of her country estates, the Contessa looked at them all.

The chapel was nestled in a copse of trees, sheltered from curious eyes, but now they felt as though they were being spied upon.

"You, whose name derives from the Hebraic Migdal, meaning tower, that has been misunderstood over the centuries. It was the title you bore in the formal ministry, within the esoteric mysteries."

"You, who wore the crown with the moon, sun and a halo of stars, which was the symbol of a powerful woman's wisdom."

"You, The Magdalene, who, together with Mariam the Mother, are earthly emanations of the Virgins of Light from the realms above. You came to earth as Messengers of Light from that Good Realm above to teach, not die for, humanity. As a product of Nazarene eugenics, you the Maiden was conceived, gestated, and raised in the ancient laws of purity and purpose, according to the ancient laws established by Elijah, Elisha and Samuel."

"You, whose marriage to Yeshua, affirmed your positions as co-rulers of the Jewish nation, based on your inherited spiritual perfection."

The high priestess raised her hands above her head and spread them wide.

"You, who always walked with the Lord Yeshua. Whose courage he praised.

You, who was pre-eminent among all those Yeshua walked with. You whose heart was directed to the Kingdom of Heaven, more than all your brothers.

You, who interceded when others despaired.

You whose spiritual knowledge was complete.

You, the teacher in your own right.

You, who alone remained steadfast in your faith under threat, understanding fully the very principles of the Nazarean doctrines.

You, whom Yeshua held in the highest esteem.

You, who were a prophetic visionary and a priestess in your own right."

We, your servants, kneel before you in awe of your wisdom and perfection."

At this the gathering of women knelt before the statue of The Magdalene and bowed their heads.

"Miryai and Mariam, let your gentle souls and love, radiate from the Good Realm above and wash over us to bless our existence," the crowd chanted.

"Help us in our time of trial, gentle mothers. Oh Holy Messengers, take our sisters who were cruelly murdered, unto your bosom and gently nourish them in the realms above, we beseech you," the priestess prayed.

"We beseech you," the gathered women, dressed in long blue robes tied with golden girdles around their waist, murmured. "Keep us safe, as the time is nigh upon us to enlighten the world, as to your true purpose in ancient times."

Large silken cushions were scattered on the floor and they sank down upon them, as enraged eyes watched them from a copse of trees, hearing their words, which were carried to the watcher from a microphone secreted in the chapel.

*

"It is not to be borne," The Cardinale was beside himself, with a rage that he was helpless to contain, as he listened to the words of le Donne in Azzuro. He had sent one of his assassins to the chapel at night, to secret the microphone. A red mist appeared before his eyes and blotted out reality, to the point of madness.

Dismissing in his mind the woman who had retained her dignity before he had her killed, his twisted psyche squirmed as though a thousand serpents were crawling over each other aimlessly seeking, forever seeking.

What he wouldn't have given to live in the times of the Inquisition. Then he would have stopped their tricks smartly and watched as they were racked and tortured, then burnt alive at the stake.

The Cardinale shivered with anticipation at the thought of the next kill. Like all psychopaths, he was escalating. It would be so delectable. What thrilled him most of all, was the mute abject terror in their eyes once the atropine had been administered and they realised how powerless they were. Powerless to resist, they were witnesses to their own death throes.

Now it was time for another sacrifice. The die was cast. He knew the viper within the breast of his own family had been allowed to carry on this ridiculous worship of the Magdalene whore unchecked. The families had been far too lenient with these spoilt women.

However, he had not uncovered the secret of the whereabouts of the betrothal contract. Now he would have to take the final step, one that could expose him, but he did not care. He would cleanse the earth of this abomination and the secret would remain hidden for all time again, once it had been destroyed.

He could see it in his minds eye now and as he relived the last death, his hand stole under his cassock and grabbed his stiff cock, standing at attention saluting the victim in her death throes. How he loved the feel of his hands that had killed, on his swollen member.

His breath came faster and faster. Harder and harder his cock became, stiffer and stiffer, as he saw in his mind's eye the erection of the cross. Faster and faster his hand moved beneath his cassock, until his entire body was one exquisite screaming mass, begging for release. As he relived his own hands thrusting the spear into the woman's side and the blood flowing, a hoarse gasp of joy and pleasure escaped him, as his climax ejaculated across the room and his body jerked in the throes of an ecstasy, which was his worship of the King of Kings. Then he moved his hands down to cup his tender balls, in order to prolong the exquisite agony of the *little death*, whilst seeing the next victim's death in his mind's eye.

As the lassitude that release brought passed, he finally rose from the leather armchair and moved across to the antique desk with its inset of tooled leather. Seating himself on the leather chair, he began to hum softly an ancient Gregorian chant from the times of the Knights Hospitaller. Putting pen to paper, his plan for the next murder took form. Of course, it would be burnt in the fireplace once he had memorised it.

His entire being required another greater release, than that he had just experienced. As wonderful as it was, it could not compare to the exhilaration of the torture and death of another human being. To realise they knew you were omnipotent, omniscient, omnipresent, as you held their life in your hands and then took it away. You were God, the taker of life from those who trespassed against God's ancient laws of the Old Testament. In secret he believed the ancient Hebraic God of the Old Testament, who distributed fire and brimstone and was the God of the Genesis, had it right all along.

Never mind this turning the other cheek nonsense of the New Testament. The Cardinale loved the Old Testament, with its smiting of thine enemies and frequent stonings against transgressors.

Musing on Leviticus Chapter Twenty in the Old Testament of God, commanding the Israelites, the psychopath could recall the text in all its blood curdling entirety.

And the LORD spake unto Moses, saying, Again, thou shalt say to the children of Israel, Whosoever he be of the children of Israel, or of the strangers that sojourn in Israel, that giveth any of his seed unto Molech; he shall surely be put to death:

the people of the land shall stone him with stones. And I will set my face against that man, and will cut him off from among his people; because he hath given of his seed unto Molech, to defile my sanctuary, and to profane my holy name. And if the people of the land do any ways hide their eyes from the man, when he giveth of his seed unto Molech, and kill him not: Then I will set my face against that man, and against his family, and will cut him off, and all that go a whoring after him, to commit whoredom with Molech, from among their people. And the soul that turneth after such as have familiar spirits, and after wizards, to go a whoring after them, I will even set my face against that soul, and will cut him off from among his people. Sanctify yourselves therefore, and be ye holy: for I am the LORD your God. And ye shall keep my statutes, and do them: I am the LORD which sanctify you.[9]

For every one that curseth his father or his mother shall be surely put to death: he hath cursed his father or his mother; his blood shall be upon him. And the man that committeth adultery with another man's wife, even he that committeth adultery with his neighbour's wife, the adulterer and the adulteress shall surely be put to death. And the man that lieth with his father's wife hath uncovered his father's nakedness: both of them shall surely be put to death; their blood shall be upon them. And if a man lie with his daughter in law, both of them shall surely be put to death: they have wrought confusion; their blood shall be upon them. If a man also lie with mankind, as he lieth with a woman, both of them have committed an abomination: they shall surely be put to death; their blood shall be upon them. And if a man take a wife and her mother, it is wickedness: they shall be burnt with fire, both he and they; that there be no wickedness among you. And if a man lie with a beast, he shall surely be put to death: and ye shall slay the beast. And if a woman approach unto any beast, and lie down thereto, thou shalt kill the woman, and the beast: they shall surely be put to death; their blood shall be upon them. And if a man shall take his sister, his father's daughter, or his mother's daughter, and see her nakedness, and she see his nakedness; it is a wicked thing; and they shall be cut off in the sight of their people: he hath uncovered his sister's nakedness; he shall bear his iniquity. And if a man shall lie with a woman having her sickness, and shall uncover her nakedness; he hath discovered her fountain, and she hath uncovered the fountain of her blood: and both of them shall be cut off from among their people. And thou shalt not uncover the nakedness of thy mother's sister, nor *of thy father's sister: for he uncovereth his near kin: they shall bear their iniquity. And if a man shall lie with his uncle's wife, he hath uncovered his uncle's nakedness: they shall bear their sin; they shall die childless. And if a man shall take his brother's wife, it is an unclean thing: he hath uncovered his brother's nakedness; they shall be childless. Ye shall therefore keep all my statutes, and all my judgments, and do them: that the land, whither I bring you to dwell therein, spue you not out. And ye shall not walk in the manners of the nation, which I cast out before you: for they committed all these things, and therefore I abhorred them. But I have said unto you, Ye shall inherit their land, and I will give it unto you to possess it, a land that floweth with milk and honey: I am the LORD your God, which have separated you from other people. Ye shall therefore put difference between clean beasts and unclean, and between unclean fowls and clean: and ye shall not make your souls abominable by beast, or by fowl, or by any manner of living thing that creepeth on the ground, which I have separated from you as unclean. And ye shall be holy unto me: for I the LORD am holy, and have severed you from other people, that ye should be mine. A man also or woman that hath a familiar spirit, or that is a wizard, shall surely be put to death: they shall stone them with stones: their blood shall be upon them.*

In reality, the insane Cardinale was a true follower of the Old Testament, which sought retribution at every turn. They were a bloodthirsty lot, no doubt about it and the Cardinale was all for it. Now the church was in crisis, he would save it by his dedication to his Lord.

There would be two victims this time. He was out of control and could hardly contain himself at the thought of it. Now that would be simply exquisite! Imagine the terror of the mother, watching helplessly, as she saw her daughter in pain and dying.

Then she would experience her own death. How he wished he could crucify her. No, he could not risk another; the first had been touch and go. Nor could he risk the ire of the group of men whose bidding he followed. They had much to lose, if the release of the betrothal contract was not stopped, but they were unwilling to dirty their own hands.

Perhaps he could use the drug to keep the mother supine and paralysed, until her time came. Prolong it, so he could visit constantly and keep torturing her mentally, spiritually and.......he shivered........physically.

The question was where to keep them? His followers would do whatever he asked them to, after all, he was the Protector of the Brotherhood and held their lives in his hands.

The more he thought about it, the more he liked it, twice the terror, twice the pain, twice the blood, twice the risk. Oh yes.

He paused for a second salivating, then as he experienced yet another climax, his eyes narrowed. This next challenge would be a climax of the mind and soul. Dealing with double the risk, only made it more exhilarating.

Chapter Thirty-two – Edoardos takes the plunge

A shadow blocked the sunlight that had been warming Edoardos. Looking up, he saw Lina looking down at him. Standing, he held out one of the chairs for her and after throwing her large shoulder bag into another, she flopped down into the seat.

"What a day." Expelling some air, she pushed her sunglasses up to perch on the top of her head.

"Buon Giorno to you too," Edoardos retorted smartly.

"I'm sorry E," she apologized contritely. "And how was your day dear?" she teased.

"Better than yours, by the sound of it," Edoardos retorted.

"I'd kill for a cappuccino," Lina looked at him expectantly.

Raising his finger, presto, like magic he caught the attention of the waiter, who skirted through the tables until he reached theirs. Their priests had that effect on Italians.

"Padre?" he queried.

"Due cappuccino, grazie," Edoardos replied. Raising his eyebrows, he looked at Lina, who grinned back, knowing he was asking if she wanted something sweet to eat.

"Grazie." Nodding her head, she thought greedily of the wonderful Italian pastries.

"Due dolci per avour," he ordered for them both.

"That is seriously good coffee," Lina proclaimed when the cup was set in front of her. Taking a sip, she leaned back in her chair, her mood improving by the minute. Noticing how contented she was, niggled at her. 'I am going to have to sort myself out.' Her feelings were running riot through her commonsense and confusing the hell out of it.

Edoardos was pleased to see her mellow, as she had appeared quite tense when she had arrived. Unable to remain still for long, while they waited for the pastries, Lina leaned forward and putting her elbows on the table, looked at Edoardos earnestly. "Now what do you have for me?"

"Not here," He looked around anxiously.

"But you do having something for me," Lina pushed him.

"Yes," he hissed. "Later."

Edoardos' words cut her to the quick, as she was still feeling decidedly fragile, which annoyed her no end. 'Get it together you stupid woman,' she chided herself. 'If you could deal with the bombs and horror of Kosovo, you can guard yourself against E's charms.'

Sulking for a moment, she stopped and considered the situation, 'Well maybe not.' Admitting her inability to control her feelings, didn't make her feel any more in control.

'When this is over you'll have to go on assignment overseas again,' she told herself firmly. 'You've had plenty of offers.' Mulling over her options failed to impress her.

At that moment the pastries arrived and any bad humour simply disappeared, as they both took a bite.

"Aaaaah," Lina sighed and licked her lips.

E grinned wickedly at her, as he leaned across the table and wiped a smudge of patisserie cream off her lower lip.

"Oh God." Emotions swept through her, kicking her in to touch. Desperately she sought a way out by drawing his attention to the fountains in the square. "I've always loved Bernini's sculptures."

"His masterpieces were inspired, but he was an arrogant genius." Edoardos commented. "He certainly didn't like sharing the glory. Poor old Borromini was constantly overshadowed and in some ways he was the better architect. Bernini overstepped the mark when he built the bell towers onto St Peters for Il Papa Urban VIII."

"True," Lina also knew her art history. "Determined to outdo his rival Borromini, he made them far too large for the unstable marshy ground, they eventually cracked and had to be pulled down."

"Fell out of ☐avour with his great patron in a big way," Edoardos agreed. "Well, there were no half measures for Bernini, the boy from Naples, who set out to outdo his sculptor father and he certainly succeeded by becoming the toast of Italy."

"He certainly provided color to the palette of the times he lived in," which Lina thought was a riot of colour anyway.

"There was enough going on then, without him adding his lira's worth." His thoughts drifted to the goings on between the church, state and nobles of the time. "What a circus it must have been at times."

"Nothing changes in Rome, but I'm so pleased I live here. It feeds my soul," Lina echoed Edoardos' previous thoughts. "Every day is an adventure when you walk out the door."

"Especially if you're driving in the traffic." The priest shook his head in dismay at the chaos, and then both of them fell silent, content to just be in each others' company.

That was until Lina spoilt the moment. She just couldn't help being the dedicated journalist. "What about le Donne in Azzuro?" she murmured. "What is happening there?"

"Leave it alone," Edoardos muttered darkly.

"I can't let it go," she cried out.

He realised that Lina could not be expected to understand the power his family still enjoyed, after centuries of service to the Holy See. They were bound to each other, by the secrets each carried close to their hearts and deep in their souls. Seeking to reassure her, he reached out his hand in a gesture of reconciliation. "You have to. We protect our own Lina, just as I would protect you with all my being."

"I know," she muttered darkly. "But this is about women's lives. They're being picked off one by one and they all belong to le Donne in Azzuro. Adelais could be in danger."

A chill travelled up Edoardos' spine and into his head as time seemed to stand still. "We've all considered that and she has extra protection now. Everything possible is being done." He looked at her pleadingly. "Please understand how it works."

"And you believe this is enough?"

"This is the way such matters have been handled in our families for centuries." Edoardos' feathers were being ruffled once again, "and I've spoken with Adelais once again, begging her to be careful. She refuses to have bodyguards assigned to her though."

Spying an opening, Lina was on him quicker than a rabbit down a bolthole, "What did you say to her?"

"Keep your voice down," he hissed, then spying a waiter, he signalled him to approach.

Looking up at the sky, Lina saw streams of dark grey clouds scudding by and gestured to them. "God obviously got out of the wrong side of the bed this morning." Having drawn Edoardos' attention to the weather, they began to gather their things, while he asked the attentive waiter, "il conto per avour." When the bill arrived, he put some cash on to it, waving away the change.

"Grazie Padre," the grateful man said, recognising a well heeled priest when he saw one.

Making their way back to Lina's apartment on Via Margutta, each were as relaxed as it was possible to be under the circumstances.

*

Once inside, E wordlessly hefted his briefcase on to the dining room table and removed a manilla folder which he put down on the surface.

"What have you got here? Is it OK to touch them?" Lina exclaimed as she excitedly turned over the pages. "Did you take them out of the Archives?"

"I can hardly take any documents out of the Archives, Lina. I would be hung, drawn and quartered, with my head placed on a pike outside Sant Anna Porta. These are notes I scribbled for you, about the different offices I think could be relevant, as well as anything I could find of interest about Mary Magdalene.

"Where did you find the documents?" Lina's longed for request had finally been fulfilled and she was so excited her voice was tumbling over itself with enthusiasm.

"The Archives are massive and I discovered them in many different places. I don't know what their relevance is for us at the moment, but I thought we could mull over them."

Bending their heads together, they looked at his notes and discussed them at length.

"A lot of this is common knowledge now," Lina tentatively pointed out to Edoardos, not wanting to diminish his findings.

"I know. That's why I'm becoming frustrated, attempting to tie Mary Magdalene to the Knights of Malta." It was proving to be a more difficult task than he had expected. "I need to ferret out the documents pertaining to Mary Magdalene, which have been placed in the subterranean basement. There's a great vault there for the most important documents, some of them detrimental to the faith."

"The Big V categorically denies any such documents exist," Lina pointed out.

"I know," Edoardos admitted.

"Well they would, wouldn't they?" Lina mocked the priest sitting alongside her. "They have a vested interest in anything controversial remaining out of sight."

"Don't you ever breathe a word of this," he warned her. "Don't speak about this to anyone."

"Would I do that?"

Edoardos just looked at her rolling his eyes up in his head. "In a heartbeat! Who is after a Pulitzer Prize?"

"Who moi? Never," she teased him, trying to lighten the mood. "Perhaps it's that white mouse that just ran across the floor."

"Or perhaps it's the elephant in the room," He replied scathingly, as the atmosphere tensed once more. "OK, let's have a look at this lot," E bent to the task again.

"We know the Nag Hammadi texts, are the Gnostic's challenge to the Nicene Creed."

There had been great excitement when the Nag Hammadi texts were unearthed in nineteen forty-five bound in ancient leather bound books.

"The church couldn't suppress those and it's a healthy thing E."

"I don't deny that, it's how we clawed out way out of the dark ages."

"If the church had its way, we would still believe the sun revolves around the earth. They gave old Galileo a hell of a time."

"We're getting off the subject. Look here," pointing with his index finger, he drew Lina's attention to notes regarding the Arian Christian's postulations about Jesus' divinity, which Constantine had clamped down on very firmly. "There are Arian Christian cults out there now on the Internet."

"There are sects that revere Mary Magdalene, but have never been able to prove their theories about her." Lina had dismissed many of them as fantastical, as they went too far, but she was willing to believe that Jesus and Mary could have been married. "You know Judaism was a very strict theology. It would have been extremely unusual for a Rabbi in Jesus' time to have remained unmarried. This lends power to the argument he was married to Mary."

"It's not what Christian history tells us," The priest was sticking to the theology he knew.

Lina raised her head and looked at him. "Anything that validates these claims, wouldn't have been received well by the Holy Roman Catholic Church."

"That is the responsibility of the Office of the Doctrine of the Faith. I leave it to them to deal with any claims that go against our doctrine." Edoardos frowned as he looked at some of the notes.

"But the church is losing ground, as they fail to interest young men in the ecclesiastical life these days."

Edoardos sighed and admitted. "It is an uphill battle most of the time."

"That's why the church is seeking converts in poor countries like Africa or South America, where the corrupt regimes aren't interested in bettering the lot of the populace. They're more interested in selling off the natural resources and shovelling the mountain of ill gotten gains into their personal Swiss Bank accounts."

"You have a very cynical view of life Lina," he said brusquely.

Acknowledging in her profession she had seen atrocities that had opened her eyes to the many heinous crimes committed in the world, she shrugged. "It's undeniable E."

"I hang around with you too much," Edoardos complained. "No wonder I'm becoming dissatisfied with my life and role."

"Caspita (*good heavens*) E, this is a turnaround for you." She was taken by surprise, when he admitted to being a little unsettled. "I think you were probably questioning your role when you met me long ago, or you wouldn't have kept me around for light relief," Lina flirted with him. "You need me to keep you on the straight and narrow."

E made a moue of derision, "If I relied on you to keep me on the straight and narrow, I'd be plunging over the precipice. I haven't had a good night's sleep since you became a journalist."

"Let's get back on track here." Lina brought their attention back to his notes. "In Two hundred and ten AD we have Mani-Hiya declaring that Yeshua and Miryai, his bride, were co-messiahs/co-redemptors. This was before Constantine put his stamp on Christianity."

"There are still followers of Manichaeism," Edoardos had to agree, but then the world was full of crazies with their theories of Jesu Cristo and his life. He preferred to stick with the biggest player in the game, the Big V.

"But do you feel fulfilled?" Lina persisted.

"I thought I did. I really did," he anguished. "But I have to admit these murders have shaken me to the core of my being."

"But are you part of the Church's family?" Lina was relentless, not prepared to give one inch. "The entire world knows it is riddled with corruption and intrigue like every other bureaucracy. No-one believes the fairy tale any longer."

"But it's our fairytale Lina. It's what I know. It's who I am."

"No, it's not who you are. You are the sacrificial lamb for your family," Lina challenged him. "Do you want to let them dictate your entire life for you?"

Edoardos shrugged off her cutting remarks. "Why not, if it helps me achieve my ambition? It's a life I like, Lina."

"Are you sure about that?" Sometimes she had her doubts. Did he hanker for a normal life; with a woman he loved by his side?

'Stop with the daydreaming you idiot,' she berated herself.

"Yes I am Lina." Edoardos reaffirmed his contentment with his celibate life at the centre of the Big V politics. "If this crazy idiot wasn't killing women, my life would be on track." E moved in his chair uneasily. "If he belongs to the Knights, or the Church, he won't bring the Holy See down. We have survived worse than this and we now have a man of integrity and humility as Il Papa. Whoever he is, I think he's simply run of the mill psychopath."

"I don't," Lina protested vehemently. "He has to be part of a group that has an agenda against either, or both, Mary Magdalene and le Donne in Azzuro. That is what makes them dangerous and puts the group at risk."

Lina's statement echoed the fear in Edoardos' heart, but he still refused to rise to her bait.

"We have to stop this guy whoever he is." Lina looked at him wearily. "Where do we start?"

"We start at the beginning," he responded, as he reached out and held her hand tightly. "All those years of study at the seminary will pay off now."

"For arguments sake, let's say there is something about le Donne in Azzuro this killer despises. What office of the Curia would be most upset about her being portrayed in high esteem?"

"There is nothing new in the worship of Mary Magdalene by le Donne in Azzuro, that hasn't been heard a thousand times before." Edoardos knew the Church of Rome, had simply shrugged such rumours off its shoulders and continued as before.

"How do you know that?" Lina's curious was more than piqued. How indeed, did a Vatican priest, know of the creed behind Donne in Azzuro's worship?

"I believe it's the same old Gnostic/Arian creed. Adelais hides nothing from us, and we're content to let her dabble in her mysteries without becoming involved, or looking too deeply into the doctrine." Edoardos dismissed it with a shrug of his shoulders. "Ever since the Nag Hammadi documents were aired, it's all over the Internet, but the Church remains as strong as ever."

Lina looked at him from under her eyes. Surely he could not really believe that. The church had been losing ground for decades now. Many of the faithful, had departed in their tens of thousands or merely paid lip service these days.

The sexual abuse scandals had been very damaging, particularly when John Paul II swept them under the carpet, by reassigning the paedophilic priests so they could re-offend. Now they were paying the price. Seeking new converts in Africa and South America, they were not making any friends in the western world with their scaremongering about the use of condoms in Africa, when the need to control the spread of the Aids virus was a top priority.

Still she didn't want to argue the point with E. The wounds were too raw and he was her very dear friend.

Changing the subject, she focused on the board around the neck of the first victim. *Magdalene – Whore*. What was that all about? "So, whoever this killer is, he obviously cannot cope with Mary being an educated woman, who is now held in high esteem." Searching for a reason for such hatred of Mary Magdalene, was beyond her. "What's tipped someone over the edge at this particular point?"

"Perhaps it was the apology Il Papa John Paul II made to her, acknowledging she was not a prostitute."

"That was years ago and it doesn't seem enough to start killing people," Lina looked dubious.

"No." E looked thoughtfully at the different offices of the Curia in front of him. "But we don't know how deep his psychosis is, do we? He still appears to be fixated on the whore part of this."

They both looked at the notes in front of them.

"Let's go through a few of the offices and see what we come up with," he proposed.

L'Ufficio della Dottrina della Fede -The Office of the Doctrine of the Faith

"This used to be the Office that was responsible for the Inquisition." Lina thought of the heinous crimes, committed in the name of the church. "The consistent torture and murder of human beings, who dared to express different beliefs to those of the Roman Catholic Church."

"That was a very dark period in our history," Edoardos agreed. It was pointless arguing otherwise. It was an abomination. A blot on the Church since the Middle Ages.

"These were the religious Jesuit nutters, who were responsible for the madness." Lina shuddered at the thought of the helpless victims that had been sacrificed. "They were the forerunners of Opus Dei."

They both looked at each other at the mention of the lay organisation that Pope John Paul II had made a prelature and canonised its founder, whom he called the *saint of ordinary life.* He had been repeatedly accused of waving a soft hand over the powerful secretive right-wing Catholic organization, as well as the Legion of Christ, whose founder was later found guilty of the rape of his seminarians.

"Their madness must have run so deep, it beggars belief. Where was Christ's mercy and goodness in that?" she challenged the priest seated beside her.

"Lina, I can't change the past and you have to look at this in light of the times, where murder and mayhem were the norm."

"That's no excuse for the atrocities that were carried out in the name of the Church." Lina defended her position to the hilt, hands akimbo on hips.

"Contrary to popular opinion," Edoardos tried to make Lina understand, "the Inquisition did not begin in Spain with Ignatius Loyola and his Jesuits, which he founded in the 15th century. It actually started in France during the twelfth century in order to persecute heresy within the church. It was not intended to persecute other religions," he said, quietly admonishing her.

"Well it certainly got out of hand," Lina went back to her history lessons and drew on them.

"Let's not get into an argument about Christ's message and the way the people of the Middle Ages interpreted it Lina," Edoardos begged for her understanding of the Church's behaviour in those dark times.

"For God's sake E, it lasted for 605 years. Why didn't anyone try to stop it?"

"I know," E had the grace to look shamefaced, "and it will forever be a stain on the Church's reputation."

Employing the rack, the iron maiden, the skull crusher, the nail chair and other horrendous tools of torture, the Inquisition more often than not, ended with the ultimate in terror, being burnt alive at the stake. Those who confessed to their purported heresy were strangled first, those who refused to confess, were burnt without strangulation.

During the middle ages, the Inquisition had defended their practices, by claiming burning cleansed the soul and did not spill blood, which was forbidden by the Catholic Church. One finds it hard to reconcile this stance, with the oceans of blood shed during the Church's crusades over the centuries.

"When did they change the name from the Congregation of the Holy Inquisition?"

"Pius X changed to Congregation of the Holy Office, but it did not change to its present name the Office of the Congregation of the Faith until Paul VI."

"Good move." Lina could see the sense in shedding the badly tarnished name of this particular office.

"To give credit where it's due," Edoardos pointed out to Lina, "Before he became Il Papa, Cardinale Ratzinger was the prefect of this Office and opened up the long sealed Inquisition archives dating to nineteen o-three"

"True, but they're lagging behind the other Vatican archives, which go up to nineteen twenty-two." Lina corrected him while thinking ahead furiously. "However, I wonder if there was anything in any of those archives, which might be of interest to us."

"That's one of the places I looked," E hastened to reassure her. "I can only look at a few at a time and I'm trying to be as low key as possible, so I don't raise any suspicions and lose my privileges which are extensive."

"Well, could we argue that the Doctrine of the Faith would be upset about le Donne in Azzuro?" Lina proposed. "After all it is their job to keep the canons intact."

"Perhaps," E conceded.

"So who runs this office now?"

"Cardinale Contardella. His family and mine will now be joined with the upcoming nuptials. I can't see him encouraging a group of madmen to run around murdering defenceless women. He's a cleric who is very much in control of himself and his Office. I believe he would dismiss le Donne in Azzuro as a joke. As far as I can tell, nothing on the internet about Mary Magdalene and the various New Age cults surrounding her, bothers him."

"What's he like?" Lina's curiosity was getting the better of her.

"He runs a tight ship." E looked at her, wondering what to tell her. "The family has gotten to know him a little better since the engagement. He's a cold character, who is arrogant and ambitious. Not known for shows of emotion. I've never seen him lose his cool."

"And what does that really mean? These arrogant cold guys are often homicidal psychopaths, because they have suppressed everything."

"Psychopaths escalate during their killings. I can't see him in the role."

"He could be a very good actor and perhaps he just gives the orders and he has a crew of Jesuits to carry out his dirty work."

"Why are you focusing on the Jesuits?" The priest was trying to get Lina off this particular train of thought without much success?

"Oh come on E. Who was behind the Inquisition?"

Edoardos took pains to point out, they had ceased the practice centuries ago.

"So apart from burning people at the stake, what is the role of this Office of the Doctrine of the Faith now?"

"Well it's pretty tame in comparison to its former role," he admitted. "It's about theological orthodoxy."

"Duh," Lina rudely interrupted. "That's just churchspeak. What does it mean in reality?"

"God, woman you'll be the death of me yet," he protested laughingly. "Let's see, basically its defending and reaffirming official Catholic doctrine, including birth control."

"Oh no, not that hot potato again." Lina brought her hands up to her ears and covered them. "What else?"

"Homosexuality. I know I know, down girl," he protested, making a show of raising his own hands in protest, as Lina raised her eyebrows and gave him a hard look.

"First clean up your own house."

"We're trying our best. It's also responsible for promoting inter-religious dialogue with other faiths."

"Not much headway being made on that one is there?" Lina said disparagingly. "They keep banging on about being the true faith, which pretty much puts a damper on any meaningful dialogue with other beliefs."

"Your parents must despair of you."

"Pretty much, as far as religion goes," she admitted, "but otherwise we're good."

"Except for marriage and bambinos," E pointed out.

Lina laughed out loud, "Yeah that too."

"This for a good Italian family pretty much covers everything."

"Well, you're not doing much to swell the ranks of the flock are you?" she shot back in jest, ducking out of the way as he reached out to swipe at her gently.

"So, do we give them the big tick, or put them on the nasty list?" she wanted to know.

"Why would they bother?" Edoardos just couldn't see them getting involved in such outrageous mayhem. They're the oldest of the congregations of the Roman Curia, and they're ahead on points. Why would they go batty over Mary Magdalene? Alessandro Contardella has more sense than to let any of his clerics get involved in something like this."

"Il Papa Benedict XVI was Prefect of the Office of the Doctrine of the Faith before he became Il Papa wasn't he?"

"What's that got to do with the price of fish?" He wondered where the hell Lina was going with this line of questioning.

"Just asking," Lina replied innocently, which didn't fool him for one moment.

Yes," he admitted, "he went through a terrible period with the sexual abuse scandals." Edoardos was embarrassed by the futility of it all, and the damage to the children and young monks who had been abused. Their lives were ruined. He knew the church should have looked after its flock better than that, and decided to change the subject.

"Do you know he was one of only seven people, who have actually read the Third Secret of Fatima?"

"Really?" At this statement Lina looked up with interest. "Was there any mention of Mary Magdalene in it? Did he ever discuss it publicly?"

Edoardos pondered how to phrase the answer to her question, knowing what she was after. "He issued an ambiguous statement in the Pauline Sisters' newsletter explaining the message dealt with *dangers threatening the faith and the life of the Christian; and therefore of the world*, but nothing explicit."

"Well it could have had something about Mary Magdalene and her disclosures."

"I think you're reaching a bit far now Lina," E retorted scathingly.

"It's typical of the Christian faith," Lina defended her position, "to believe that some revelation that would affect them, would be the end of the world."

"He said it *threatened* the world, not that it was a doomsday prophecy." The priest jumped to Ratzinger's defence.

"Well I've never believed in these prophecies anyway." Lina contemptuously dismissed them out of hand. "They're just another way to control the masses."

"You think Nostradamus was working for the church?" he countered.

"His prophecies were so oblique and after the fact, it's very simple, for anyone who has a vested interest, to make a prophecy fit." Lina dismissed them out of hand. "We're just as superstitious today, as we were in the Dark Ages."

Edoardos couldn't argue with that line of reasoning. Since time began people had pursued the answer to life and death, but they still clung to the mystery beliefs based on unquestionable faith.

The Darwinian theory of evolution, simply scared the pants off many who were less than happy with their current lifetimes and sought recompense in the hereafter, or the chance to have another go at it. Given this premise, the Catholic Church's creed was no better or worse than any of the others. "It's not quite that bad Lina."

Lina moped for a moment, but you couldn't keep her down for long. "Let's look at some other Offices then."

"That's why I'm here." E was pleased to move on and picked up another sheaf of papers, coming to his own Office of the Administration of the Patrimony of the Holy See.

Ufficio per l'amministrazione del patrimonio della Santa Sede - The Office of the Administration of the Patrimony of the Holy See

Try as hard as he might, Edoardos could not imagine his own Cardinale Vendetto, who ran the Office of the Administration of the Patrimony of the Holy See, as a shadowy dangerous defender of any threat to the Church's existence. The notion appeared absurd, as Edoardos thought of the ascetic priest banker who kept a firm guiding hand on the finances of the Holy See.

Distant? Yes. Unapproachable? Not once you had overcome Cerberus, the three headed dog from Dante's hell in the antechamber, whose ferociousness to anyone lesser than Il Papa, defeated many a brave soul. Perceiving everyone as a threat to the Cardinale's very existence, in his zeal to protect him with his life, Monsignor Galasso made few friends and not a few enemies.

"My God Edoardos," Lina put her hand to her forehead theatrically, as she exclaimed. "Surely you are not this nasty piece of work who is going around murdering innocent people."

"Very funny Lina."

Once again, he was fortunate to have entre to the Cardinale through his family connections. The man had personally mentored Edoardos' career, guiding him past the dangerous ravines that riddled the big V's politics, into which the unwary could fall, never to be seen again.

His Cardinale's devotion to Il Papa was beyond question. His unswerving loyalty to the church and its doctrine went without saying.

Would he harm anyone who stood in its way? Edoardos thought he knew Cardinale Vendetto as well as any man could no another, but admitted to himself he had no way of knowing the inner workings of a man's mind. In his heart though, he believed it was not possible.

Having met him in social circumstances, at his own family palazzo, as well as inside the Big V, he believed he knew a true arrow when he saw one.

"It's simply impossible," he assured Lina. "I'm part of that office and believe me I would know if someone was running around killing women."

"Are you sure E?" Lina looked at him searchingly.

"Underneath his aloofness, Cardinale Vendetto is a good and honest man, who has guided me diligently, through the intricate steps of survival in the Big V, ensuring I never put a foot wrong. He has Il Papa's ear and his trust, and he is genuinely focused on running the Office of the Patrimony to the highest levels of transparency and efficiency."

Edoardos couldn't begin to imagine, the Cardinale taking part in some archaic ritual to eliminate some imagined scourge from the face of the earth. "Anyway I'm sure he's not a Knight."

"What about that awful secretary who looks after him."

Edoardos gave a start as he thought of all the neuroses Monsignor Galasso carried around with him, but he still could not bring himself to condemn him as a killer.

"No. Difficult as he may be, he's no killer. Resentful, neurotic, envious, but no," here Edoardos shook his head emphatically. "He's no killer Lina. He is devoted to Cardinale Vendetto and would do nothing to bring harm to him, or his name, or our Office."

Sighing he wondered what made him infallible in the matters of a man's soul, and couldn't rid himself of the doubt that niggled at him, whilst he castigated himself for admitting it was there. "I have to put it aside for now. I cannot believe this of him."

Turning aside, he hesitated to mention the next congregation on the list, knowing she would go on the attack over this one.

Opus Dei - *The Work of God*

"What about the infamous Opus Dei?" Lina looked at Edoardos, beseeching him to be open minded and not close down on her.

A highly secretive and fabulously wealthy Catholic faction, described by one authority as sinister, secretive and Orwellian, both Il Papa Paul VI and John Paul II, had continued to sanction its activities.

"They're a lay society Lina." He ran his right hand through his hair, to relieve the headache he felt coming on.

"With their weird beliefs in self flagellation to clarify thought and cleanse the spirit, they are also taught to avoid natural human feelings. What could be in it for them?" Lina plopped down on to the sofa with a sigh.

"Look Lina, being admonished to have a *reticent and guarded heart* doesn't make them Satanic," the priest defended them. "I'm not a supporter of them by any means and the new Il Papa does not favor them as others have, but we can't condemn them out of hand."

"Yes, I think we can." Lina was adamant. "The current Il Papa is a wonderful human being, but whoever this rogue Cardinale is, will not be dissuaded by him. He will whip up his crowd and they will simply redouble their efforts." Rising from her seated position, she began to pace agitatedly.

"Simmer down Lina," Edoardos admonished her. "What makes you think a Cardinale has to be behind this?"

"It has to be someone of great authority, in order to have a following that will obey his instructions." She replied stubbornly, which didn't resonate with the priest.

"It still doesn't follow it has to be a Cardinale."

"I don't believe that." Lina stuck stubbornly to her theory. "We have to find out who he is connected with."

Edoardos gave up at that point. Why not go along with her way of thinking. He had no other clues at the moment and neither did the police or his family. Everyone was at a loss to explain the disappearance. He could hardly wildly accuse some Cardinale, so he didn't bother.

"Why should he necessarily be connected with Opus Dei any other Catholic organisation?" he asked her. "He may be acting alone."

Lina looked at him sympathetically, knowing how he was personally suffering. Placing her hand on his arm, she gently suggested. "That's unlikely. It would take a team to pull this off. There are more crazies out there, helping him with his vicious delusions."

"Look, I'll go along with your idea, but don't expect me to raise it with anyone else," he argued, placing his own hand over hers. "This is wreaking havoc within the Vatican."

"Then we're back to the Knights of Malta."

"What makes you keep insisting on their involvement?"

"Because of their proximity to the first murder site," she insisted.

Looking at her keenly, he wondered where her wonderful reporter's balanced and judicial eye, had disappeared to during this investigation. "Then how do we explain the second abduction." Lina was nothing if not stubborn, and once she had made up her mind, it was almost impossible to change it.

"I have this gut feeling and it won't go away."

"It's not enough."

Lina rubbed her eyes, which were irritable from lack of sleep. "Maybe not, but it seems I just seem to be going in that direction, despite my normal inclination."

"Alright, let's keep looking through the different offices of the Curia." Knowing it was unlike Lina to go off on an irrational tangent, the priest capitulated. After all, what other leads did he have? "Let's get back to Opus Dei. They're harmless enough Lina," he sought to reassure her.

"I'm not so sure of that. They're modern day Jesuits." Lina was well aware of the secular lay organisation with its arduous demands upon its followers.

"The Jesuits do a lot of good work now," he protested. "As well as their high profile in missionary work, human rights and social justice, they're Colleges and Universities are world renowned."

"And where does Opus Dei fit into all of this?"

"As you know they are a lay prelature."

"They were only a lay society, until Karol Woljtya made them a personal prelature. Why did he do that?"

"It's looked upon world wide as a catholic cult," she continued. "They're highly secretive, fanatical, and their members are highly controlled by the organisation. They also recruit aggressively, yet we point the finger at other cults for the very same things."

"They have a far more moderate leader now that Josemarie Escriva has died," Edoardos protested vociferously.

"For God's sake E. They're into self flagellation." Lina shuddered at the thought and it would take more than a simple denial to convince her they were harmless. "Their doctrine would throw the Church back into medieval times."

"Well they no longer enjoy the protection of Il Papa, as they did under Il Papas Pius XII and John Paul II."

Lina mumbled and grumbled, for all the world like Mount Aetna working itself up for another explosion.

Edoardos was determined to avoid that at all costs. "OK." Employing commonsense, he was determined to lead them away from this load of dynamite that was getting Lina so wound up; she was now pacing around the room, making him quite dizzy as he tried to follow her perambulations. "Let's take stock and see what we have here."

Congregatio Cultu Divino et Disciplina Sacramentorum -The Congregation for Divine Worship and the Discipline of the Sacraments

"OK E. Who are they and what do they do?"

"Well they handle most affairs about the liturgical practices of the Latin Church as distinct from the Eastern Orthodox. They also deal with some technical matters relating to the Sacraments.

"Like what?"

"Oh," Edoardos waved his hands in the air, "The regulation and promotion of the liturgy, primarily of the sacraments."

"As in the bread and wine?"

"That and celebrating the Eucharist. They draw up and revise liturgical texts. Review the calendars and proper tests for mass, sacred music and art."

"So they're responsible for all those Madonnas and bambinos."

He laughed and nodded, "Over the centuries."

"Have you seen some of those paintings of God's wrath; and angels in battle?"

"Pretty explicit I agree. Oh you'll like this one."

"What?"

"They examine non-consummation of marriages."

"Such as Princess Caroline of Monaco's to Philippe Junot you mean?" Lina grimaced at the hypocrisy. A visit to Il Papa and a few Hail Mary's and your unwanted marriage is history, if you're wealthy. Try that one if you're a poor Catholic. What a travesty. It made a mockery of the sanctity of marriage that the

Church bangs on about, and proved to the world there is one law for the rich and another for the poor."

"The ordination of priests," the priest continued, as though she had not interrupted him. "And they regulate holy relics."

At this Lina burst out laughing, unable to help herself, but wisely kept her counsel before she got herself into more trouble. "OK OK. I get the message and I give up. Unless it's about relics of Mary M, I can't see why someone here would get their holy knickers in a twist."

"No, seems pretty tame to me."

"Who heads them up?"

"Cardinale della Rovere."

"Like the guy who was Rodrigo Borgia's rival for the papacy, and his deadly enemy?"

"That's the one. The family disappeared into obscurity after they married a daughter off to the Medicis, but there has been the odd distant relative floating around."

"What's he like?"

"Who Alesso?" Edoardos' mind went back to the past when he was a young boy. "I don't really know him that well, as he's ten years older than me. He was more my brother, Landro's playmate than mine. He still comes over to the house from time to time, but I'm not always there, and I don't really come across him in the day to day running of the Vatican."

"Does he seem harmless enough?"

He shrugged his shoulders. "I've got no reason to believe otherwise."

"Nothing seems to be leading anywhere," Lina said miserably, then immediately perked up, "so the Knights of Malta are still top of my list."

"Oh God," Edoardos groaned and threw up his hands. "I give up."

Chapter Thirty-three – The Choice

The warmth of the sun upon his back felt very pleasant as the Cardinale walked in the garden with the Contessa. Related by marriage, he had spent many a pleasant evening dining with the family. He liked the intellectual discussions he had with the Count, but disparaged the Contessa's heretical belief in the fallacy that the Magdalene had been married to Christ.

"Adelais, you mustn't tease the poor man," her husband continually chided her. "He is part of our extended family."

"I cannot help but mock him Tonio, he gives me the creeps," she would reply.

Many evenings they had locked horns about the Church's doctrine and its treatment of women. Why on earth his cousin had married outside the Italian nobility, the Cardinale would never know……..and a Catholic who only paid lip service to the Church to boot. What was happening to Roman Society? It would not have been tolerated half a century before.

At least she was French and not some boorish American. He shuddered at the thought. If she had not spouted such heretical nonsense, he would have enjoyed challenging her intellectually, as she was a well educated woman.

Passing on her ridiculous doctrine to her children, simply could not be borne. He had mentioned this many times to his cousin, who was overly tolerant and loved her very much, so let her have her head. The true believers of the Church were dwindling in numbers every day, even in this most Catholic of countries; and to have such heresy within his own bloodline was beyond forgiveness. It begged retribution.

"It is a beautiful autumn day. The worst of the heat of summer is behind us now," the Contessa ventured. She was a slim, beautiful woman, with shining coppery hair that reflected the rays of the sun like a golden helmet. Bedecked in Prada from head to toe, she was the epitome of Roman aristocratic society.

"It is my favorite season," he admitted. "Tonio will be enjoying the waters of the Pacific now I have no doubt." The Conte was an enthusiastic, experienced sailor who kept a racing yacht moored at Savona. An avid follower of the America's Cup, which was now an international race that landlocked countries participated in, he was also a close friend of Alinghi's owner, Ernesto Bertarelli. The Contessa was tolerant of her husband's many absences, as he followed the yachting adventures around the world.

Being the heir to a pharmaceutical fortune enabled him to fund this expensive interest, and his many absences. The business was a family affair and they were happy to let him indulge himself, as the business was a well oiled functioning machine, which did not require his presence 24/7. Now they were branching out into the latest technologies, where even more vast sums of money could be earned. One of the richest families in Italy, they had built on the fortune that had amassed over centuries.

"When does he return?" The Cardinale politely enquired of the Contessa

"Oh, you know Tonio." Shrugging her elegant shoulders, she looked at the Cardinale through her Prada sunglasses, which shielded her beautiful emerald green eyes from the strong sunlight. What was really going on behind his cool demeanour? What were those black gimlet eyes hiding from the world, covered over by his religiosity?

"Only too well," the Cardinale agreed. He certainly did know his cousin and his obsession with sailing, which left his wife to dally with the unholy sisterhood of le Donna in Azzuro. As if her position in the upper echelons of European society did not fulfil her enough. Spoilt, indulged, the expected crowning apex of their lives being motherhood, what more could she want?

'This was the problem with educating women,' he sneered to himself. 'No matter how intelligent, their minds flitter off into romanticism,' and he had no patience with it.

Little did it matter, that his church was based on romanticism and was full of romantic symbols, by the most romantic of painters and sculptors.

They continued strolling through the beautifully laid out gardens, with large cypress trees shading the paths they chose.

"Are you going to the country soon Adelais?" he enquired.

The family owned a country estate in Tuscany, which they visited several times a year.

"No. I might go up to the villa at the Lake," Adelais responded. They also owned a beautiful villa on the shores of Lake Como. Not only could they enjoy the magnificence of this area in the summer months, but it was close to the Tyrol for the skiing in winter.

"When do you think you might leave?" he asked innocently enough.

"Oh, probably not for a month or so." Her hand reached out, as she bent down, cupping a rose in full bloom, the colour of ripe raspberries. She breathed in deeply the wonderful smell, reminding her of the perfume that she had specially made for her. The note buried in the perfume which she wore today, reached out gently to its origin and blended in the warm air surrounding her with its delicate scent.

The Cardinale watched this wife of his cousin covertly. This foreign interloper into the bosom of Roman society. High born she may be, but welcome she was not, in his book. Descended from the despised Trencavel family, with their worship of the church of the Nazarene, he believed the Guilianini family should have rejected her. It would not surprise him, if she had brought the wretched belief system with her and corrupted those women she mixed with, in her role of Tonio's wife.

He should have been aware, that the belief of Le Donna in Azzuro had spread throughout northern Italy and Mary Magdalene had been worshipped in the seat of Catholicism for centuries. Adelais had simply hooked up with them when she married Tonio.

However, it justified his madness and she had become a focus for his hatred.

Unable to stop his cock hardening under his cassock as he watched her, rather than admit his obsession and lust for her, he turned it against the object of his desire. In his eyes, she deliberately tempted him, attempting to make him stray from his dedication to the Lord, using disgusting artifices learnt from the Magdalene teachings.

His mind seethed and festered as he plotted, wheedling the information from her that he needed to plan how he would separate her from his cousin for all time; and punish her for trying to tempt him from his celibacy and love of his Lord. The fruit of her union with Tonio, must be destroyed as well.

It was time she produced another child. An Italian wife would have given Tonio more than one child and a male at that. He simply glossed over the fact, that science had proven the father's genes determined the sex of the child. He had a passing relationship with science, preferring the well documented facts of religion, on which to base his life.

"Perhaps we could take a run out into the country. Would you like that?" His handsome patrician face, concealed the loathing he felt.

Inwardly she shuddered, knowing there was little love lost between them. This man had shown his contempt for her on many occasions. Patronising her in public continually, she could not abide him. "I will be so very busy in the time between, but thank you for thinking of me. Your offer is most generous." Rather a walk around the roman forum with hungry lions stalking her, than an afternoon with him. He made her blood run cold within her veins.

*

Again they met at the monastery of St Gerard and the Cardinale had to convince his followers.

"It's dangerous to keep a prisoner now," one ventured, although noone was willing to stand up to the Protector.

"It's more dangerous erecting two crosses and carrying out two executions on the same spot. Don't you think they will be vigilant and watching that area for months to come," he sneered.

"That's true," the group muttered, but still uncertain, he had not won them over yet.

"Listen to my plan," he bullied them.

These were severe men, but the risk involved in one crucifixion was enough and their concern was apparent.

"We move to the next stage of the pageant." The Protector's head was down and as he clasped his hands together in front of his groin, his eyes raised to look at them from under hooded lids. "We bury her alive in the catacombs. Let's see if her false idol Mary Magdalene comes for her."

As one or two of the less strong stomachs revolted at the thought, he looked at them expectantly.

"How can we do that?" The Abate looked mystified. "Someone could hear her screams. It's far too dangerous."

"Do I have to do everything for you?" The Protector looked at the head of the monastery in disgust. "I will be the one who will have to bring them here and we use something to keep them malleable yet unable to move. Once I get them here we will use atropine to paralyse her. The mother can watch as we wall up the younger one until it's her own turn. They die alone in the catacombs."

"But atropine wears off," the dotorre priest amongst them volunteered.

"We would need to administer a dose large enough to last a day and a night, yet not kill them. Oh no, I do not want them dead, just paralysed and laying in the darkness of Lazarus's tomb. Let's see if her Miryai comes for her then."

"It's dangerous to administer such a large dose, she could die," the doctor insisted.

"No, I do not want her dead," the Protector snarled, seeing his exquisite plan unravelling. He would not allow it, as he desperately wanted to prolong this one's suffering. "We will not administer the dose for a day or so. You can then administer the largest safest dose, returning to top it up as required. That will see them out." His ice cold green eyes glittered like polished emeralds. "Keep the child as weak as a kitten and then with terror, grief and no food or water, she will die relatively quickly, but not before the third day."

"I still think it is risky, someone could see us going in and out," the doctor muttered reluctantly, knowing it would be he who would have to take the risk of administering the injections.

"There are catacombs that run under the monastery into the hills, we can use those and enter from within the building," the Protector reinforced his plan which had been worked out to the smallest detail.

"It would be dangerous bringing her in to the monastery and carrying her down to the catacombs." The Abate still looked unsure.

"Do I have to do all your thinking for you, as well as take all the risk? I will bring her in at the dead of night. I know her route to Lake Como and once I know the time, I will intervene by making sure the vehicle is faulty and will breakdown some miles into the country. I will turn up fortuitously and disable the car, before I transfer them to my vehicle and bring them here."

"The other brothers will see her then and wonder why we have her," one of the friars protested.

"Then make sure they are not around when I arrive with her. The dottore can administer to them." He nodded to the priest who would carry out the task. "Then we will put take them into the catacombs late at night, when all your brothers should be slumbering in bed, while one of you will drive my car to where theirs was left and move it away as though they have continued their journey to the Lake."

"It could work," one of the clerics murmured.

"It will work," the Protector growled. "I have planned this to the smallest detail."

"Well sometimes one of our brothers will wander into the chapel to pray or perhaps seek water in the kitchen."

"I don't care how you clear the halls that night, but make sure that you do. No-one must be about on that night."

The group looked at each other uneasily, wondering if The Protector was going too far this time.

"See it is done." His command was law and they dare not refute his idea. Angrily he walked around the inside circle that was gathered around him and spat out at them.

"Reconnoitre. Are you not God's army? The ancient Knights would not have hesitated," he challenged them. "Find the safest way and the safest catacomb. We'll stuff them behind the wine cellar. It has walls three feet thick, hewn out of the rock."

Chapter Thirty-four - The Arma dei Carabinieri's Utter Frustration

"Christo Santo," thundered Primo Capitano Carlino Fanelli. "Another woman has been abducted, this time with her child, a girl who is only eleven years old."

"The entire city of Rome is in a furore and our heads will roll if we do not find them before there is another sacrifice." He looked expectantly around at his men as though they could produce the missing persons from behind their backs. "What are you doing about this?"

Glumly his team looked back at him. Shaking his head, Carabiniere Claudio spoke first, inwardly cringing at the onslaught he believe he would unleash. "We haven't got a clue. Where would we begin to look?"

"How the hell would I know?" The expected retort rained down on their collective bowed heads. "That's what you lazy bastards are paid for. What have you done to find them?"

Heads turned towards the Crime board where the photos of the woman and child had been added to those of the other two women who were members of le Donne in Azzuro. All looking quite pitiful as there were too few links connecting the profile that gave them the trial they desperately needed. They had been taken, but to where, no-one had a clue.

"We have tried to trace their movements along the roads they should have taken to reach Lake Como." Rocco offered.

"There were no traces," muttered Guido sullenly. "They appear to have driven off and just disappeared."

"Oh gone to France for a holiday have they?" Tenente Ferdinand sneered in frustration, knowing he was being utterly unfair to his men who had worked their butts off, "and didn't leave a note for the family."

The team knew they were in trouble when the tenente turned acerbic and dumped on them.

"It's a possibility," volunteered Gianfranco.

"For God's sake, idiota. The family has rung half of bloody Europe trying to find them," the tenente looked at him witheringly, "and they speak half a dozen languages, so are familiar with the playground of the rich and famous throughout Europe. They aren't having any trouble being misunderstood."

The team decided discretion was the better part of valor here and sat mutely.

Umberto stepped in and tried to soothe the troubled water which was threatening to drown the squad.

"We've run up a profile on the killer or killers."

The team looked at him expectantly, glad to have the Lieutenant's focus diverted from them.

"We all agree a group has to be involved. It would be impossible for one person to have carried out these crimes without some help." Rocco looked at the board glumly, hoping for inspiration which did not come.

"We agree with you." Umberto signalled to his case leader *carabiniere scelt*, Gianni. The two teams had united to try and resolve the murders.

"We narrowed it down to a leader and followers." Gianni looked over the group and was pleased to see the resentment disappearing from the Arma di Carabinieres' faces. They were so frustrated by now they would take any help they could get.

"The most important one of the group is always the leader. He dreams this up, sets the direction and the others follow in his wake."

"So what do you have?"

"He's a charismatic leader in a position of power"

"Christo, he would have to be to get some maniacs to do this for him."

Gianni nodded in agreement. "Right. We figure he's late 40's to late 50's."
Now he had everyone's full attention. "Problems with women, probably mother
related. Self esteem issues which he internalises, appearing cold to others. On the
outside he appears confident and in charge, but on the inside when his control
mechanism is pushed and this would have to be an external jolt, he flips and reacts
with violence. In order to function with what appears to be normal, he functions
inside a highly structured organisation, with a very definite hierarchy. He sits
somewhere near the top of this group."

"Jesu," Rocco chimed in, "are you saying this nutcase could be in the church?"

"No, no," Umberto hastened to reassure him. "Although deep down he is
probably a religious fanatic, but you do not have to be in the church structure for
that."

"What, you're talking about someone in say a lay organisation connected with
the church, like Opus Dei?"

"It could be suicide to a burgeoning career, to openly make statements like
that," Umberto warned. "Let's just focus on this and see where it takes us."

"Allright," sighed the Capitano now he had vented his spleen, which
unfortunately did not make him feel better at all. "Scatter, try and plot something.
Turn the house upside down again. Ask questions. Look for the damn car that
seems to have disappeared into thin air. This is an important family and the husband
is powerful, not someone we want to make an enemy of. We've got enough of those
already."

"This family appears to have connections to the Vatican," Rocco gingerly
espoused, not willing to give up the religious fanatic connection.

"Every noble family in Rome has connections to the damn Vatican." The Primo Capitano snarled wishing Umberto had never brought up the subject. He had enough on his plate without Il Papa or one of his bossy Cardinales getting on his back. "So what?"

"Well….." Rocco dug his heels in not willing to give up the only lead he felt they had. "Should we at least make enquiries about those that are close to the Guilianini family? You never know what we might undercover."

"Great. Bring the Vatican down upon our heads as well. Clever idea." As the Lieutenant rounded on the poor fellow the others in the team were pleased they had not opened their mouths. "Next thing you'll be telling me the Knights of Malta are in on it because their mansion is on the top of the sodding hill where the last body was found."

"Well, someone mentioned a Cardinale was seen entering the Guilianini's son's palazzo during the day recently," the persistent fellow refused to give up what he saw as a lead.

"Good God man, don't you know how it works. Cardinales and monsignors are in and out of all the noble houses, eating fancy meals. The noble families have been providing the Church with high ranking priests for centuries and half the Vatican belongs to the Knights of Malta."

"Well, just a thought." Rocco looked embarrassed and shut up.

"Forget it. What would a Cardinale want with a woman and child, he's hardly setting up house with them in the Vatican is he?" With that the Primo Capitano stormed out and slammed the door muttering to himself, imagining the flak he would get if the squad got in Rome's nobility's collective countenances.

"How's the search for the wooden beams and bolts going?" Umberto thought some face saving was required.

"De Niente," Ferdinand said glumly, his aching feet reminding him they weren't about to cooperate for much longer. In fact a two foot rebellion was going on down there.

"Porca vacca," Rocco vented his frustration. "I think we should be looking in the area where the car disappeared. We're making enquiries about centuries old timber beams and bolts. Let's look for a monastery in the area."

"Well, that should narrow down the search," Ferdinand piped up sardonically. "There's only one around every damn corner in the countryside."

"Yeah, well you'd better get at it hadn't you if you want to complete the job this century." With that aside Umberto up and followed the lieutenant's recent escape route.

Muttering and cursing amongst themselves the two teams huddled together to decide their next move, even if it was simply polishing their gun of choice, the Beretta Model 12S 9mm submachine, with variants specially equipped with silencers, scopes and laser aim-point devices, ready for the charge of the Alamo when they finally found the culprits.

"I wonder if a traitor lurks inside one of these well connected families?" Ferdinand looked around the squad who stared back at him in alarm. One didn't mix with those heavy hitters.

"Just a thought," he shrugged.

Chapter Thirty-five – The Reconciliation

On the second night a figure appeared at the entrance of the tomb. Gaunt, shaggy and wild eyed Kepha slipped inside.

At the sight of him, Miryai caught her breath and held her daughter tight to her breast.

Yeshua gazed sadly at the broken wreck of a man before him. A single tear ran down his cheeks, as he exclaimed, "Kepha!"

The large man broke down. Tears streamed down his face and he sobbed so inconsolably. he could hardly speak. "Forgive me Yeshua, I have failed you twice. I do not know what came over me."

Turning to Miryai, he begged her forgiveness as well, "It was like the devil possessed my soul and I could not see or think straight."

He doubled over in agony and knelt before Yeshua who said. "Kepha, look at me."

Kepha was so ashamed, he shook his head. "Strike me dead now, so I cannot bring harm to you and Miryai."

"Kepha look at me," Yeshua commanded.

Reluctantly Kepha raised his eyes, to look upon the countenance he had loved so dearly.

"I tell you now. You are not to blame," Yeshua gently reassured him.

Kepha broke down again, "I turned my face from you when the soldiers arrested you my king. And because of my jealousy, I, who adored you above all men and believed I would protect from all evil, have attempted to destroy you and those you love."

"Kepha, take heed of me." Yeshua reached out to take Kepha's hand. "Like Judas Iscariot this was your destiny. It was out of your hands."

"Lord," Kepha raised his eyes, a dim light of hope gleaming. "It was my doing. It was my jealousy of your love for Miryai and the thought of losing you whom I adore with all my being, that made me betray you. I should kill myself like Judas."

"No, Kepha. That would pain me more than I could bear." Yeshua tried to explain to this simple rough fisherman, "my destiny was written as was everyone's. This was your fate to be tested further than you have ever been tested before."

"Why Lord, why?" Kepha was bewildered.

"This is the dance of life Kepha and everyone must play their part. I am no longer strong and healthy, therefore I must flee and you must remain here."

Kepha reached out with both hands and grasped Yeshua's tightly. "Let me come with your Lord, please I beg of you. Let me protect you all and be your rock."

Yeshua winced at the pain, that Kepha's grip on his damaged hands were causing and Kepha gasped when he realised and let go. Yeshua reached out and took hold of Kepha, although every movement caused him intense pain. It was almost too much for Kepha to take and he trembled violently.

"Listen to me Kepha. My time has come. I cannot make the journey to Egypt with my family. I was never intended to. I will go as far as I can, and then I will give up my spirit and return to the Inner Realms."

Kepha desperately tried to grasp what Yeshua was telling him.

"I have taught you the art of enlightenment through meditation. To look inside yourself for your link to the source who created us and whom we call Yahweh." Yeshua continued in a gentle voice, which soothed Kepha and calmed him down. "It is your time to practice this art. You must let go of cravings and attachments that will drag you down and anchor you to this earth plane."

"My Lord, as long as you remain on this earth plane, I want to be here to share it with you and protect you. I must make up for all the damage I have caused."

"No, Kepha. Be my rock. Your destiny is far greater."

The red mist that had clouded Kepha's thinking seemed to lift from him, and for the first time in days he could think clearly. "Yeshua what is it you need of me then?"

Although every movement hurt him, causing Miryai to draw in her breath, Yeshua reached out to draw Kepha close to him, and looking deeply into his eyes, told him of his destiny.

"Kepha, I want you to continue the teachings of the Brotherhood of Light. Lead my followers to safety and watch over them, so their numbers multiply and my word spreads throughout the world."

Looking at him quizzically, Kepha listened.

"Now you must be their rock, for I can no longer lead them."

Kepha flinched and whispered. "I am such a weak man. What if I fail you again?"

"You are strong enough Kepha. My family and my followers will be hunted and persecuted in Judaea whilst Herod lives, and you must protect them."

"Lord, I will do as you ask, though it breaks my heart to leave you." Turning to Miryai he begged. "Please forgive me for what I did to you. I was out of my mind with grief and jealousy."

Miryai had as much insight as Yeshu, and knew that Kepha's destiny had forced him to behave as he had. Now he would be much stronger and could look after the flock they had left behind. "I understand Kepha. It was your destiny and there is no forgiveness required."

At this, Kepha visibly relaxed and releasing a huge sigh, gazed upon them all with such love. "May I hold the child, just once? Please."

Miryai handed Tamar over to him. As he took her in his burly hands and massive arms, both she and Yeshua knew everything would be alright.

Kepha gently stroked the baby's face and his face glowed with love. Looking at Yeshua and Miryai he said. "I would like to go with you and protect her from harm whilst she is growing up."

The couple knew their own destinies and that Kepha's lay in another direction.

"Kepha I need you to look after my followers," Yeshua reminded him gently. "I need you to lead my flock to safety, as they are fragile and you must lead them in the art of the brotherhood as I taught you. The pure teachings have been corrupted by those who sought power. There is no need of priests for intervention with Yahweh, the source of all energy." Yeshua's face began to glow as Kepha listened. "Joses will help you."

Kepha's eyes lit up at this promise, as he did not know where he would get the strength from to look after himself let alone others, once Yeshua left them.

"I have taught you that it is wrong to sacrifice animals to Yahweh, as the priests do. It is an abomination in Yahweh's eyes, that the priests have set themselves above others and demand money to intercede on their behalf with him. This is why I was enraged with the money lenders in the Temple, as well as with the priests and the temple itself. The teachings have been perverted and my anger was great."

Kepha handed the child back to her mother and leaning forward, put his large head gently in Yeshua's lap. He breathed in the smell of his Lord once more, then raising his head he sat back on his haunches. "I will do as you say Yeshua."

"My destiny, was to be the sword that cleaved the priesthood's power and teachings. My throne is not destined to be an earthly one. The people turned their face from the heir of King David. Now is the time to teach about love and compassion for oneself, and all living beings on this earth."

"I hear you Yeshua." Kepha's soul found peace from his master's words, as he had during his life with him.

"You are not on your own Kepha. My 0x0d Joses, (James) will be by your side."

"I want you to know that in countries distant from here, two more prophets were born in recent times, who have also taught enlightenment to their own peoples. Everyone is able to commune with Yahweh directly. The Kingdom of Heaven lies within. The inner realms can be discovered."

"The secret of creation will be revealed to those who practice this art and they will go home to the source without fear or grief, for both of these emotions must be conquered. It is the cravings for the attachments of this world that blinds us and gives the power to negative emotions which rule us." Yeshua leaned back and sighed. "The priests are so corrupted by their love of riches that their hearts are cold and their minds clouded. Yahweh does not hear them, no matter how much they pray in his name, for they have closed the portal to him, with their greed and avarice for power."

"Who are these other people Yeshua? Will I ever meet them?" Kepha felt stronger, now he knew that in spreading the truth he was not on his own.

"You can meet them in the Inner Realms. One is called Siddhartha. He is a prince, who gave up all his riches and power, to go out and live amongst common men, to teach them the truth."

"Can I find him?" Kepha's eyes were shining.

"He lived in a country called Sakya (*Nepal)* and will come to you Kepha if you call for him. He has passed on to the Inner Realms now. Your power comes not from another person, but deep inside yourself. You can speak with both of them, if you go into the Inner Realms and ask them to come to you. They will understand our language, but you will not understand either of their earthly languages."

Kepha had struggled with the concept during Yeshua's ministry, preferring to be the bodyguard and protector of a royal line,

After three years of living with Yeshua and being trained to meditate, it was finally sinking in. He had been with his master every step of the way, when Yeshua needed the protection of a rough fisherman, but now was the time to leave anger and force behind. The mission against Herod and the Sanhedrin was over. It was time for a new mission, one of love and compassion and he could only achieve this, if he stayed in touch with the Inner Realms within himself and Yahweh would answer him.

"Who was the other person Yeshua? May I know?"

Yeshua's eyes shone, Kepha was beginning to question, to push out beyond his personal narrow boundaries. He had not been mistaken when he had chosen him to be his rock.

"Of course," he replied. "His name was Lao Tzu. He lived in Cina (*China*) and he showed the common people the Way, which he called the Dao. Another sage called Confucius lived there also, and he was very wise. His writings will survive through the centuries, but his message was for the aristocracy and the court of that land, to urge them to rule more wisely and benevolently." Yeshua smiled at Kepha.

"It was not for the common people, so Lao Tzu taught them the Way. He would not write down his teachings, as he believed they would become corrupted and turned into dogma." Yeshua reached out and put his hand on Kepha's arm

"What does that mean Master?" Kesha was a simple man, which is the reason that Yeshua had chosen him for his rock. An intellectual would be tempted to turn his teachings into dogma.

"It means the teachings can never be questioned."

"Is that not a good thing Master?" Kepha looked at him questioningly.

"No Kepha," Yeshua knew he had to reach this simple man before he left him, so he could help others. "Everyone must think things out for themselves." Here Yeshua touched his finger to his forehead. "They must not blindly follow other men and what they say. This is why the Romans and the Pharisees have such a hold over Judaeans. They must break their minds free. Not accept blindly what they say."

Kepha frowned and tried to get his head around this. "But they punish us if we do not do as they say, or think as they say we must think."

"What is punishment Kepha?" Jesus asked. "Is it working out for yourself, what is right for you and your family? Or allowing others to enslave your mind, telling you what to think and do? Is life worth living then?"

Kepha thought for a moment before agreeing. "Nooooo." It was a new concept for him and quite difficult to grasp. However, he was prepared to give it a go. A light went on in his brain. "And that is why people are rebelling against the Romans and their rule." A smile spread across his countenance and he looked at Yeshua proudly.

"That's true, but they must also break free from the Sanhedrin, who have a vested interest in telling them only the priests can talk with Yahweh." Yeshua tried to put it into simple terms, to reach this man he was relying on to help others. "That is not true. Everyone can speak directly to Yahweh. I have taught you this."

"Most of the time I do not feel Yahweh hears or answers me, Master." His face screwed up with the effort, of accepting the responsibility for his thoughts and feelings. Kepha looked at Yeshua anxiously.

"He hears you Kepha, but you do not hear him. You were afraid when you thought I would leave you. Afraid of how you would manage without me. You were still leaning on me weren't you?" Yeshua smiled at Kepha so gently and with so much love, that tears started in the disciple's eyes.

"You are right Master. I am beginning to understand. But I am still afraid to be without you."

"Trust me Kepha, when I say you are stronger now. You have fought your demons and are willing to stand alone now and let me go. You are my rock and will be the ray of light for those who listened to me. People will believe you. They would not believe a learned man. Trust me."

"I do Master." Kepha humbly knelt before Yeshua and kissed his tortured feet.

"Then arise Kepha," Yeshua lent forward and raised Kepha's head, then indicated with his hand that the latter must stand up straight.

"Stand proud and tall, Kepha. Do not kneel before any man. Be my rock. Be my light. Joses will stand beside you. You are not alone."

"I will serve you for the rest of my life," Kepha said simply and honestly.

"This is why I must entrust you with my teachings. I too fear, that if they are written down, they will be corrupted and become a dogma that unscrupulous men seeking power, will seek to rule in my name. I do not want this. You cannot read and write. Tell the stories and by the way you live your life, my truth will be known."

Yeshua knew that even the tradition of passing on doctrine orally, would corrupt his teachings, which is why the people must be taught self reliance and to seek within themselves, not rely on others.

"The knowledge is not only for the rich and powerful. It is time for the common people to be led back, to that which has been lost to them. They must know that the responsibility for their lives lies with them, and the course of their lives will be determined by their thoughts and actions."

"They will return lifetime after lifetime, until they reach the balance. There is no right, nor wrong, just achieving equilibrium. Only then they will be free of this earthly plan. They *can* do this. That is why prophets come to show you the way.

Teach them what I taught you about reincarnation and meditation. There is more than one life Kepha. Be honest and kind in this one and strive to reach the Inner Realms."

Kepha marvelled, that Yeshua thought him worthy of this knowledge and trusted him to tell others. "How do you know of these men who live so far away from us here in Judaea?"

Yeshua was delighted he had stimulated Kepha's mind. Now he knew all would be well. People would learn from a simple man, not a grasping, greedy intellectual, with only his own self interest at heart. "Because the teachings connect me to them and Yahweh who is the source of all things. All knowledge is made available to those that follow this path. Will you take on this task and lead the common people to enlightenment in my name Kepha?"

"I will Master." Kepha stood and looked upon the people he had lived with and loved for three years. He realised how privileged he was to have been part of it. His shoulders set and his bearing grew straight and tall, as he became Yeshua's rock once again. "I will do as you bid me and I will spend my time in meditation, until I reach Yahweh and your friends."

Bending down, he kissed Yeshua then turned to Miryai who reached up to him and drew him down to kiss his cheek.

"You will see us both in the Inner Realms when you meditate Kepha." Yeshua assured him. "I will come to you, when you call for me."

"And I Kepha," Miryai promised.

Gazing once more at Tamar, Kepha reached out his large gnarled hands and gently stroked her head, then turned and walked out with a backward glance, the tears starting in his eyes.

"Go with Yahweh, Yeshua and Miryai. Know that I am your rock Master, and I will not let you down again. I will question, I will ask and I will find out and keep my own truth for all time."

Yeshua raised his hand in blessing to Kepha, watching as he slipped out of the tomb. Sighing, his gaze fell upon his family that he loved so dearly and knew he must soon leave. Quietly he closed his eyes and drew within himself, accessing the inner realms through the portal at the base of his skull. A golden light streamed down through the top of his head and down his body, then expanded, protecting him and giving his strength to face what lay ahead.

*

On the third night there was no moon and no stars. Iosef brought four donkeys, one for each of them. Yeshua, Miryai who was cradling the baby, Mariam and faithful Joses.

Shimon, Yeshua's 0x0d was there to say his goodbyes. "OmO (*Mother),* may

Yahweh travel with you at all times. Yeshua wants me to remain and help Kepha, or I would be there to protect you on this perilous journey."

Mariam drew him to her breast and kissed him, "I know that my son. Yahweh will keep us safe and Joses will protect us."

Tears fell down their gaunt faces as they bid farewell to Iosef, who looked upon them sadly, believing he would never see their dear faces again in his lifetime.

Reincarnation was part of their belief and he knew he would meet them again in another realm, Yahweh be praised. If he was willing, Herod would pass from this life and they could return safely to Judaea. Maybe he would still be alive, but he doubted this, as he was an old man now and time was short.

As he watched the two women in their blue robes and head coverings ride a donkey out of this life of his in Judaea forever, he was contemplative.

The donkeys picked their way carefully up the Mount of Olives and began a journey that would take the fugitives into Nabatea (*Jordan).* Here they would remain until it was safe to journey on to Assyria, then Egypt and in time, once

Herod had died, return to their homeland. It was a dangerous journey, fraught with risks, as brigands and soldiers laid in wait to kill and loot from wayfarers.

Yeshua's health suffered, and despite the ministrations of friendly physicians and apothecaries along the way, as they sheltered in caves and the homes of supporters, he could not stop long enough, to rest sufficiently to heal his broken body and soul. Eventually they reached the town of Nitzana, a station on the incense route, in the capital of Sela (*Petra*), where they rested in the house of Hellel, a wealthy Judaean merchant.

The Nabateans were one of the most resourceful people of the ancient world. A nomadic Arab tribe, who mastered the desert as no others had done before them. When they settled down, bringing not only their merchandise but, more importantly, cultural and spiritual ideas from Asia to Mediterranean Europe during the Roman period, their cities became model centres of agriculture and horse breeding. Their ingenious water management systems, which are still studied today, permitted them to build magnificent cities, leaving the legacy of their most wondrous rose coloured Petra.

Resting in the courtyard which was resplendent with black iris, tartar lily, wild tulip and oleander, all cascading down from the balconies leading off from the main rooms of the two storey dwelling, Yeshua's head hung low.

Soft footsteps approached and he raised his head to gaze on Miryai, wearing the blue robe that was her right as a Virgin of Light. Her long black hair fell down around her beautiful face, as he gazed into her deep brown eyes that drew him down into the depths of her being when they were together. Her dusky skin was like satin when he caressed her. The past year had taken its toll on her. The once strong body had lost the flesh from her bones and was so light under the robe; it reminded him of a dandelion on its delicate stem. One puff of breath and perhaps she would dissipate into the air, like the flower he felt she resembled now.

His strong minded Miryai from Migdal, the fishing village, on the Sea of Galilee with her will honed with her early teachings, as his had been.

One soul formed from two. Both knew their lives would be short, as they carried out their purpose on Earth for this lifetime.

"You must go on without me," he begged Miryai, as she sat down beside him. "I can go no further."

"I will not abandon you," Miryai protested and put her hand on his, as it lay listlessly on the bench. Holding his shattered hand in hers, the tears began to fall again. These days, they appeared to constantly shine in the depths of the windows of her soul. Then like a constant soft rain that falls from the heavens, they would trace a delicate pattern on her beloved face, but alas without the power to renew Yeshua.

"Soldiers have been making sorties into the countryside after us and we must reach Egypt where we will be safe," she urged him.

"I cannot make the journey," wearily he turned to her, urging her to leave. "You must take the child and see she is safe. Get her to Egypt."

"I will not leave without you." Again Miryai shook her head and held on to him, her eyes fierce and determined.

Joses walked into the courtyard and wandered over to them. "We must get ready to move on." Gently he put his hand on Yeshua's head. "My 0x0d they seek us."

Yeshua raised his head and looked lovingly at his older sibling. "I know, but I can go no further."

Fear beat in Joses' breast like a small mouse caught in the talons of a falcon. "0x0d (*Brother*)." Dropping to his knees in front of Yeshua, he begged him, "you must find the strength."

"I want to Joses," Yeshua assured him, but my body and spirit are too broken. Look." He gestured to his feet and hands which were twisted where the bones had not mended straight where the nails had broken them. "What use am I to you?"

"We only want to care for you," Joses wept and looked imploringly at his mother, who shook her head sadly, "as you have always cared for us."

"My time is over Joses." Yeshua put his crippled hand on Joses" head and caressed his hair. "You must be the head of the family now and take them where they will be safe. You will travel faster without me."

"Aha, if we can move past Antioch Herod will not pursue us further." Joses sought to bring strength to Yeshua. "The Romans do not care about us. A radical activist in Judaea means nothing to them, once he is defeated. The movement was put down and the fire put out. Rome does not fear us. As long as we are not in Judaea, the Sanhedrin and Herod do not fear us. Move on to Assyria with us and we can rest there longer."

Yeshua shook his head, "Joses, my time has come. I know. I must accept it. "

The little group gathered together and wept bitter tears. They had been through so much in the past four years, during Yeshua's mission.

The unfulfilled promise of peace on earth. So near, yet out of reach for them. Deep down inside, they knew the truth. If they insisted, Yeshua would die on the way. Here he could die in peace and some measure of comfort.

"You must stay here Yeshua," their host insisted. "We will care for you and see your last days are peaceful. You will be loved." Turning to Miryai he confirmed Yeshua's words. "You must go on, your child is important to the house of David."

Miryai tore her hair and rent her robe. "I will not leave without my husband." Desperately she began to wail.

"Miryai," Gently Yeshua spoke to her. "There is nothing to fear. I accept my fate. I cheated death once, but the spirit moves over me now, waiting to take my hand and lead me to heaven."

"No, my husband, no." Miryai clung to him in desperation.

"Miryai." a soft voice said and a gentle hand went out to stroke her hair. Lifting her gently to her feet, Mariam begged her, "Your duty and your child must come first. I cannot bear to lose my son again. I lost him once before, but we are of the House of David and know our duty. You must do as Yeshua bids you."

Miryai fell to the floor wailing again, renting yet more of her robe, as befitted an Aramaic woman in mourning.

Yeshua rose painfully and sunk down beside her. "Miryai, you are the dearest thing in this world to me, but I beg you to take our child to safety. Teach her to sing and dance as a young maiden, play the cymbals, spin a top. Leave me."

Raising her head, she gazed upon the man she had loved for twenty five years. They had known each other since he was eight years old and she six. Trained by the Nazarenes from young children and married by them at the age of eighteen and sixteen, leaving together on their studies in Egypt.

"I will see you again Miryai, in heaven as promised. For it is written, we will not need to return to this earth again." Yeshua held her as tightly as he could in his weakened state, kissing her eyes, her face and her lips.

Taking his hands, she kissed them then standing up, she lifted him and placed him on the bench in the courtyard. Bending down, she uncovered her long hair and washed his feet with her tresses.

"Oh Miryai." Tears rolled down Yeshua's face and fell on to her head. "How I have loved you."

Turning to Mariam he held out his gnarled hand. She went to him and sat beside him. "OmO, I have loved and honoured you above all others." Lifting his hand, he gently stroked her hair and face, the love shining out of his eyes like a beacon, his face softening as he bent to kiss her.

"My son," Mariam was heartbroken as she looked on her son, the heir of the royal bloodline who had been chosen to ascend King David's throne. She could not bear to see him like this. The price had been too high.

Placing gentle kisses on his face and hands, she knew she had to leave him. Being part of the Royal House of David was hard, perhaps too hard to bear.

Miryai stood up and sat down on Yeshua's other side. Together the three of them mourned, whilst Joses watched.

"I will not leave you," Miryai was determined and Joses and Mariam knew she was determined to remain. "I will tend you for as long as you have," she told her true love.

Mariam, Joses and Yeshua looked at each other, knowing Miryai would not be convinced otherwise.

"Joses." Yeshua drew himself up as best he could. "Take OmO and Tama, to safety."

Miryai looked at him as though he had struck her. "Yeshua, no," she protested.

"Either you go and keep her safe, or you let her go Miryai. Choose." Yeshua implored her, hoping she would leave.

All hope fell from Miryai. Her head hung down and her body slumped. In a few moments, she had aged ten years. How could she make such a decision? It was unbearable.

"Miryai," Mariam whispered. "We must go," and she held out her hand and lifted Miryai's chin, looking into her eyes with such a deep love and intensity, that the younger woman felt overcome. "This must not be the end of the Davidic lineage."

"It is my destiny to remain with Yeshua," she whispered. "Take Tamar, I place her in your care, Omo and Joses." Raindrops from her eyes fell to the ground and the sun turned them into little pools of sparkling pain. "If we survive, I will follow you."

"Let me remain here with my son," Mariam implore her, "and you go with your child. You still have much work to do."

"No OmO." Miryai knew deep in her heart, that their time had come. She had learnt her religious instruction well. If it was time to return to Yahweh, so be it. If that was part of the eternal plan she could not change it. "Our time has come," she declared.

"I must stay with him. You know that." Imploringly she looked at the older woman with the wonderful serene face, who had been like a mother to her. How she loved her and trusted her completely, to raise Tamar. She would keep her safe and keep alive the memory of her mother and father.

Indeed Mariam would. This was the way it had been since they were children. The plan had failed and now they would pay the price. Her heart wrenched with pain when she thought of how close her son had come to death, been saved, only to die this short time later.

Herod still feared Yeshua greatly. If the heir to the *divine* bloodline of the House of David remained alive, he count mount another challenge against him to call himself King of the Jews. He had not succeeded in killing her son yet, but he would not stop until Yeshua was no longer a threat to him.

Bowing her head, she accepted their fate and her responsibility, hoping she could make the arduous journey and see the child to womanhood.

Joses went into the house and brought out Tamar, a gentle, quiet child who was now one year old. It was almost as though she knew of the fate that hung over her family and appeared wise beyond her years. Going over to her OmO and Jwhyhb0, they embraced her and washed her face and hands with their tears of love.

"Go quickly." Miryai's voice cracked and she turned her head away. "Omo and Joses, love Tamar and keep her safe until I come to you."

"Always sister," Joses promised, his own eyes full of pain and tears as he doubted she would live to make the journey. "We will wait and look for you."

Turning to Yeshua he enfolded him in his arms. "You Aha, I honour and respect above all men and shall always hold you in the highest esteem. In times of turmoil, I will see your radiant face before me and I will call upon you to guide me in your wisdom."

"Joses, I will ever be with you," Yeshua promised. "Stay in Assyria or Egypt, until Herod dies. I can tell you now it will only take five years. Then it will be safe for you to return to Judaea. Once the Sanhedrin knows I am dead, they will not pursue you further."

Their host led four horses into the courtyard. "You must travel more swiftly than you have. Legionnaires are on your heels." They mounted the horses, Joses placing Tamar in front of him. "I am sending a trusted servant with you and here is money." He handed them bags of coins refusing their protests. "It is an honour to serve the House of David."

Gesturing to the fourth horse which had saddlebags and water bags slung around it. "There is also food and water for three days."

Yeshua and Miryai watched the forlorn little band leave the courtyard and ride out through the gate. Joses and Mariam turned back once and gazed upon the couple in the courtyard, feasting their eyes upon them. Mariam knew this was the last time she would see her son and Joses must now be the leader of this small family. How she prayed Miryai would come safely to join them.

Chapter Thirty-six – The Taking of the Woman and Child

All had gone as planned and now the Cardinale paced the floor in his excitement, pure hatred oozing out of every pore as his maniacal eyes lanced the terrified woman and child.

"Whore," he spat the word out disdainfully. "How dare you pass your evil daughter off as the daughter of a nobleman." He spat on them both.

"Mama," the child whimpered.

"Silencio," the Cardinale roared so loudly, the child shrank back into her mother's arms, burying her head into her bosom to hide from the madness emanating from this tall figure, who strode around the room like the three furies from Dante's hell.

"Leave my child alone," the woman defied him.

"Your whelp will be destroyed along with yourself. Your ilk will not be allowed to walk this earth," the monster bellowed.

Watching her beloved daughter shrink into herself at the vicious onslaught, the Contessa tightened her arms around her, and once again defied him. "You're mad. Tonio will kill you when he discovers what you have done, to the woman and child he adores."

"Adores?" the Cardinale roared at her. "When I tell him the truth he will be through with adoring. He will hate the very sound of your names."

"You are a poisonous snake," she retorted bitterly. "All these years in the bosom of our family and your fanaticism has rotted your brain away."

"Heretic. I serve my Lord," he hissed at her, "and you with your games of the Magdalene whore. You dare to suggest my pure and precious Lord married a prostitute."

"She was no prostitute. She was Miryai, the co-redemptor and priestess in her own right, and they were married. Your precious Church subverted and twisted the truth, to serve the ends of evil men such as yourself." Although terrified, something gave her the strength to lash out at this man she had known all her married life.

Sneering he bent over her and raised his hand as though to strike her, then raised his other, until his robes once again billowed around him, giving the impression of a vulture about to sink his beak into the dead flesh of his victims and rip them to shreds.

"You will be cast into the inferno, where your despicable Magdalene is made to suffer in that eternity outside time." As the sewer that passed for his mind festered and fomented, he snarled. "They nailed My Lord to a cross like an ordinary thief." Suddenly he spun on his heel and swept out of the crypt, slamming the door behind him. Hearing the key turn in the lock she despaired for herself and her child.

Striding up the stairs, emotions tearing at his soul, he hurried to the chapel where he prostrated himself before the altar with the image of his icon hanging from the cross above his head.

Chapter Thirty-seven– Yeshua's Death

Seated in the courtyard, they awaited their fate, serene in the knowledge they would ascend to the Inner Realms together. It was a warm clear day and the courtyard protected them from the sun, filtering the light and heat, so they were bathed in a cocoon of serenity.

A beautiful metalmark butterfly fluttered around their heads and landed on Miryai's shoulder. It was exquisitely marked, being predominantly black with white spots, whilst its front wings were bright orange in the centre with the black and white spots at the ends; and its body metallic blue. Smiling, their eyes locked, together in love, and they felt as one.

"What is the butterfly doing here so far from the sand dunes?" Miryai whispered.

"It has come to lead us home," Yeshua's tone was deep. Miryai had always loved the deep timbre of his voice, which reached deep into your heart, as it had done with the people of Judaea. He could tune your emotions like a lyre player with his instrument, and just being in his presence, you would hear songs in your soul. It had been enough to share his life and now it was enough for her to be here with him now.

As members of Royal Houses both Mariam and herself had been conceived and reared according to ancient Nazarene laws of purity and purpose. They had come to teach humanity alongside Yeshua and rule.

As Virgins of the Celestial light they had worn the blue robes whilst the community as a whole wore white garments. Women descended from David's House, or marrying into it wore the blue robes and Mariam and Miryai's roles were defined at birth.

In Judaean times, a Virgin meant a young maiden from the Aramaic-Hebrew *bethua*; and does not deny or imply any prior sexual activity.

The Nazarene studied all religions, such as the teachings of the ancient Chaldeans, Zoroaster, Hermes Trismegistus, the Revelation of Enoch, Moses secret instructions and a form of Buddhism. Each religion was considered another stage of the revelation of the whole.

They knew they would only remain on earth for a short time and it was important to keep their eternal souls pure by strict discipline, not to compromise nor bear false witness or falsehoods. They were the guardians of the Divine Teaching. How she had gloried in the very ancient manuscripts that had opened up their minds. Translating and reproducing them, so they could be passed on to future generations and show them the way to Eternal Life.

Both Yeshua and herself had loved being in the Brotherhood/Sisterhood, on the path of evolution that would take them through the cycle of their incarnations, until the purity of their souls finally reached their apex and there was no longer a need to return to earth.

They came, as they knew they would, the Roman soldiers who were carrying out the bidding of the Sanhedrin. Yeshua and Miryai were ready.

Firstly came the clattering of horses' hooves, followed by heavy footsteps and the shouts of the soldiers, seeking their prey, as they had done since time immemorial. Fists hammered on the door. Loud voices demanded admission. They could hear the chatter of nervous servants, running helter skelter in panic.

"Miryai my beloved, you must escape," he begged her. "You must pass on the ancient beliefs to a struggling world, which has been deprived of them for so long."

"No Yeshua, I will not leave you." Miryai drew him close to her.

"Please my beloved. You must." The anguish on his face tore into her soul, as he insisted. "You must continue the royal bloodline and also teach the people the truth. Teach them they are part of the Divine Being and need no priest to intercede for them. God listens when they speak."

"The ministry is now yours alone and the disciples *will* follow you. You must ensure that Tamar carries on the word *and* the bloodline after yourself. Her children must carry the knowledge forward and each generation into the far future, must pass this on to the people."

"No," she wept. "They will not listen. They did not listen to us."

"Aah my beloved." Reaching out, Yeshua put his finger beneath her chin and lifted it so her eyes met his. "You know better. An enlightened age will arise and the truth will be accepted with joy."

The strong deep voice of their host questioning the intruders' presence, penetrated to them, as he opened the door. They heard the soldiers brushing him aside, demanding to know where Yeshua and Miryai were.

They could hear the chattering of the soldier's pleated leather skirts and the clumping of their sandals, as they clattered into the courtyard. Finally, they were surrounded by the intruders, loud voices berating them. "Ha, King of Jews! Look at you now."

Rough hands pulled them apart, forcing them upright then striking them both.

Yeshua collapsed as his frail body was unable to withstand the rough treatment. Clutching at his chest, he heaved, trying desperately to draw breath.

Miryai uttered little cries of love, as she tried to reach him. The soldiers, led by Basius, cursed them both, as they watched Yeshua. They had been instructed to take him back to the Sanhedrin in Jerusalem, who would judge them both.

Miryai broke free and flinging herself down beside him, she cradled his head in her lap. His eyes opened and gazed with love at her. She heard, rather than saw, the sword fall before it struck her.

"Don't! The leader screamed at the unfortunate soldier, who had drawn his sword, and attacked. "Put that sword away. Our instructions are she is not to be harmed."

The unfortunate man flushed and his sword fell to his side.

Miryai felt, rather than saw the warm blood cascade out of her, as her head swam and everything went out of focus.

Yeshua reached out his hand to her and with her last piece of strength, she took it and they lay together, her mind returned to happier times. Whilst their training had been rigid and austere, there were happy carefree times.

The young men and maidens of Judaea were taught to express themselves through song and dance. The rhythmic swaying of the maidens' bodies and their nimble steps, spelt out the dance of the creation. The tinkling notes of cymbals, as their melodious voices sang songs and psalms of praise.

Miryai heard Yeshua breathe his last with a gentle sigh, and felt him leave for the Inner Realms, to rest in peace for all time.

It was as though the very essence had been torn from her body. Collapsing beside him, she rejoiced at his release and waited to follow him, but her spirit remained stubbornly bound to the earthly realm.

"He's gone. What do we do now?" a soldier asked of their leader.

"Herod wants us to return to Rome with his body, to reassure himself he is dead."

"Will they crucify him again?"

"I wouldn't think so. The family will be allowed to bury him."

"What about her?"

Miryai felt a heavy sandal nudge her body.

"Stay your hand and sword," the leader warned the soldier again. "We will take her back to Herod. He can decide her fate. Bind her wound."

Bundling them both on the top of a litter, Yeshua's body and Miryai were dragged back to Jerusalem. Miryai begged to be allowed to die, but it was not to be.

Brought before Herod, as the Sanhedrin wanted to wash their hands free of stain once again, once he was reassured Yeshua was truly dead, he told Miryai.

"You are banished from this land," he told her. "Take him," he sneered and gestured to Yeshua's body, "and bury him. Then you leave, never to return to Judaea in your lifetime." He snarled. "If you do, you will be crucified."

Standing before him blood caking her head where she had been struck and on her robe, she challenged him. "Why? What threat are we to you?"

"None at all," he sneered. "You are banned for practicing sedition."

Turning to Iosef of Arimathea who was supporting her, she looked at him bemusedly.

"Come Miryai," he encouraged her. "You are exhausted and I need to heal you."

"What will I do?" she asked of him.

"I will heal your body, Miryai and then you will follow Mariam and Joses to Assyria, where you will be safe. When Herod dies you can return to Judaea."

Reluctantly she followed Yeshua's last wishes and joined the little family in Assyria, where they remained, as they had found the safety they sought. It would be fruitless to continue on to Egypt.

"Miryai," Joses came to her respectfully. "You are my 0x0d's OaRKHiYMeA (*beloved one*). You must have a protector and Tamar a Jwhyhb0. I will marry you Miryai, in order to provide you with all that has been taken from you."

It was the Aramaic way. And so they were wed, and Joses and Miryai produced two sons, which enabled the royal bloodline of David to continue.

When Herod died five years later, as Yeshua had predicted, they returned to Judaea and carried on the ministry of the Nazarene.

Together with Yeshua's disciples, Miryai ran the ministry that he had began and with the disciples spread his word, until she slipped from the world at the age of fifty-three, leaving their daughter Tamar and her sons byJoses, to carry on the teachings.

From small beginnings, the ministry and its flock grew, left in peace by the Romans. The women dressed in robes of blue and carried on the role of Miryai.

Chapter Thirty-eight – Edoardos in The Secret Archives

Under the guise of further research for his department, Edoardos had returned to the Secret Archives in the Tower of Winds, which were guarded by an enormous pair of brass doors with a bas relief of Old Testament scenes.

After passing through these, he ascended a narrow winding staircase until he came to the Index Room and continued on until he reached the Old Study Room, with its high vaulted ceiling and life-size statues of saints set into niches in the walls. He never tired of the view from the large windows which overlooked the Vatican Gardens.

Due to his position, he was indeed fortunate that he enjoyed privileges that gave him licence to explore at will, without hindrance. There were no restrictions on what he could access and over the years had been privy to some of the most important secrets of the Vatican. Wisely he had kept his counsel, as to do otherwise would have meant with the end of his career, and would have besmirched his reputation for life. Of course he had to tread lightly, or he could bring down his family as well.

One kept faith with the Vatican, or risked the likelihood of being utterly destroyed; literally, if the rumours regarding Il Papa John Paul I were to be believed. Earlier Papas had been poisoned and murdered, but it beggared belief that this could happen in this age. There was no denying the suspicious circumstances regarding his death, and the secrets of The Vatican was paramount, as the institution fought to retain them, against the ever invasiveness of the electronic media.

Pausing in the Study room with its card catalogues and rows of desks with reading lights and power plugs for computers, he plugged in his laptop, then logged in and entered his password. Pulling up the computerised file indexes to see if a particular title caught his eye, if he felt it was relevant to their quest he would open the file and quickly skim it.

It was slow and laborious work, so taking a stab in the dark, which was all he could do, he started by earmarking any reference to Mary Magdalene. Not wanting to call undue attention to himself, he chose two from the highly secretive vault cache and another four from easily accessible ones.

"I can spread the risk this way," he reassured himself, looking around the Study room. "After all, I've been down here quite a bit lately." If he did not find what he was looking for amongst the smaller areas of the 84 kilometres of shelving in the Vatican Archives, he could search the Vault which had recently been completed and ran the full length of the Vatican Museum.

"Hmmm," his memory gave him a gentle nudge. "You weren't asking for documents about Mary M at that stage." Giving his memory a nudge to move over, he continued to pore over anything that held a glimmer of hope.

To seek out the document he had been tasked with finding for Monsignor Galasso, he took the elevator down to the vast fireproofed subterranean vault with its climate control to protect the ancient papyri. Gazing upon the row after row of utilitarian metal shelving housing would be intimidating, if he had not noted the exact location and he went directly to it.

Whilst in this closely guarded area, he would take advantage of the opportunity to pull up some Magdalene documents. It was a slow process, as he could only remove and work on one file at a time.

When he had located the document for his superior, he took it over to one of the tables, turned on the goose necked lamp and spent a half an hour poring over it and making notes, then returned the file to its location.

Glancing around to see if he was alone, he spent the next half an hour removing one file at a time, that he thought might be of interest to Lina, but failed to find anything of relevance to their quest, so he took the elevator back up to the Archive of the Secretariat of State, with its rooms of seventeenth-century walnut cabinets. As the file he wanted was out of reach, he hauled over the tall library ladder and clambered up to bring down the box.

Tables and the goose necked lamps favored by the Vatican had been set up in the area and he carried the box to the nearest table, laid it down and lifted the lid. Inside lay a treasure of ancient texts. Pulling on thin white gloves, with the greatest care, he eagerly looked through the parchment scrolls. To his disappointment, there was nothing illuminating about them.

"You have not found what you seek have you?" Startled, Edoardos looked up to see the Head Archivist, Archbishop Ruggiero standing beside him with a rolled scroll of parchment in his hand.

As Edoardos gazed at him, he continued. "For three days now I have watched you pore over any documentation relating to Mary Magdalene.

"Well," he sputtered, not knowing what to say, anxious he would put a foot wrong. "To be honest, I am not really sure, I'm checking cross references, which I hope will prompt me to find whatever it is we seek."

"We?" the archivist looked at him searchingly, then smiled. "I have seen you come away, your face reflecting your disappointment."

Edoardos dropped his eyes, to the document on the table in front of him. Another fruitless search and doubtless it showed.

"Let me replace these documents." Placing the rolled scroll of parchment down, the Archivist carefully retrieved the documents Edoardos had been searching through.

"Here are fresh gloves." Placing two thin white gloves on the table in front of Edoardos, he bid him put them on. "I suggest you carefully scroll down to the middle and move forward from there."

As Edoardos' frustration was eight, on a scale of zero to ten, he was willing to give anything a go at this stage. Puzzled he watched the archivist leave the room, before taking off the gloves he had been previously using, pulling on the fresh ones and turned to the bound ledger.

Carefully unrolling the scroll which appeared to be a record by Justus of Tiberias, the most well known Jewish historian of that era, he wondered at the relevance, as previous research of his writings had not elicited a mention of Jesus, although he lived not far from Tiberias.

The Jews were meticulous administrators and although many records were lost during the destruction of the Temple of Jerusalem in 70 AD, some writings had survived from those times. As well as Justus, there was Philon of Alexandria and Josephus Flavius, who had penned Jewish Antiquities, but his later writing of *"Testimonium Flavianum"*, conveniently discovered in 300 AD when Bishop Eusebius was recording the history of the Christians for the Emperor Constantine, was generally dismissed as a forgery.

Studying the text in front of him, it appeared they were records of some kind. What were they? Names, places and dates appeared before him in ancient Hebrew, which he had studied at Theology College.

The scroll was almost to its full length now and his eyes alighted on the record on the third line across. He froze, as though he had been turned to a pillar of salt.

Yeshua haNotzri(Yeshua of Nazareth), η Μαγδαληνή Μαρία (Miryai of Magdala). Betrothal – Marriage- Cana

The words swam before his eyes, spitefully refusing to make sense, so he blinked rapidly to clear them. Refocusing, he read them through again, then shaking his head to clear it, tried to take in what he saw.

Although it was indistinct, he could make out the words, although he peered until he was almost blind, he could not make out the date and found himself holding his breath.

"Breathe Padre," a soft voice urged him.

Discord settled in his mind and body, jangling his nerves with icy tendrils that tangled through his fogged brain that was trying to make sense of what he saw before him.

Hearing a rustling sound beside him, he lifted his gaze, as the Head Archivist smiled and sat beside him. "Why?"

"Because it is now time," The Archbishop answered.

"Why would you show me this?"

"One of our own is now in danger."

Rubbing his forehead with the heels of his hands, Edoardos tried to focus once more. "Where did you get this?"

"My family has kept this treasure from the 13th century, when we lost our lands and titles in the Albigensian crusade."

"You were Cathars?"

"No, we were the followers of the Church of the Nazarene, which flourished in the Languedoc but the crusaders made no distinction. They killed everyone in sight."

"How did you survive to this day?"

"A few fled to Cordova, where some recanted their faith and became Catholics."

Edoardos was so flummoxed, he was lost for words.

"Padre, I am going to trust you with a highly volatile secret. We kept out faith deep in our hearts and some returned to the Languedoc when it was safe once more, while others ensured they buried themselves deeply in the Vatican."

"The church would not have fallen for that? How do you explain your position here?" Edoardos found it hard to believe what he was hearing.

"Oh indeed. It took a long time to prove the sincerity of our conversion and obeisance to the Holy Roman Catholic Church."

Edoardos simply did not know what to say but gave it his best shot. "Why would you trust me to keep your secret? I am a priest of the Holy See."

"I have been told that you will hold this close to your heart."

"But what are you doing here?" Edoardos' mind tried desperately to grasp the connection and made a sweeping gesture that included the entire Vatican, while he waited wondering how the archivist would respond.

"You know the saying Padre, *Hai Capito bene?* The safest of all hiding places is in plain sight."

Yes, Edoardos did understand the reasoning behind this, but how did a man who had maintained the simple belief of the early Christians, become the Head Archivist in the Holy See? It beggared belief.

"But how did you achieve this?" Reasoning he should be considering this bombshell such a treacherous act, he should immediately report it to his superiors. Instead he found himself listening for the explanation.

"Centuries of patience Padre. It took until the 16th century for one of us to become the Head Archivist and we have ensured we retained that position until now."

"Why now?"

"The time is right and she is the last."

Startled Edoardos grasped the man's arm. "What do you mean?"

"Now the truth will be known. All we ever strove to be were good men and women Padre. I leave you to do what you will." Gently removing Edoardos' hand, he gathered the scroll and made his way back down to the basement. Placing the scroll in a secret compartment only he knew of, he locked it carefully and sat quietly to meditate.

Edoardos sat in silence, until he felt he could breathe comfortably again. Retracing his steps, leaving the archivist to ensure the tower was secured; he returned to his office and began work on the paper he was tasked with delivering to the Under Secretary Monsignor Galasso.

Hours passed when he finally raised his head, stretched fully and let his mind wander back to the scroll he had been privileged to see. He knew the die was cast. Knowing what he had seen with his own eyes, he knew he could not turn back now.

His mind in turmoil, his faith in tatters, he reflected on his heritage and wondered if it had all been worthwhile. In the pursuit of power and wealth, the Guilianini family had been complicit in perpetuating the fable that Pope Leo X, born Giovanni di Lorenzo de' Medici in the 16th century, had no hesitation in openly declaring "*this myth* of *Jesus has served us well.*"

After centuries of loyalty to the Church, could he break the bond that bound the Guilianini family to the Vatican, and incur their displeasure?

Did he care whether they disowned him, if he left Holy Orders and made a life with Lina?

After all, the aforesaid Pope Leo X, the second son of *Lorenzo il Magnifico* of Florence, was one of many Pope who had been married.

Edoardos was well aware that the concept of celibacy had been introduced into the Roman Catholic church by Pope Leo X's cousin, Giulio di Guiliano de' Medici, who succeeded him as Pope Clement VII. The aim had been to ensure the wealth remained safely, in the Church's coffers which previously had been endangered by priests' wives making claims on it.

Clement VII had also been a Knight of Rhodes, the forerunners of the current Knights of Malta, which Lisa was hell bent on exposing.

Feeling decidedly out of sorts, he picked up the phone and called Lina, committing himself to the cause and arranging to meet her on the following day.

Chapter Thirty-nine– Edoardos' Crisis of Faith

Edoardos' family were out of their minds with worry about Adelais and Tamar. They had simply disappeared from sight. No ransom demands, nothing.

Every favor from well appointed people had been called in, but nothing had come to light.

Edoardos had shared with Lina, the secret that the head archivist had shown him and how he was now experiencing a crisis of faith.

"Do you really believe you could walk away from your life?" Lina was doubtful.

"I don't know," Edoardos admitted miserably. "It's what I do. It's all I know."

"Then you will not break away." Lina was convinced of this.

"I have considered it."

"Then break away and get a job as a banker."

The priest derided that suggestion, "I could not get a job as a banker, if I walked away from my appointed destiny. My family would feel completely betrayed and I would be cast aside."

The thought filled Lina with pity for him, as she tried to persuade him he could be wrong. "Surely not, in these modern times," and she chewed her bottom lip as she waited for him to continue.

"Is that how small and weak I am?" Anguish showed on his face, as he looked inside his soul and questioned himself. "Is that all there is of me? Am I just an extension of an ancient system?"

Lina went to him; and put her arms around him. "Edoardos, you don't have to be this incredibly strong and powerful person, who has to do someone else's bidding."

He put his arms around her and leaned his head towards hers. "How do I know? I have never been forced to face it until now," he whispered, softly taking in the scent of her.

"I'm so sorry." Tears started in Lina's eyes and rolled down her cheeks. "If I hadn't started this investigation, you wouldn't be here questioning and doubting yourself."

As he pulled his head back and looked at her, he raised her chin and wiped her tears with the sleeve of his cassock. "It's not your fault. I would have come to the crossroads one day. Every time I kneel before an altar now, I feel such a hypocrite."

Snuffling, she wiped her nose on the sleeve of her t-shirt

"Oh that's so elegant Lina," Edoardos softly laughed. "Your lack of pretentious is what I love about you."

A wet smile flowed across her face. "It's who I am and I'll never change."

"And that's what I love about you. You are true to yourself."

"You've never been a hypocrite," she asserted. "You are the most honest man I know."

Suddenly Edoardos dropped to his knees on the floor, "But am I? I have no God to pray to, now that I am questioning him. Has my faith been merely lip service, just a means to an end for both myself and my family? Is my real faith, my family and not the church? If this is so, how do I destroy that faith and my allegiance to them?" he questioned. "Do I give in to my feelings?"

Lina drew back in shock. "You are a highly intelligent, strong man E. You must make your own decisions." Placing her hand over his, she pulled him alongside her on the sofa. "I don't have that kind of power over you."

"Oh yes, you do," he finally admitted, as their eyes met and he drowned in hers. "I have denied it for years and so have you."

Lina dropped his hands and moved away, her heart aching for him. "No Edoardos, you haven't. You come to me because I am safe. You use your faith to erect a wall between yourself and any personal desires. Your family determined you would stifle those feelings for them and you have obliged them."

"Lina, I don't know what's happening to me. I have never doubted my place in life before. Now it has become so complicated." The priest rose up from the sofa, to avoid the temptation he felt so strongly now. "Maybe I am searching for a simpler life," he pondered and shook his head emphatically. "Perhaps I *could* put this life behind me and we could be happy together now."

"My dearest friend." Lina rose, and placing her hands on either side of his face, she gently stroked his cheeks. "You know the depth of my feelings for you, but how could we survive the schism between yourself, your family and the Church that would arise?" Lina looked doubtful at the very thought of such devastation.

"I know." Looking shamefaced, he bent his head in contemplation before he raised it again and declared, "I want to be with you more than anything else, but there will be so many pressures on us it would probably destroy any relationship," he reluctantly agreed, "but I want to try. I want to find out what I'm really made of." Then making up his mind, he reached for her,

Melancholy stole into the room like a ghost, bringing with it doubt and shame.

His aristocratic family's wrath would engender his expulsion from their sight. With all their expectations of their children and their progeny, his leaving the church would be unacceptable in their eyes and would shame them before the world. As a family, they would suffer also, as the family was so closely intertwined, it would be difficult to preserve the status quo.

Could Lina and E form a relationship and survive being shut out in the cold? She had no doubt her own parents would find it impossible to understand and live with, so a slight shudder went through her body. "Let us wait and see what develops in our quest. Once we have time to devote to each other, we can see where it takes us." Desperately hoping that he would make the commitment and spend his life with her, she knew it would be far from simple.

Looking doubtful, he nodded his assent, kissed her on both cheeks and took his leave of her.

Once he had left she turned out the lights and sat for a while in the drawing room. Outside the weather decided it was time to clean up the city. She loved the sound of the rain spattering on the terrace outside. It cleared the poisonous air of Rome's polluted streets as motorists fought for supremacy on the roads.

Wandering over to the bifold doors, her gaze was captured by droplets caught on the plants, hanging there like trembling tears ready to fall at the slightest impulse. Other big fat drops splashing onto the table and chairs bounced, as they hit the terrace washing it clean. From the roof, they traced their way down the bifold doors and refreshed her world, as she opened one of them slightly and breathed in deeply and satisfyingly.

It ran off the eaves of the red tiled roof two storeys above her, then traced another path off the edge of the terrace and ran in rivulets down the sixty nine steps to the street below. "Was it taking her dreams of a life with Edoardos with it?" she wondered.

Reminding herself to keep breathing, she watched as it wiped away the Roman grime from the buildings in partial shadow around her. As her eyes gazed out to the Medici Villa and the Borhgese Park, she thought of the treacherous path both families had trod in their colourful famous world, until the demise of their power.

Edoardos' family had followed the same path and would recoil from anything that upset their dignified existence.

Despite the horrors she encountered in her job, suddenly her world appeared uncomplicated, fresher and cleaner. Sighing to herself, she knew deep in its soul that ancient Rome still kept sway over this modern city.

Then her eyes fell upon the roof of St Peter's Basilica towering above the other rooftops, which had silently kept watch, as the stately dance of intrigue and corruption had woven its path through the centuries in its halls below and wondered how different life might have been for humanity, if one man had not had empirical ambitions.

Chapter Forty - The Roman Emperor Constantine and the Rise of Christianity

Through a lucky stroke of fate, three hundred years after the death of Yeshua, Constantine Emperor of the West won the royal crapshoot for control of the Roman Empire, between himself and his brother in law Licinius, who co-ruled the Eastern half.

Not content with his share, Constantine set out to defeat his rival Licinius and unify the Roman Empire with its huge amount of territory, not caring one jot that he had involved the country in civil war.

Whether as he claimed, the Christian God helped him win the day, by personally assuring him he would be victorious and crowning that with a vision of a cross of light, the mists of history have obscured. Maybe he was just a very good military leader.

After all Constantine was an aggressive young man, with an energetic military vocation. He lived at Diocletian's court and received a formal education, as his father, Constantius', successor. His military career under Diocletian and Galerius, saw him fight many campaigns in Assyria, Mesopatamia, Asia, and in Germany, serving with distinction and achieving the status of a tribunus ordinis primi - *tribune of the first order.*

Deciding the introduction of a monotheistic religion (*the worship of one all seeing, all knowing God*), was the way to unite Empire, both politically and culturally, he cast his eye around and decided the new religion of Christianity was a good fit.

For whatever motives, he became Christianity's champion, and with the willing assistance of the Christian bishops and Eusebius, the Bishop of Caesarea, who became a favorite scribe, he set about abolishing the pantheon of Gods and superimposing Jesus Christ and Christianity over the current main religion of Sol Invictus, (Mithra) the Sun God. This way, he would not have to stray far from the beliefs that were familiar to the populace.

After a period of religious and cultural tolerance when Rome was relatively peaceful and open minded in the 1st and 2nd centuries, people of many cultures were allowed to retain their heritage. During this period, the Romans were a pretty open minded bunch, seeing value in the culture of the Jews, Christians, Babylonian astronomy and astrology; and other cultural elements from Persia, Egypt and India.

Their own talents lay in government, law and architecture, so they absorbed and perpetuated the art, literature and philosophy of the Greeks and left the Western world a legacy of rich cultural elements. With the spread of their own Latin language, this culture spread through the legionnaires posted in defeated territories.

The Emperor Diocletian figured he had enough worries with the Goths, who were seeking a better climate for their farming endeavours; and Vandals, who contributed nothing to society, invading the Roman Empire, without the Christians spreading the word amongst the poor and slaves, that all men were created equal. Well not in Rome, where there were very distinctive class and gender divides.

Add to this numerous civil wars within the Empire and a cluster of Roman Emperors who were simply not up to the job, and the country was in a bit of a pickle.

With Diocletian's burning of the Christian scriptures, it was possible for Constantine to revise Christianity to suit his purpose. After all, where was the written proof that refuted his version?

As the Emperor was God's conduit to the earth and all things thereof, Constantine could bring his people to heel with this God, who resonated with that of Sol Invictus. So he appointed himself head of the church, which was founded on the name of a man the empire had crucified 300 years, before as a radical activist.

If this necessitated taking liberties with the truth about Yeshua and his life, it worried Constantine not one jot.

The Christians had left themselves wide open by clambering up on their soapboxes and squabbling amongst themselves, as to whose version of Yeshua's life and words was the *true way*. History has shown, perhaps because of man's inherent inability to get along with his fellow man, it is generally impossible to form a cohesive religion.

Different factions arise, all clamoring that their *truth* is the right one, then turning on each other in the age old tradition of might is right, in order to enforce it upon those unwilling to bend to their belief. It's a sad state of affairs.

In Three-seventeen AD, Lactantius a Christian scholar was called to the Emperor's court as advisor, ostensibly to guide Constantine's religious policy as it developed. He was also tasked with the education of Constantine's eldest son, Crispus, in the fundamental elements of classical scholarship, as well as the tenets of the Christian religion.

As political, military and cultural stability had been achieved throughout the Empire, it is most likely Constantine who had received a minimal classical scholarship, took advantage of the situation to sit in on the lessons.

The family of Constantine would be the first to agree,he was far from a spiritual being, as he later murdered Crispus and his mother, who was the emperor's second wife.

History obscures the meeting of minds, but the legend of the icon of the Christian church, Yeshua, reflects in remarkable detail, that of Sol Invictus, (Mithra) who predated him in Rome by 300 years.

Legend has it, that Mithra was incarnated into human form in 272 BC. He was born of a virgin Anahita, who was called the Mother of God. Mithra's birthday was celebrated on December 25 and he was called *the light of the world.* He performed miracles and had 12 disciples. After teaching for 36 years, in 208 BC as the *great bull of the Sun,* he sacrificed himself for world peace and ascended into heaven, which obviously failed to bring about the desired result.

Mithraists believed in heaven and hell, judgment and resurrection. They received baptism and communion of bread and wine. They believed in service to God and others.

As most of these tenets were familiar to the populace of the Roman Empire, Mithra having previously transformed into Sol Invictus, Christianity co-existed happily with the other religions, after the Edict of Toleration was issued. Only 5% of the Roman Empire converted to Christianity which Constantine tolerated, as he himself was not baptized until he was on his deathbed, by his old friend Eusebius.

Constantine had further deliberated with his close friend and historian Eusebius, Bishop of Caesarea, whilst promulgating the doctrine of his new religion.

"Yeshua must remain pure and unsullied. Like Sol Invictus, he remained celibate throughout his life, valuing self-control, renunciation and resistance to sensuality."

Oops, what to do with Miryai, Yeshua's wife and their child Tamar? Eusebius faltered before responding.

"That could pose a problem Augustus." The Bishop lowered his gaze as he continued. "She is widely accepted as his wife and partner in the ministry and it is public knowledge they had a child, Tamar."

"His wife Miryai, can have no place in our church." Constantine looked at Eusebius from beneath his furrowed eyebrows.

"It will be difficult to write her out of history Augustus," Eusebius tried to reason with the Emperor. This was a tricky situation indeed. "Yeshua was a rabbi and it is their duty to marry. It was arranged when they were young children, as both were of the royal bloodlines."

"No, it cannot be." Constantine was adamant. "She will weaken the religion. Women know their place in our society Eusebius. They are submissive to men at all times and must remain so. Our new religion must enforce this."

'Riiiiiight!' thought Eusebius to himself, as he smiled guardedly at Constantine. 'Miryai had been a strong woman, but she will obviously have to take a back seat in the interests of progress,' he thought to himself. 'Truth be told Miryai had more or less been sidelined by the movement over the past 200 years anyway. The disciples Paul and Luke had seen to that.'

"In order for Christianity to prevail over the old Gods, the doctrine must appeal to the wealthy and the poor." Constantine was adamant on this point.

"May I be so bold as to make a further suggestion Augustus?" Eusebius literally held his breath, not knowing how this would be accepted by the Emperor, who believed himself to be a god on earth, or the regent of one.

However Constantine was a very astute and clever man and was not averse to taking suggestions from time to time, so he waved him on.

"Perhaps we need to address human needs, better than the old Gods did Augustus." Eusebius promulgated

"Yes, they were a pretty selfish lot weren't they? Demanding sacrifices and throwing tantrums." Constantine smiled wryly at some of the shenanigans he had seen and taken part in, on behalf of the pagan Gods. "But how do you suggest we do that?"

"By accepting Yeshua's teachings, that all men, wealthy and poor alike are equal," Eusebius suggested.

"You mean distribute the wealth evenly?" Constantine looked horrified at the suggestion.

"No Augustus," Eusebius protested mildly. "They receive equal status on a spiritual level only. Only by their own efforts will they be able to change their circumstances."

"As slaves, this will be impossible." Constantine gave the poor a brief thought. They didn't have a chance. The way the system was rigged, wealth would always remain in the grasp of the nobility.

"Yes, Augustus. However, have you considered abolishing slavery?" Eusebius held his breath, wondering if he had gone too far.

"Are you mad Eusebius?" Constantine was appalled at the suggestion. "How can you expect the Empire to run profitably without slaves? The economy would be ruined."

"Of course Augustus," Eusebius hastened to assure him. "One of Yeshua's precepts was, that no man should be a slave to another. That all men were created equal and should remain so."

"Well Jesus never attempted to run a country," Constantine snarled.

Eusebius drew back slightly. "Perhaps we could find a way freed men could be involved in trade. Give them a chance to change their status in time."

"The nobility and merchants would never stand for it." Constantine was in a bind here.

Eusebius tried another suggestion. "You could issue a decree for the better treatment of slaves."

Constantine was prepared to consider this proposition. "I'll need time to think about this." Whilst deliberating, he called for a servant to pour more wine, for both himself and Eusebius.

Then he perked up as a bright idea that would get him out of the dilemma, fired the synapses in his brain. "I will order all Christian slaves to be freed."

"That is an excellent idea Augustus, but........." Eusebius looked at Constantine expectantly.

"No, no. I cannot free non Christian slaves." Waving his hand dismissively it was obvious, he was not prepared to discuss the matter further. "It is out of the question."

Oh well, the concessions he had gained would have to do in the meantime and Eusebius was not going to fret over the issue. He understood the ramifications of freeing all slaves.

In order to promote the Christian religion above all others, he was willing to quell his conscience over Yeshua's commands. After all His Lord had been crucified for less and Eusebius did not wish to suffer the same fate.

*

Ten years hence and the Christians were driving Constantine crazy. What really got Constantine's pistons fired up, was the continual squabbling between the different factions, regarding Yeshua's divinity. Like theologians throughout the ages, they had to find some fine point to niggle about.

Constantine was reclining on a couch, eyeing his scribe Eusebius, who was feeling decidedly uncomfortable and cursing a presbyter named Arius, an eloquent speaker who was busy promulgating the Samosatene Doctrine, which eventually concluded that Jesus Christ was a created being, not uncreated as God was. This meant that Christ was less than fully divine. "How could God so alter Himself as to have a human form and a human life?" raged the argument.

Furthermore, if He had died for humanity's sins, how precisely did this happen? Can God die at all and remain God?

Well Constantine had news for Arius. It was his way, or the highway and this *was* his highway. In fact, they were all his highways in the Roman Empire, and he'd be damned if he was going to sit back and let them destroy his hard work, bringing it all down like a house built on sand.

Damn it, hadn't he taken Christianity under his wing and protected it. He had pushed through the Edict of Milan, allowing religious tolerance for all, showered them with blessings and gifts and the populace had accepted the deification of Yeshua……..and now this.

He'd had it up to here! Now he was going to quieten them down and unite them on the doctrine once and for all.

Eusebius was a scholar of history and theology who had written many books and was Constantine's choice to help him in his mission. He had already written Constantine's account of his vision, after he came to power.

"It hadn't been easy being Constantine's favorite scribe," Eusebius reflected, seated at a highly polished stone table with pen poised, whilst the Emperor rose from the couch and commenced stalking the room of the Imperial Palace in Constantinople, like one of the large cats his predecessors had let loose on the Christians in the Coliseum

"The Christian bishops have called upon my help to decide what a Christian is, and what they should believe." Sighing mightily, he ensured Eusebius was aware of the burden the bishops were placing on his shoulders.

"Have I not exalted the church and its bishops?"

"You have indeed Augustus?" Eusebius was taking this cautiously, as he had learned to do so when his master began with the pacing routine.

"Have I not made the followers of Yeshua safe from persecution?"

"You have Augustus."

"Have I not given the Christian Bishops many gifts?" Constantine stopped in his pacing to sulk grievously. "Did I not sponsor the building of great churches?"

Eusebius thought of St Peter's and St John's Lateran Basilicas in Rome, the Basilica of the Holy Cross in Jerusalem and the Church of the Holy Apostles in Constantinople, which he could see from the Imperial Palace.

"The Church has benefited mightily from your generosity Augustus," he agreed, wishing to remain in his cushy position.

"Have I not accorded the same privileges to the Christian clergy, which priests of other recognized religions enjoy, including tax exemptions?"

"Yes, Augustus, you have." Eusebius was sticking with a policy of agreeing with the Emperor and exalting his achievements.

"Have I not made exemptions for Christians from military service and forced labour?" Constantine was beginning to get worked up. In his opinion he had been more than generous and was having difficulty with the ingratitude of the bishops as a whole. "Have I not allowed Christians to will their property to the Church?"

Eusebius thought this was going a bit far as the Church was the beneficiary here, ensuring its wealth and continuing power. However he acknowledged that under these circumstances, the numbers of the clergy of the Church had risen considerably, before Constantine had woken up to the scam and put a stop to it. "They have indeed been honoured Augustus."

"Now I have to put up with them squabbling over ideology and Yeshua's divinity is in doubt." Constantine began to pace around the room, like one of the caged tigers his ancestors had kept, to dine on Christians. "He is the Christos, the anointed one." Pausing for effect, he turned back to Eusebius whose mind was scrabbling around like a couple of wild ferrets, trying to keep up with him. "Arianism teaches he was mortal. We can't have this."

Again he began his pacing of the room, which Eusebius tried to ignore as it made him quite nervous. "Well, if they want me to help them make up their mind, I will. I'll convene a Council and it shall be held at Nicaea. All the Bishops of the church throughout the Empire, and those outside, will be invited to attend."

Eusebius wondered if Constantine had, or would bother, to consult Pope Sylvester I on this matter, or he would just take the lead in ecclesiastical matters and risk pissing him off. Mentally shrugging this off he thought, 'The bishops had better get their act together, as Constantine has not yet made his break with Sol Invictus, and if they wish to retain his goodwill and sponsorship, they have got to decide this issue about Yeshua's divinity.'

The schism in the church would have to be settled, and Arius silenced.

"This troublesome priest comes between the Creator and the Emperor, and this I will not tolerate." A superstitious fellow, Constantine was alluding to the Highest Divinity being moved to wrath, not only against all mankind but also against himself, to whose care by celestial will, God had committed the management of all earthly affairs.

Wisely Eusebius remained silent.

"What is Arius postulating now?" The man was exasperating Constantine no end.

"He has made a statement Augustus." Eusebius ventured, as he inwardly cursed Arius for making his life more difficult.

"Read it to me." Constantine gestured with his right hand, encouraging Eusebius to continue.

Eusebius picked up a parchment scroll and proceed to avail Constantine of its contents. *"We are persecuted, because we say that the Son has a beginning, but that God is without beginning. This is the cause of our persecution, and likewise, because we say that he is of the non-existent. And this we say, because he is neither part of God, nor of any essential being."*

Broadly speaking this meant the Arian belief in One God, meant Yeshua was not God, or a part of God. Behind this, was the fundamental issue of the deity of Christ, which Arius was denying. For him, the Son was not to be identified with God himself, but remains the first and greatest of God's creatures.

Constantine calmed down and thought things through. In reality, the Christian bishops had given him carte blanche to superimpose Yeshua over the cult of Sol Invictus. Well, he would give them another tradeoff. If they adopted Constantine's canons at the Council, in return for this, the Church of Rome would officially become the *Catholic Church of the Holy Roman Empire*, giving it enormous credence. That should nail it once and for all, and give that troublemaker Arius, something to really feel persecuted about. He didn't know the meaning of persecution, but he was about to find out.

Constantine walked over to the table and sat alongside Eusebius on the stone bench. "Then we need to give them some canons to consider, which will help them to make this decision."

Eusebius waited patiently wondering where this was going now.

"Write these down for me Eusebius," the Roman Emperor commanded.

Church of Rome "officially" will become the "Catholic (Universal) Church of the Holy Roman Empire"

Formulate a creed concerning the *Trinity* based on that of Anthanias' that Jesus was of the same substance as God the Father

Change Verses of Bible

Eliminate certain verses and books from the Bible

Declare Arian's belief in the Unity of God *heresy*

Change the day of worship from Saturday to Sunday

Change the date of Jesus" birthday to December 25th

Introduce a celebration for the resurrection of Yeshua during the "Feast of Ishtar")

"There may be a problem with the latter Augustus," Eusebius ventured timidly, as this was the pagan Saturnalian celebration, which he thought Christians might object to their Savior being associated with.

"That will be easily quelled," Constantine assured him, "as the people love a celebration and this will assure Jesus' divinity." He was not about to be thwarted over any decision. Lost in reverie, he bestowed a beneficent smile on the historian. "We will continue to hold a symbolic celebration every year to celebrate the rebirth of the divine. They will love it."

How could anyone not? Family and friends getting together to celebrate with feasts, overindulgence, giving of gifts, and decorating their houses with festive greenery. Of course they would love it.

Privately Eusebius thought this was overdoing things a bit and it might be a hard sell to the Christians, but on the other hand, everyone liked a good celebration where they could let their hair down once in a while.

However, Constantine was not finished yet. "We also need a celebration of Yeshua's death and resurrection, so I am proposing replacing the festival of Ishtar which is the celebration of the spring equinox. This will symbolize his rebirth and ascension into heaven," he uttered smugly, looking ever so pleased with himself.

Eusebius swallowed hard, his mind working overtime. 'It could very well work. Replacing a pagan festival with a Christian celebration? Hmmmm. Please the Christians and still give the pagans a holiday." Figuring the odds silently to himself, he decided, 'I believe he could swing it.'

Turning to the Emperor, he brown nosed unashamedly. "That's brilliant, Augustus."

"I thought so myself," Constantine preened.

Eusebius wondered if he could relax a little bit now.

"So, have we covered everything?" Constantine arose from the couch he had been languishing on and looked over Eusebius' shoulder. "Have you got everything down?"

"Almost. Augustus." In fact, Eusebius was still writing frantically, listing the main points.

Whenever he was around Constantine, Eusebius was always on guard, as the Emperor's moods could be mercurial.

Discussions alone with the Emperor could be volatile to say the least, as Constantine could suddenly spring up from the couch in one fluid movement, to stand over Eusebius to read the words he was recording, even whilst eating.

"This is one of those days." Sighing to himself, Eusebius watched carefully as Constantine strode around the room, dictating further canons to him.

*

Resplendent in purple and gold, Constantine made a ceremonial entrance at the opening of the Council of Nicea. Obviously hoping to win brownie points, Eusebius' description of Constantine as *"himself proceeding through the midst of the assembly, like some heavenly messenger of God, clothed in raiment which glittered as it were with rays of light, reflecting the glowing radiance of a purple robe, and adorned with the brilliant splendor of gold and precious stones, "* was slightly over the top.

Seated in the largest hall of the Imperial Palace at Nicaea, the Emperor gazed upon the assembly of some one hundred and fifty Christian Bishops he had brought together. The overflow was deliberating in the Principal Church as some three hundred out of the eighteen hundred invited had accepted his personal invitation, wherein he had respectfully begged they come promptly to Nicaea to come to a consensus through this assembly which was representative of all Christendom.

Arriving from Asia, Assyria, Palestine, Egypt, Green, Thrace and even Persia, which was outside the Empire. Pope Sylvester 1 was represented by four priests.

"This Council," he addressed the assembly, gathered before him in a semi circle, seated on wooden benches, "has been convened with the express purpose of producing a theological confession, which will be entitled the Nicene Creed.

"You are tasked with drawing up the ecclesiastical doctrine and liturgy of the worship of Jesus Christ." Looking at them all seated on stone benches within the great hall, he let his gaze wander over each and every man present.

A rustling issued throughout the great hall, as they turned to each other and murmured in low tones. This would set the Christian Church's political ideology for many centuries, and firmly establish Constantine's reputation as the first Christian Emperor.

They set to the task with great zeal, deliberating over the points Constantine had outlined, until they reached the consensus Constantine had directed they achieve.

There was much to be gained by following Constantine's directives. Only 2 of the 318 did not vote against Arius, pleasing the Emperor mightily. The rest of his suggestions were passed without dissent.

Amongst other resolutions, with the power of the state behind them, the Bishops managed to slip in, that no-one was to be made bishop, except by other bishops within their particular province. This effectively stopped the common Christians from choosing their own bishop.

The resolution of the main issue before the Council, culminated in the first version of the Nicene Creed, which is repeated at each mass in the Roman Catholic Church.

We believe in one God the Father all powerful, maker of all things both seen and unseen. And in one Lord Jesus Christ, the Son of God, the only-begotten begotten from the Father, that is from the of the Father, God from God, light from light, true God from true God, begotten not made, Consubstantial with the Father, through whom all things came to be, both those in heaven and those in earth; for us humans and for our salvation he came down and became incarnate, became human, suffered and rose up on the third day, went up into the heavens, is coming to judge the living and the dead. And in the Holy Spirit.

And those who say "there once was when he was not", and "before he was begotten he was not", and that he came to be from things that were not, or from another or substance, affirming that the Son of God is subject to change or alteration these the catholic and apostolic church anathematises.

With the Council of Nicaea, Constantine had changed the structure of Christianity, turning it into a well-organized, quasi-political institution that would survive for centuries and influence world politics.

Using the church as a tool, he held together the crumbling Empire, at the cost of diverting a culture based on the tolerance of diversity, to that of a rigid all encompassing power. It handed the divine right to Kings, Emperors and Popes, who would rule in the name of Christianity and open the way for Christian world dominance.

By ensuring the Church came under the Emperor as *Divus Caesar*, the Christian bishops became his imperial officials, who administered law and justice, as the church flourished. The Emperor dominated the church, with the bishops answering directly to him. By approving a uniform sacred ecclesiastical liturgy for use throughout the Empire, the Church and State effectively became one.

His decision would affect civilization for almost two thousand years.

Chapter Forty-one – Edoardos faces up to facts

Edoardos and his family were shattered at the loss of Adelais and her daughter.

Antonio rushed back to their side and the family closed ranks in their grief.

"You are not going to like this." Lina bided her time, then cautiously approached E, watching him warily for his reaction.

"Oh dear, now what?" Edoardos braced himself, his face mirroring the dismay he felt at her words. He was very downcast and didn't know if he could cope with Lina's flights of fancy at the moment.

Knowing Lina as he did, he was expecting her next words could lead them both of them into another pit, from which they would have to extricate themselves with great difficulty. His hitherto comfortable life was fast disappearing into oblivion and he wondered if there would be any return to it in the future.

"I've been speaking to my contact at the Arma Carabinieri." Tentatively moving forward physically towards the priest, she hesitated.

"And your point is?" Edoardos prompted.

"Well, it's a bit difficult and I don't want you reacting before you consider the possibility."

"For heavens sake Lina, get on with it. Spit it out." Edoardos' stomach dropped, as his anxiety levels rose to an uncomfortable level. "It's not like you to be reticent."

"OK." Taking a deep breath, she faced up to him and blurted out. "Apparently a Cardinale was seen going to your brother's house shortly before that day."

The priest looked at her in dismay. "So what? Cardinales move in well connected circles. My family frequently entertain them."

"Be that as it may," Lina retorted defensively. "We have to consider all options."

"You're not serious? Next thing you'll be telling me, the iniquitous *they,* saw Papa there and he is a suspect."

"E, please don't reject this out of hand," Lina wheedled, turning on all her charm. "I really need your help on this now. I can't snoop around in the Big V, but you are there every day."

"What?" He was shocked to the core of his being. "You want me to snoop around the Vatican, tracking down some Cardinale you believe is a thug. Do you want me to be kicked out of the place?"

"E please," Lina pleaded with him. "Don't close your mind to the possibility. I beg you. It's not as though the Vatican isn't steeped in intrigue and scandals," she tailed off weakly, not wanting to offend him further.

"We're not back in the times of the Borgias you know, where larceny and murder where frequent affairs," Edoardos raced to the defense of the establishment.

Lina returned to the fray. "Well that's not really true. Look at the Holocaust and the Ratline, the mysterious death of Papa John Paul I and the assassinations during the Vatican Bank scandal."

This touched a nerve with Edoardos. "I'm going to get really pissed off at you in a moment." He moved away from her.

Not to be outdone, she followed and took his hands in hers. "There are women's lives at stake. Can't we just consider this and maybe just look around from the inside."

"You're out of your mind Lina." Angrily he pulled his hands away and glowered at her, seeing his career pass before his eyes from the heights he had achieved into a pit of the blackest despair, from which he would never be accepted by the Church or his family. "I'll not risk everything for your desire to win a Pulitzer Prize.

"I admit my quest started like that, but now I am acting out of concern for these women. There is a maniac loose in the streets and he has to be stopped before he destroys any one else."

"Then let the police handle this. It's their job."

"They are stumped and you know how much corruption there is in high places."

"Well, that's their problem," Edoardos flatly stated, determined not to be drawn into the investigation.

"And what about the women of Italy?" Lina was losing her cool fast. "Must they live in fear each day?"

"Look the Carabinieri will catch the murderer," he emphasised.

"I don't believe the assassani is acting alone."

"What? You think there's a club of them?"

Lina looked at him seriously. "Yes, I do. There is no way a single assassani could have carried out these murders."

This stopped Edoardos dead in his tracks. Together they had discussed this many times and he saw the logic in it. His nerves began to ripple as though a thousand serpents were crawling beneath his skin, and shivering involuntarily; he talked over to the sofa and sat down, cradling his head in his hands. "Oh God, what have we become?"

"The world has always been this way." Lina hurried over and dropped onto her knees before him. "There is nothing new in the nature of man."

He reached up and tousled her hair in a familiar manner, which made her heart beat faster. "Where has my objective reporter gone then?"

"I'm back in the Priory." Shaking her head, she looked at him glumly. "I can't get them out of my mind."

"What now?"

"I'm going back to see what I can find out about Adelais and her daughter."

Edoardos started and took both of her shoulders in his hands. Shaking her gently he admonished. "You can't go snooping around there. It won't do you any good."

Taking a step back to release his hold on her she shook her head again. "You can't dissuade me. Somehow I know there is a link. I can't explain it, but I'm going with my instinct."

He rubbed the back of his neck to ease the tension he felt. "Lina be very, very careful. You are poking around in an ancient world, full of mystery and not averse to treachery and murder."

"I'm well aware of that, but I'm not an investigative reporter for nothing," she protested as she looked at him, and he at her. "My mind's made up. I'm going back there."

The priest sighed from the depths of his soul and shrugged, knowing any further protests were futile.

"I have to go Lina." Hurriedly he rose, looking down at her. "I'll be in touch."

"Please do not think too long," she pleaded meeting his gaze, "lives are at stake.

Holding back her resentment against a church which dithered over obscure theological interpretations while their followers suffered, she watched Edoardos close the door quietly behind him and damned the self serving Emperor Constantine, whose influence remained into the present day.

*

"Hear us, Miryai and Mariam, as we pray for our lost ones. Please protect them and return them to us.

As you made your perilous journey out of Judaea to Assyria, returning only when Herod Antipas was dead, your courage protected the lineage. We have carried his lineage through to the present time for you and now we stand in danger.

As the word spread through Egypt, into Byzantium when Constantine made Christianity the religion of the Roman Empire, it continued on its journey when you taught into Assyria, then spread throughout Europe, as the followers of Yeshua as our descendants moved away from persecution in the Middle East. The message spread through Palestine and Lebanon into Turkey and across the Bosphorous, through Macedon, Greece, the Germanic countries and into Gaul, now known as France.

It was a treacherous journey but they kept your lineage alive and your secret safe."

We know neither your husband Yeshua nor you ever sought to be worshipped. We know neither of you would approve of the worship of him, that is the core of the Christian churches today. "

The enlightened age has arrived. It is time for the Miryai's testament to be shown to the world."

"We stand ready to do this for you so please keep the Sacred Casket safe and sound."

Chapter Forty-two – The Glorification of Constantine

Constantine was feeling his age. After all, sixty five years was a good length of time to survive in these turbulent times. Furthermore, he appeared to be in the grip of an illness he could not shake off.

He had wanted a place in history and by God he had achieved it. As well as establishing the city of Constantinople, which history taught him could be destroyed, he sought a more lasting legacy.

"I have done great things, Eusebius," he declared, reclining wearily on a couch, whilst concerned physicians hovered over him.

The elderly Bishop nodded in agreement, waiting to see which way the wind blew on this fine sunny afternoon.

The autocratic emperor raised himself with great effort, from the couch he lay upon and propped himself up on one elbow.

"I rewrote history and will forever be known as the Christian Emperor." Constantine indulged in some well deserved self satisfaction. His achievements had indeed been spectacular.

"What you write," Constantine studied the Bishop of Caesaria, although his gaze was less fierce than before, "must stand up to scrutiny. Christianity will survive throughout the ages as a testament to my power and glory."

"Be assured I have your best interests in mind whenever I put pen to parchment." Eusebius had been around Constantine for a very long time now and felt justified in dropping the titular title from time to time.

As history was always written by the victor, reflecting their version of events, Eusebius knew he could fulfill Constantine's desires.

"I am honoured you have asked me to write about your glorious life." Eusebius was genuinely fond of the man before him and sad to see him in such a distressed state. He was not averse to a place in history himself, so documenting the life of the man in front of him, was no mean feat.

Constantine lay back on his couch once again while his mind drifted back to the earliest times in his reign as Emperor.

"Do you recall my learned friend?"

Eusebius' face lit up. "Augustus?" He waited, but the Emperor appeared to have subsided into lethargy.

"You have fulfilled prophecy," Eusebius hastened to reassure him. "The disappearance of the Jewish state and Rome's rise as an Empire is part of a divine plan. As Augustus, you have brought peace to the earth, by expunging a multitude of rulers and gaining mastery over nations, which was prophesied. The fortunes of Rome have reached their zenith under your rule."

Constantine looked well pleased with his trusted historian.

"You have united the Empire," Eusebius continued, "and the nations have found rest and respite from their ancient miseries."

Rising from the couch, with an enormous effort that left his physicians greatly distressed as he waved them away, Constantine reached for Eusebius who supported him.

"Take me out to the terrace, so I may survey my beloved Constantinople once more."

Concerned servants followed them, but the Emperor would allow no-one by Eusebius to help him.

"I have been criticised for making Constantinople the heart of the Roman Empire, rather than Rome, but it is here that I feel most at home." Surveying all before him, he put his hand in the middle of his chest. "This is where my heart lies."

"It is a magnificent testament to your glory," Eusebius had to admit. Seeing the emperor weaken even more, he sat him down upon a stone bench.

"I am not well, Eusebius," Constantine admitted.

"This illness will pass Augustus." His scribe felt he need to reassure himself, as much as the sick man in front of him.

"I fear not." Constantine had never been afraid to face up to the truth, and he had a fierce premonition that his time had come. "I want you to document my life and times beginning now."

"I would be honoured to do so Augustus." Eusebius had been by Constantine's side for a very long time and had documented many events. He would rely on these and his memory, to ensure Constantine was portrayed as the great man Eusebius truly believed he was.

"And how would you write it my learned friend?" Constantine turned his scrutiny to the man in clerical garb beside him.

"I will write it in the most favorable terms Caesar." Eusebius bowed his head in honour. "Yours has been a long and glorious reign and you have achieved mighty things."

"Tell me some of those things Eusebius."

"You moved the Roman Empire away from many states and rulers. Before you united the Roman Empire, cities were at war against cities, nations at war against nations, and humanity continually rushed madly into mutual slaughter, enslaving one another and wasting one another's cities with sieges." Eusebius glossed over many of Constantine's methods for becoming Emperor of the Roman Empire.

Make no mistake; Constantine did a great deal for Rome which should be acknowledged, as it affected Western civilization for the next twenty centuries.

"You restored the senate, when it had disintegrated considerably and was at its lowest ebb." This was respect well earned. "You remoulded Roman law and culture."

Eusebius glanced at his Emperor, who was listening thoughtfully. Knowing he had little time left, who could blame him for indulging one last time in memories of his successes.

"You abolished crucifixion as a legal punishment." True, it had been replaced by hanging.

"You forbade the cruelty of the gladiatorial games."

As this had been a staple of Roman entertainment for more than four centuries, it took some years for the citizens to give up the wholesale slaughter of human beings, to replace them with chariot racing.

"You enabled the smooth transition of Christianity as the main religion in the Roman Empire." Eusebius owed much to this man by his side. Without this achievement, he himself would simply be a Bishop in a nondescript cult.

Constantine nodded his assent. "I believed that was for the best."

"And so it was. The Empire is stronger today than for many decades."

Eusebius smiled at Constantine, as he continued. "The Government established by you, is the system and method of government for all states. As in heaven, so be it on the earth."

"You have done well my friend." Constantine looked upon his friend with true affection. "You most certainly are my faithful servant and your reward will be great. You will share a place in history with me."

"I can only stand in your reflected glory."

Constantine looked at him wearily. Time was running out. "I believe it is time for me to be baptised in the name of Jesu Cristo."

Eusebius face lit up. "Augustus," he proclaimed with delight.

"Let us proceed now." Rising he led the way inside, collapsing on to a couch, much to the relief of his physicians and servants.

And so it was, Constantine the Great, Emperor of the Holy Roman Empire died a Christian.

Chapter Forty-three – The Brave Carabinieri Struggle On

"Terrorists, anarchists, or serial murderers? What the hell are we dealing with here?" Ferdinand was leading his men through the latest kidnappings.

"Anarchists have given up killing people decades ago," his *carabiniere scelto* Rocco replied. "They realised it only makes things worse. They focus on inanimate objects like buildings now," and he turned to look at the others grouped around on chairs.

"So is it the work of terrorists?" Truth be told, Ferdinand was at his wits end.

"No-one's claimed the killings in the name of any well known terrorist organisation," appuntato *(corporal)* Giovanni replied.

Ferdinand glared at them all. "*Don't* bring up Osama bin Laden's name. Don't even go there," he warned.

"He gets blamed for everything else and he would be convenient," one cheeky lad ventured.

"I said I don't want to hear his name," the squad leader threatened. "He's the scapegoat for every damn thing that happens in the world, now the Russian Bear's claws have fallen out. I've got my doubts he's even alive. Who the hell has seen him for years?"

"Yeah, and I pissed my pants laughing when the Americans released the last known tape of him speaking from a lectern." Rocco waved his hands around and hooted with laughter. "A lectern? Per amor di Dio, the bat cave in Afghanistan must have been well fitted out."

The rest of the team broke into laughter, welcoming it releasing some of the tension that was making the room feel like a fog of doom had descended upon them all.

"The CIA probably superimposed an old photograph of him over George Bush at the lectern," Giovanni threw in the ring for a bit of light relief.

"Anything's possible when that crew were at the helm of the USS USA," a dour old sergente – sergeant - fronted up. "The Americans must think we are all idiots out here."

"Yeah. Bush would have had a better image, if he had old Osama's looks and charisma. Old George sure wasn't in line, when they were given out." The team broke up at a new member's comment.

"His old Dad's connections, plans and money didn't make a statesman out of him," Rocco said gleefully.

"I thought I said not to mention Osama Bin Laden and we've nearly written an essay on him," Ferdinand growled but his claws were retracted knowing this bit of fun was good for the men who were under a great deal of stress.

"Sorry Tenente," chorused the team, still sniggering.

Rocco rose from his chair and walked to the board. He pointed to the spot of the crucifixion. "Let's take a look at the buildings in the location," he said. "Maybe they didn't drive up the hill. Maybe someone whoever lives there is responsible."

"Oh come on. Why would a pack of rich people want to do something this horrible and stupid?" One of the group felt himself duty bound to denigrate this stupid suggestion. "Why would the rich and famous bother? After all they had everything they could want..."

"God knows, perhaps they have too much damn money and are bored," Rocco replied looking disgusted. "A lot of them like to get their kicks in perverted ways. Maybe the new victims are locked up there in one of those homes."

Everyone looked at him sceptically.

"We can't go raiding all the houses on the Aventine Hill based on a hunch." Ferdinand was dejected and tired.

"That's right but maybe we could leave the ones on the perimeter and approach the nearest ones to the killing ground." Rocco turned around and looked at the team expectantly.

"Whoever it is will have them well hidden," Lucio answered with a distinct lack of enthusiasm. "We can't go foraging down in the cellars. They'd get pissed off and ring their friends in high places to stop us. We all know how this works in Italy."

"They're pretty scared though." Rocco was determined to push this one through. "Since the last abduction, they are all screaming for protection."

"We don't have enough manpower to mount a 24 x 7 watch on all those houses." Ferdinand was thinking of his budget and blanched at the thought. The Commissioner was not all that generous and he was managing on a shoe string most of the time.

"True," agreed Rocco, who was the ablest man Ferdinand had in the team and was the reason he was his 2 i/c. He was he best strategic thinker they had. "But we can sniff around those in close proximity to the kill area. They are the most nervous. We could offer these people, two men 24 x 7 couldn't we?" He looked to his Tenente for confirmation.

Giovanni spoke up leaning forward with his hands on his knees. "It would make them feel a bit safer and they would probably let us in. We've worried it to shreds, asking if anyone saw anything and of course no-one did. No-one ever does." Shrugging his shoulders, he looked around and saw that almost everyone in the room agreed with him.

Ferdinand chewed on his lip for a moment and looked around the room. The room looked back at him hopefully. "OK," he agreed, "but for one week only. We covered them off after the killing, we cannot stay forever. This will be the last."

"It could be enough." Rocco was happy he had gotten this small respite. "Personally I think they are somewhere else, but maybe someone will drop something. Sometimes serial killers return to the scene of the crime also, so we need to be very vigilant," he reminded them as he looked around the team.

"We went through that just after the first killing," a young dark lad who had joined them from Genoa spoke up. He was very excited at being with the famous Carabinieri and wanted to contribute. "We couldn't pick out anyone."

"You never can," Rocco spoke directly to the lad from Genoa, who was thrilled at being singled out. "It is a waiting game and you have to wait for them to make a mistake. We are looking for a clue as to why these women are being chosen, and now a child as well.

As he returned to his seat, the team began to speak among themselves and plan their return to the crime scene, so they could cover off this question and still look for the missing woman and child. The Tenente left them to their planning which they were good at and he trusted them to come up with a worthwhile one.

Most of them were married and each one knew how he would feel if it was his wife and child that had been abducted, hidden away under God knows what conditions and waiting for their impending death. It was enough to send them over the edge, never to return mentally and emotionally to their families, even if they were returned physically. Judging by the Caribinieri's record to date, that was not at all certain.

Italy was full of plots. The Caribinieri was as susceptible as any other department. Since the carabinieri have units down to the village level, the Commander-in-Chief is an unrivaled position in which to keep his finger on the pulse of what is going on. He would also be excellently placed to take some undemocratic initiative against the established system, were he so inclined.

Would the Unit cover up something as horrific as this?

What kind of people were the Caribinieri were up against?

Chapter Forty-four - Into the Lion's Den

Unable to take a back seat, Lina determined that she would continue her own investigation whilst Edoardos looked further in the archives at the Vatican, so she dressed herself in black, grabbed a balaclava she had bought for the expedition and headed back to the site of the murder.

"Damned weather," she muttered to herself, as she pulled the jacket around her tightly and clipping the fastener zipped it up until it fitted snugly around her neck, then pulled the attached hood over her had

Tonight she had taken a calculated risk and parked outside the Church of St Sabena, then doubled back through the Orange gardens to the rear of the Knights of Malta priory.

As she battled her way around through the park, the wind howled and hooted around her like Dante's three furies, buffeting her and tearing at the hood of her jacket trying to pull it off her head. Her hands flew up to hold it on her head and it became a battle for possession of it.

"What the hell am I doing here in this weather? My God, who would be a journalist?" Even as she muttered the words, she knew she was obsessed with the Knights of Malta as a suspect. Her gut instinct told her so, and had served her well in her career on many an occasion.

The financial state of the country was deteriorating beyond salvaging, along with other European Union countries and her thoughts about the politicians running the country were beyond dark.

The wind continued to tear at her making progress slow and Lina's patience was wearing as thin, as the weather which appeared to be in sympathy with the mood of the country. At long last, Italians had cried 'enough' and ousted the arrogant self serving politician who had brought the country to its knees after three terms in office.

"Porca miseria! *Bloody hell!*" she cursed as she struggled valiantly on.

Her eyes swept all before her, until she gazed once more at the rear of the Priory with the wall surrounding its environs. Running alongside the Santa Maria Priory Church the wall increased slightly in height, but there was a gate set in the wall.

"They most certainly could have carried it out from here from there. What if here's a secret entrance that comes out underneath the priory somehow? They used to build them like that in the past as quick exits were often necessary."

Peering around for guards or anyone else in sight she tried the gate, but found it locked, so pulling the balaclava over her head she focused on the wall surround. "Thank God E can't see me doing this."

"Oh well, nothing for it. Have to do this the hard way." Jumping as high as she could, she managed to grab onto the top of the wall with both gloved hands, then heaved herself up and over the other side landing unsteadily on her feet. Regaining her balance she looked around once again and seeing the coast was clear she headed towards the building with the tower.

In front of her stood a thick wooden door leading into the building, which effectively blocked her way. She was certain it had kept intruders better than herself out for centuries.

"Merda!" Gazing at the ancient iron handle in the shape of a ring she crossed her fingers and turned. Nothing happened.

Then she noticed the large old keyhole. "Merda and merda again," she cursed wholeheartedly. "Of course there is a sodding key." Stumped for the movement, she cast her eyes around the immediate environs wildly seeking a hiding place. "Please don't be locked from the inside," she begged the angels or whoever on high listened. "I just *know* it will be." Her body slumped and she sat on the ground in despair, gazing around desultorily.

Her eyes lighted one of the stones of the building. Surely it was protruding slightly. Holding her breath she reached out, her fingers closing around the stone.

"Please be loose," she begged. The stone remained still. "Oh God," she muttered, "it has to move, lives are at stake. I know this place holds the secret."

Bringing up her other hand she began to work the stone from side to side until it gave a little. "Just a little more," she breathed. Suddenly it moved forward and she eased it out. "Yes," she exulted quietly. There lay a key.

Carefully she put it into the lock and turned, praying it did not stick or make a great clanging noise that could be heard from the inside. "Who would be down in the bowels of the earth anyway?" Desperately trying to convince herself, she turned further until she heard a soft click and pushed. Nothing happened.

"Oh no," her stomach lurched. Wildly she looked around and thought "The iron ring. Of course. How stupid of me."

Turning to the ring, she reached out with both hands and carefully turned. When it moved easily, she muttered under her breath. "Hah. Someone's oiled this and been using it lately." Cautiously she pushed and to her amazement, although heavy it opened when she pushed against it. "Whew. Obviously it can be opened from the outside as well as the inside." Letting out the breath she had been holding in, she tentatively stepped inside the door.

Peering into the darkness, she saw a tunnel ahead of her. Cautiously turning the torch on low beam, she shone it into the blackness, and then took a few tentative steps forward. Navigating her way through the tunnel with one hand against the wall to guide her, she came to a large cavern. Looking around, she noticed some steps that lead upstairs, obviously into the body of the priory.

Stilling her thoughts which were running around like ferrets on the prowl, she used a meditative technique to centre herself. Drawing her breath deep down into her naval area, she built her chi (energy) then slowly released it through her body and mind.

Placing her foot upon the bottom step, she cautiously ascended until she reached the top, where to her delight; there was no door to impede her progress. As she moved cautiously into the Priory, no-one was around to challenge her. In the depth of night all was still, so she moved slowly along the corridor.

Suddenly she heard footsteps, echoing on the polished floor behind her.

"Cacca!" Desperately seeking a hidden space, she saw no niches or curtained alcoves where she could hide. Scooting along as silently and quickly as possible, she came upon a door. Turning the handle as softly as she could, she heard a slight click and the door gave.

Pushing against it, she slipped through a gap and quickly turned to push it to once more, but did not close it completely. Hardly daring to breathe, she heard the footsteps pass by. 'Phew.' Wiping away a few beads of sweat on her forehead, she let her shoulders relax and after another 30 seconds, allowed the latch to catch and became aware of her surroundings.

She was in a large room with curtains framing mullioned windows. Gazing around, she saw bookshelves surrounding three of the walls, with each shelf housing exquisitely bound leather books of indeterminate age. Normally a magnet for her, she allowed herself a moment to let her glance fall on the gold lettering of the spines.

She appeared to be in a library and could only begin to imagine what treasures were housed here, but she had no time to find out.

Ahead of her was an oak panelled wall with a door set in the right hand corner. In the centre of the wall above head level, were three portraits in gilt frames, of gentlemen in the full regalia of the Knights of Malta. Each one obviously took himself very seriously indeed, if their respective miens were anything to go by.

"Pronto," she urged herself. "Someone could come."

As she tiptoed forward towards the door, which was conveniently slightly ajar, she became aware of a low murmuring. Carefully peeking her head around the door, she looked through the narrow slit, which showed a smaller room; and just stopped herself from gasping.

Suddenly she heard voices and froze on the spot. Again, she stilled any panic and breathed slowly out, realising she was up against dangerous forces.

"They've been taken to the monastery," a dry arrogant voice, full of authority stated.

A second voice queried nervously, "do we need to prepare for two crucifixions?"

An eerie silence filled the space where she lingered. To her chagrin she could not see the figures inside.

"No," responded the first voice. "I have something else in mind."

"And what is that Vostra Eminenza?"

Lina drew in a breath. "A Cardinale," she thought. "A Cardinale *is* behind this. I was right all along." However, she took no pleasure in the verification of her suspicions.

"They will be buried alive in the walls of St Gerard monastery."

"Merda," Lina felt as though the air had been sucked out of the room and she could hardly breathe, as she felt chilled to her marrow. "I can't believe my ears. Here is a Cardinale of the Church of Rome, openly discussing walling up a woman and child, as easily as if he was ordering a cup of coffee in a trattoria." The very thought made her stomach revolt.

The library spun around her. Placing her hand against the wall for support, she focused on calming her breathing.

"Empty your mind of the poison you are hearing Lina. Let it drain away." Recalling a technique she had been told to employ in times of fear and ultimate stress, she tried to empty her mind and not react to the horrific suggestion that had been made by the Cardinale, although it was difficult. "Your mind is a receptacle. Like any other it can be filled and emptied at will. Imagine a plug in the bottom, ull it out and let the horror and fear drain out." Willing herself, she felt the urgidity it had caused begin to drain. "Now refill it with clean clear thoughts."

Apparently the listener had been silenced by the plan, as there was no esponse.

"Let us drive there now and discuss this with our companions, as I want to set his up for three days from now." With a rustling of a black robe broken with the ed sash of a Cardinale, the man arose from the chair where he had been seated. Seeing his face for the first time with the red biretta on his head, she frowned as he was no-one she recognised.

"If these women want to be part of a secret society then they will pay the ltimate price for discovery. The church did not hesitate in centuries past. Now they will be silenced forever."

Out of the corner of her eye, she saw the Cardinale take two paces towards the loorway she was standing behind.

Lisa looked around frantically for a hiding place, but could see none.

"Vostra Eminenza," the other voice caught the Cardinale's attention and with a econd rustling of clothing suggested, "let us go out of the side door. No-one will ee us that way. If we go through the Priory someone could see us together."

Lina hardly dared to breathe, as she waited for the Cardinale's response. To her elief, he nodded in agreement and took a step back, turning to follow the other man who was dressed in a long brown robe with a girdle.

"He's a monk. What on earth is going on here?" Taking a deep breath, Lina ulled herself together quickly and sped silently across the library cautiously pening the door once more. After checking the corridor and seeing no-one, she led back the way she had come, leaving the library door ajar behind her. She had to move and fast.

"These people seriously need an attitude adjustment." Down the steps and out through the tunnel she raced, almost tripping over herself in her haste.

As she came out into the night, she pulled the door to and locked it, then replaced the key and stone.

Throwing herself back over the wall, she tumbled to the ground where she crouched low. The sound of a motor starting alerted her and as she sped through the grounds and skirted the back of the church, the sound of a car backing out of its parking space inside the grounds of the Priory, carried on the night air despite the winds.

"I have to beat them to Via di Santa Sabina." Her mind could hardly accept the sentence she had heard, that was to be the lot of the captured woman and child.

Recklessly she ran to her car and sat there panting, waiting for the vehicle to pass by. A black Mercedes glided down and as it passed, she clearly saw two faces recognizing the pair of churchmen from the Priory. Grabbing the notebook she always left on the passenger seat with a pen, she copied the registration number of the vehicle.

Putting the car into automatic gear, she put her foot on the accelerator, and then pulled out to cautiously follow them, while muttering anxiously to herself. "Talk about the rotten Inquisition. These guys must have this same crap in their genes."

As they wound their way through the city and into the hills north of Rome, she stayed unobtrusively on their tail.

Thirty kilometres from the city the Mercedes turned into a driveway. Slowing the car, she parked it under some treesone hundred meters from their destination which was a monastery.

Locking the car she slipped the keys under the front wheels, took a deep breath and moved in. Finding a way into the cellars of the monastery was not going to be that simple. Her heart was beating fit to burst out of her chest, leaving her lifeblood behind her.

Coming across a side door at the back of the monastery she noticed it was lightly ajar. It appeared to be the kitchen and was empty.

Cautiously looking around she tiptoed inside and crossed the floor until she to an internal door that was ajar. Noticing steps leading down she made her way to the cellar. All remained silent and casting her eyes around the walls, she sighted a tunnel leading off to the right hand side. Not daring to breathe, she stole past wineracks and entered the tunnel, more terrified than she had ever been in her life. These were catacombs lined with bones and skulls looking back at her.

Creeping forward one step at a time, she faintly heard voices and what sounded like sobbing, after five eerie minutes. Gliding forward and trying not to make a sound, she heard what she had come for.

"Do not think I can be swayed from my path." A cold voice emanated from behind an open door, causing her to retreat into the darkness of a niche where oaken barrels holding wine stood.

"I will leave you now to contemplate your fates. Firstly your daughter's while you watch and then your own. I promise it will be a painful, lingering death for daring to cast aspersions on Our Lord's holiness, in the name of that whore you worship. You're all whores and should know your rightful place, which is to produce children to populate our mother church and glorify our Lord. In all else you are second class citizens, who should submit to their husbands and remain out of sight behind closed doors."

'What a bastardo.' Lina imagined all the nasty things she would like to do to this creep.

"You're insane," a woman's voice cried out in despair.

"Be that as it may," the voice loaded with disdain hissed, "but I am the instrument of your death and I promise it will not be a pleasant or easy one."

The atmosphere emanating from the room was toxic, and Lina could feel it steal across her body, mind and soul, clawing at her senses. She could only imagine what it felt like in the room itself.

As she remained hidden in the crevice, knowing she had struck gold and found the missing pair, she heard the whispering of a gown upon the stone floor of the ancient building.

"There's no need to lock you in. You're going nowhere," the ice cold voice was implacable. "There's no need to gag you, as no-one will hear you from here and if they did, they belong to me and will not rescue you. So do not waste your time."

With that he walked to the door, switching out the light, plunging the area into pitch black darkness, where it was impossible to see your hand in front of you.

As Lina pressed herself further into the crevice to remain unseen, the black cassock billowed in passing, while her mouth twisted in a grimace. "Merda, that was close."

With her heart pounding wildly in her breast and waiting to leap out of her chest again, Lina waited until the footsteps receded up the stairs, thanking God when the Cardinale left the door ajar.

Making sure no-one else had followed her from the cellar, or was coming down the stairs, she felt rooted to the spot with fear. Urging herself forward her feet would not do as they were told.

"Move, move," she bullied herself. "You have to move, or you'll be joining them and all will be lost. Thank goodness I brought a torch."

Willing her reluctant feet forward, she stole towards the door, fearing what she would find. Hearing the murmuring of the woman, as she sought to soothe her terrified child, she slipped through the door and turning the torch on low, she looked at the pitiful sight before her.

Raw emotions were tearing at the woman. It was consuming her, as she pulled her daughter closer to her. Courageously struggling to push the fear aside for her child's sake, she looked up startled.

"Ssssh," Lina admonished them, as they gasped at the sight of her, "do not say a word," she cautioned. "I know Edoardos and am your friend."

The woman, who could not see behind the torchlight, looked in Lina's direction with astonishment.

Lina moved towards her and tried pulling at the chains bolted into iron rungs in the floor, but they would not release their victims without a key or some mechanical means. Putting her finger to her lips to caution them to remain silent, she was glad they had been placed together

As she shone the torch around the cavern, she suddenly blanched as she realised they were in an ossuary or burial chamber, where the skulls of past monks were viewing the scene from hollow eye sockets.

Keeping it together for the sake of the woman and child, she shone the torch on the walls noticing how thick they were. This would be their tomb if she could not rescue them.

In wonderment, she watched the woman's lips moving and realised she was praying silently. Waiting respectfully until she opened her eyes, Lina heard her comfort her daughter. "Don't be afraid cara mia," she whispered through parched lips. "Miryai will protect us.

Lina hoped she was right.
"I know Mama," the child's voice was muffled. "I feel her presence."

Adelais was concerned. Her daughter's heritage had made her vulnerable and she was still a child who should not be experiencing such horrors, but she was only too well aware that the madness of men throughout the eons, had scorched the souls of the innocent. However, she had not expected this attack on them would come from within their family.

Stretching out her hand, Lina covered the woman's. "I'm here to help," she told her simply.

"How?" The woman looked at her in despair, wondering how on earth one woman on her own could achieve this. It would take a cavalry.

"I've found you. I knew the Priory was involved," she whispered excitedly, "and I followed the trail."

"Where are we?" Adelais had no idea where they had been taken.

"In the Monastery of St Gerard in the countryside."

"I know of it." The woman was obviously worried as she looked at Lina. "Do you know who is behind this?"

"I know the Knights of Malta are involved."

Adelais looked at her in surprise. "What do they have to do with this? The Cardinale who left here is a member of my husband's family."

"Merda," Lina exclaimed before she could help herself and immediately apologised. "He obviously belongs to the Knights, as he has access to the Priory on the Aventine Hill. I followed him from there to here," she concluded.

"I don't take that much notice, of who belongs to all the male secret societies in Italy."

"What is his name?"

"He is Alesso della Rovere."

Lina's breath caught in her throat. "My God he is the Prefect of one of the offices of the Curia."

"I know." Adelais bit her lip and frowned. "I can't imagine why he is doing this."

"He's obviously unhinged," Lina replied. "There's no other explanation."

"Well he has kept it well hidden until now." Adelais thought of all the times he had been in their homes and noone had ever suspected he was deluded. "And yet, there has always been something about him that I could not put my finger on." She shuddered. "At times he made my skin crawl but never did I dream……" she was unable to complete the sentence.

Lina looked at her as confounded as the other woman. "He runs the Office of the Liturgy. What has he to gain?"

Adelais simply shook her head in sorrow and remained silent.

"Why would he want to harm you and your child?" Lina simply could not connect the dots.

"The only explanation I can come up with Lina, is that I am a descendant of the Trencavel family of the Languedoc, who protected the Cathars and Jews."

Lina started, puzzled that Adelais with her background, had married into one of the Ancients of Venice families, who had aided and abetted the Roman Catholic Church at every turn.

"I thought they were imprisoned after the Albigensian Crusade, when Il Papa Innocent set the French crown against them."

"They were virtually exterminated." Adelais" eyes teared up at the thought of all her ancestors had suffered. "A few of my ancestors escaped to Cordova, along with the Cathars."

Lina shuddered at the thought of the horrors they had endured.

"So Mary Magdalene did make her way to France then?"

"No, she did not." Adelais looked at Lina calmly, while the latter wondered how on earth she could keep her composure, under the circumstances.

Lina simply raised her eyebrows.

"Her descendants did."

"So Jesus did survive as some claim?"

"No he didn't."

"I'm utterly confused here."

"Let me tell you the true story of Yeshua and Miryai. They were Aramaic, Lina, and these were their given names."

Lina looked around nervously, wondering if the Cardinale or once of his henchmen could come back at any time.

"He will not return, and neither will anyone else come in," Adelais assured her

"How can you be so sure?"

Adelais just smiled sweetly and gestured for Lina to sit on the floor. "What do you know of the Trencavels?"

"Not very much at all," Lina admitted.

"What people do not understand today, is that the Jews saw the Davidic bloodline as divine, and were awaiting the messiah who would re-establish their rightful place on the throne of Judaea."

"I think it is widely accepted that Jesus was a descendant of King David."

"And Miryai was brought up to be his wife. She came from the Hasmodean Priest line, the Kings of Syria."

"I think this is pretty common knowledge as well." Lina couldn't really see where this was leading.

Patiently Adelais drew her in. "Yeshua's main mission was not to minister to the poor and the weak, but to rally them behind him, for the restoration of the Davidic bloodline to the Throne of Judaea. He really was meant to become King of the Jews."

Lina gasped. "No wonder Herod was so pissed off."

"He was, and of course Yeshua failed." Adelais' eyes became pools of sorrow, for the man and his tribulations. "The people did not get behind him."

Sorrowfully, she considered the repercussions that had awaited a failed contender for a throne. "When he came into Jerusalem on what they now call Palm Sunday, he was presenting himself to the people as the rightful King of the Jews."

Lina looked at her aghast, as her mind flew back to those ancient times in Judaea. "The Jews were looking for the promised messiah, but they were fickle believers."

"Well, they were confused." Adelais had a lot of sympathy for the common folk of those turbulent times. "They expected him to come with an army to overthrow Herod and the Romans, which of course was impossible. Herod was not a popular King, as he was an Idumean and not Judaean and the royal house of David thought Yeshua's argument about this would carry the day."

"So everyone miscalculated somewhere along the line."

Adelais sighed deeply. "Everyone did. You have to understand the mysticism that existed in the Jewish religion in those days. They constantly referred to the Old Testament for messages. This was no longer the Israelite army of the Old Testament. The Jews were a conquered, defeated nation."

"John the Baptist had been sent ahead to pave the way for Yeshua and named him the messiah. John was instructed by the Essenes, who were an ascetic faction. A male dominated isolated society, completely out of touch with the real world. They were a sect that practised celibacy and had no time for women, who were forbidden in their midst."

"When it came to the crunch though, the people couldn't understand that if they stood behind Jesus, a passive revolt would carry the day."

Lina relaxed, getting caught up in the lyrical adaptation that Adelais was bringing to an old story.

Lina nodded her understanding of the whole sorry situation. "I guess they thought Jesus was another David with his slingshot. One stone and he would bring down Goliath again. Where was Jesus, during the three years noone knows about. Was he with the Essenes in the desert?"

"No." Adelais shook her head, "he was in Syria receiving instruction from the followers of Buddha and Lao Tzu.

"Oh wow." Lina was overwhelmed by this remark and parked it, until she was ready to consider its validity.

"However Quirinus was ruling as Governor of Syria, so he had to keep a low profile," Adelais continued.

"And Mary Magdalene?" Lina was becoming so involved in the story Adelais was relaying, she had almost forgotten about the danger they were all in.

"Again she came from a line of priest/kings from Syria and was trained in esoteric knowledge."

"You have to study the Roman Imperial struggles, which resulted in the assassination of Julius Caesar, Brutus and Cassius, to understand the background of Judaea. Rome's time had come, but to be dominant she had to conquer the older Parthian Empire. Unfortunately the Jewish leaders swung their alliance from one nation's party to another, in the struggles for global power and control, so Judaea became the boiling point. Regrettably, the Maccabean king, Mattathias Antigonas, had aligned himself with the loser, the Parthian nation. So they paid a high price."

Lina was doing her best to follow the tale. "So how did Herod usurp the throne of Judaea?"

Adelais paused here, as she re-gathered her thoughts. "Herod became the Hammer of Thor, as the imperial Roman powers sought to control the destiny of the Jewish people."

Lina was flabbergasted by the depth of Adelais' knowledge of Jewish history, as well as her erudition as she continued.

"He was an Idumean, whom the Roman Senate installed as the king of Judea in 40 BCE, with the backing of two legions of Roman forces. This affronted the Jewish people, but there was little they could do about it. Their time had come and gone. Then his son Herod Antipas succeeded him."

Lina was spellbound, listening intently. Here, finally, was a version that made perfect sense to her.

"I don't have time to give you the complete history of the Davidic bloodline," Adelais continued, "save there were five branches. By 4BCE, they had died out, the Maccabeans having defeated each other in their quest for power and greed.

In Thirty seven BC Sanhedrin approved the Abiudite Line from the Babylonian wife, Abytis and the father and grandfather of Iosef, Yeshua's father, making them eligible to become Princes of Israel."

"So Joseph was Jesus' real father?" Lina had never believed in the virgin birth.

"Of course he was," Adelais confirmed.

"Yeshua relied on the spiritual aspect of his training to win the day, but these were turbulent times, with too many different religious factions and he couldn't pull it off."

"They would never defeat the Romans, who were amazing military leaders," Lina thought of the ragtag bunch of followers Jesus had gathered around him and the capricious crowd.

"You are quite correct," Adelais nodded in agreement, "but remember these are highly superstitious people, who believed that Joshua's trumpets brought down the walls of Jericho, so the Israelite army could march in and defeat the Canaanites. They expected the messiah to perform to this standard. Yeshua couldn't carry it off without their support."

"Then his descendants regrouped and started the Church of the Nazarean movement."

"The Christian movement, as it were?"

"No, just keeping the legend of the Davidic bloodline alive." Adelais shifted about, trying to get more comfortable on the cold floor with her daughter nestling into her. She simply wasn't dressed for an abduction and incarceration in a cellar.

Now Lina's eyes teared up at the thought of the whole sorry mess. "Good grief," she spluttered. "The Holy See will not like this version."

"No they won't. Their church is founded on lies."

"Commencing with Constantine I gather?"

"No, beginning with Luke, the supposed apostle," Adelais corrected her.

"What did he have to do with all this? What about Peter?"

"Aaah, this is the crux of the matter. Kepha was an uneducated simple fisherman. He was a follower, not a leader, so Luke became the pre-eminent disciple, after his conversion. This effectively hellenized the Church of the Nazarene." Adelais looked pensive for a moment before continuing,

"The Church of the Nazarene which honoured Yeshua kept his message alive. Not until Luke arrived on the scene, did Yeshua become Jesus Christ. Christo is the Greek word for messiah and the Judean followers morphed into Christians. Do you know that the letter j does not exist in Aramaic or Hebrew?"

"That gives rise to some speculation," Lina agreed and this prompted another thought. "Somewhere in the back of my mind I read, the letter *j* did not appear in he English language until the fourteenth century and in fact its usage was not popular until the seventeenth century, so I see where you are going with this."

Adelais visibly relaxed, Lina was not rejecting her story outright. "After Luke's epiphany on the road to Damascus, he found the perfect opportunity to lead the movement into a religion based on Yeshua's ministry. He was probably fed up with the pantheon of Greek Gods and Goddesses, and saw an opportunity for a monotheistic religion, which he could spread throughout the known world."

"So he was on one big ego trip?" Lina was pretty disparaging of poor old Luke, considering him just another opportunist.

"I wouldn't say that," Adelais hesitated. "He knew the truth of course. After all, he was a friend of Saul, who originally persecuted the Nazarene church, then became a follower," Adelais paused, looking thoughtful. "I guess Luke was no different from people throughout the aeons. Searching for something to believe in and he found it in Yeshua's esoteric teachings."

"But what makes you and your daughter such a threat?"

"Well, the purity of the bloodline is everything in the Jewish religion. They had no problem with Yeshua being a mortal being, who failed at an attempt to restore the Throne of David."

"But obviously," Lina took up the thread, "they weren't having a bar of him as the messiah."

"Not when it came to standing up to the might of the Roman Empire. So Luke took up the baton and ran with it. Then things got worse for the Nazarene followers."

"In what way?" Lina was more than curious, she was fascinated.

"In Seventy AD, the Romans destroyed the Temple of Jerusalem, which was a huge blow for the Jewish people. It destroyed them with it. By this time, Luke's Hellenised version of the Nazarene movement of equality for all men had spread far and wide, appealing to the poor and meek, who were searching for a way out of their predicament."

"Unfortunately the church hierarchy's began to squabble amongst themselves, with each professing their own to be the one true way. Their egos got in the way as usual and weakened the movement." Adelais pressed on with her tale. "It left the way wide open for Constantine to come in and take over."

Lina shook her head in dismay. "So by this time, Mary Magdalene has died," "and her daughter's bloodline went to France and became the Merovingian Kings?" Lina was struggling a bit here.

"No." Adelais corrected her once again, while Lina waited expectantly.

"A woman on her own could not survive in biblical times, so it was an Aramaic tradition which is still honoured amongst some Arabs, that when the husband dies, his brother will marry his widow."

Lina's eyes flew open in shock, as she could see what was coming.

"Yeshua died Lina," Adelais tried to be as gentle as possible. "Joses, (James) Yeshua's brother, had gone to Syria ahead of Miryai, with his mother Mariam and Tamar. When Miryai arrived, he made her his second wife. They had two sons from which the bloodline could continue, as he was Yeshua's full brother. When you take the nonsense of the Virgin birth out of the equation, the family settles back into its true lineage. He brought up Tamar as if she was his own." Adelais watched the journalist closely hoping she could cope with this.

"I thought he married Esta," Lina spluttered, trying to get her head around Adelais' words. From her travels through the Middle East to war zones, she was aware that some Arabic tribes still maintained this tradition, so she could accept the premise. "And where is the proof of this?"

"There is an appendage to Miryai's testament, which outlined the truth of Yeshua's mission and also that Joses became her husband to protect her and Tamar, to ensure royal line continued."

"Then how did they end up in France?" Lina looked at her puzzled. It was becoming too much for her befuddled mind to take on all at one time. Surely she should be the one comforting this woman before her, who was shackled and under threat, rather than the reverse.

"It was during Constantine's era, when the heirs approached Il Papa Sylvester , to complain about the purity of the Nazarene Church of Yeshua being corrupted by the takeover of Imperial Rome. They wanted the control returned to them, believing they were the rightful ones to run it."

"If I remember correctly," Lina was dredging around in the recesses of her mind for barely remembered information. "He gave them a short shrift, looking to his own secure future. He liked his job and wasn't about to abdicate for anyone. So he told them in no uncertain times, that the power of salvation did not rest with Yeshua, but with the Emperor Constantine, for whom the right of Messianic inheritance had been personally *reserved since the beginning of time!"*

"Which brings us up to the time whenYeshua and Miryai's heirs, left Judaea and resettled in France."

"As the Merovingian Kings?" Lina prompted, recalling one of the theories about Mary Magdalene.

"No," Adelais looked horrified. "They were of Germanic origin and their reputation was less than beneficent. The bloodline settled in the Languedoc and as they treasured the memory of Miryai, this is how she became to be worshipped in France."

Now Lina was looking sceptical once again.

Chapter Forty-five – The Magdalene Gospel

Miryai knew she had little time left on earth and wanted the simplicity of Yeshua's teachings to remain uncorrupted. The light from the oil lamp was dim, and her eyes teared up from the smoke. After returning to Judaea, the family of Joses had returned to his mother, Miriam's house and Miryai instructed the followers of her Nazarene from there.

She picked up a papyrus and laid it on the table, then reached for a quill and blackened it on the wick of the oil lamp.

"I already sense that in their quest for power," she confided to her daughter Tamar, who was seated beside her, "men will pervert Yeshua's words and teachings. Therefore I must pen the truth and our bloodline must ensure it is passed from generation to generation, in the hope they remain as pure as when he uttered them," and with her failing strength, she began to write in Aramaic.

As a Rabbi, Yeshua diligently studied the Scriptures and wished to pass the truth on to the people. Simplifying his teachings so all could understand the message:

All men and women are equal in the eyes of God the Father;

In the scriptures there are riches for all men and all women;

If you would manifest riches on earth, firstly look inward for the riches of the soul;

All beings are part of the divine source from which they emerged into this world;

Divinity is within every being, therefore look inward for riches, not outward;

Man does not have dominion over women;

No man or woman has dominion over another. To seek this is to upset the natural order of the Divine Source from whence we all come forth;

All beings are connected. All is balance. Strive to preserve the balance;

All beings are born again until they achieve the purity that enables them to return forever to the divine source from whence they emerged;

The wealth of each land should be shared equally amongst its peoples;

Treat others as you would wish to be treated. Harm no-one, or you harm yourself.

Miryai's strength grew weaker and she knew her time on this earthly plane was close. On her deathbed, she requested all leave her except Tamar, to whom she showed a small golden casket. "My Frbd (*daughter*), I must charge you with a sacred duty."

"What is it OmO?" Tamar leaned forward and placed a kiss on her OmO's forehead.

Miryai smiled lovingly at her. "You have been a good daughter and I know you will keep faith with me, when I have passed over and gone to join your Jwkyhb0 (*father*)." At his name, her eyes misted over. "Inside here is a treasure," she told her daughter.

"I always wondered what was in such a beautiful casket, that you kept so close to you." Their life had been a very simple one, without riches.

Miryai smiled sweetly. "Hold it closely to you. It is to be passed on to the eldest daughter of our matriarchal line for 2000 years."

Tamar gasped, unable to conceive of such a timeframe.

"Trust me," Miryai insisted. "This will be a more enlightened age and when the time is right, our bloodline will know. Then the casket can be opened."

Her Frbd looked at her in amazement, despite knowing her OmO's acknowledged powers of divination.

"I have seen this, along with other miracles and I know that men will pervert your Jwkyhb0's words and teachings for their own self interest."

"OmO, he would be heartbroken?"

"Indeed my child." Miryai looked at her with sorrow. "He was aware that the masses will continue to suffer greatly at the hands of the wealthy and powerful, until they all have learnt to read and write. This will free them to make their own decisions."

"Can we not do that now OmO?"

"No my child," Miryai's sweet countenance clouded as she thought of the plight of the ordinary people. "The masses minds are shackled by the temples and the priests. Unfortunately this will continue in your Jwkyhb0's name."

Her Frbd (daughter) looked horrified at the thought.

Miryai reached out and took her hand in hers. "They will build temples and elect priests, who will fight amongst themselves and foist their own interpretations of his teachings on the followers, and it will be so for 2000 years."

Tamar gasped in amazement, as she gazed at her OmO who continued. "When this time comes this casket must have survived, as it will serve as proof of my descendants' rights to our bloodline."

"To what purpose OmO?" Tamar could not imagine such things could be.

"It will open men and women's minds to their own power and possibilities." Placing the casket in Tamar's hands, she tasked her with keeping it safe during her own lifetime. "Charge your eldest Frbd with its safekeeping. She in turn, will charge her eldest Frbd and so on down the matriarchal line," she instructed. "Each generation *must* produce a girl child. This must survive, my Frbd."

"I will treasure and guard it with my life, and it will be so OmO. I make you this solemn promise," and Tamar put her arms around her OmO and held her lovingly, singing quietly to her until she saw her spirit was about to leave her earthly vehicle. Stroking her face she said. "I release you OmO. Go. Be with whyhb0 *(father)*, who is waiting for you on the other side in the light."

Holding Miryai in her arms until she breathed her last, Tamar saw her OmO's face transfigure into that of a smiling angel, who was reunited at last with her Yeshua, who showed himself plainly to Tamar, as her OmO's power of divination now passed to her as the keeper of the legacy.

And so it was. Each marriage produced the necessary girl child, in order to perpetuate the matrilineal line of Judaism and they taught the simple message of Yeshua, calling themselves the Church of the Nazarene.

In the Eleventh and Tweflth centuries the bloodline grew strong and became very powerful in the Carcassone area of southern France. With a patina of Roman Catholicism, in secret the Trencavel family practiced the teachings of the Nazarene Yeshua, and protected those of other faiths.

The women dressed in robes of blue, recalling Miryai and Mariam's dedication to the Virgins of Light were initiated into the secret mystic teachings which they carried forward, calling themselves The Women in Blue.

The casket continued to be passed down through the bloodline to the eldest daughter, who held it safe until the time it was safe to tell the world the truth.

*

"Lina, I have proof of all this," Adelais sought to convince her, seeing her drift away from credibility.

Lina did a doubletake. One thing after another, was getting to be a bit much to swallow in one mouthful.

"I have proof that Jesus was simply a mortal man, doing his best to reconquer Judaea for his people, because it was expected of him."

"How can you possibly have proof of this?"

Adelais drew in a breath sharply. "I have the document between Yeshua and Miryai, which the bride kept until the consummation of her marriage. As you know all betrothals and marriages were recorded in ancient times. It is how the Jewish people traced their lineage, which was very important to them, particularly when they were both connected to Royal houses."

Lina looked at this from with a jaded journalist's eye. It certainly made more sense to her than virgin births and Jesus' divinity. She had lost her belief in that theory during her journalistic career, having been exposed to too much horror. "They certainly took a census which was mentioned in Matthew's gospel. I suppose it is highly likely they recorded births, deaths and marriages."

"They did and the family kept the original document."

"It may be in tatters now. Two thousand years will destroy most things."

"Look at the gospels that have been discovered at Nag Hammadi and the Dead Sea Scrolls," Adelais persisted. "They survived in just earthenware pots that were sealed tight."

Lina had to agree with this. Ancient documents had survived thousands of years. "Well that will put the cat amongst the pigeons."

"Miryai also documented the true purpose of Yeshua's mission. She believed his mission and words would be distorted in the future, so she wanted to record the truth."

"I thought the Emperor Diocletion had destroyed all the documents relating to Christianity."

"He tried his hardest but the family knew how to hide these documents to ensure their survival."

"That's sounds promising, but how do we know it is not a forgery?" Lina was still playing the devil's advocate.

"Carbon testing will prove it is not. This is why the documentation could not be produced until this era, where carbon and DNA testing has progressed to a point people trust it."

"I wonder if Jesus and Mary's DNA would have survived?" Lina was reluctant to buy into the delusion, but decided it was worth thinking about.

"We are hoping so."

Lina looked at her keenly. This would set the Roman Catholic Church on its ear, if this information panned out under carbon dating. "The Christian churches won't like that. Not just the Holy Roman Catholic Church, but many other demoninations."

"I have further proof," Adelais admitted. "Miryai foresaw the chaos that would arise from his simple teachings. So she ensured there was a family heirloom that was passed down from her, to the eldest daughter of her bloodline, throughout the centuries."

Lina's head jerked upwards in shock and her senses swam. What had she gotten herself into now? This sounded as outrageous as the Church with its crazy relics.

"Please trust me." Adelais whole demeanour begged for understanding from Lina. "I am not crazy. This has survived. I have it safe."

"Good grief." Lina tried to grapple with this latest revelation. It was beginning to move into the realm of implausible credibility.

"Please believe me Lina." Adelais begged for understanding. "I know it sounds outlandish, but we have no doubt."

"May I know what the heirloom is?" Lina couldn't help herself from showing a little cynicism. It was all just too pat for her liking.

Adelais looked at her searchingly, then cocking her head to one side looked past Lina to somewhere only she was able to travel at that moment in time. A brief silence followed, then she gazed at Lina and said. "It is a baby tooth that Miryai's mother kept from her childhood along with a lock of hair. They were no different than we are today in that respect."

Lina blinked, but kept her mouth shut. 'The woman is deluded,' she thought with pity. "What will this prove?"

"It has her DNA."

"Won't this have deteriorated so badly, it will be unable to be tested?"

Adelais shook her head firmly. "No, the casket was hermetically sealed at the time and this has not been opened for two thousand years."

"You cannot guarantee this."

"I believe it is so Lina, and I trust."

Privately Lina wondered if trust was going to be enough. "And what if it disintegrates when the seal is broken?" she pressed.

"It won't. Trust me," Adelais beseeched her.

"It could still be the DNA of any woman at that time," Lina persisted.

"Miryai signed the marriage document with both their names on. Her DNA is on papyrus. It will match."

"But that will have deteriorated so badly, it won't be able to be tested," Lina argued.

"Lina, I have faith that when the casket is opened, everything will be in good condition. Look at the documents found at Nag Hammadi and the Dead Sea Scrolls. They were only buried in earthenware pots, then sealed and they survived in good condition."

Lina could not help but give her that one. "God, it will need to be in pristine condition to prove all of this."

"Both my daughter and myself will be able to be tested for the bloodline through the tooth."

Lina shook her head from side to side in denial and looked down at the floor, trying to hide her cynicism. "This alone won't prove Jesus existed."

"I understand your scepticism, but there is more," Adelais told her gently.

Lina looked up expectantly, willing to listen, if not to believe.

"In ancient Judaea, just as today, when a man approached a woman's family for permission to marry their daughter, he gave her a betrothal ring. This is also in the casket."

A flutter of excitement went through Lina, and she stopped breathing for a full thirty seconds. "That could very well have Jesus' DNA on it."

"Very likely," Adelais agreed.

It sounded incredulous, but could she believe it? No wonder the Cardinale was beside himself. She wondered if he knew there was a casket and what was in it.

"And do not forget the testament Miryai penned about herself and Yeshua. As they were both from royal families, they were taught to read and write. This is also sealed in the casket I hold safe."

All this was very difficult for a sceptical journalist to absorb. However, if it was true and the DNA held up, the impact on the world would be nuclear.

'But would this be a good thing?' Lina asked herself, as she lowered her gaze to the floor. "It could destroy the foundation of the Christian churches and throw the world into further chaos." Mentally shrugging off her doubts, she decided. "On the other hand it could be the best thing that could happen."

One of the reasons she went into war zones, was to try and better the lot of those who were bearing the full brunt of it. Did she have the right to destroy any faith that underpinned their lives? 'I've covered too many wars, where religion was the underlying cause. The result of mankind's inability to coincide alongside another's ideas and ideals, without having to prove them wrong,' ran through her mind.

Lifting up her eyes again, she faced Adelais. "I have to think about this."

Anxious to convince Lina about the proof she had to offer, Adelais pressed on, "We don't have a lot of time." Understanding that Lina was a journalist who worked with facts, not speculation, and could reject her tale out of hand, she took a deep breath before continuing.

"Miryai had the power of divination and knew what was in the future, including the discovery of DNA testing. She alludes to this in a testament she wrote and this is also in the casket. The secret has been handed down by word of mouth through each generation." Adelais never doubted for one moment, that all the links would come together to provide irrefutable proof to the world that would stop the madness forever.

"You know this is beginning to beggar belief," Lina scoffed, despite her sympathy for the woman.

"You have to understand Lina, this was a different time from that we live in today. The mysteries of the cosmos were taught and accepted as a matter of course."

"Yes, to put shackles around their minds and lives," Lina retorted sharply.
Adelais knew it would be fruitless to pursue this with Lina. It was now straying into the realms of suspended disbelief. "Then let us leave it in Miryai's hands and await the outcome of the tests," Adelais insisted.

"If you live that long," Lina cried out in despair. There was no denying Adelais' charisma and she desperately wanted to save her from the terrible fate the Cardinale had for her and her child.

"We will Lina. I have no doubt of that." Now the situation was reversed with Adelais attempting to console Lina. "My daughter will be tied to Miryai through the

DNA in the tooth. Then Miryai will be tied to the tooth, through her DNA on the testament she penned and the marriage document."

"What if it is proven to be a forgery?"

"Everything will check out," Adelais could not be swayed from her belief in the validity of the document. "It is written on papyrus, not parchment. It can be carbon dated. It will not be proven a forgery."

"I'm not sure that will be sufficient." Lina's mind was busily trying to follow the threads. "The Roman Catholic Church has untold wealth and can, and will, pay off anyone who attempts to disprove Jesus Christ's immortality. They have too much to lose. They will say it could be any woman's DNA from that time."

"The marriage document has both their DNA on it." Adelais looked triumphant as Lina's resistance began to break down.

"Will this prove the existence of Jesus?"

"That will be more difficult. There was no male child with the Y chromosome passed on from him, but there has always been a girl child, with the mitrochondrial DNA in the matriarchal line from Miryai." Adelais looked at her elatedly.

"How can you be so sure?" Lina's reporting skills had come to the front and she would accept nothing less than proof positive.

Adelais looked at her searchingly. "I have never shared this secret with anyone. My daughter would have been told when we presented her to the world." She seemed to look past Lina to a place only she could see. "Miryai has told me to trust you, as you are honest and compassionate and will not betray us."

Lina was not too sure of that, because there was a sensational story here.

"Miryai knows you better than you know yourself Lina," Adelais assured Lina. "The time will come when this story can be told to the world and you have been chosen to carry out this important task. You will not divulge the secret that I will tell you now, until the time is right."

"Adelais, I am a reporter, how can you trust that I will not race out and print this?"

"You have much to do Lina, before you write your story and the world reads it." Adelais smiled sweetly. "You will receive a Pulitzer award in the not too distant future, but events must take place, before the story is complete."

"Adelais?" Lina looked searchingly into Adelais beautiful green eyes, twin emerald pools in which she thought she was drowning, to try and read her thoughts behind her statements. However, with this came an understanding that was beyond her and she put a hand down to steady herself, as her senses swam until she thought she would collapse.

"Lina." A gentle voice that sounded like tinkling bells, brought her back to the present.

"Adelais?" she queried and looked at the woman in front of her, who gazed upon her serenely.

"No Lina that was not my voice."

"Then who?" Lina knew the answer, the moment she asked the question and shook her head in denial.

"Yes, Lina," Adelais voice resounded around the cellar. "That was Miryai."

Lina looked around her, but saw nothing.

"She is not a physical being Lina," Adelais endeavoured to explain. "She is a vibration that you can feel and see, only when the veil is taken from your eyes."

Lina felt a tremor go through her body, from the tips of her toes to the crown of her head. As she tried to hold onto the hard reality of the earthly plane, a feeling of unreality enveloped her.

"She also penned her testament stating the true aims of Yeshua and confirmed his death and her remarriage to Joses. There was no resurrection. It was all the doing of the Emperor Constantine, in his zeal to form a united Roman Empire."

"I know the Catholic Church will protect its very existence. They will fight you every inch of the way and they have the wealth to do so."

"I know, but Miryai has prepared the way. Il Papa who sits on St Peter's chair is a good man who truly cares about the people of this world."

"I don't believe the Catholic Church would kill over this." Lina protested vehemently.

"Nor do I," Adelais agreed.

"But *they* will." Lina's thoughts were churning.

"Who are they?"

"Cardinale della Rovere, the Knights of Malta and the Abate of this monastery. It will destroy all *they* hold dear."

Adelais gasped, "I thought it was della Rovere alone. Are you saying all the monks attached to this monastery are involved?"

"I do not believe so," Lina shook her head in denial "but I have to treat everyone in the building as an enemy."

"Why on earth would the Knights of Malta be involved?" Adelais wondered aloud.

"There are power structures in this world that want the status quo to remain exactly as it is. It enables them to manipulate people through fear. They strike at the most vulnerable and play on their fears. This keeps money flowing into their coffers and they do not want anything to deprive them of this."

Adelais looked at her bewildered. "I find it hard to believe the Knights of Malta could be so sadistic."

"Oh I can believe it." Lina did not doubt it for one moment. "If their power and wealth is threatened, they will do everything to in their power to ensure their existence is not threatened."

Adelais nodded in agreement then looked puzzled. "But what has Alesso got to do with such people?"

"This man has serious problems, which they obviously believed they could use for their own ends." Lina knelt down before Adelais and the child knowing time was running short and she still had to retrace her steps to escape herself. "Many people in this world have been waiting for the proof that the Christian religion was built on a lie. Some will not like the truth, as they will have to become responsible for their own lives. Many who have built fortunes on the premise that Christ was immortal; will be destroyed and unable to manipulate their congregations. You won't be very popular at all."

Adelais looked at her sadly. "I am aware of that, but I also have a document in Miryai's own writing that has been handed down from mother to child, instructing the bloodline to tell the world the truth in 2000 years from her time."

"How would she have known a religion would be formed in Jesus' name which would make a mockery of all he believed and taught?"

"The Jewish mystics could pierce the veil between the two worlds in those days. They could communicate with the spiritual world and she was told this would happen."

"Why has it not been exposed before now?"

Adelais looked at her sorrowfully. "I don't understand why the world had to endure the suffering the Church inflicted on the world. I only know the bloodline had to wait 2000 years."

Lina looked thoughtful, "I guess it remained buried, until the shackles were taken off people's minds and they were free to form their own opinions without repercussions. The lot of the common folk in past centuries has been pretty miserable, under the yoke of the wealthy and the church."

"You are right, of course," Adelais agreed. "If they could not read nor write, they could not reason for themselves. It took a long time. I don't know about the morality of it all, nor do I know if there is a greater plan for this world. It seems a cruel vision to me."

"I think it is more likely that the chaos theory rings true," Lina promulgated, "This world was created out of chaos. Out of chaos must come order, as in nature, and it took time to evolve. This will turn the world on its ear, but we need changes now the masses are stronger and more vocal."

"I just hope it does not lead to anarchy before it is all over," Adelais looked worried. "But I have to carry out Miryai's wishes. Far too much horror has been perpetrated by all churches in Yeshua's name, for 2000 years."

Lina looked sceptical. "I don't think you will find the Vatican is behind this. Since the discovery of the Gnostic texts at Nag Hammadi and the Pistis Sophia, there are millions who now accept Jesus was a reformer, not the son of Yahweh. I think we will find it is the work of a deranged mind and now we are aware who he is we can bring him to justice, along with his cohorts." Lina's eyes went to the young girl.

"And that makes it the right time to release the proof." Adelais' tone of voice would brook no opposition.

"If this is true, don't you realise what the Cardinale will do to you?" Lina was horrified knowing the lengths the man had already gone to. "He will stop at nothing to recover the testaments and relics, to destroy them along with you and your child."

"I would rather die than reveal its whereabouts." Adelais' face showed her determination.

"And what if he tortures your daughter in front of you?" Lina was a dyed in the wool realist.

Adelais' straightened and looked at Lina proudly. "We are prepared for that."

Lina looked at her in horror. "You would martyr your daughter for this?"

Adelais nodded sadly. "We are both prepared to die."

Lina was outraged. "I don't think I my mind can grapple with this. Would Jesus and Mary Magdalene have wanted another sacrifice on their hands? Surely not." Desperate to convince Adelais this way lay madness, she pressed her advantage knowing one woman and a child were no match for a deranged psychopath and his cohorts.

Although Adelais looked disconsolate at Lina's response, she held firm to her faith in Miryai. "It will not come to that."

"And what do you think will intervene."

Adelais looked at her lovingly. "You have already intervened in the Cardinale's plans," she said softly. "Do you think you have become involved by pure chance?"

"I am a reporter who will follow a good story. I don't put much credence in being chosen by illusory spectres."

"Lina, please do not reject what I am saying to you." Adelais gazed at her earnestly. "This is precisely why you were chosen. Once you are convinced and you present this in an unbiased form, you will give credence to our claims."

Lina seriously doubted they had *chosen* the right person, if they were looking to her to validate their claims. Even E wouldn't tackle that one.

'What is wrong with these people?' she asked herself. 'Should I leave them to their illusions and fate?' Then realising she could never do that, she tried to convince Adelais.

"The Cardinale will stop at nothing to silence you, if you can provide this proof." Lina was concerned that Adelais was not facing up to reality, but decided to go along with her in an effort to make her see sense. This man of the church was highly dangerous. Adelais and her daughter could not fly in the face of the threat he presented.

"In fact, he isn't bothering to wait for proof, he wants to destroy it rather than let it see the light of day. He has already murmured two innocent women." Lina's fears for Adelais and her daughter were very real. "He is capable of anything."

"Then we are both prepared to die to keep the secret but," and here a look of pure bliss, shone from Adelais beautiful emerald green eyes, "it will not come to that. Miryai will save us."

Lina looked at her doubtfully, wondering if the woman had taken leave of her senses. After all, she and the child had just been through a terrifying experience, which was not over yet.

Lina felt something inexplicable, something she could not put her finger on. What the hell was it? Wildly she looked around. Nothing she could see, but a feeling a presence was there. 'My nerves are getting the better of me,' she thought. 'Get a grip. And get out of here.'

Suddenly the woman straightened and placing her hand under her daughter's chin, and raising her head, spoke softly to her. "She is here." Her face and eyes reflected the glory of something only she could see. "We are not abandoned. Miryai is here with us."

Lina peered into the gloom, but could see nothing.

Her mother smiled gently at her daughter. "No matter how threatened they feel, it is time to introduce Miryai's descendants to the world."

The young girl raised her head higher and looked where her mother's gaze lingered. "Mother, I feel a strength flowing through me. I am no longer afraid."

Lina looked at her doubtfully, wondering if the experience had driven them crazy. After all, she and the child had just been through a terrifying experience, which was not over yet.

Lina looked around the room, searching in vain for answers that eluded her. They lurked in corners, teasing her, refusing to come out into the light and help her make sense of the senseless.

Exhausted she leaned against the dank stone wall, from which emanated the strong musty smell of ancient intrigues, her head pounding, heart racing.

"I must go. I cannot free you on my own." Willing herself back to reality, she knew she must leave them, "but I can lead the gendarmerie back here and rescue you."

"You may not have time," the woman was losing her strength and her resolve weakened. "He will be back. The Cardinale hates us so."

"It's a risk we have to take. There is no other way." Lina felt terrible as she knew the woman would have pinned her hopes on her, but there was nothing to hand, that she could break the chains with. "I know you have three days before he will harm you. I'm going to leave now, but I promise you I will be back and you will be saved.

"How do you know we have three days?" Adelais looked at her hopefully.

"Because I overheard his plans for you both," Lina admitted, determined not to reveal them and distress the pair further.

"What are they?" Adelais swallowed hard and looked at Lina beseechingly.

"Nothing you need to worry about now," Lina reassured her gently. "Trust me. I will not let you down."

Wrenching herself away from the woman and child, feeling their despair at their plight, she understood the fear the woman held for her child.

Mentally shaking her head, the situation appeared surreal to Lina. "I must go." Smiling at them both one more time, she tore herself away and crossed the cavern. Once more she turned back to the shackled woman and child, who looked back at her serenely. "I will bring help," she promised meaning every word.

"We know you will." Adelais smiled at her. "We are no longer afraid."

'Well, if it's up to me, I have to do something on this physical plane, no matter what's going on in their world,' she reminded herself, although she had to admit she was touched by the mystery.

It was time to be practical and Lina knew it was time to get a move on, if she was to help them further. Slipping back through the door, she tentatively began the journey back the way she had come, ever vigilant for the slightest sound.

Barely breathing until she reached the door, which was still ajar and slipped out into the night.

Then she slipped through the grounds until she reached her car, still feeling in mortal peril and caught her breath as she started the motor, only releasing it when she was a mile down the road.

Chapter Forty-six– To the Rescue

"We have to go to the Carabinieri, E," Lina begged the reluctant priest.

"We cannot do this, Lina. The scandal that will arise will bring down the Church." Edoardos was agonising over his decision, but his first duty was to the Holy See.

Lina could not believe what she was hearing. "How can you possibly say such a monstrous thing? This is a member of your own family, your sister-in-law and your niece," she cried in despair. "Are you prepared to sacrifice them for the sake of the Vatican? Don't you understand we have no time to lose?"

Edoardos' face twisted with pain and despair, as he was torn between his love for and duty to his family; and his duty to the Vatican. "God, this monster is one of our own. Let me think, please Lina," he whispered, trying to clear his confused mind.

Collapsing onto the sofa in her apartment, where he had hurried safe from prying eyes and ears after her frantic call to him, he cradled his head in his hands.

"Lina, stop," he had ordered, as she began to blurt out her story on the telephone. "I will come to the apartment and you can tell me what you want." The risk was too great to let her continue on a Vatican phone. God knew who could be listening or watching.

"Please hurry," she had urged him. "There is no time to lose."

"Why are you so fixated with the Knights?" he asked quietly. "Why is this, such an emotive issue for you? A reporter is meant to report the facts, remain detached, not colour them with emotion."

"I'm not built like that." Her eyes defied him. "Emotions are running high over these murders and I need to get inside the murky head of the perpetrators of this horror so I can report on it."

"Don't inflame an already volatile situation for headlines, Lina," E cautioned her.

"How can you say that?" Her eyes filled with tears which she angrily wiped away on the back of her sleeve. "You sit in that Bloody Vatican detached from all feelings while they weave their web around the world, ensnaring the unwary, the desperate and the poor, controlling their lives with unrealistic dictates and the fear of excommunication, purgatory and hell. As if the poor and weak don't have enough to contend with. How bloody reasonable is that?" she flung at him.

Stung, he drew back and bit his tongue, knowing she had touched on a sore point. Gazing at her, he put out his hand in a gesture of peace and she reached out tentatively and grasped it. In silence they sat still and looked at each other, until church bells pealed, recalling them to the world around them.

The rain fell down in sheets. "There'll be flooding somewhere if this continues," Edoardos said, looking out the window at the sky, as his mind tried to escape from the reality of the situation. "This is unseasonable."

"The heavens are weeping for those poor women; and Adelais and her daughter," Lina cautioned him.

"Perhaps you are right," Sighing sorrowfully Edoardos capitulated. "What do you want from me?"

Now she had to beg him for help, "We have to stop them and bring them to justice E." Falling to her knees before him, she pulled his hands away from his eyes. "We have to round them all up, the bastards. We can only do this with the Carbinieri."

"Lina we cannot destroy the Church. A scandal of this magnitude would bring it down around our ears," he insisted. "Let me think."

"This is not time for thinking," she complained unable to hold back her words. "I'm not going to get bogged down in rhetoric. It's time for action. Let's take a leap of logic, not a leap of faith."

"I know," E remained determined to protect the church. "Nor is it time for some hasty ill thought out action, which could bring repercussions down on our heads. The Carabinieri will doubt our story and we will lose more time."

"Then what are we to do" she asked in despair? "We have no time to lose, every second is important."

Edoardos' face set like stone. "I must go to Il Papa. He is the only one I can trust. I must convince him to instruct the Vatican Carabinieri to take action. To arrest the Cardinale while he is in the Vatican and rescue Adelais and Tamar."

"What about the rest of his merry bunch of murderers?" Lina countered.

"Il Papa learnt from John Paul I's mistake, and does not involve those he does not trust," he assured her. "He fully intends to complete what John Paul I could not."

Lina contemplated both him and his words. Would this Pope be given the opportunity, to carry out Albino Luciani's intentions, or would he also be silenced and stopped. "And how the hell do we hide this from the authorities? The crimes have been perpetrated in the Italian State, not the Vatican State. It is the State Carabanieri's bailiwick, not the Vatican's."

"Il Papa will find a way. It must be swept under the carpet Lina." Edoardos looked her in the eye.

She flinched, gasped and pulled away from him. "The Vatican has spent 2000 years sweeping its dirty little secrets under the carpet. It is time it stopped."

"You don't understand the repercussions Lina," Edoardos insisted.

Bitterly she went on the attack again, "I can't believe my ears. You would hide the truth of these atrocities from the world."

"It has to be." He was adamant. "Il Papa is as humble and kindly as John Paul 1. Like his predecessor, he does not distance himself from the people. He uses the ingular *I* instead of the royal *We*. He refused a papal coronation, insisting on an nvestiture only."

"What about your sister-in-law, and her child?" Lina cried. "How will you ilence them?"

"Aaah Lina, my family has been keeping the secrets of Vatican City for enturies. They know it will be important for this to be handled discreetly rather han in the public domain."

"Why? Why do you ask this of them?" she cried out bitterly. "They will never now peace of mind again."

"Adelais knows if we bring down the Vatican, we bring down the financial tructure of the world and it will collapse into chaos. Il Papa will find a way. He is ne reason I am a priest."

Lina wrung her hands, looking confused at his last words. "What do you nean?"

"Trust me Lina. Trust Il Papa. He is a great man. My family have spent a ecade, ensuring he became Il Papa," Edoardos knew he was taking a risk being so onest with Lina, but it had to be.

"He has no use for rich ecclesiastical displays, nor panoply, and continues in ne vein of John Paul I, by encouraging parish priests to sell precious vessels and ther church valuables for the benefit of the poor. He is going to ensure that John aul 1"s plea to the wealthy churches of the west is carried out. They will give one er cent of their income to the impoverished churches of the third world. In fact," espite the seriousness of the situation, his eyes twinkled briefly. "In fact I have it n very good counsel he has upped the ante and made it 5%."

"Now I must go to the Reverendo Padre," he told her softly. Walking towards ne door, he stopped and turning to face her extended an invitation to join him. Give him a chance. Come with me."

*

They hurried down the steps from Lina's apartment to the street below where Edoardos had scored a nearby park. A miracle in traffic clogged Rome.

"Get in. Quickly!" he insisted. "We have no time to loose."

Clambering into the low slung sports car, she looked at him balefully, as she still could not accept his reasoning, despite his protestations of the Pope's intentions.

Putting the car into gear, he pulled out into the chaos that Rome called traffic and drove as fast as possible without killing them both to the Vatican.

Entering the Via di *Porta* Angelica, he drove up to the Porta di Sant' Anna, where he was waved through by one of the two Papal guards on duty; after showing his credentials and vouching for Lina.

Driving to one of the areas reserved for officials who worked in Vatican City, he parked the car in a cobblestoned piazza. The Holy See was a hive of rarified activity, with clerics in flowing black robes and even crimson skullcaps sweeping past, whilst carrying on conversations on their cellphones. This was the modern face of the Church of the Nazarene.

Limousines and cars passed by, some disgorging monsignors, archbishops and Cardinales from God alone knew where. Lina stepped lively to avoid being run down by some out of control nuns, at the wheel of a Fiat.

Picking up the pace, Lina followed Edoardos down a laneway running along the stone ramparts of the Apostolic Palace, until they came to an entrance. Once again he was granted instant access into the Vatican Palace. Being familiar with the layout of the building, he took the stairs two at a time with Lina hurrying to keep up with him and spluttering "How do you know he will be there?"

Striding down corridors until he came to the Papal office on the first floor, which also housed Il Papa's private chapel, he stopped for her to catch up before he entered. Two floors above was the Papal apartment, with its famous balcony over the Piazza St Pietro.

"At this time of the day, I know he will be. Strangely enough, there have been no appointments announced. This is most unusual," he tossed over his shoulder at her.

Assuredly he moved towards Il Papa's private study, Lina lagging behind, unsure of her position in these hallowed halls.

Passing through official rooms, he finally came to his goal where the Papal Chamberlain looked up from his desk and frowned as they knocked and entered unbidden.

"What are you doing Padre? You cannot come here without Il Papa's invitation or my permission," he rounded on Edoardos imperiously.

"I must see His Holiness on a very urgent mission," Edoardos insisted.

"You do not have an appointment." The man was astounded at Edoardos' temerity. Who did he think he was? "You cannot see His Holiness." He endeavoured to turn them away.

"This is urgent, it will not wait. The very future of the church is at stake," E was determined to hold his ground until he achieved his purpose.

The Chamberlain shook his head just as determined to make his stand, but unseen forces were at work behind the scenes.

A diminutive figure clad in a simple white cassock with red slippers on his feet and a white zuccetto on his head, appeared through the door leading into Il Papa Callixtus IV's private study. "Who is it Benito?"

"Vostra Santita," the Chamberlain stuttered to His Holiness. "The Padre does not have an appointment, you cannot be disturbed."

"Something has impelled me to leave my desk and come to the door," the Sovereign Pontiff replied, reaching out his hand to Edoardos. "Come in Padre. I know you have something urgent to tell me."

Edoardos' face registered its surprise and he moved forward towards St Peter's Vicar on earth.

"And who is this you bring with you?" Il Papa queried gently.

Lina froze to the spot, in the face of the quiet power of the man clothed in white robes before her.

"She is a reporter, Vostra Santita." Edoardos swallowed hard, as he addressed the most powerful man in Christendom, who smiled at him encouragingly.

"Is she now?" Il Papa smiled mischievously. "Are you asking for a story for your paper?"

Lina had never been so tongue tied in her life.

"No, Vostra Santita," Edoardos stepped in and replied for her. "She has a story to tell you."

"One that reflects upon the honour of our Mother Church I believe," he quietly dropped a bombshell at their feet.

"Hhhhhow do you know Vostra Santita," Edoardos stammered?

Il Papa just smiled quietly, as though at some secret. "Santo Padre (*Holy Father)* will suffice Edoardos." And he beckoned them forward while the Papal Chamberlain stood to block their way.

"Leave us please Benito," Il Papa gently requested of him. "Come with me Edoardos," he requested when the priest remained rooted to the spot, astounded that Il Papa knew his name

The Papal Chamberlain was dismayed. "But Santo Padre," he protested vehemently. After all he was the guardian of this inner sanctum and he took his role very seriously indeed.

"I am perfectly safe." The man in white reassured the concerned man, who was completely loyal to him and would protect him with his life if need be. "Go about your duties."

Reluctantly the man turned and went towards the desk in the antechamber, where he had been seated.

"Come into my office," Il Papa invited Lina and Edoardos, who were overawed but they did as they were bid.

"Sit down." Indicating a grouping of three renaissance armchairs, he seated himself and waited until his visitors had done the same. As they did so, he made a steeple of his fingers and looked at them solemnly. "Now tell me."

Edoardos looked at Lina and began to relay the sorry story to one of the most powerful men in the world.

They had Il Papa's full attention, as he nodded from time to time.

"My sister-in-law, who lays claim to the bloodline of Jesus Christ, knows where the original testament penned by Mary Magdalene is secreted."

"It is the Third Secret of Lourdes my son."

Lina gasped while the colour drained out of Edoardos' face. "This will be the end of the Church," he whispered.

"Not necessarily my son. Have faith." The Pontiff smiled gently. "There will still be the faithful that will choose our direction. Many people cannot handle the responsibility of their own lives and will remain with the Church, looking for its intercession on their behalf."

"Now my dear," turning to Lina he urged her. "Tell me about your role in this matter."

She was not used to being overcome by a presence, but it emanated so strongly from the gentle, educated man, she was momentarily thrown off balance.

Hesitating for a brief second, Il Papa realised she was overwhelmed. "Please," he encouraged her.

"I'm sorry." Lina then proceeded to bring him up to date, whilst thinking to herself, *'Oh my God, he will think we are crazy and have us thrown out.'*

Suddenly Il Papa surprised her. "I will not do that," he reassured her, although she had not spoken a word. Looking at him in surprise, she hesitated again.

"I am not so out of touch with what is going on in the world," he told them both, "and in my prayers, I am often guided by another world."

Shocked, Lina stammered out the rest of her story, finally urging Il Papa to help rescue Adelais and her daughter.

"We will do so," he reassured them both. "I will instruct the Vatican Carabinierei, and we will enlist the help of the State Caribinieri, who have jurisdiction over the monastery."

Lina sighed with relief, that Il Papa was going to do the right thing, but suddenly he raised his hand to silence them both. "Ssshhh. Trust me Lina." Cocking his head to one side, he bade them, "listen."

Suddenly they heard the scurrying of running feet and a voice raised in alarm. Voices murmured in to the antechamber.

Il Papa arose and crossed the room to the door separating the two rooms and opened it. "What is it Benito?"

The Chamberlain's face was solemn and the messenger clothed in a black cassock was ashen.

"Santos Padre, I have sad and serious news," he declared.

"Proceed," Il Papa encouraged him.

"Cardinale della Rovere has been found in his study. He has had a massive stroke, which has left him severely impaired."

Il Papa smiled gently. "Has he been seen by our doctor?"

"He is with him now."

"Thank you Benito," he said kindly to the Chamberlain who hurried out of the room.

Turning to Lina and E, he beckoned, "come." They followed him out of the apartments and through the halls of the Basilica until he came to a door, where hushed voices were murmuring.

"Vostra Santita." The people dropped to their knees, in deference to the most revered man in the Catholic world.

"Stand up," he commanded them, turning to the doctor who had been called. "What is your prognosis?"

"Vostra Santita, I am afraid the Cardinale is paralysed."

"Is he in a coma?"

"No Vostra Santita. He appears to know what is going on around him, but can neither move nor speak."

"Like being bricked up behind a wall?" Lina whispered, feeling a wave of nausea assail her.

Il Papa, who had overheard her, nodded sagely.

"Will he recover?" he asked the doctor.

"That is very doubtful Vostra Santita." The man shook his head. "You may get a second opinion, but in my own, he will remain as he is."

Sighing, Il Papa said sadly, "I would like a moment alone with our brother."

Moving forward, he gestured for Lina and E to follow him and they gazed upon the man who had moved out of this physical sphere, sitting as though in repose before them.

"Is this the man you saw?" he asked Lina.

"Yes," she whispered as she looked upon the inert figure in the chair.

Il Papa bent his head in prayer, as he raised his hand to bless the Cardinale with the sign of the cross.

Turning he left the room, asking Lina and E to follow him again. When they were seated in his office again, he turned to them. "Forces greater than us are dealing with this matter in their own way," and he raised his hand to bid them to remain silent, as the telephone rang in the antechamber.

The Papal Chamberlain appeared in the doorway which Il Papa had deliberately left open. "Vostra Santita, may I approach?" he asked tentatively.

Raising his hand Il Papa beckoned him near. "What is it Benito?"

Agitated and confused the Chamberlain looked at Il Papa. "The Grand Master of the Knights of Malta has died."

"Well he was very old. It will be a natural death." Il Papa gently reassured the Chamberlain, as the telephone rang once again and he motioned to Benito to return and answer it. Again he raised his hand to Lina and Edoardos, asking them to remain silent and wait.

Again the Chamberlain appeared in the doorway, wringing his hands. "I do not understand Vostra Santita."

"What is it Benito? What has upset you so? Come. Come," he beckoned him forward.

"The Abate of the Monastery of St.Gerard, has had a heart attack."

"Is he dead?" The man in white waited quietly as though he already knew the answer.

"Yes Vostra Santita."

At the door, the Chamberlain turned back, "I don't understand?"

"What don't you understand?" Il Papa asked quietly.

"Why should these two calls have come through to your office?" He knew how unusual this was. Normally Il Papa would not have been advised immediately. The information would trickle through to him in time.

"There are forces greater than Our Lord's humble servants on earth and sometimes they move in mysterious ways," he told the confused man, as he turned to Lina who could not believe her eyes, as despite the gravity of the situation, the Supreme Pontiff of the Roman Catholic Church winked at her.

With this, the Chamberlain left the room closing the door behind him.

"Your work is done," he told Lina, who looked at him in amazement and was reduced to silence for the first time in her life.

Turning to Edoardos, he motioned to him to approach. "Now you and I will start the real work that we are destined to do. It will be difficult and dangerous, but we have been chosen and we must see it through to its conclusion."

"Vostra Santita." Edoardos looked at Christ's Vicar on Earth. "I am just a humble priest."

"Be that as it may Edoardos, but you come from an ancient lineage, who have dues to pay to the Church. You and I must work together now."

Edoardos dropped onto his knees before Il Papa, and raised his eyes to gaze into those intelligent serene ones of the man before him. "I am not worthy," he began.

"Oh yes you are," Il Papa assured him. "Do not question those imbued with higher authority than your own. You must tread the path of your destiny, which will be a hard and dangerous path that you may not survive. Are you willing to do this for your Saviour and his Church?" Il Papa reached out his hand to him.

Edoardos felt more humbled than he had ever felt in his entire life. "I will follow you into the fires of hell if need be," he told the holy man and meant every word of it.

"Then get off your knees my son. I will inform the Chamberlain to contact the Vatican Carabinieri, who will meet the civil Carabinieri at the Monastery, to free Adelais and her daughter. They will be returned to your family home and remain under my protection. They will not be harmed."

Lina sat gazing in wonder at this extraordinary scene, wondering if what she was seeing and hearing was real.

"What if they the monks close ranks and refuse them entry?" she interjected.

"And who would be so bold as to stop the Vatican Carabinieri, when they are following out the instructions of the Santo Padre?" Il Papa leaned towards Lina and earnestly assured her. "They will be in disarray with the death of their Abate. Furthermore, I will instruct the Papal Chamberlain to ring the monastery and let them know that I know everything; and that if the woman and her child are hurt, I will excommunicate them all. They will not disobey me."

Lina continued to look doubtful, wondering whether the punishment of excommunication carried the weight it used to in past. Then decided to put her trust in Il Papa.

As if to reassure her he took her hands in his. "I am also instructing my Secretary of State, to contact the civil Arma dei Carabinieri, to offer our assistance in this matter.

Lina was speechless as His Holiness' integrity shone through like the sun breaking through the clouds when the storm had passed. And the rainbow that appeared to shine around him, to her was a measure of his honesty and greatness.

"My dear," picking up her hands, he brought them to his heart. "The Church owes you a great deal and I would ask one more thing of you."

"What is that Santo Padre?" she murmured.

"Go now write your story. I will ring the owners of La Republicca, and it will appear on their front page in the morning."

After the initial shock, feeling began to return to her body as he lay her hands back in her lap again. Tears welled in her eyes and standing, she dropped to her knees before him, seeking to kiss the Fisherman's ring on his finger.

"No, no," his humility was genuine. "I do not ask others that they venerate me. I am a simple man of plain faith and do not need gestures of supplication."

Lina stood again in the presence of Il Papa.

"Benito has organised a driver and one of the Papal Guard will escort you to your home and remain with you whilst you work."

The Reverendo Padre blessed them both. "Leave me now. I have much to do."

When Edoardos started towards him, seeing how tired he was Il Papa reassured him. "Edoardos I will meet with you first thing tomorrow morning. Please send Benito into me as you leave. Until then sleep well."

Once they had closed the door behind them, he sank tiredly back in his chair, his eyes reflecting the deep sorrow he felt at the state of his Church, and prayed he had time to make things right before he left this earth. Hopefully go to another realm, where he wished to reside with all his heart and soul.

When his old friend Benito entered, concern for Il Papa clouding his features, the Reverendo Padre reassured him.

"We have much to do, you and I. We must act swiftly and surely now. Please do as I instruct you and let no-one near me unless I personally approve the appointment. You will personally supervise the food and drink for all my meals I know this is an onerous task but it is vital if I am to survive this challenge."

They might as well have been living in the 15th century under the Borgia papacy, with a sacrificial lamb, who was appointed as Il Papa's food taster in case it was poisoned.

Tears started in his faithful aide's eyes and he fell to his knees before Il Papa Callixtus IV, who blessed him and standing raised him to his feet and embraced him. Holding Benito, he urged him to listen as he gave him instructions he wished carried out.

When he had finished, he dropped back into the chair. "I have Our Saviour, his Father and all the Angels of Heaven on my side. When my task has been completed, if they seek to take me to them, I will gladly do so, but I must be able to face my saviour knowing I have done all I can to right great wrongs."

After Benito had departed to organise the rescue of Adelais and Tamar, he made his way into his private chapel. As his slippered feet whispered over the white marble floor, he looked up at the Christ cast in gold, suspended in the floor to ceiling concavity of red marble, behind the simple and elegant altar with its white lace covered table holding candles and a Bible. Lowering himself to the red velvet kneeler, he humbly asked his saviour for guidance.

Chapter Forty-seven– The Storm Breaks

Lina's story was on the front page of La Republicca the next day and flashed around the world. Television interviewers were fighting over her. Her name was made.

Everything she had dreamed of and yet? Something was missing. What was it?

No longer feeling innocent or naïve, she along with the rest of the world, faced up to reality.

Il Papa had ordered the Vatican Carabinieri to go to the Monastery of St Gerard, where they had released Adelais and her daughter, returning them to the Guiliannini family.

Then they searched Cardinale della Rovere's ascetic cell in the building, where hidden behind his sleeping pallet, they found secreted in a cavity under a loose stone in the floor, a list of the members of the Brotherhood of the Cross.

Working with the state Arma dei Carabiniere, they arrested them and they were held over for trial.

The world watched on with horror and fascination, as the stories with Lina's byline continued to update them of the unfolding events.

There was worldwide admiration for Il Papa who refused to hide the Church's malefaction. The brave man who had opened the closet, to air it completely for the first time in its history, became their hero.

His courage saved the Church, as his flock did not desert her, but gathered behind him. More than ever, they needed a shepherd to guide them through this tortuous world that could be capable of such evil.

In searching the Abate's office, they found a safe and discovered that only Cardinale della Rovere held the key that would open it. Searching his office in the Vatican, they located it.

Amongst other documents, including his last will and testament, they found a list of the rogue element of the Knights of Malta. Enjoying diplomatic immunity, with Il Papa's blessing and insistence, these men who held positions of immense financial and political clout throughout the world were also arrested by the authorities of their own countries, as the present Il Papa withdrew his protection from the Order.

The intelligence services' investigations, uncovered their use of the Knights' aircraft and trucking fleets, used to smuggle illicit diamonds from countries that had no qualms about the treatment of their labour to mine them, and used to fund the illegal, but extremely lucrative armaments trade.

Crates purportedly ferrying in goods for humanitarian aid, had in reality, illegally smuggled in those very guns and rifles, to despots who committed genocide, in the name of personal greed and corruption.

The world was reminded of the lines in Aldous Huxley's novel: *After Many a Summer*:

The people who make wars, the people who reduce their fellows to slavery, the people who kill and torture and tell lies in the names of their sacred causes, the really evil people, in a word – these are never the publicans and the sinners. No, they're the virtuous respectable men, who have the finest feelings, the best brains, the noblest ideals.

Deeming these to be crimes against humanity, the world chose to try them in The International Court of the Hague, as a warning to others, that they were finally prepared to take action against the obscenities the world had been living with for too long.

Pope Callixtus IV stayed his hand against The Knights of Malta, but watched as them scramble to undo the damage. Previously viewed as a venerable organisation, it had been tainted.

The Order could not be destroyed. Might as well try and destroy the Bilderberg Group. Nevertheless he made a vow that as long as he remained as Pontiff on this earth, they were answerable to him.

*

The following morning Edoardos received a summons from Il Papa Callixtus V, to meet him in the Papal Gardens.

"Sit with me Edoardos," the Vicar of Christ invited him, placing his hand on the bench beside him.

"Vostra Santita, I cannot," the priest protested, as he knelt before him in fidelity. "I am not worthy."

"Of course you can Edoardos. Stand up and sit by me." His hand patted the bench until Edoardos sat beside him. "I do not want to stand on ceremony here."

"I am a simple man and could not understand why the Cardinales elected me to the Chair of Peter, for I am as outspoken as Pope John Paul I. However, I learned my lesson from his demise and I do not share my innermost thoughts with anyone. I have elected my own papal secretary and the nun who looks after me. They believe in the love of our sweet Lord and do not fear death, if that is what it takes to protect me and my works that I intend to carry out."

"This time the plan must be in place, before any announcement is made, when I will make the world aware of my intentions. By then I must also have put measures in place, which will occur should I meet an untimely end.

"I have reflected at length, and will need your youth and strength in the months to come. When I send for you again, it will be at the last moment. Until then, do not let anyone catch a glimpse of what you know, or show your disillusionment in the meantime. You are to be the greatest actor the world has ever seen, as I will. Only then, together can we deliver the script we must prepare."

"My decision will end the Church as we know it and take it back to its simple roots, before the Emperors and Il Papas built their own desires into the simple philosophy of our Lord and Master Jesus Christ. The Mother Church is strong and as it builds itself again, I believe we will attract the faithful in greater numbers than before and their lives will not be constrained in the name of wealth and greed. They will be able to live free, full lives and be joyful. I am determined to release them from the bonds of poverty."

"Governments may turn against me in fear of the loss of their power over the people. My Church could rise against me, as they will fear their own loss of power and realise their personal ambitions will not be realised. That type of thinking has no place in the Church on my watch."

"I believe the peoples of the world want a return to simplicity. If I am able to live long enough, I will lead them back into a simple faith, which will sustain them in their daily lives and provide for all in this world. If I am eliminated, then steps will be in place, to ensure the plan will be carried out to its successful conclusion.

"Mother Earth will be a simpler place with a chance of survival. I will work with governments to restore the balance of power equitably and fairly across the globe. The few, cannot be allowed to hold the rest of the world, in thrall.

He rose from the bench, his body exhibiting the horror he felt at the deeds of servants of the Church. Placing his hand on Edoardos' shoulder he bid the younger man, "I will need you by my side."

"Together we will need all the strength and energy of your youth. Will you stand with me, against all who will resist us with all the might at their disposal?"

The priest had never felt so humbled in his life and dropped to his knees before this Holy Man. "My body, soul and life are at your disposal, Vostra Santita."

"Good, then let us return to the Vatican and make preparations." Gently he smiled at Edoardos. "There is one more thing."

Edoardos waited patiently.

"You will become a Chaplain of his Holiness. This will be announced tomorrow."

"Vostra Santita," Edoardos dropped to one knee before the diminutive figure, "I am not worthy. I do not need any rewards."

"You are wrong on both counts my son," the man in the white cassock told him and holding out his hand he grasped Edoardos' and raised him to his feet. Looking deeply into his eyes, he said, "I know of no other man who is as worthy as yourself. The world owes you and your friend an enormous debt. You have done me a great service and if you remain by my side. You may pay the ultimate price, so reflect on my demand of you overnight and let me know your answer in the morning. I want you with me Monsignor, as I trust you implicitly, and you deserve more than this honour should you join me."

*

Il Papa Callixtus IV made a brief appearance the following day, apologising to the world for the actions taken in the name of his Church. He also took the opportunity, to apologise for the Inquisition in the Renaissance period. To him, it had set a precedent for others to follow.

"Terrible crimes which I abhor and for which I apologies profusely to the world, have been committed in the name of the Church. This I not the first time, but intend it shall be the last.

"Men can live in the heart of Christianity, without Christianity touching their souls.

"God has punished the leaders of these atrocities and those that took part have been arrested and will be dealt with by the State Police. I promise you there will be no cover up of these monstrous acts.

"Never again," he promised the world.

The cheers and applause that rose from the assembled masses in St. Peter's Square reached to the very heavens. A television audience of two billion people, including those of the Islamic faith, turned to each other in wonder.

The kindly man in the white biretta and cassock held up his hands for silence.

"It is time to clean the church of its centuries of corruption and intrigue. Of its irreligious and imperfect behaviour. I make this pledge to you today, before the Tomb of St. Peter."

Again spontaneous applause broke out, while Il Papa Callixtus IV, waited until it had died down.

"The Church has aligned itself with corrupt and greedy ancient families for centuries and it has brought her to this unholy state. She will no longer be part of the devious control, which threads through the fabric of the intricate financial systems of this world.

In the name of my saintly predecessor, Il Papa John Paul I, I propose that the church will return to the simplicity of Our Lord Jesus Christ's message.

There is no need for luxurious citadels which were built by Emperors' and Il Papa's to serve their own vanity and in the hope of reflecting their own glory for all time.

Against the admonishments of Our Lord Jesus Christ, we have recreated the hierarchy of the Temple of Jerusalem and its corrupt practices, which he believed to be against Judaic law."

He made a vow to the peoples of the world, there would be massive reforms in the church, even if his investigations reached into the highest levels of governments in his own and other countries; banking, finance, major corporations, none could expect evasion or protection from him.

Giving notice to those who would harm him to stop him, he publicly announced he was in extremely good health and he would remain alive to see them fulfilled. If he suffered an early demise, it would be investigated with the full force of the law until the perpetrators were brought to justice.

And still his reforms would be carried through, as he would set the wheels in motion and it could not be stopped.

"I will speak again with you on these subjects. Bear with me for two months when I will again speak to you in greater detail."

Thunderous applause greeted this diminutive, yet so powerful man in the white biretta, cassock and stole, as he stood on the steps of St. Peter's Basilica. Following his speech he walked unafraid amongst his people, who wept with emotion as he passed yet never attempted to touch or crowd him in any way. Wherever he went, this charismatic kindly man carried them with him by his sheer presence; humble, dignified, holy and utterly determined.

*

Edoardos took Lina in his arms and looked deeply into her large brown eyes which swam with tears. "I cannot turn my back on him."

Her heart pounded like a Buddhist temple drum creating the roaring sound of thunder. "He asks too much of you?" she cried in agony.

"No." Edoardos shook his head slowly and firmly. "He asks far less of me, than he asks of himself."

Melancholy stole into the room like a wraith, infecting the atmosphere with doubt and fear.

Placing his finger under her chin, he watched the tears well up in her eyes, then drop to the floor, as the dream she had held on to for the briefest of moments, was crushed beneath the weight of a greater need. Lifting his chin he assured her. "You will win your Pulitzer Prize."

"But I will lose you," she sobbed and her tears soaked his cassock, where her head had burrowed into his shoulder.

His hand slowly stroked her hair and for the last time he breathed in the scent of this woman he loved dearly. "You will never lose me. I will be your friend forever."

"But isn't there a chance that things could change and we could have that which Yeshua and Miryai had?" Hopefully she sought an assurance she knew would never come.

"Viaggiatore (*homing pigeon*), there was never the remotest chance of that," Edoardos sighed into her hair, as he held her ever closer. "We can only choose one or the other at this moment in time."

Pulling back to gaze upon him once more, the air redolent with the strong feelings flowing from one to the other, and her long slender arm reached out to brush her fingers across his face to trace every plane and angle. Gently biting down on her lower lip, the concern she felt for him and the grief at their personal loss, chased shadows across her face, highlighting her high cheekbones and natural beauty.

The light behind her beautiful dark brown eyes dimmed, as they searched his own trying to pull answers from him that he could not give her.

"What if I choose you?" She raised her head and looked into the reflecting pools of his eyes, in which the truth shimmered, blinding her.

"But you won't," he replied as he held her at arms length. "You would always be torn and disappointed that you had lost the one chance to achieve the ultimate goal of any reporter."

Lina bit her lip, acknowledging the truth. "And could you walk away from the Big V and your family."

"You know the answer to that *viaggiatore*." Edoardos searched her face for a glimmering of doubt. "Il Papa will need men to stand firm behind him. His life will be at stake once his declaration is made. What type of coward would I be, to turn away from an honest man who would risk all? I cannot do that to an honest Il Papa. There have been too few of them."

"But you belong to the Ancients." She shook her head in bewilderment.

"I know," he agreed. Releasing her he walked over to the window and looked down upon the ancient city that was Rome. "That is why my life will be forfeit." Turning back to face her he continued. "This is my choice. My family decided ten years ago, to make reparation for their part in the intrigue that surrounds the church. Despite this, they will be unable to protect me from the great forces that will band together and my life is now forfeit."

"Il Papa may win the first round, but they will find a way to strike him down. And this will also be my fate. I am aware of the penalty. We must strike swiftly and effectively. All my energy must now be focused on the declaration and the twelve months following. You and I have no future together now."

As she walked towards him, to stand at the window alongside the man she loved, she felt him move back and stand behind her. Catching his reflection in the window as darkness fell swiftly, a diffused light was reflecting around his head like a halo. Suddenly finding it hard to breath, she drew in a sharp breath.

'No God no,' she pleaded silently, knowing the invisible would not answer her plea. 'No, don't take him. You have thousands more to choose from. Spare him!' she begged.

Coming up behind her, he gathered her in his arms once more. "The chance that I will be dead within twelve months is high, as the Ancients are not going to allow Il Papa to dismantle their Synarchy. If he acts fast, he will let it be known to the world that he intends changing the Catholic Church forever."

"The Knights of Malta will be forced to clean house, and this in itself will be enough for the time being. Once Il Papa and I are no longer walking this Earth, we must have achieved targeting them in the heart and the Synarchy will begin to implode from within. Their structure is now unsound and the eyes of the world will be upon them, as they elect another of *their Il Papas* and struggle to maintain the hold they have upon the Vatican's and the secular wealth throughout the world." His chest heaved, as he took several long deep breaths.

"I don't want you to die." Lina's sobs began anew.

"What is my life in comparison to the dismantling of the miseries of the world?" he asked her gently.

"It is everything to me," she retorted, smarting under his rejection.

"Except for your Pulitzer prize?" Placing his hand under her chin, he lifted her head up and looked into her eyes. "My life is forfeit now. Nothing can save me. There is nowhere I can hide. Not even if we run to the ends of the earth."

"But the truth will free us and keep you alive."

"Don't be naïve Lina. You of all people know that is not true. The Knights have always won in the end and they will regroup and begin the long road back, but they *will* regroup and place their feet upon that path that they know so well, until they gain the power again."

"The world will not let them," she cried out in her agony.

"The world has never been able to stop them and the world will temporarily become unafraid, then sink back into avarice, apathy and inertia within six months, which is why we must act swiftly before the attention of the world turns to the next sensational happening.

"The world does not want its middle class values and comforts turned upside down." Wearily Edoardos stood, kissed her on the top of her head and holding her tight again him, he inhaled the sweet clean smell of her recently shampooed hair.

"Please," she begged once more.

"It cannot be Lina." He sorrowfully shook his head, then breaking away; he let himself out of the apartment.

Lina's mind was whirling as she ran to the terrace to watch him navigate the steps, never once looking back, while she stood like a pillar of salt.

Finally, the gentle beaming of the silvery moon seemed to touch her heart with gentle fingers, reaching into her soul to heal the torment she felt at the probable loss of her best friend, her soul mate.

Her eyes filled with tears which she let spill down her cheeks, making no attempt to wipe them away, feeling the droplets scourge the knowledge she now carried in every cell of her body and allowing them to release her from the paralysis she felt.

Stumbling back inside she sunk into a soft chair that enveloped her as though providing her with the sanctuary she sought whilst she cried to some uncaring invisible force that was taking E away from her, "I don't want to feel. I don't want to spend each day without E. Let me turn to ice." Rocking back and forth in her agony, tears of bitter salt fell, until they dissolved the ice around her soul."

Leaning forward, she brought her knees up under her chin, then pulled the long thigh length sweater she was wearing down to cover them and sat there miserably with her head bowed, arms clasping her knees, contemplating a future without E. It was too much to bear. It would be like losing her right arm, as well as her heart. "Could she survive it? Why had she ever begun this horrible investigation?" she castigated herself.

The tears flowed down her cheeks and dropped on to the sweater, her mind spinning, unable to reason and she remained like this for what seemed like eternity.

Oh My God, I cannot envisage life without E.

"Hold him in your heart and soul, but I promise you will live and love again." A soft sweet voice whispered in her ear, while a warmth enveloped her body.

Startled, she looked up; her eyes unfocused to perceive what appeared to be a fine mist. Blinking, she tried to clear her vision, but it was not to be. Her eyes went out of focus again and to her amazement, in her mind's eye she saw the outline of a woman wearing a soft blue robe.

"Who are you?" Dreamily she seemed to float outside herself and found herself able to communicate with the figure.

"You know who I am Lina," the figure smiled at her.

"It cannot be true." Her mind was whirling with the impossibility of the existence of the vision. She tried blinking hard but the image was still there. "It cannot be," she whispered. "You cannot be Miryai." This was something she would have given no credence to before, yet now it somehow seemed natural and wholly believable

"I am the truth for you Lina, therefore I am." A soft breeze wrapped around Lina as the figure reassured her.

Lina untangled herself and leaned forward in the chair. "Why would you appear before me, an unbeliever?"

"You are not an unbeliever Lina. You have accepted the truth in your soul."

A burst of joy spread through her body and a warmth and peace she had never experienced previously suffused her entirely, but her mind would not stay still needing to castigate herself. "I have destroyed the person I value so highly in this world. I have doomed him."

"Ooh no, far from it." The figure's head moved slowly from side to side. "This was meant to be."

"Why?" Lina's voice broke, "Why Edoardos?"

"His fate was determined before he entered this world and his time on earth was always short. You have performed a great service to my followers and the world." The figure moved forward and held out her hand. "Edoardos will forever be with you and you will be able to communicate with him whenever you wish to. In act as easily as you are speaking with me now." Slowly the figure retreated and egan to disappear.

"Don't go," Lina cried out in agitation. "Please come back. I know so little."

"You know everything Lina," and the figure dissipated in front of her stonished gaze, while time past unheeded.

As she slowly became aware of the familiar surroundings her entire body ibrating as though the great bells of St Peter's were tolling in the room with her, he sank back into the chair and began to accept what Miryai had told her.

Somehow she would find the strength to move forward once again and face hatever horrors lay there, for her to discover and expose. And more importantly ome to terms with a life without Edoardos in it.

Chapter Forty-eight – The Arma dei Carabinieri

Capitano Carlino Farnelli, called his team together and addressed them with Umberto Orsini at his side.

"You have carried out your job with distinction and I am very proud of you all."

"What the hell did we do Capitano?" Rocco asked sombrely. "It was handed to us on a plate."

"You all worked hard and diligently and you were on the right track when I derailed you, and for that I apologise profusely."

The men looked uneasily at each other. They didn't want their commander to humble himself to them. To a man, they respected him and knew that under very difficult circumstances, he looked after them and their interests.

They were all tired to speak at once to reassure him of his value to them and of their respect for him.

"Do you know," he mused, his eyes gazing into the distance, "much good will come out of this. There will be greater cooperation between Vatican City and the nation, including its law enforcement."

"I agree." Umberto stepped forward. "I am of the Roman Catholic faith, but mainly paid lip service. Il Papa has reignited hope in my heart. Hope for the future, hope for his faith, hope for him and the world. How can we lose with him at the helm?" Looking at them all he added. "I want you all to know, it has been a pleasure working alongside you on this case and I speak for everyone in the del Centro Nazionale per l'Analisi dei Crimini Violenti."

Moisture collected in the corner of all of these hardened men's eyes and they surreptitiously wiped them away. Nodding in agreement with him, they did not trust themselves to speak just yet.

"Your profile was spot on Ispettore." From Ferdinand, this was high praise indeed.

"I wish," young Carabiniere Ignatio started, then hesitated.

"What do you wish son?" Carlino looked at him.

"I wish," again he hesitated, but the rest of the team encouraged him to continue. "I wish we had been able to save the other two women. I dream of them at night," and burst into tears.

"It's OK son." Rock hard Rocco went up to him and placed an arm around his shoulder. "We all do, not just for them, but the multitude of horrors we've seen," and as Ignatio continued to look shamefaced, he whispered to him, "and we all shed tears as well."

The rest of them agreed, cheering and clapping, thereby dispelling the sombre mood that prevailed in the room.

"Let's go and get a glass of wine," Carlinos invited, beckoning them to come with him. As a man they rose and followed their Capitano into the gates of hell if need be.

Chapter Forty-nine – The Magdalene Inheritance

When the dust had settled, Adelais met with Lina and Edoardos.

"You have saved my life, and now I must safely recover the casket and open it." Looking searchingly at them both she entreated, "I would be honoured if you would escort me to its secret hiding place and back, and be present when I open it."

Edoardos and Lina looked at each other in amazement. Stepping forward, he put his arms around his sister-in-law and held her close. As he stepped back he held on to her hands and looked into her beautiful emerald eyes, the mystical quality that had drawn his brother into their depths, now worked their magic on himself and Lina.

"Are you really sure you want me present?"

"Of course I do Edoardos," Adelais hastened to reassure this dearest of brother in-laws.

Edoardos hung his head, "Because I belong to the Church Adelais, which has been your family's enemy for centuries.

"Aaah, I cannot allow the actions of a single religious maniac to reflect upon the church and Il Papa, for whom you have great admiration."

Lina stepped forward and took Adelais" hands in hers. "I am a nosy journalist who has her sights on a Pulitzer Prize. Do you really want me present?"

"Of course I do." Adelais stepped forward and folded her into her arms. "Without your determination and courage, I would not be alive to present the findings to the world. Who would I rather entrust that responsibility to, if not my good friend."

Tears spilled over from Lina's eyes and ran down her cheeks, as she held on to this precious woman for dear life.

"Adelais, we must recover this quickly," Edoardos urged her. "The rogue element of the Knights of Malta, still have a vested interest in destroying the betrothal contract, and the other contents of the casket. I am sure there is an arduous journey in front of us and we must make plans."

Adelais smiled sweetly at him. "Where else would I have hidden the casket in this day and age, if not in plain sight?"

Lina and Edoardos gasped and spoke in concert, consternation showing plainly on both their faces. "What do you mean?"

Leaning forward, Adelais whispered in both their ears, stepped back and watched them laugh joyously.

The Swissair flight 992 landed at Zurich and they booked into the hotel. Not an uncommon occurrence for this wealthy high profile family. Welcomed by the discreet management they were shown to their rooms and left in peace.

The following morning they proceeded to Credit Suisse, the large international bank where the Guilianini's held their most precious possessions in a strongbox in the bank's Vault.

After being escorted to the vault, the officer of the bank discreetly withdrew and they were left to open the box in privacy. When Adelais drew out the beautiful ancient casket, they drew in a collective breath, not daring to release it, as she withdrew a chain from around her neck and turned the key attached to it in the lock.

With a soft click it opened and there before them lay Miryai's baby tooth and lock of hair. "We must not touch them. They could dissolve or become corrupted."

"I know Edoardos, I am being very careful," Adelais reassured him. "Let us take it home with us to Italy."

Placing it in a sealed case with a combination lock, they rang for the custodian who returned the strongbox to the vault and escorted them out of the bank.

*

Arriving back at the Palazzo that evening, they gathered in Adelais' sitting room where they laid down a silk cloth and drew on soft thin white gloves. Once again the casket was opened and gave up its secrets.

"There is the ring that Miryai wore." Standing around in awe they could not speak despite the emotions tumbling out of each and every one of them like jewels scattering from the night sky's myriad of stars which twinkled in the heavens and watched their endeavours.

"There are two documents here." Peering into the casket, they hardly dared to breathe as Adelais reached in and lifted out the first with a pair of fine tweezers.

Gently pinching the end of the papyrus in her thumb and forefinger, she took her other hand and very carefully unrolled the papyrus, praying it would not disintegrate and turn to ashes in their hands. "It's their betrothal contract." Tears fell from Adelais' face and she stood back quickly so they would not land on the papyrus.

Reverently they each read the lines, which told of Yeshua's and Miryai's forthcoming marriage. Simply gazing on the rings in the casket, they did not dare to touch them, for fear of corrupting whatever secret it may hold.

"And the other one?" Ever curious Lina's excitement was mounting by the minute, electrifying her body and soul. Her hands were trembling and her whole body began to tremble as she awaited Adelais' next move.

Adelais drew in a breath. "It will be Miryai's testament." Looking at the two of them she reached out her hand and took it out of the casket. Again, laying it down, she carefully unrolled it. Immediately it broke in half as they gasped with dismay in unison.

"Its allright," Edoardos reassured them, "it is still complete."

Then their astounded eyes read what Miryai had written in pure Hebrew Aramaic script two thousand years ago.

Barely able to comprehend what they were reading, they struggled to keep their composure.

Miryai told the story of their betrothal when they were very young and the marriage that took place between two descendants of King David in their teens.

Yeshua was tasked with reclaiming the Throne of Judaea from Herod the Idutean, for the Royal House of David, whose father had so feared the birth of the King of the Jews, that when the Magi told him of Yeshua's birth, he had ordered all the firstborn in Bethlehem killed.

The family had protected the baby Yeshua and when he was a teenager he had been sent to the Nazars (Nazareans) the *Sons of the Prophet*, who were Chaldean Kabalists. They were persecuted by the orthodox synagogue, which was led by the Sanhedrin who enounced their beliefs including resurrection.

At this time, there was great religious turmoil in Judaea, with many factions vying for supremacy.

The Zealots, Jewish political revolutionaries who wanted to expel the Romans by force of arms in the tradition of the Maccabees, King David, Joshua, and others who fought military battles against oppressors or foreigners in God's name.

The Hasideans or pious ones, who believed in the *foreign* Hellenistic culture of the Greeks which appeared to be influencing the Judaean religious beliefs, were in conflict with the Torah.

Out of this group came the Pharisees, who were religious fundamentalists and the current religious leaders, focusing on strict observance of the Jewish laws, ceremonies and traditions and leaders in the synagogues.

The Sadducees were also Jewish religious leaders, primarily from the upper-class, who preached tolerance for the Romans as they sought to maintain their aristocratic positions in society.

These two groups were at odds with each other.

The Sanhedrin (the Judicial Council of the Jewish people) was comprised primarily of Sadducees.

As he grew to manhood Yeshua, ever aware of the greater role he was expected to fulfill, sought even greater wisdom to help him rule wisely and well. Hearing of the Essenes, who were the converts to the philosophy of Buddha-Sakyamûni, he spent three years in the desert with them.

Realising the futility of raising an army against the mighty Roman Empire, Yeshua's revolt would be a passive one, mainly of religious reformation and the claim to the throne.

His path had been paved before him by his cousin John the Baptist, whom Herod had purportedly beheaded for criticising his illicit marriage to his brother's wife. As he feared John's power over the people, this was more likely.

John had announced to the people that Yeshua was the Messiah the Jews were waiting for and bade them follow him, so he had to be silenced. As Yeshua's popularity gained ground, Herod began to fear him, as did the Pharisees who were appalled at the reformations he preached.

He would debate with the Pharisees and priests of the Temple and show them the error of their ways. Well versed in the Scriptures he was a Rabbi and a good debater and orator.

All had gone as planned and as he rode triumphantly into Jerusalem on a donkey, to show the people his humility in the face of such a huge undertaking on their behalf, the Jewish people lining the streets waved palm leaves.

Herod's fears were coming true, as he watched the procession and the people cheering the coming of their messiah. Immediately he sought audience with Pontius Pilate and demanded Yeshua's arrest.

Yeshua then challenged Caiaphas, the Head Priest, by raiding the Temple, attacking the moneychangers for defiling a holy place and telling the people the practice was against Jewish Law.

Caiaphas, who fearing Jesus' followers, as well as his popularity with the people, would be challenged, tried him before the Sanhedrin, who were essentially a bench of judges. There was no jury as in a modern trial, only the witnesses for the accuser and the accused. The Council were the final authority on Jewish law and any scholar, who went against its decisions, was put to death as a zaken mamre (*rebellious elder*). As a Rabbi, Yeshua was naturally a scholar.

They had the power to convict but not sentence, so Caiaphas took him to the Governor of Judaea, Pontius Pilate for his decision. At first Pontius Pilate sent Yeshua to Herod, whose authority he is also challenging. When he will not make the decision, he was returned to the Sanhedrin who again took him before Pontius Pilate.

Fearing that Jesus had the charisma to lead a guerrilla uprising against Imperial Rome, despite its unlikelihood, Pontius Pilate finally approved the death sentence.

As Miryai wrote of the sad outcome of the Davidic line's peaceful attempt to restore the throne to Judaea, including their flight to Assyria and Egypt, her descendants, with her friends alongside her, wept for the dashed hopes of the bloodline.

Even with Herod gone and Yeshua's family able to return to Judaea, their time had come and gone. Without Yeshua and his charismatic presence, they set out to continue his Nazar/Buddhist teachings, calling it the Church of the Yeshua, the Nazarene.

Each lost in their own thoughts; they watched as Adelais carefully folded the two papyri and laid them back in the casket. Locking it again, she looked at them both.

"My God," Lina breathed out slowly, while Edoardos looked on in shock.

"Why did Pontius Pilate hesitate the first time?" Edoardos was still bemused.

Adelais had remained serene, as she had long known the truth about Yeshua, Miryai and their earthly and spiritual quests

"He was well aware of the different ways in which the leading Jewish families competed for social prominence and influence," she answered him. "So he may have seen this case as an attempt to use Herod as the Roman authority, in a game of Jewish factionalism, albeit at Yeshua's expense."

"Why didn't the crowds stay with him?" The disappointed priest cried out in agony, for the gentle reformer.

Lina had recovered and answered him. "As we know crowds can be so fickle."

"So we're saying that Yeshua needed to deliver a humungous miracle, right there then, or he was the man of the past." Edoardos had his feet back on the ground and his head out of the clouds. His family had been so aligned with the Church for centuries, that deep inside their core, the divinity of Jesus Christ had been etched into their genetic makeup.

"That's the one," Lina was returning to her normal self.

"What are we to do with this?" Adelais appealed to them both.

"Adelais do you trust me?" Edoardos reached out and took her free hand.

"Of course I do Edoardos, you know that." Her face turned towards his, so full of trust that he hesitated, praying she would not misunderstand his intentions as he urged her. "We should take this to Il Papa Callixtus IV."

"What?" Both Adelais and Lina were aghast.

"He is the most trustworthy person I have ever come across and he will tell us what to do."

"But he will bury this in the archives, or destroy it as he will fear it will tear the Church apart and it will tumble down like a pack of cards."

"Please trust me and Il Papa," he beseeched them both. "What else can you do with something as explosive as this?"

Like his predecessor John Paul I, Il Papa Callixtus IV had not been a front runner to the Chair of St Peter, but in an uncharacteristic move Edoardos' family had put all their powerful resources behind him, after deciding it was time for them to make amends for their part in the election of many despots to the Vicar of Christ, ably assisting the Church's centuries of abuse of its power.

Lina and Adelais looked at each other, acknowledging the truth Edoardos was uttering. Where could they turn, that the casket and its secret would be safe now? The Barbarians were at the gate and before the walls fell, he could think of no other person that he would entrust with this secret.

Reluctantly they nodded their agreement and he hurried off to request an audience.

*

"Does it really matter whether Jesus really existed or if he was wed to Mary Magdalene? Whether his mission was to minister to people as a Rabbi, or rule them as a King?" he continued.

Lina, Edoardos, Tamar and Adelais looked at Il Papa in shock, unable to believe their ears.

"Vostra Santita, am I really hearing you correctly?" Adelais asked

The Pontiff smiled gently at her. "He would have been a good and spiritual King my dear."

Lina and Edoardos considered whether the Four Horsemen of the Apocalypse were whipping up their mighty steeds to head for planet Earth and wreak havoc and destruction upon the inhabitants.

Adelais felt as though a mighty wind had blown her off her feet.

"Yes," Il Papa gently reassured her. "There is so much written about the subject today and much doubt, but the Church's duty is to carry on his ministry and look after the poor and the meek."

"Maybe we have not succeeded very well over the centuries, but I promise," and here he reached out his hands and took both of Adelais' in his, "that under my reign as Il Papa, we will do a lot better."

"How will you achieve that Reverendo Padre?" Adelais still doubted his integrity. She did not know him as well as he himself did, or indeed as Edoardos did.

"I do not believe that the faith of the meek and poor will be crushed, if they accept that Jesus was a mortal man, married to Mary Magdalene and attempting to make himself King of the Jews." In an attempt to explain his reasons to them, Il Papa prayed to God, that he could make them believe his utter sincerity. "I do not believe they will turn their face away from us, as we offer hope, in a world beset with the whirlwind of political intrigue and the greed of the powerful."

"But the church itself?" Adelais protested.

Il Papa held up his right hand to stave off her protestations. "I agree and I can share with you now, that you have given me the perfect opportunity to speed up my plans for decentralising church power, simplifying its canons and using its wealth to help those in need, as my predecessor Il Papa John Paul I intended before his untimely death."

Laying his hands on her head, he turned her face up to his as he bent down to where she was seated. "I do not perceive you and your daughter as a threat, as my predecessor Innocent III did with the Cathars. They were good holy people and I intend to publicly apologise to them."

"I have always liked the tenets of their faith. They lived it and attended to the poor and the meek. They were indeed Bon Hommes and Bon Femme. Your family protected them and suffered alongside them. Now it is the Church's time to attend to the underprivileged and helpless and to protect them."

"Our role is to provide hope where there is none. Some of them live under the most corrupt of political systems. Dare I say most of us do, and it is time to change that." His warm brown eyes, flecked with gold, took on a steely cast and his face and demeanour exhibited a determination that would not be thwarted.

"Can you blame these people for turning to the Church for help or salvation, after the horrible lives many of them are forced to endure? We can try and stop the intrigue and corruption around the world which has existed since time began, beginning with me calling on all of Christendom and other faiths to do the same."

"Men must cease this intolerance to other men's beliefs which breeds hatred and violence."

"The church will proclaim man was not born of original sin and free them from the burden of self hate.

If we can give our people the hope of eternal life and help them to face yet another day, is that not a worthwhile thing?"

"Of course it is and if you can do so, it will be a miracle." Adelais astonishment showed on her face.

Il Papa smiled at her and it was if the sun had reached inside the room and was suffusing it with love and hope. "This new information will not be the end of the Church altogether, just the Church as we know it. The one the world loves and despises in part. In fact, the truth will set us free, and we hope mankind with it?"

As Lina and Edoardos tried to come to terms with what they were hearing, they fervently hoped Il Papa could make it work.

"I wield considerable power in this world," the Sovereign Pontiff spoke not from arrogance but from humility and surety. "And I will not hesitate to use it for the benefit of all mankind, particularly those who cannot help themselves."

"We are now at a crossroads. Our currencies are collapsing, our economies are in ruins. Nations have frivolously and recklessly accrued debt to such a massive extent, ignoring the repercussions, and they are unable to pay them.

"There will be chaos, starvations, death and destruction as nations crumble if this cannot be corrected. This could be followed by anarchy, as people strike out at those that took away that, earned by their hard work for years."

The Vicar of Christ nodded sagely as he looked from one to the other. "The church was losing its credibility when it became part of this shameful corruption. It no longer gave young men and women a reason to serve it devotedly. It is time to return to grass roots. "

"We were so nearsighted and to afraid to look further than the noses on our face, that we lost our flock because of our poor shepherding skills. We need to move forward boldly if we wish to continue administering to the poor and weak. I am determined we will carry them through these turbulent times and what lies in front of us."

Nodding slowly he looked at each of them. "I promise you reforms will be carried out. The ban on birth control *will* be lifted. I cannot bear to see starving families, living in abject poverty and misery because of this edict.

I intend to apologise to all those we have persecuted, including the Cathars. So I may die at peace with myself and my Lord."

"They will stop you Reverendo Padre." Edoardos moved forward, seeking a sign from the man in front of him.

"They can try Edoardos," suddenly this humble diminutive figure appeared seven feet tall, "but they will not succeed. I learnt the lesson well from my predecessor, John Paul I, and I will see his spirit at rest."

"I cannot bear to see more bloodshed in the name of Yeshua the Nazarene who was my forefather." Adelais was torn between wanting to believe the man who stood before her with Edoardos by his side, and the doubts that assailed her.

"I give you my solemn promise there will be no more carried out in the name of the Holy Roman Catholic Church. I cannot speak for all denominations and all faiths, but I intend to reach out to them and try."

"Yeshua said no temples and no priests," Adelais cried. "How will you run our church without them?"

"As the Lord and his disciples did. We will meet in our followers' homes. We will meet in the fields. We will carry on and spread the word."

A slight smile crossed Il Papa's kindly face. "Churches that can no longer afford their upkeep will be turned into homeless shelters run by the church. In some instances they will be sold and the money will go toward low cost housing. We will try and establish true socialism throughout the world."

"The wealth of the church will be distributed to the poor. Not as handouts, but rather to help people to enable themselves. Programmes and projects will be set up to ensure this."

"So many of the funds from well meaning projects and programmes that are set up to help the poor end, up in the hands of their corrupt leaders. The money never reaches those for whom it is intended," Lina appealed to him to right this wrong.

"I understand your misgivings. If we do not set up a bureaucratic dinosaur, it will work," he smiled at her.

"The Vatican bank will continue to manage the monies." Upon seeing the doubt on their faces he hastened to reassure them. "It will be an entirely different bank, I can promise you that."

Turning to Adelais, he asked her if she would permit him to progress the matter of the DNA testing, by ensuring the best laboratories in the world handled the matter, and the Holy See would cover the costs.

Adelais looked doubtful. "I do not like to let these precious relics out of my sight."

"I understand your suspicion." As he lifted his hand and made the sign of the cross, the room seemed to fill with the breath of fresh air that blew away the cobwebs lurking in the corners of the Vatican, that the holy dusters of the household nuns had been unable to eliminate for long. "I promise you this will be managed in the greatest secrecy by someone you trust." Turning to Edoardos he smiled. "I task you with this my son."

"Me Vostra Santita?" He had taken Edoardos' breath away. "I wouldn't know where to start."

"But with my help you will find out." Turning back to Adelais he queried, "Is that alright with you my dear?"

"Thank you," she accepted graciously.

Turning to Lina he held out his hands. "Go win your Pulitzer Prize, as this final part to the story will ensure that you do."

"Do you think that if the truth were known to the world, that Yeshua was a mortal man, a Rabbi married to Miryai with a daughter Tamar, that mankind would refrain from revering him?" Yeshua's descendant pleaded. "He was a good man, a reformer who sought a better life for every man."

Il Papa nodded. "I believe they will, and I will ensure his wishes are carried out. It is time," Il Papa reassured her. "You are a wise woman."

Lina looked on in amazement, as these two disparate followers of Jesus carried on a conversation that was alike in many ways. When it all came down to it, their desires were the same. To see the poor elevated out of their misery and the wealthy forced to share the benefice of the world with all. This was true Christianity, and all it stood for, in action.

With bated breath they all waited for the results of the DNA testing. So many centuries had passed, it was impossible to prove Tamar's lineage to that of Miryai's, but did prove the existence of the ethnicity group.

However Jesus' were inconclusive. The degradation of the DNA on the papyri was too advanced. It had been far too long, for any of his DNA to remain on the papyri, which would conclusively identify him as the man who gave the betrothal ring to Miryai. However the betrothal contract and the entry in Josephus' ledger could not be denied. Both DNA on the rings were insubstantial, and there was no close male relative in the present whose DNA could be tested against that of the males.

The marriage contract would have to be taken on faith, but carbon testing had dated it back to the first century AD.

True to his word, two months later Il Papa Callixtus IV called out to the world with another announcement from St Peter's Basilica with television exposure the pundits had calculated would be watched by over two billion people.

He had regained the respect of leaders of all Christian denominations and other religions, including the New Age practitioners.

The steps for reformation were in place and it was time to release them to the world that was waiting with bated breath, together with a warning he knew he also had to invoke.

The crowd was silent, wondering what was coming.

Epilogue

Again St Peter's Square was filled to capacity and overflowed into the streets of Rome, as far as the eye could see. Huge television screens had been erected in the famous squares of Rome, and in sporting stadiums, where people gathered to hear what Il Papa had to say to them.

In cities all over the world, crowds had also gathered in public places, where the authorities had erected huge plasma screens, so they could see, as well as hear him.

They assembled, from far and wide, people of all colours and creeds, waiting patiently to hear his words. The world seemed to have a need to gather together, as they waited for his announcement, to share with others their admiration for this man and support for him, and mankind. In him, lay their hopes for a better future for this planet Earth.

The world of commerce came to a halt as office workers' eyes were riveted on their computer screens, which were streaming this historic event. Smart phones and laptops were bringing the message to their users. Service halted in restaurants and cafes.

Governments and boardroom oligarchs in the West and the East were glued to their television sets.

The world waited for the words of one small Italian, who held them in the palm of his hand with his honesty, integrity and mesmerising words.

Raising his hand in benediction, he blessed the crowd. The air was hushed with expectation when the diminutive smiling man in the white biretta, a simple white cassock and slippers addressed them.

"I am Our Lord's representative on Earth," he stated simply, "and I must do his bidding.

I am not here today with obscure words; for I am a simple man and I speak plainly to you this day.

I am the servant of Jesu Cristo and St Peter, but I am also your servant and I stand before you today and pledge that I am prepared to make the radical changes to the Church that Il Papa John Paul 1 intended before his untimely death."

The square broke out into a tumultuous roar of approval and support for this courageous man of God standing before them on the famous central balcony leading off the library of St. Peters.

"I am today declaring War on Poverty."

"Christ's message has become tainted by those that led the Church seeking wealth, power and prestige throughout the centuries. We will return to Christ's Gospel.

The Church has become an anachronism in the time of an exploding world population. This planet will be unable to sustain mankind if this continues. We must all do our best, to ensure our legacy to the generations who follow us, is a sustainable one.

I announce to you now, that I am issuing an encyclical that from this day forward that the Church approves the use of birth control devices for our followers, in particular, the use of the contraceptive pill.

The long awaited permission to his flock had finally come. Throughout the square and around the world, cheers and applause followed this announcement. He waited patiently until it had died down before continuing.

I intend to fulfil my predecessor Il Papa John Paul I's stated intentions to carry out massive reforms in the Church. These have been set in motion.

I intend to modernize the Church and make it a force for peacemaking and social justice, to ensure work for all, dignity in that work and fair wages. The Kingdom of Heaven can be achieved in this world, right here and now.

Leading by example, the Church will abide by its traditional vows of poverty, asceticism, and communalism. Jesu Cristo was a simple man. The panoply and excess of wealth in the church, will cease. We will return to Christ's simple message and be his simple Church.

Let me now address the 'wretched of the Earth.' Christ is on your side!" he proclaimed, hands lifted in benediction, to the rapturous applause that heralded his words from every soul in St. Peter's Square and the two billion he could not see, around the world.

"I am reforming the Holy See. I am decentralising the power of the Church and sharing it with the bishops of the church throughout the world, who are able men.

Firstly, as Il Papa, I own and manage the Institute for Works of Religion, known as the Vatican Bank. I have made changes to its management practices and appointed personnel who will see these carried out.

This bank was established for the purpose of funding Religious Works and its current resources will now be directed to fulfilling these purposes.

This institution will no longer be under the director of an outside Chief Executive and I have appointed Cardinale Bellino to take over this role.

I am going to unravel the financial operations of the Vatican.

The church is going to divest itself of the trappings of great wealth, as I firmly believe this is what Our Lord Jesu Cristo fought against in his ministry on earth and it is unseemly for his house to go against his teachings.

I am selling all of the Vatican's assets in a controlled manner over the next fiveyears. These monies will be used to relieve the intolerable burden of the poor and disenfranchised, to restore dignity and comfort to them.

These programmes will not be hand outs. The monies will be used for practica income generating projects and programmes, for ordinary people to earn a fair wage in return to the effort and time they put into a job. It will help to set up micro enterprises that will change people's lives, one person or family at a time.

These monies and programmes will be under the direction of trustworthy priests, whom I will entrust to the bishops to personally choose and charge upon the salvation of their soul, with managing the successful outcome of each and every undertaking. No hands but theirs will touch the monies put aside for these programme.

The wealthy dioceses of the industrialized countries have been instructed to end 1% of their annual income to the Third World dioceses, to compensate for the injustices our consumer driven world has committed against them.

I will commence by divesting the Vatican's finances and its holdings into currency that can be used for the benefit of all mankind.

The Sovereign Pontiff decreed then continued to amaze all with his pronouncement:

I deplore the accumulation of obscene wealth which will, in turn, become worthless, because of the endemic corruption in the financial systems of this world.

It has brought this world to its knees".

Gasps of amazement arose from the crowd gathered before him, as they struggled to come to terms with what he was saying. Never before had a Pope been so honest and transparent about the shenanigans at the Vatican, as he declaimed the state of the world.

It was incomprehensible. They could not take it in all at once. When a glimmer of understanding began to filter through, tumultuous applause and roars of approval rose to the heavens themselves. The Roman Catholic Church as they knew it would no longer exist, but they were with him to a man, woman and child

"The Church must lead by example," the diminutive figure in the white biretta, simple white cassock and slippers, continued. *"From today forth this is the clothing*

you will see me wear and that of my clergy. We will divest ourselves of opulent garments to celebrate the simplicity of Christ's message.

I have no desire to destabilise the currencies of the world, nor the financial markets, which are in crisis, but I will not stand by idly and watch the greed and corruption continue unchecked."

Had he just warned the financial community? Bankers, financiers, stockbrokers and accountants looked at each other in dismay, and then shrugged. After all, what could this isolated Pope do about it?

"In order not to further destabilise the financial and currency markets, I will slowly sell the Church's shareholdings in corporations, investment funds and real estate. Some buildings will be retained to be used as shelters for the homeless.

Commodities being held in banks for the Vatican will be sold at their current value and used in the war on poverty."

The Bankers, financiers, stockbrokers and accountants faces turned ashen, along with the heads of governments, their intelligence agencies and oligarchs of both the West and the East.

"This money will not end up in the hands of despots.

It will reach those who have the right to it.

We cripple them, shackle their minds, heart and souls if we say, "They Cannot."

We say "They Will" and "They Can," if they are given the chance, the funding and the support to do so.

If we do not clean our houses, a bleak future is staring us in the face.

Let us close the doors of our world to the Four Horsemen of the Apocalypse, Conquest, War, Famine and Death. It stalks our lands and is an abomination not only in God's eyes, but in man's as well.

I appeal to all peoples of the world. Make peace not war. Put aside your religious differences.

Let us refute the obscenity of arms merchants. Refuse to kill your fellow men. Let us join in passive resistance to change things we can no longer tolerate."

Every person in the Square or watching on the television held their breath.

"I call on every man, woman, creed or race or colour of their skin.

Open your eyes and hearts to your neighbour. Make peace with your neighbour

I am anxious to pursue union with other denominations."

Again, applause broke out until he again lifted his hands to quieten the crowd.

"Israel and Palestine, I call upon you to put aside your differences. You are brothers. The Patriarch Abraham/Ibrahim is the father of both your religions.

Let us reach out our hands to each other. Come to the Vatican as my honoured guests. You will be safe within our walls. Let us broker peace between our three religions. Let us set an example to the rest of the world.

I beg you, let me help broker peace between your two nations and see a State of Palestine established.

While the Knesset of Israel, which was watching to a man in Givat Ram, Jerusalem and the leaders of Palestine gathered in Gaza, sat in stunned silence, the world held its breath, at such a bold move by the Pope, the bravest of men in their eyes.

I am setting aside monies that the Vatican may have accumulated as a result of the Holocaust and will give it to Israel with no conditions. I apologise.

I am setting aside monies the Vatican may have accrued as a result of the Crusades and I am giving it to Palestine, with no conditions. I apologise.

I am setting aside other monies that the Vatican may have acquired as a result of the Crusades and am giving it to Iraq, so she may rebuild herself on her own terms.

Come; let us make peace among ourselves.

Tears streamed down faces of all colours, whether present in the Square or watching through the medium of television. People turned to each other in wonder and joy. Surely these nations could not refuse such a generous offer.

They will be able to tell their grandchildren, they were there at this historic moment.

It is time to put good Governance in place worldwide. All men are created equal and the wealth of the land and resources belong to all, not a favored few.

Governments have recklessly incurred massive debt, without a thought for the final reckoning. They encouraged their citizens to accumulate personal debt they could ill afford, and brought many to their knees. Now it is time for reparation.

I now invite the leaders of the large wealthy countries and the smaller poor nations, to come to the Vatican in one month's time, where a special Congress will be held to work out way out of this crisis. In order to right the wrongs of this world and bring about reform in the shortest possible timeframe,

Let us work on a 10 step plan to:

Eliminate poverty

Pay off debt

Cease the manipulation of food prices and supply

Eliminate corruption from the financial markets

Eliminate the manipulation of commodities and currencies

Restructure your utility companies to a level people can afford

Acknowledge the natural resources of a country belong to the people and cease the manipulation of them

Cease spending your citizen's tax dollars on armaments

Cease the destruction of the forests, rivers and seas of this world

Disarm nuclear capability

I call upon the citizens of the world, to focus, not on what they do not have, but on what they do.

Simplify your lives. Be content.

And how will I, a small Italian man, who lives in a large palace, simplify his and his family's life.

I recall my father's struggle to put food on our table and keep a roof over our heads.

The world also knew his story. The tireless work he had done in the parishes he had for the working man. How he had fought their battles. As he rose through the ranks, he did not forget nor desert them.

The people who live in the Vatican will live simply and frugally.

Patting his slim hips with both hands, he grinned at the people as they roared with laughter. There were certainly some corpulent priests who could lose a few kg.

We will budget like any normal household and we will meet our budget.

I urge you to eat simply and put an end to obesity and ill health. Let us return to the ways of our forefathers. Support your local farmers markets and producers. Eat seasonally and congregate over food in your own homes.

Whilst the people were with him, he turned and gestured at the magnificent building behind him.

"I admit," and here he chuckled, *"it will be difficult to find a buyer for our home."* Laughter erupted throughout the square, as people took delight in his humour. It lifted their spirits and they waited to see what other pearls of wisdom he had for them.

My house will be run from the entrance fees the public pay to tour it and marvel at its treasures. Its many treasured paintings and sculptures, must not be lost to the world.

However, jewelled crosses and chalices and luxury trappings, are not a prerequisite to celebrate mass and I will sell these to add to the offerings for the poor.

We will put away the meaningless ritual and panoply, as our Lord would have us do.

Powerful forces will align themselves against me, but I am determined the Church will return to its roots and all mankind will benefit.

Be not afraid my children." He reassured mankind. *"Be strong. Stand with me."* He raised both hands in benediction. *"We have seen the outcome of greed and corruption, from which only the wealthy benefited, and the working peoples of this world have suffered once again; through no fault of their own. No more."*

As a stunned world listened to his address being beamed by satellite to two billion people on the planet, he continued

"To paraphrase Il Papa John Paul I, it makes no difference whether or not Christ ever lived. What is important of Christ's life, is not His link to the Old Testament and not His life on earth, nor even His death. All that is important is what He left behind, Love thy Neighbor as thyself and Sell all that thou hast and give the proceeds to the poor."

How could the governments and those who maintained an iron grip on global finances, ignore his pleas made in front of the entire world? People could simply not believe their eyes, or ears and held their collective breath to catch his next words.

"I intend to return the Holy Roman Catholic Church to the simplicity of his mission and teachings. I believe he would be dismayed, to see the ravages carried out in his name for 2000 years."

With this he raised both hands above his hands, while the masses roared their approval and a wave of absolute love from them washed over and blessed him.

"I give warning to the corrupt and evil. Your time has come."

Again spontaneous cheering and applause continued for ten minutes, while he ought to control them.

"I am in full health and as these people are my witness," here he gestured to the 200,000 thousand people gathered in the St Pietro Piazza, *"should I suffer an unexpected demise, I have left instructions that my death will be investigated in full view of the world and those responsible will be handed over to the State Police to answer for their actions."*

With this oblique reference to the death of Il Papa John Paul I, a mighty roar burst from the throats of the assembled crowd. Holding up his hand once more, he continued.

"I call on the major religions of the world to cease their hatred of each other and allow men to live in peace with their own faith. This has brought us to the brink of extinction.

I call on all governments who have nuclear capability, to cease the obscene practice of building nuclear weapons and channel this money to improve their peoples" lives."

He paused again as the crowd roared their unabated approval for five minutes, despite his best endeavours to quell it.

"I call on people of different races to put aside their differences and live in harmony. What does the colour of man's skin, matter? Our Lord was dark complected, with Semitic features, yet throughout the ages, he has been portrayed as a fine featured, light complected personage. We have denied the Lord by doing this.

If we do not work to resolve these problems, I fear in the near futur, the world will dissolve into anarchy, as people try to feed themselves and their families. I will not allow this to happen on my watch."

A collective sigh of relief rose from the crowded square to engulf him. At last, a Pope of the people.

Having thrown down the gauntlet, His Holiness gave a final blessing to all, while the men and women of the world, turned to each other with tears and hope in their hearts for the first time in many centuries.

With a final wave, he turned to go inside, Edoardos by his side. Two brave men re-entered the Vatican, knowing their days were numbered, but desperately hoping they would be able to achieve their goals before they lost their lives.

FINITO

Printed in Great Britain
by Amazon

79154697R00241